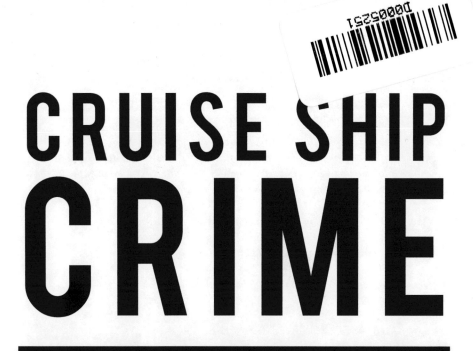

# CRUISE SHIP CRIME

## A MEDICAL MURDER MYSTERY

### PAUL DAVIS MD

iUniverse, Inc.
New York   Bloomington

iUniverse books may be ordered through booksellers or by contacting:

iUniverse
1663 Liberty Drive
Bloomington, IN 47403
www.iuniverse.com
1-800-Authors (1-800-288-4677)

Because of the dynamic nature of the Internet, any Web addresses or links contained in this book may have changed since publication and may no longer be valid. The views expressed in this work are solely those of the author and do not necessarily reflect the views of the publisher, and the publisher hereby disclaims any responsibility for them.

ISBN: 978-1-4502-1227-4 (sc)
ISBN: 978-1-4502-1229-8 (dj)
ISBN: 978-1-4502-1228-1 (ebook)

Library of Congress Control Number: 2010901919

Printed in the United States of America

iUniverse rev. date: 02/18/10

*This book is dedicated to my Mother who taught me an appreciation for writing at a very early age. Also to my sister; and all the friends, co-workers & passengers I worked with on cruise ships over the years.*

# PREFACE

How does one become a ship's doctor? Hundreds of years ago when motors did not exist, the ship's doctor was the one who was a bit more adept with the blood letting equipment than the next guy. Sometimes it was the fellow who the captain knew had learned a bit of homeopathy, but was equally adept with the sails or other aspects of the multi-masted sailing vessels.

As the sailing industry advanced, so did the qualifications of the person responsible for the health of the ship. Often it was a "bright young officer who can keep a level head in an emergency and has had some training in first aid", this according to the company manual of a shipping company in 1904. One manual put it this way in 1924 "… "if he has had experience in the great war tending to casualties, he should be able to attend to the potential medical problems that may befall sailors".

Designation as a trained medic became a requirement on cargo ships as years went on, and on the larger ships carrying passengers, a licensed physician was required. Unfortunately, sometimes the doctors that were hired, had little or no emergency or family practice experience. The quality of medical care was very dependent on the luck of the draw.

Eventually, standards were developed and certain certifications were required. Most large cruise line companies now adhere to these standards, especially if they deal with US, Canadian or European passengers. Most hire through a medical agency that contracts with various shipping companies to provide doctors, nurses and medical directors for specific fleets of ships. The fleet medical directors have the job of hiring the staff, trying to sort out major problems, going to the board meetings of the shipping company, and occasionally having to fill in a spot on a ship when a physician can't make it.

# CHAPTER ONE

*December 6, 2009: Boston*

ALAN LOOKED AROUND HIS neat and tidy little apartment for the last time; he felt like one of those old whaling captains of long ago, preparing to embark on a long sea voyage. Well, he was going on just such a trip, but this time, he was to be a passenger. He stood by the window and looked out over the shoreline before him: such a pretty view. Smiling, Alan thought it so typical of him – he always had to be within sight of water.

Turning, Alan's eyes swept the living room. Ah, Jo Ann had always been such a fastidious woman: a place for everything and everything in its place. The fingers of his right hand curled about the gold ring on his left hand. He wondered, should he keep it on, or leave it here? Experience had taught him that many ladies on the ship wouldn't care one way or the other.

Yet, Alan was torn. That phase of his life was over. But, how does one put aside so many years shared with another person and just ignore them? He chewed his lip. He knew the answer – by *not* doing it! He would do what he felt was best; he would honor that most noble of ladies by keeping the ring right where it always belonged.

Problem solved.

Alan stepped over to the hallway mirror and looked himself over. Huh, that patch of gray in his beard was getting just a bit bigger. He wondered - should he shave it off? Jo Ann had always said he looked younger when he was clean-shaven. Since her… departure from his life - he'd stopped shaving. It had only been this morning that he'd at least trimmed the beard down so that he looked nice and neat.

Rubbing his hand across the fine hairs on his chin, Alan grinned. Jo Ann had always complained that his whiskers felt like sandpaper against her soft skin. But now, with the hairs grown out, they had softened and felt quite nice. No, he'd leave them. Hey, maybe the ladies on the ship would think he looked distinguished! Besides, Alan's days of trying to look younger were well and truly behind him.

He pulled on his coat and cupped his hands before his mouth, blowing a warming breath into them. Oh, the place was just a bit too chilly for his tastes. Of course, all those years serving in the Caribbean had tended to… thin his blood just a bit. Still, with ten generations of New Englanders in his genes, these cold winters weren't too terribly much for him to endure. No, Alan wasn't heading south to escape the cold; he knew that, and had to admit it to himself. This trip was about one thing – the need to forget.

Alan picked up his bag, fished his keys out of his pocket and headed out the door. The hallway was rather narrow but not as narrow as he was used to on board ship. He locked the door and headed down to the elevator. A short ride later, Alan was strolling across the pretty little lobby area. Ah, it was all decked out for the holidays and he could see a bit of snow and slush outside the large glass doors.

The doorman saw Alan approaching and pulled the door open for him.

"Good day, Dr. Mayhew," he said brightly. "Call you a cab, sir?"

Alan nodded.

"Yes, thank you, Frank."

Frank waved to a car down the block, and one of the city's many yellow cabs was soon approaching.

"Off to spend Christmas with the family?" Frank asked.

"Not this year," Alan replied. "Alexa and the boys gave me a rather odd gift…"

"Oh? - Odd in what way?"

"They're sending me on a cruise…"

Frank laughed.

"Oh, that *is* priceless! You sure it's not a gag gift and they're expecting you to redeem the ticket?"

Alan gave him a weak smile.

"No, I'm sure. They set it up that way. They think it'll do me some good."

The cab arrived, and Frank popped the back door open.

"Hey, it's already done you some good; this is the first time I've seen you smile since… well, a while. Who knows - after all you've done on ships over the years, I wouldn't be surprised to hear they let you go up to the bridge and drive the boat. So, you go have some fun."

"I intend to," Alan said, handing the cabbie his bag. "My best to your... wife. Oh, and Frank - it's *steer* the ship."

With that, Alan climbed in, and they drove off. He gazed out the window at the city and thought of all his years there. It's said that the best cities in the world are the ones you feel comfortable walking around. Well, that must be true of Boston; in all the time he'd lived here, he'd never once bothered to buy a car. Did he even remember how to drive one?

Jo Ann had known. She drove like a New York City cabbie and cursed like one too, at times! Ah, driving out to Arlington or Fitchburg, or out to Amherst to see Alexa at school had always been an... adventure. Sure, Alan's life often flashed before his eyes and he returned white-knuckled, but life was never dull with her around.

Now that he was retired... and without her... what would life be like? Time to find out. On this drive to the airport, Alan may have looked over the city but he didn't really see anything; he was lost in thoughts of the past. He was actually startled when the door popped open next to him.

"He'e ya go, fella; Logan Ai'po't, te'minal A," the cabbie said.

Alan blinked his eyes and climbed out.

"Yeah, right... thanks."

Alan stuffed some bills in the man's hand, grabbed his bag and made his way inside. Once again, he really wasn't aware of what was going on; his body just sort or knew the routine. After all, he'd done this so many times in the past. A cold wind blasted at him, practically picking him up and scooping him through the big double doors. Alan barely felt it; it was so much colder inside his soul than outside.

As if in a dream, he just sort of floated along with the crowd. If anything, Alan felt as if he was having an out of body experience. He seemed to hover over his body and watch it get jostled about like a sheep or cow in amongst a herd but not one going to slaughter, he hoped.

He had been reading a lot since the passing of Jo. Could it be that a person's beliefs have at least some bearing on who is likely to have an out of body experience (OBE)? Could it be that a person who believes in soul survival is more likely to have an OBE than one who does not? The answer, according to some surveys by psychiatrists, seems to be - yes!

Alan knew enough to know he was not crazy, but he really wasn't in control of anything, was he? He was just going with the flow and letting events drag him along.

Well, what of it? Maybe that's just what Alan needed right now. He'd been trying to control his life to the nth degree ever since he was a young man. Why not relax and let someone – or something – else do the steering for a while?

## December 6, 2009: Miami

THE PLANE FLIGHT WAS uneventful. Or, at least, Alan didn't remember anything about it. So what did it matter, one way or the other? When he stepped out onto the sidewalk outside the terminal, his mind snapped awake. Oh yeah, this was south Florida; the temperature and humidity were positively stifling.

A bunch of cabbies tried to hail him, but he ignored them. He knew the drill with the ships; there was a shuttle that took passengers to the dock. Ah, now wouldn't this be a switch? All those years taking the crew entrance and now he was going in the front door. The shuttle was very nice; the air conditioning made the trip much more bearable.

Funny - so many years spent down in this area and yet he still hadn't gotten used to the climate. Oh well, once they were out on the water, he'd feel right at home. The Miami skyline hadn't changed much since his last visit and the dock area was just as he remembered. Yeah, that area wasn't about to change; too much money was generated by the cruise ships. They were here to stay!

The ship Alan was going to travel on was of course, docked at the pier. In many ports, one has to take a tender out to the ship. The massive groups of people just gather at the portside, usually in great long queue, waiting for the tenders (often the lifeboats from the ship) to take them aboard. Shipping companies usually pick a port where they do not have to do that at the beginning of a cruise. The logistics are much easier if everyone – and their luggage - can merely walk or be wheeled aboard.

Miami is one of those ports where everything is designed to make it easy for the passenger to get aboard, and for the cruise line company to get the largest number of passengers on board in the shortest time. The faster the turnaround from disembarking passengers to loading a new group of pocket books, the more cash the company makes.

My God, no matter how many times Alan shipped out on one of these, he never got used to their massive size!

"You going the wrong way, sir," a porter called out.

Alan looked around, having lost his bearings for a second.

"Huh, what…?"

He looked up. Yep, he was heading toward the crew's entrance. He laughed: force of habit. It seemed his feet knew where he belonged. Giving his baggage to one of the pushy porters, he headed inside and got in line for the ticketing.

The place was huge: a large open room with thick, rich patterned carpeting. Alan sort of felt like a visitor to Disney World; after all, there were all those queues carefully set up to weave and wind their way from the glass front up to one of the massive numbers of ticket counters.

Plenty of people were already in line and Alan joined them. Standing there, slowly shuffling along, his eyes played across the myriad of people there with him. He smiled. Oh yeah, this was always the fun part for him, back when he was on the other side of the barrier. He'd look over the different people waiting to board, and he'd play a little game with himself: what was the story connected with a person, couple or family?

Some were easy. The couple all giddy and happy and with stars in their eyes: newlyweds. The couple with three or four little ones: a family trying to go on vacation in peace, and without poor old Dad having to do a lot of driving and Mom doing the baby sitting; (the opportunity to dump the wee ones in the Kids' Corner was the main reason many families went on cruises).

Alan thought back to his first week-long cruise as a member of the crew. How long ago had it been; how many years? Oh, he didn't want to think about that! Yet, he couldn't help his mind wandering back to those times when he had first gone aboard ship to work…

# CHAPTER TWO

*July 9, 1984: Galveston*

ALAN HAD NOT BEEN just any member of the crew of the ship *Ocean's Quest*. No, he was Dr. Alan Mayhew - the ship's doctor – the name had a nice ring to it, he thought, but he knew the connotations that entailed; many of the ship's old passengers still remembered *The Love Boat*, and insisted on calling him "Doc". He didn't mind. After all, there was a time when a ship's doctor had an altogether different meaning. In the "Old Days", a ship's doctor was usually about one day ahead of a lawsuit – or arrest - and wasn't known for his expertise.

Alcoholism was high among the old time ship doctors, probably as a way of dealing with the impossible situations that they were often put in the middle of - both medically and politically – aboard ship.

Oh, if those happy tourists coming on board only knew what really went on behind all the glitz and glamour of a cruise ship… what it was really like to work on one of these floating cities! One day he'd have to write a book. He was already planning that day; his notebook went everywhere with him. One never knew when one of the well-heeled passengers would let slip a real gem of a quote and Alan wanted to catch it.

Alan knew that when you worked for one of these cruise lines, you got a view of more than the ship itself. The company you worked for was usually quite sizeable. Of course, Alan wasn't directly involved in the corporate goings-on, but he was responsible for the budget and various other financial aspects of his department. As an officer, he also had to attend Captain Halverson's weekly meetings and various other management meetings. He knew the drill; the company made its money on the volume of passengers they carried, and all the extras that they sold: the novelties, drinks, tours and so on. Yes, there was profit in running a cruise line. But what would the ship's doctor know about that?

The young Dr Alan Mayhew stood on the small deck just off of the bridge. It was a great Monday morning: clean skies, a few fluffy white clouds and a light ocean breeze. He inhaled – deeply and slowly. Yeah, Alan loved the sea. The smell of the salt air was positively invigorating; this was where he was meant to be.

Captain Halvorsen stepped out next to him.

"Well, Doc, you ready to head down to the main promenade and 'press the flesh'?"

Alan gave him a smile. Captain Halvorsen was a fine figure of a man: tall, with a solid build and his salt and pepper hair gave him a very distinguished look. Alan had always felt that was deliberate. After all, as Captain, he had to look commanding and all-knowing, even when he wasn't.

"A full load this time, sir…?"

Captain Halvorsen nodded.

"As always; after all, July is our busiest time. Should be good, though – a real mix on this cruise, Doc; not just the Golden Oldies. Should be fun. Besides, you know how the ladies go for a man in uniform."

Alan cringed. He was always rather embarrassed by the attention that the uniform seemed to draw from the young ladies on the make. Shy and somewhat reserved by nature, Alan would love to find the right girl – 'The One' – but he knew 'the one' for him would have to see beyond the swanky uniform and the prestige that comes with being 'Doc' on board ship. No, he'd leave the chasing the booty to the Captain and other more forward ship's staff. He was hopeful that 'Miss Right' would appear on ship one day and spot Dr. Alan Mayhew going about his daily business of tending to the truly sick and the pampered people aboard the cruise ship. He had pictured her many times – not so much the physical details – he was hazy on those - but the personality… now that he knew. Miss Right for Alan would be a real lady – fun, not stuffy, but… demure. She'd not be one of these gannets at the dinner table, eating all she could because it was included in the price…

Alan's attention was diverted from thoughts of the one true love he had yet to find as the first few over-sized passengers waddled onto the deck before them as he and the Captain stepped out of the crew elevator – the one "behind the scenes" – and made their way onto the Promenade Deck, the public area. Once through it, they took up their usual positions near the main hatch to the gangway.

Alan looked around him. Unlike so many of the crew, who had grown immune to all that the ship had to offer, he was always delighted to look over the unrelenting parade of humankind and its many manifestations and often the humor it provided and then of course, the beauty around him – the ship's architecture – while many other crew members had their eyes firmly on the young female eye candy tottering up the gangway.

This area was the most open part of the ship's interior; it went up four decks and was capped by a dazzling glass ceiling. A bar sat at the center of the room and then the excursion desk was against one wall, opposite the entryway. Then there were the glass elevators. Alan smiled; oh, the number of handprints the cleaning staff had to wipe off of those every night!

Captain Halverson's elbow tapped the Doc in his stomach, bringing Alan's forcibly attention back to the matter at hand – the new passengers. He painted a big smile on his face; this was the hardest part of the job. While he loved being around people - after all, he was a doctor - it was just difficult smiling and saying the same sorts of greetings to the same sorts of people week after week.

The passengers began filing in and there they all were: all the usual stereotypes. There were the old retired couples – the husband with his short pants up around his chest, and the black socks and sneakers. Then in came the families – half a dozen children decked out in colorful clothes. Oh - and there was a newly married couple; they were in their fanciest clothes and had eyes only for each other. There were also middle-aged women who had scraped every last cent together to come on the cruise and buy clothes they otherwise could never afford, all in an attempt to get a husband. There was a sprinkling of matronly females of ripe old ages, mostly widows, hoping to find that retired or also widowed male to take care of them in their reclining years. And of course the dance hosts. These guys were often retired, divorced, or widowed and not in the best of financial situations. Their hope was to latch onto some wealthy older female, who could financially support them in their reclining years.

The Captain leaned toward Alan and whispered.

"Have you seen Michael?"

"No, not since the staff meeting."

"He's our new Tour Director! He should be here."

"Do you want me to go look for-"

Captain Halvorsen shook his head, cutting Alan off mid-sentence.

"No, don't bother. I'll… discuss it with him later."

"Maybe he and his… partner are… busy."

"You can say boyfriend, Alan; I'm okay with their relationship. Are you?"

Alan nodded.

"Sure; means all the more ladies for me!"

Captain Halvorsen grinned. He knew the Doc was not one to go chasing the skirts, but he did draw a fair amount of female attention. Privately the Captain thought it was a shame that Alan didn't let his hair down and enjoy some of the perks of the job, such as having beautiful ladies throw themselves at him. The Doc always said he was too busy, or the woman in question was not his type. Captain Halvorsen thought Alan was nuts hanging back for the girl of his dreams when the reality was that a lot of hot girls on board were happy to have a fling with a crew member and be on their way at the end of their cruise, with no recriminations. Still, it was fun to tease the Doc.

"Ah… I see; so that's why you like being here for the boarding. You checking out your next conquest?"

Alan laughed.

"Ahh well as Captain of the ship, I think it only fair that you take your pick first, sir," he teased back, squirming a little.

The Captain gestured with his nose, pointing at a gaggle of young ladies – they looked to be in their twenties, and all were decked out for fun – and with all over suntans. They were just the kind of ladies that would make Alan run a mile, but he knew the Captain was impressed by what he saw.

"What…? Them?" the Doc said. "You think you've got a chance with one of them?"

"*All* of them, my dear Doc. They're young, single, and check out the clothes; they're itching for some action! You just need some confidence, man!"

All four of the ladies were in snug little hot pants that hugged the curve of their firm bottoms and short crop tops that left little to the imagination. It was obvious that none were wearing bras.

"Well, not all of us cut such a dashing look as you, sir."

With that, the Captain moved off to speak to the four 'Bouncy Babes", as he'd now dubbed them, but he would have to wait to see what effect his status as Captain of this ship would have on these young, impressionable ladies. He was snapped back to reality, spinning on his heels, as a loud woman's voice yelled,

"Are you the manager?"

Alan turned and saw that two women, clearly a mother and daughter – their resemblance made that obvious - had successfully accosted the Captain.

"I'm the Captain," Anders Halvorsen replied. "Miss…"

"Mrs. Ellie Temple," the old woman shrieked. She gestured at the other lady. "And this is my daughter, Divinia."

At first glance, Ellie looked to be in her eighties and the years had been kind, but not the technology. There was something strange about her. Her eyelids were very young looking, as was the tightness of the skin of her neck. It appeared to be very taut and closer examination, with furtive looks in her direction, gave the Doc the feeling that he was looking at a fish, not a human. Her nose was quite prominent, but had a cute Doris Day shape and her full lips had obviously had collagen injections as they were unnaturally full – the Marilyn Monroe pout. The rest of her face had obviously been pulled and chopped in a rather aggressive way over a long period of time. Some of the surgical scars were obvious to Alan's trained eyes, even with her expensive make-up trying to cover it. She had obviously had one too many facelifts and some failed BOTOX injections. It allowed the scowl furrows to show through and a bit of lid lag on the left; the surgeon had either nicked the nerve or paralyzed the nerve with too much BOTOX. She'd also had various collagen injections and a number of them were a bit off center and consequently gave her face a lopsided appearance.

She was well dressed and demure, but unfortunately stone deaf. That much was clear by how loudly she spoke, and the two hearing aids and some sort of contraption that apparently magnified sound that hung around her neck along with the rather large diamond necklace. She held the cone-shaped portion of this contraption in her hand and sort of pointed it at whoever she was talking to. It looked like a bit of a mix between *Star Wars* technology and something from *Mork & Mindy*.

Alan and the Captain gave them both a smile and a gently handshake. These two definitely would make great characters for a book!

"Hello, Captain!" Divinia chirped, showing off her capped teeth. She turned to Alan. "Are you the first mate?"

"This is our ship's doctor, Dr. Mayhew," Captain Halvorsen replied, giving the ladies a curt nod.

Divinia's smile spread ear-to-ear. "Ohhhh, isn't that nice? So, if I'm sick, you'll be the one… examining me, yes?"

The Doc struggled to keep the smile on his face. "Yes, but I'm sure you'll stay healthy, Ma'am. We want all our guests to thoroughly enjoy their cruise…"

"Oh, I'm sure Mom and I will have a great time. We're here to celebrate my birthday; I turn twenty-five in a few weeks. Would you believe I'm that age?"

"Absolutely not," Alan said, and he was being completely honest.

While the years had been kind to her mother, the same could not be said of Divinia. What was that phrase that Alan's Dad had always used? It was something to do with horses. Ah, she 'looked like she'd been ridden hard and put away wet'.

The ladies were looking up in adoration at the Doc and the Captain. An expectant silence fell as Captain Halvorsen stared intently at the obviously surgically enhanced faces, and the Doc struggled for something complimentary to say.

Just in the nick of time to save them all, Michael, the new tour director, who had so far been conspicuous by his absence, flounced over. He could see that the Captain wanted an out, probably to go and scope his hot prospects. Michael was sure Captain Halvorsen would also have one or two questions for his so far absentee tour director – and that was a conversation Michael just did not want to have.

"Well, hello, ladies!" he gushed, sweeping up behind the two and embracing them as far round each shoulder as he could reach with both arms outstretched.

"Welcome aboard and boy have we got some wonderful things lined up for you - on and off the ship!"

Michael was only thirty-four years old but his fondness for living life to the fullest was already showing, in contrast to the two ladies he was now sweet talking. He had been in the cruise industry sixteen years and consequently had no idea how to cook a meal, but he was definitely overweight. He was more likely to be seen in the staff mess eating a snack of bacon and sausages than he was in the ship's gym.

Michael had just joined the Gold Cruise Line, having been contracted to the parent company for quite some time before that. The company had lost its contract, but Michael and his partner, Alfonse, had impressed people enough to grab the job of Tour Managers for Gold Cruise Line, despite many derogatory comments made by passengers that they would never buy a shore tour 'from those gay guys'. The Captain – and Doc – knew they would change their minds when the sun and free-flowing alcohol and food got to them on board.

Michael and Alfonse had an 'open' relationship. What you saw was what you got with those two and they wanted everyone to know what they were. They were often on the lookout for a sexual conquest aboard ship, although he and Alfonse had been 'married' for the past fourteen years.

Michael's eyes never once met the Captain's as he deftly turned and swept the two women down the promenade deck in the opposite direction, giggling like girls. Ellie and Divinia were now sure they had been singled out for particular attention, and they were highly flattered.

Captain Halvorsen knew that happy passengers spent more money, and that was fine by him. Let Michael schmooze those two. He'd keep. Anders even had a secret smile to himself, wondering if Ellie and even Divinia realized in their flattered excitement that they were on to a non-starter with that particular 'Romeo'. And at least Michael going off with the ladies was unlikely to rile Alfonse. Captain Halvorsen thought that man rather volatile. Already, rumors were circulating about Alfonse's angry outbursts. The Captain would have to keep a close eye on that one, he knew.

He had known all along it would be a challenge to have a couple working together aboard ship, but he hadn't realized that Michael would be sneaking off for… whatever he had snuck off for with Alfonse, his boyfriend… before the ship had even cast off! He didn't even consider that thought in the least hypocritical, as he took the opportunity of not having to talk with Michael to scope the deck and cast his eyes upon the Bouncy Babes once more.

Pushing his shoulders back and puffing out his chest, Captain Halvorsen strode toward the girls.

"Hello there, ladies. Allow me to introduce myself… Captain Halvorsen. I do hope you will enjoy your cruise with us."

With an effortless ease that Alan envied, the Captain offered,

"Would you ladies care to take a tour of the ship with me – orient yourselves a little? We want you to feel at home here."

'I'll bet you do,' Doc thought as he went, chuckling, to check out the sick bay, to make sure all was in order there before they left port.

# CHAPTER THREE

*December 6, 2009: Miami*

ALAN'S MIND WANDERED BACK to those early cruises as a ship's doctor as he got ready to board ship now as a passenger for the very first time. The sounds, the smells – those were what he remembered most, and they hadn't changed. But he had to forget about the past for a little while. The children had known that. Maybe this cruise would be a good idea, after all.

Once Alan had his ID card and had checked his baggage, he made his way to the gangway. All around him were the other vacationers and he started to size up who he would be spending the next couple of weeks with. No longer 'Doc', he wouldn't have the security of his sick bay to retreat to alone, and he didn't want to spend his whole vacation in his cabin. He had brought his laptop along, though. Like with all his travels at sea, Alan wanted to keep a journal so he could look back on it and spark his memories. He could always bury himself in that if the incessantly happy cruisers got to be too much for him.

'Why, I may even get started on the book I've been promising myself to write for years!' he thought to himself, chuckling.

As the passengers shuffled on board, Alan among them, he scanned the crowd with a practiced eye. Quite the mix! About a dozen young hotties within sight, and easily twice that number of "ND's" (Newly Divorced), but there also appeared to be a good number of middle-aged men and women, some traveling alone, just like Alan. He began to relax a little.

Entering the main foyer, Alan looked around. Yes, it was a good ship. A big beautiful bar was center stage, flanked by the usual glass-encased elevators.

He had to grin; he remembered the *very* good time he and a young lady had enjoyed in one of those once. It had been four in the morning, and Alan was exhausted by that hour of the morning, which had certainly helped him grow a little braver with the lady in question.

She had called it a game of 'The Quarterback and the Cheerleader'. Alan had never understood the reference; after all, it wasn't like they wore any costumes or anything. That had been one of the wilder times that Alan had had on board ship as the ship's doctor.

It was fortunate that that ship had an older clientele that retired early, and a staff captain that was already occupied with a hottie. If Alan had been seen carrying on with a passenger, he would have been severely reprimanded -and possibly even fired depending upon how quickly they could find another Doctor and how much it would cost the cruise line. Really, he looked back now and realized he had some great times, but not many that he would be ashamed to tell the grandchildren about. No, the Doc had been the steady one, a people watcher, fascinated by those around him. And he still was, to this day.

Alan entered the main foyer of the ship, feeling a whole lot happier about his vacation now he didn't feel like the token single guy who would stick out like a sore thumb. Across the open area of the foyer were two desks, one on either side of the lobby: the one for excursions and the one for the assistance of the ever-questioning passengers.

If you ever spent time with the front desk personnel, as Alan had when he was a ship's doctor, one would hear many tales of just how stupid passengers could be. It appeared that passengers, in general, usually 'check their brains' when they get aboard a ship. It was common to be asked questions like "where is the elevator that goes to the front of the ship?"; "what time is it?" (Even with the four or five clocks with the various time zones in front of them.) To the question of "where do the crew sleep?" Alan used to particularly like the standard response: "At night the crew gets into that little boat that the big ship pulls behind, and then in the morning, they haul it back to the ship and let the crew go to work". Unfortunately, some passengers believed it. The list went on forever.

For now, Alan would skip both the desks. He thought he would just wait a while and just see how he got on before booking anything else – feel his way around in this new territory of 'the single guy on a cruise ship', so to speak. He also didn't need to bother with the usual boring orientation lecture; he knew his way around a ship, no problem.

So, Alan headed up to his cabin. He knew it had been a bit pricey to get the Gemini Suite, but it was also very effective in getting him some much needed personal space.

Yes, when it comes to cabins, bigger *is* better! So, Alan unpacked, slipped into his new bathing suit and headed down to the Promenade Deck. Now, he knew from long experience that the casino would not be open yet; that was not allowed while they were in port. No, he wanted to stake out a prime relaxation point for himself.

So, once down there, he grabbed a lounge chair, got himself an iced tea and pretended to read a book. That was another key element to being left alone. It didn't always work, but Alan was feeling a little raw and exposed right now and he thought it was worth a try!

As it happened, another gentleman – albeit quite a bit older than Alan - chanced to sit next to him. Alan did not object to this, reasoning that at least this would save Alan from any unwanted female attention that a single guy – even one of advancing years – might attract.

"Hi there, young fella," the newcomer said, extending his wrinkled hand to Alan. "Dr. Fillem… how you doing?"

Alan grinned – 'young fella'? Oh, he liked this guy already! And a doctor too. Ah, perhaps he'd have someone to talk to on this cruise, whenever he got bored. As a ship's doctor, Alan had often been forced to entertain other physicians at dinners. Generally, it was interesting to meet other colleagues, even if they'd been out of practice (and what was really happening in any field of medicine) for some twenty years or more. Sometimes it was a royal bore, sometimes a test of Alan's diplomatic abilities to quell wars between opposing sides of certain esoteric arguments; sometimes he got to meet some very interesting people (often the wives), and sometimes it was very amusing.

From a historical point of view, it was interesting to listen to how medicine was practiced in 'Podunkville' thirty years ago, and to realize how medicine had advanced since then. It was also often illuminating to realize that some of these practitioners of medicine actually helped people with their often outdated beliefs and practices.

Alan surmised that it was often better to have had some assistance medically than none at all. When Alan had done volunteer work in developing countries, this 'better than nothing' dictum was always present. One often had very limited supplies of medicines and antiquated or non-existent equipment to use, but somehow, he was always able to help some and teach others some basic medical facts and ways of being able to help ('pearls', as they are called in medicine).

Occasionally Alan would meet people who called themselves "doctor" but who used a rather liberal definition of the title for themselves. There had been Dr. Zetisman, an "honorary doctor of letters for having raised the most money from alumni for the schools scholarship program". Oh, he had truly tried Alan's patience.

'Dr.' Zetisman was in the habit of doling out lots of advice about anything remotely medical. Where he got his information from, God only knew. Most of it was way off the mark. Unfortunately, some of the advice was dangerous, and Alan had to reverse what he had done, just to keep the person safe, and to try to do it diplomatically.

For some unknown reason, Gold Cruise Lines had bestowed a privileged status to 'Dr.' Zetisman. He would get special perks and made good use of them. Rumor had it that he had twisted the arm of the university he was associated with to get the nephew of the general manager of Gold Cruise Lines into some acceptable program after he had failed to get into even a junior college.

'Dr.' Zetisman would also use the title 'Dr.' to gain access to the beds of 'certain ladies of a certain age' (at least eighty-five). They were most impressed by his title and apparent wealth. (He wore many items of gold jewelry.) Dr. Z. also favored certain men, usually younger, so he was quite free with his attentions while at the same time being quite a miserable and unpleasant character – quite the opposite to the delightful Dr. Fillem with whom Alan now sat.

Alan took Dr. Fillem's frail hand now and gave it a gentle shake. Hmmm… quite a bit of muscle weakness and osteoarthritic changes there: far more than age would normally cause.

"Nice to meet you, Doctor," Alan replied. "What's your… specialty?"

He'd learned over the years to be… diplomatic in asking such a question. In this case, it was entirely appropriate. Dr. Fillem was – no joke – apparently a "Doctor of Dentistry", from some unknown school (probably defunct by now, even if it ever existed). He admitted that he hadn't practiced in thirty some years, and that when he had, it was in the services. Alan noticed that Dr. Fillem did seem a bit vague about whether he had gone to dental school before or after the services.

Over the course of their chat, Alan also learned that during his time in the services, Dr. Fillem had been injured in a plane accident. No, it hadn't been in combat, but when he and some friends rented a plane to go for a party at some distant airport. His wealth was apparently due to a very generous ex-wife that gave him the alimony, and a disability insurance plan. The current Mrs. Dr. Fillem (seated next to him the whole time), was your typical trophy wife: young, curvy, blonde and with a bust you could do chin-ups on.

It was also obvious that Dr. Fillem had suffered some form of brain damage; his speech pattern was a bit… hesitant - and indicative of brain damage to the speech centers; he also walked with a decided limp and held his arm in a typical right sided hemiplegic stance: old stroke.

The bar area utilized flower vases to put nuts in. They were placed throughout the deck area, and anyone could easily see that they were nut containers. At one point, the dear elderly dentist started stuffing some of the nuts into his pocket.

"Are you going to store up some protein for this evening with the nuts?" Alan said.

"Oh no, I intend to water these and make some new plants during the rest of the cruise," he replied, with total honesty.

Trophy wife said nothing.

It was all Alan could do to keep a straight face. Oh, these two were going in his notebook! Characters like this were just too good to forget.

In an effort to quell his laughter, he lay back on his sun lounger and found himself daydreaming. In an effort not to laugh and upset his new found companions, Alan tried to think of something serious. From nowhere, a name popped into Alan's head.

Michael.

Alan's heart beat a little faster, remembering that man. Finding his body; realizing that there was no pulse, no respiration, and a classic pallor indicating that he was long past being resuscitated. That had been bad enough. But what really had Alan sweating now as he lay back on his sun lounger was the recurrence of that nagging subconscious thought he'd had pricking at his conscience a few years ago. That Michael had been murdered!

# CHAPTER FOUR

*July 10, 1984: Galveston*

A FEW HOURS AFTER Michael, the absentee tour director, had put in an appearance on board and then promptly disappeared again with two girls he wouldn't have a clue what to do with, the ship was well beyond sight of land; the Captain was practically walking on air, which was good for all the staff. The four lovelies were all fresh out of college, and anxious to let down their hair and have some fun. Hell, if Captain Anders Halvorsen played his cards right, he could bang all of them before the ship made it back to their home port. He might even be able to create his own "Girls Gone Wild" video to help him remember the good times.

Captain Halvorsen checked his watch. Yes, he had time to change and primp himself for dinner. He'd already talked to Maitre'D Gilbert, and he would be seated at their table tonight. So, step one had been completed.

A few minutes later, though, Captain Halvorsen appeared in the sick bay, in need of the Doc's attention. He had a small laceration to his face that definitely required suturing because of its location and the fact that it was bleeding rather profusely, along with a few other scratches.

"What happened to you, sir?" Alan asked, stepping closer to him to examine the Captain's injuries.

"Oh, you know Helena, the buxom front office manager…? She has been a fairly steady new girlfriend. She got angry that I haven't gotten a divorce yet. So, a slight battle ensued, but I'm only a bit worse for wear. Can you hurry and clean me up?"

Alan moved about the snug little sick bay. Like everything on a ship, it was built small and efficient. Medical departments tended to be much smaller than the financial office or the tour office, since they did not provide any ostensible profit for the cruise line. Space was money, and although a medical department was required, it was not high on the priorities. Consequently, it often ended up being on one of the lower decks.

Fortunately, designers often put the medical department in the center of the ship. This allowed sick patients to be in the most stable part of the ship in rough seas. It is not easy to try and start lines and read cardiograms on a heart attack patient when you are otherwise trying to hold onto the walls as the ship is bucking high waves.

Only a few of Alan's assignments were on poorly designed ships where they had placed the medical department (or room as it so often was) way forward or aft so that one got the full effect of rough seas. Once, Alan had a job where he was the designer of a ship's medical department. That was placed not only amidships, but had portholes and real light and easy access to passenger and crew areas.

Yet, since a ship's medical department had to handle a plethora of medical matters and there was no local pharmacy down the street, most were well stocked and kept up to date with current medicines and basic equipment that worked.

The Doc quickly got out the gauze, suture material, tetanus shot, xylocaine and a syringe to administer the local anesthetic.

"Leave it to me, sir; I'll have you fixed up in no time."

Captain Halvorson gave him a smile.

"Good man. Can I ask a favor of you?"

"Anything. What, you want me to sedate Helena with some valium and clip those 'claws' of hers?" Alan said with a grin.

"Not quite; although that *is* a thought… No, I can't show up to dinner looking like this. Take my place at the Captain's table tonight…?"

Alan gave a small jump – and nearly pulled too hard on the suture on which he was working.

"Ah… tonight, sir? Well…," he said slowly.

Captain Halvorson grinned.

"Come on, Alan, be a pal; one night won't kill your chances with the lady."

What the Captain didn't know was that, unusually for him, Alan did have his eye on a young lady this cruise. That thought amused Alan and so, with no real choice anyway, he conceded.

"Oh… all right," Alan said, feigning a hurt tone. "After all, I can't have my Captain scaring the passengers with a face like this!"

They both had a good laugh; the Captain retired to his quarters and Alan did the necessary paperwork and wrapped things up a few minutes later.

That evening, Alan got into his good dress uniform and headed down to the main dining hall. Standing at the entrance, he paused to take it all in; it was an impressive place. A large curved room with two levels, the Captain's table was right in front of him, dead center of the lower level. All around it were the tables for the passengers in the fancy suites. The grand staircase – somewhat reminiscent of the one from the Titanic – was on the other side of the room from the main doors.

Alan looked over to the side, where it was quieter due to less reverberation of the sounds of all the diners and where there was a little more privacy and fewer tables from which to be observed directly. That was where Alan *would* have sat tonight, had Captain Halvorson not gotten into trouble with his latest conquest! Oh well, tomorrow was another day.

Needless to say, a few of the people at the table were a bit upset that Alan was substituting for the Captain. When the ship doctor or Captain is scheduled to eat with passengers on a six star ship, the reception office in consultation with the Maitre'D and/or the Food and Beverage manager would send out the appropriate invitations that are necessary. These are hopefully sent out in due time so that the passengers can respond, and so that they are not caught up in having to make a choice between 'eating with the Captain/doctor' or 'having dinner with drinking buddies'. So, the people Alan was to dine with would have been expecting Captain Halvorsen.

Of course anything that has so many hands involved is bound to have glitches. It is the doctor's job to try and get the appropriate number of 'doctor-passengers' on board with him for a meal or so during a cruise. Sometimes it feels like trying to herd cats. Sometimes invitations are not sent out at the appropriate time for a formal night or not sent to all the people they were supposed to; sometimes they were sent to the wrong people, wives or husbands not included, etc. And in the spelling of the names, Alan had to chuckle as he once he was sent an invitation stating that Dr--- would like the company of Dr--- at dinner. His first response was to hope that he was going to be present at his own dinner and be cognizant enough to know that he was there.

But, this time, there were no such problems and once they learned he was the ship's doctor, it gave them the chance to give their respective "organ recitals", giving long renditions of their various maladies and expecting the Doc's expert advice over the appetizers and free of charge, of course. Now, most people do not find such things to be polite dinner conversation – unless it's their own medical malady they're talking about. For Alan, it was no problem; it never dampened his appetite, even when someone went on in great detail about their abdominal bloating and the horrific gas it produced, or people gave numerous renditions of "how I threw up when I was seasick".

The Doc was seated at the head of the table, of course, and on his right was Mrs. Temple: the woman he'd briefly spoken to that morning. This was Alan's true personal introduction to Mrs. Temple and her daughter.

"My husband is a very famous plastic surgeon in Beverly Hills," she said. "He's done wonderful things for me, as you can see…"

She stood up for a moment and showed off her profile and youthful looking body – at least the general shape covered by expensive clothes. Alan had to admit, for an older woman, she cut a fine figure. She sat down and gestured to Alan's left, to her daughter.

"This is Divinia, my, twenty-something daughter. Isn't she beautiful? See what a good plastic surgeon can do!"

Alan plastered a smile on his face, even as he heard some others at the table snort. Clearly, they were fighting the desire to burst out laughing. First of all, Divinia was anything but in her twenties; double that, maybe even triple it and you were closer to the ball park of her age. Divinia was quite the contrast in weight to her mother. She weighed in at probably a hundred and ninety pounds, touching the sky at maybe all of four foot four inches. Her BMI (Body Mass Index-the scientific way of determining if someone is overweight) would have definitely been way over the recommended 25!

Alan studied her with a professional eye. Yes, a good portion of her girth had recently been removed by liposuction and she made no attempt to conceal her breast implants. It looked like the heads of two bald men were desperately trying to escape from her tight spandex top. For some reason, the phrase 'Twin Peaks' flashed through Alan's mind. Wait, hadn't there been a TV show by that name? Well, the term suited her to perfection. He'd have to make a note of that. She had a large amount of hair, probably mostly hair weaves considering how it was clustered around the crown, and it was colored a deep unnatural brown. Her eyes, unlike her mother's, were deep set and very beady, like a hawk. In the case of her nose, it was well shaped and proportionate to the rest of the face: an A-plus on that one to the surgeon. She had also had collagen injections, as her lips were quite puffy. It was clear that her cheeks had been altered, but the Doc was unsure as to just what she'd had done to them. Implants, maybe. With her neck, it was taut and relatively well done and the rest left nothing to the imagination. Divinia spent most of the meal leaning over Alan's lap, so that there was no question as to whether or not he was able to see down her cleavage.

Although, the views down her cleavage were more like looking between two volcano peaks. She was dressed in a see-through lace bodice that minimally covered a few black straps that suspended those architectural monuments.

Although her stomach had been liposuctioned; there was evidence of what are known as "banana deformities". These occur when a plastic surgeon isn't careful at suctioning evenly. It leaves small gullies and bulges, and they were recognizable through her see-through gown. Other cosmetic techniques had probably been done, but Alan was trying not to get too long of an "Organ Recital" from her. The crew serving the table was very impressed with the protuberances Divinia gleefully showed any male within view. Later, many of the crew commented on "how lucky" Alan was to have been able to view these up close and personal all evening. How little they knew!

The other members of the table were overshadowed by the overbearing presence of "Twin Peaks" and "Fish Face". Divinia seemed quite disappointed when Alan didn't invite her back to his cabin for the night, but instead, rather politely said goodnight at the dinner table.

As a doctor, Alan had the perfect excuse:: he had to go see a patient. He'd made sure of that! The mobile Intra-Ship cellphones that were used onboard could be programmed into vibratory mode and/or tone mode. Also, the really clever doctors would program it to call them hourly. When they wanted to leave, they'd make up some inane one-sided conversation on the phone ending with,

"I'll be right there, please meet me in the clinic,"

or

"That sounds quite serious, please get the IV ready and give her…"

If Alan was in a playful mood, and had a nurse who knew what he was doing, he'd have her call him and play the same game to get him out of an uncomfortable or totally boring situation. One of Alan's favorite things was to end the conversation with instructions on the type of medication that he wanted to give to the obnoxious or boring individuals he was sitting with. Unfortunately a large dose of Haldol or Largactil is not socially or professionally allowed, but the thought of it helped him to keep his sanity by at least mentioning it in those fake calls to his nurse.

In any event, Alan was able to make a gracious departure, and hid in the medical center to finish up some reading through some medical reports on the passengers on board this trip. He decided he'd wait until well after dinner and then swing by the dance hall to see if there were any lovely ladies around. Who knows, the Doc thought, if he played his cards right, maybe he wouldn't have to sleep alone tonight.

But things did not work out as he had planned. First, a whole slew of children were brought into the sick bay by their parents, complaining of various maladies. It didn't take a brain surgeon to know what was wrong; it was a combination of seasickness and the rich food. Kids who were used to peanut butter and jelly, and Cheerios, found that their gastrointestinal tracts did not react well to the ship's other kinds of foods like rich cream sauces, highly fatted cuts of meat, soups that did *not* come from a can, etc. Oh, and then there were the unlimited sodas, desserts and chocolates.

When all those foods blended together in their tiny tummies and then the rocking of the ship was added in, however gentle that might be - oh, the things that would spew out of their mouths! Anyone who has ever seen the movie *The Exorcist* will know about the "*vomitus infantilus*" that they can produce. Unfortunately for Dr. Mayhew, they produced a lot of it – all over him and his office. Fortunately, ships have 24/7 cleaning crews and very expedient dry cleaning services.

Many hours, many patients and two clothing changes later, he was informed that "Twin Peaks" had not retired for the evening. Everyone's guess was that her hormones were raging. Alan thought it more likely that it was her empty pocketbook.

In any event, quite late in the evening, or rather, in the early hours of the morning, Alan was summoned to the "Ten-4 Club" located up near the bow. Arriving there, a waitress informed him that "Twin Peaks" had, after consuming a fair amount of alcohol (or so it was politely put forward as an explanation for her behavior), had removed her panties and tossed them seductively at several of the males still left in the bar. She then proceeded to "lap dance" and remove the black straps holding her "Vesuvial" monuments. On ships one often sees clothes and adornments that are totally out of place. Sometimes, one also sees clothes and adornments that are so humorous that it takes all one's willpower to not laugh hysterically.

The Doc remembered getting onto an elevator once and noticing a woman with a rather stylish hairdo, beautiful jewelry around her neck, a boutique type T-shirt, and designer jeans. The t-shirt was of a very fancy cat with a funny smile on the face and the rest of the body in a standing position. The color of the T-shirt and the appliqué were all in good taste and various shades of pink. The wearer had obviously dropped a bit of food onto the T-shirt as the food was still there. It was very inappropriately placed under the tail of the cat and was brown in color. This in combination with the funny smile on the face of the cat was enough to raise a very amused smile with the Doc.

This was probably not even close to being as funny or as tragic as Divinia's chosen evening attire, though. With only the see-through lace bodice now gracing her body, she gave quite a show.

Most people aim to wear their best clothes on a cruise and perhaps that is what Divinia thought she was doing. There are many examples of people going to extremes in buying and bringing the best for a cruise. This goes for not only the clothing but also the jewelry. In reality, for many cruisers, it is often the only time that they are able to wear their best. A cruise is a once in a lifetime, or at least a once in a number of years, taste of luxury in an otherwise mundane life.

Fortunately on a ship, you have a closed system and if there is a notorious jewel thief on the prowl, he/she can usually be caught. There are safes in most rooms and if there is a question about storing some fabulous diamond tiara, it can be stored in one of the giant safes that the ships have to have for cash payments to ports, crew and various other payouts. On a ship, for the most part there is one class travel and most of the people are not going to mug someone on their way back to their suite. Unfortunately this is not the case in cities like London, Mexico City, Cape Town, New York and the like. In one of these cities, if a lady were seen at a function with the type of jewelry often seen on a ship, they would be followed home by either one of the less wealthy guests, one of the serving staff, or someone tipped off by a less than honest staff member. They would be mugged either en route home or their home marked as a likely place to be robbed. On ships one also sees celebrities who get to show off their jewels and couture clothes without fear of the paparazzi photographing them and letting the whole world know of their possessions.

A complete opposite of Divinia was the delightful Lady Brogate from England – the last descendent of an old family who had no children to whom to pass down her wealth and her title. She was now a seventy-two year old woman who was a 'lady' in every sense of the word. Alan liked her and although he often had to attend to her because of her cardiac disease that limited her ability to take many shore tours; she would get exercise intolerance very easily. She always dressed elegantly and chose the finest accessories to any outfit. She was also a charming dinner companion and given a choice, the Doc often sought out the company of Lady Brogate and her husband at dinner. The Doc had missed them at dinner so he was pleased to be able to take a seat with them and their companions that night as he kept an eye on how the situation was progressing – or deteriorating – with Divinia across the bar. She was certainly drinking a lot and flirting even more, but at the point the Doc did not feel inclined to go over and intervene. He was sure that the young, handsome barman had more than enough experience of fending of unwelcome female attention – if in fact the flirting by Divinia was unwelcome; who was he to judge!

So, keeping one eye on the bar area, the Doc resolved to relax and enjoy the company. Sir Brogate was pleasantly plump and very doting upon his wife's needs and wants. And one of the wants was the desire to have jewels. And jewelry she had in abundance. Every night of one hundred and twenty days at sea, she would have a new brooch, new chain, new necklace, and matching earrings, all gold or diamonds and other precious stones like rubies and emeralds which matched her beautiful, kind green eyes.

It made no difference that Lady Brogate was the sweetest, most affable of ladies. Her obvious wealth and good taste often drew disparaging comments from her fellow passengers such as how some of the jewels were 'the size of a goose egg' or 'as big as my thumb' etc. In fact, everything that Lady Brogate wore was in the best of taste, as was her conversation at all times.

'This is something that should really never be seen in public,' the Doc thought.

The Doc was often saddened to think of how much Lady Brogate missed out on, being unable to participate in most of the on-shore excursions. As well as her cardiac problems she had asthma, was afraid to expose herself to new germs on the ground in strange places and was claustrophobic in tunnels and any other confined places. The reason that Lady Brogate took cruises was that she was afraid of being inside the confines of a plane and even the thought of that was sometimes enough to trigger a rather unpleasant asthma attack.

Sir Brogate did what he could to make up for these restrictions, being her doting companion throughout most of the cruise and only taking an occasional trip ashore himself to go buy another 'bauble' for his wife, although the 'bauble' would cost more than most people, even on a five and six star cruise liner, could make in a month.

Alan, knowing the Brogates' good humor would sometimes joke that packing up all the jewels acquired on the cruise would take them another three months.

Not that clothes – or jewels - make the person, but there are generally accepted items of clothing that one should not wear to a meal - especially a semi formal meal like the dinner with the Captain. These include a t-shirt stating in red letters 'My Farts Smell Better than Yours'; plaid shorts and a striped shirt open to the navel revealing a beer belly and 4 gold chains; or, as in Divinia's particular case now, a skin tight lycra body suit on a 350 pound female under five foot tall.

'This something that should really never been seen in public,' the Doc thought.

True to their breeding and class, the Brogates and their companions averted their gaze and deafened their ears to Divinia's little show, instead carrying on their conversation of more innocent pleasures. It didn't surprise Alan in the least to find that Lord and Lady Brogate, in their younger days, had been practical jokers and they still were, given an opportunity. Now, Alan had sometimes as an adult been too self-conscious to make himself the center of attention through practical jokes but he had taken gleeful delight in them as a boy and was a little pleased to find they were part and parcel of life aboard ship so he had some tales with which to join in the conversation.

"Ho-hoooo! I'd never do such a thing!" he declared, as Lady Brogate affectionately related the story of how her husband had short-sheeted her bed the night before, much to her confusion as she had tried to slip between the sheets without turning on the lights.

Lord Brogate snorted with laughter.

"Don't believe a word of it, Constance!...These chaps aboard ship... always at it... what!... Oh... Oh... always playing practical jokes on each other, I mean!... Charlie, really! Ladies present!"

The male of their companion couple, Charlie Saunders as the Doc later found out, sipped his whiskey, attempting to control his hilarity, although his thoughts had turned to one of his best practical jokes and that made it difficult to quell his giggles.

"Reminds me of when I first went up to Oxford... Cling film... ah... what do you ... *guys* call it... saran wrap?..." he enquired for Alan's benefit.

"Anyway – that stuff – across the ladies' lavatories. Great fun hanging around the corner and waiting for the squeals when the little ladies' feet got wet!"

Alan grimaced but he had to admit that he would have found that funny too, although he had never personally taken a practical joke that far. He did admit,

"My best... worst?... practical joke took some time to prepare. One night... I can't for the life of me remember why now... I spent almost an hour pushing real tiny pins right into a toilet roll.

Charlie's wife, Lucy, who hailed from Atlanta, Georgia, was apparently as sweet and innocent as her friend, Lady Brogate. She was bemused.

"Pins in the toilet roll?...How's that so funny?"

The men roared with laughter and her husband patted her heartily on the knee.

"Damn frustrating when you want the roll and it comes off shredded like confetti!" he enlightened her, with a wide grin.

"Exactly!" declared the Doc, but then their hilarity was at an end – at least for Alan, who once again had to cast off his practical joker past and assume the mantle of responsibility.

Unfortunately, (or maybe fortunately) Divinia's impromptu lap-dancing show had offended a few of the ladies that were also there. The security officer on duty dutifully watched the bawdy show for a while and then called Alan, to deal with the medical problem this passenger undoubtedly had.

The Doc assessed the situation, and decided that enough was enough, so he made his excuses and hurried over to the bar area to help out with

Divinia. He sighed at his luck of always being the one who got the attack of conscience when he saw passengers in such a predicament. But he couldn't ignore it. Someone had to save Divinia from herself! He reassured the security guards that this was merely a matter of too much alcohol and that escorting her to her room to sleep it off was the most prudent approach to take.

As Alan watched them lead the staggering starlet from the bar, he had a feeling that they were going to break the unthinkable crew law — going to bed with a passenger in their room, for a quickie. As much as the Doc was tempted to warn them not to, he decided to let it go. Divinia was most definitely not *his* type, but if they found her pleasing, more power to them.

The following night, "Twin Peaks" decided to latch onto another passenger: John Silver. She had been told that John was quite wealthy. He wore no wedding ring, and as was the truth, there seemed to be no woman attached to him. Alan had seen him often reading in the library.

On this evening, John had just closed up his magazine when "Twin Peaks" descended on him. Alan had finally managed to pry Alison, the tall, slender redhead of the "Bouncy Babes", away from the other ladies, and was trying to dazzle her with his knowledge of Shakespeare. Of the four, she was the one with the most brains, and it was clear that she loved smart guys. So, they stood off to one side in the library and he tried his best to remember a few choice love sonnets of the Bard's.

Alison smiled, placing a gentle forefinger on Alan's lips to quiet him.

"Shh… kiss me," she whispered huskily.

"But…" Alan faltered, acutely aware of his position as ship's doctor.

Liaisons between crew and passengers were strictly frowned upon… Not that that ever stopped the Captain or many of the other crew members.

As it was, this time, Alison took matters into her own hands – literally. She grabbed hold of the Doc's hand and turned to stalk out of from the room, pulling him along with her.

"I have… uh… something I would like you to take a look at, Doc…"

The Doc shivered in anticipation, taking his hand from hers only to trace his fingers up the back of a shapely stocking-clad thigh to caress the hem of her short, tight skirt. He cupped the shapely round bottom which might have been made to fit his hand.

"Ah… I'd be… *pleased* to… uh… take a look at that for you…"

Meanwhile, Divinia, oblivious to what John was reading, made some major moves. The notorious 'cleavage viewing position' was assumed; the see-through material was amply backlit so he could easily see that she was not wearing panties and, of course, the inane chatter was put on in full force to try and lure him away from his magazine he had suddenly become engrossed in once more.

He didn't budge. She was clearly getting very annoyed with him until she finally noticed that he was looking at a male porn magazine. The light bulb went off in her head as to why he wasn't responding to her advances. She quickly moved on to Mr. Rabinovich, the eighty-three year old New Yorker.

Mr. Rabinovich seemed a quiet, decent fellow: short and a bit on the thin side. Sitting off in the far corner of the library, he was casually reading a newspaper when she made her move. The same Vesuvial viewing position was assumed before him, and it didn't take long for the widowed Mr. Rabinovich to invite her down to his room.

As they left, Alan couldn't help but think of one thing – that old show "*Mission: Impossible*". Could the two of them truly… link up? Well, if the Doc got a call later tonight about a probable myocardial infarction, he'd have his answer, but for now, he took the opportunity to make a discrete exit with Alison, down to the deserted sick bay, where he spent a very happy hour examining her skin tones… a purely professional duty to check for sun-induced abnormalities, you understand…

As it turned out, Alan got his answer about Mr. Rabinovich the next day. He suspected that nothing much really happened, as Mr. Rabinovich came to the clinic in the morning begging for some Viagra. He was very disappointed when it was explained to him that he could not use the drug because of the potentially fatal result if he should combine it with his cardiac medications, his long acting nitroglycerine patch in particular. Ah, what a way to go, though!

Because of many recurrences of sexual harassment of vulnerable but well-heeled passengers, the powers-that-be on the ship were able to convince "Twin Peaks" and her mother not to cruise with their line any more. Alan was quite surprised; it usually took a lot for a cruise line to do that and lose the potential revenue. They were allowed to finish the cruise, but must have been told to rein in the lewd activity on the ship, because in the next ten days, they were hardly seen outside their cabin much to the chagrin of the crew who enjoyed viewing 'Twin Peaks'.

It was apparent, too, that someone else was not being seen as much as he should be. Michael, the tour director, wasn't doing much tour directing unless it was some covert operation somewhere deep in the bowels of the cruise ship, it seemed.

Just as Alan found himself pondering whether he should ask security to check Michael's cabin to see if he was sick, the man himself turned up in the sick bay.

Michael had an interesting personal biography. His medical history sheet that accompanied his sign on physical exam showed no serious medical problems. He had been cleared for duty at sea by his personal physician who did not note any medical difficulties, even given his more than considerable weight and blood pressure that was sky high with a diastolic pressure of 110-140! These were just the most obvious omissions.

This is unfortunately a situation that ships' physicians often encounter with the crew physicals they are presented with. In the Philippines, where many crew get their physicals, it is well known that an extra twenty-five dollars to the doctor will get you a passing physical even if you are barely alive. Some of the clinics have been guilty of Xeroxing the physical findings and just putting a new name on the form. When the Doc encountered this one time, he had to point out to the Human Resources Department that every single crew member that they had just hired who had gone through this one clinic were five foot six inches, all weighed and hundred and fifty-five pounds, had blood pressure of 120/82 and none had *any* medical problems. The name and age was the only thing that was different on the physicals. When Alan would enquire of the crew, he'd often find out how much they'd had to bribe their shore-side doctor to "overlook" certain physical or chemical deficits so that the person could get the job. Life ain't perfect.

He'd also found that certain employees in departments that did not necessarily need regular contact with the passengers had some major difficulty with the English language, even though that was a stated requirement of being a crew member. The laundry crew was often from China, and sometimes the head laundryman could speak "some" English. When one of his workers needed medical assistance, the one who spoke 'some English' needed to be in attendance so appropriate history and treatment instructions could be conveyed.

The same went for the galley staff that would usually emanate from one major ethnic group, that is, maybe the Subcontinent of India, or potentially, Guatemala, Indonesia, etc. The head chef was usually relatively well educated and at least comfortable with English as they would almost always be from either France or England, unless a rare Austrian, American, or German chef slipped in due to extraordinary qualifications *and* knowing someone. This was common for the larger ships or the ultra luxury ships. The smaller ships and the Exploration Cruise Lines would have a varied assortment of chef nationalities.

It was also very unusual to have a wine sommelier (the head wine steward) that was not French, but occasionally a German, Swiss, or a Romanian would sneak into that position.

Americans who worked on the large ships either worked as doctors (until the recent scares over malpractice), line officers, hotel staff, financial departments, the casino, or the like. They also ended up in some of the technical departments.

Alan always had a fascination for languages - even English. He always enjoyed the colorful language that various regions of certain countries had. Personally speaking French, Spanish, Talog, Basa Indonesian, and a smattering of other languages, he was always amazed at the different expressions that emanated from the individuals who hailed from various countries and how it could enlighten and entertain.

He remembered doing a physical on a young man from Arkansas who was going to work in the engine department on a rather menial job. The man was afraid that he might not pass the test and get sent home.

"Be gentle on me; if ya ain't, I can't get da job," he'd blubbered.

It didn't take a linguist to figure out the translation for that line: "Please be kind in evaluating my physical qualifications, as I know I have some defects; (one of them obviously being my IQ). If you go by the book, I most probably will not get this job."

Among the tests Alan had had to perform, and truly loathed, was the urine drug tests. Over the years, he'd seen all the tricks in the book for trying to pass it. There were the satchels of "clean urine" that people would (if they were woefully inexperienced) strap to their waist or thigh. With the smarter ones, they'd hold it in one of several various anatomical orifices so that it could be emptied into the collection vessel and pass as the examinee's sample at body temperature.

Alan often used the containers that had built in thermometers and specific gravity testers that had a better chance of telling if the sample was or was not from the examinee. Alan had seen it all. His Medical Review Officer course (MRO) had reviewed a number of the new ways potential candidates would use to try and fudge drug tests.

Besides the strapped on vial of clean urine, there was the attempts at trying to dilute the urine with toilet water. The nurse would routinely put bluing in the toilet bowl to avoid this attempt. Of course, Alan's personal preference was to test hair and nail samples. They were more accurate for many drugs, and they gave you a much longer history on the individual's use - generally a three month picture of the potential drug use. Of course there were the 'clever' ones that would shave their head to try and avoid the hair test, never thinking that the nurse might use the body hair between their buttocks as a good sample.

The negative aspect of urine testing was that, with many drugs, all that the candidate needed to do was stop taking certain drugs like cocaine for a couple of days, and the levels in their urine would show less than the tested minimum for a positive. Ah, but hair and nails, they slowly grew over a long period; so they gave a much better history of the drug use.

Another time, one crew member was even correctly listed as a male yet in the patient information section (presumably mistakenly) it was listed that 'she' had given birth to two children. Although cruise ships do occasionally have crew members with questionable gender, for the most part, the candidates are hard working healthy individuals. Needless to say, the company terminated the two hundred and fifty dollar examination fee contract with this clinic. This was not to single out only the Philippino clinics, as there were a lot of the clinics in the former USSR countries and other eastern European countries that had similar questionable physical findings on the exams.

In between being a ship's doctor, Alan also had the opportunity to work in various Occupational Medicine Clinics and Urgent Care Clinics in the US that were the usual places that most employees get their physicals.

It was enlightening to learn that the American work force was not always the most healthy or able to work, even if the spirit moved them. Often there were hidden agendas with the American and Canadian employees, where they were expecting disability payments and they were nearly a given.

Oh, and then there was that special 'joy' that came from doing physicals with a translator present in : Cambodian & Chinese (for a clothing sweat shop in Seattle); Japanese (for a Toyota car plant in the mid west); Czech for the Roma-Gypsies from eastern Europe (coming as 'refugees'); and Kentucky'ian" (for the Hillbilly English spoken at some of the mining companies). Sometimes it took longer to explain to the translator what maneuver you wanted the potential employee to do than it took to do it – like 'breathe deeply through your mouth', or 'bend over and touch your toes'.

But at least those foreign workers were physically capable of carrying out the job for which they were applying. Oh, there'd been those security guards applying for jobs at the Wackennut Power Plant. They were obese and couldn't move easily; they had cataracts or other visual deficits and they were deaf, even with hearing aids. A couple had hernias so they couldn't lift much of anything; there was even a one-legged amputee in a wheelchair that couldn't use crutches and couldn't write because of the tremors he had.

Ah, and then there was the thirty-five year old mentally retarded man with nasty scars from the burns he'd had as a youth, healthy physically, but way down on the IQ level. Surprisingly, even with his handicaps, he was much more capable of doing a job than the seventy-eight year old who had no teeth, laryngeal surgery for cancer and refused to use any devices for speech assistance. His attitude was, if anyone wanted to communicate with him, they could write it down. Of course, it turned out he had trouble with any words that had more than one syllable, so he was essentially illiterate. It made taking a history and doing a physical a long, tedious, procedure. Alan had to shudder; these were the individuals that were guarding the US's fourth largest power plant! But he couldn't wait to get back to his cabin and jot down just some of these and other details in the journal of his travels that he kept. He met so many 'interesting' characters on board – both crew and passengers – that he was sure he would forget them in the future. He didn't want to forget a single person. These characters were gold-dust! Alan had an ambition to write all this up in a novel one day – if anyone would believe it!

A few sessions working as a doctor in shore-side clinics like that made Alan long for the sea once more; doing physicals on the wait staff for one of the cruise ships was infinitely more fun, and often very enlightening. It was even his first introduction to cross-dressing! There were a few of the applicants for whom it was very questionable as to whether they were applying as men or women. Alan only had to stretch his imagination about two-inches to guess what they did after hours. Oh, and then there were the tattoos and piercings; they were considered the most popular collectable. It never ceased to amaze him how many portions of the human body could be pierced, and how many tattoos could be fit onto one human body. It was policy on most cruise ships that obvious tattoos needed to be covered by the uniform. Piercing, other than ear lobes for women were generally forbidden. If an employee wanted nipples, belly buttons, foreskins, and the like pierced, so be it - they couldn't be seen by the general public. Whenever Alan saw the little rose tattoo on the breast of a young woman, it always made him think of an elderly woman in a nursing home with a very long stemmed rose on her breast. Time modifies things!

The regular ship's crew generally was required to have annual or biennial physicals. The nurse would keep track of when the physical was due. If the physical fell during the contract in which the crew member was still on board, the Doc was required to do the physical. When Alan started with the cruise industry, this ongoing physical job tended to be a random thing and not much of a time taker. As the companies started to realize that they did not have to pay anything extra to have the onboard physician do the physicals, and that the physicals were more likely to be more in compliance with the basic regulations of the maritime law and the companies' rules, ongoing crew physicals became a weekly job. Depending on the cruise line, one could expect 10-40 physicals per week.

These were usually done after passenger and crew hours, and of course they ate into any potential free time the Doc and nurses would otherwise have. Besides pointing to any deficits that were not documented in an original on-shore physical, it actually was a good educational tool for the crew. Oftentimes, Alan could teach the crew member about their impending diabetes or hypercholesterolemia and its consequences. Sometimes it was a simple reminder to take some of the free condoms when they next went ashore to partake of the local fauna.

Michael the tour director's English doctor may not have been on the take, but he certainly did not give a complete history on the form. It could have been that Michael had 'neglected' to mention that he had had angina (chest pain) previously and other heart-related problems, liver disease and a raft of various infections picked up from his promiscuous ways.

When Michael showed up in the sick bay this particular day, it happened that the nurse on duty with the Doc was none other than Polish-born Petra Gacek – the one who took great delight in plucking the buttock hairs of potential drug addicts. On ships that are not Canadian flagged, there is often random drug testing of employees. This is obviously to keep the ships as drug free as possible and to avoid potential disasters.

Some of the random testing is with urine or mouth swabs. Other testing is with hair samples. Hair is a great scientific way of knowing what drugs one has been taking over a three month period prior to the sampling. Drugs like heroin, cocaine, barbiturates and marijuana are metabolized and taken up into the follicles of the hair. There is virtually no way of getting them out completely even though dyeing and bleaching are a favorite method of drug users to try and beat the system. Another way that many try is to shave their body. This allows very little hair to test. Petra would find hair in the pubic areas, on the buttocks, etc. Her favorite trick was to pluck out the few hairs that someone had missed on the buttock or between the legs near the anus. She was a tough cookie!

PETRA WAS TRAINED AS a physician in Poland. In the USA she went to Physical Therapy school and became a PT at a county hospital. The Doc and his team were given to understand that she basically sat there in the PT department, as a chief would with his tribe, and gave orders. That was pretty much what she did on board ship too. Alan had his work cut out to get Petra to accept her place in the pecking order or, in this case, to go get Michael a drink of water, which he clearly needed at the time he showed up, pale, sweating and in obvious distress.

"But… you will be alone…" Petra ventured.

A glare from the Doc halted her in mid-sentence.

"But I am a *nurse*," she tried again. "It is not a nurse's job to…to fetch water."

"It is humane," an imperious Dr. Alan Mayhew sent her on her way.

Petra was near-sighted and wore thick glasses like the bottom of bottles. She was a large woman too. The Doc ventured that not too far back in her heritage were the farmer women who chucked the bales of hay and single-handedly roped the cows in rural Poland.

Petra could wolf down three portions of anything put in front of her. This is not to say that she was fit. Her girth was sizeable. The poor uniform department always had to adjust her uniforms and order special sizes. However, she was good at the paperwork that was ever present in the department. Every aspirin and band aid had to be accounted for, to justify the next year's budget and the meager salaries. When push came to shove, Petra could pitch in responsibly and help resuscitate a failing passenger, she did know her CPR and at one time had actually taken ACLS (advanced cardiac life support) and passed it.

Petra was formidable to most people but the Doc knew exactly how to play her. He had had to learn – or be forever a servant in his own sick bay. He wasn't having that!

Back in her native Poland, Petra had been eating her lunch in her office one day and 'Smelly', a guy whom it was well-known locally had raped women, came into the department and was obviously going to rape her. He was intent upon it.

Completely unfazed, Petra told him to sit and wait until she was finished eating lunch, then he could rape her all he wanted to because it wouldn't be any worse than the concentration camps she had been in. Needless to say that took all the fun out of his venture and he left, much to the relief of the other staff who had been very scared for Petra.

Once Petra was out of the way, on her begrudging refreshment mission for Michael, Doc sat on the edge of his desk, looking kindly at Michael, who was slumped in a chair looking distraught and very dehydrated. It was no surprise to Alan that Michael requested treatment for "feeling like my body is not in sync with the world" and having "weird dreams" that made his "heart race like crazy": in other words - he was having a severe anxiety attack.

Michael refused to say specifically what was going on, but just from his general clinical presentation and the fact that his pulse was tachycardic and irregular, it was clear that he was definitely having an anxiety attack and deserved something for the incident. The Doc tried to probe a little more into the etiology of the episode.

"When did these symptoms start, Michael?"

"Well, I have been very busy with trying to make arrangements for Mrs. Brightman…," he was defensive.

The Doc asked,

"You mean *the* Mrs. Brightman, the one who demands that the entire ship turn over backwards for her when she arrives for one of her extended cruises?"

He said,

"Yes - the one and only; she is currently in St Petersburg, Russia on another antiques buying trip. I've made the arrangements to send her there at least eight times. Frankly, I think she is trying to steal the crown jewels."

One could never quite be sure when Michael was joking so this caused Doc Mayhew to snap his narrowing eyes keenly into focus upon Michael's.

The other man laughed.

"No... no, not really, but she has this fascination with all things Russian from the 1850s. She buys antiques while she is there like there is no tomorrow... even old clothing of the Royals."

Michael was clearly proud as he announced,

"I set her up with Vasilov Eranowski, an old classmate of mine, who had promised to get her the real stuff not often available in the antique stores. He assured me it was all on the up and up. I am having second thoughts now, though. He called me and said that she tried to cheat him on a very rare couch and matching chairs that apparently had been given to the Royals by Queen Victoria. She called in a day later and said that he was trying to get her to buy a fake and she would have no part of it. She also told me that Vasilov had taken her to some pretty seedy parts of the city and 'seemed to know everybody ugly'."

Now, it was a fact widely accepted on board that Michael knew all the right people – all the ones likely to get genuine antiques - so he was clearly offended by this slur on his honesty and his connections. Michael was English - very English. He came from what was termed 'a good family' that had sent him to the best of public schools in whatever country he had been. Public schools in the British tradition are of course, private schools, in contrast to the American system that calls its taxpayer supported schools "public schools".

Michael's father was a career diplomat who had been assigned to interesting posts all over the world. He, of course, took his family with him. Accordingly, Michael had attended school with a variety of people who had also been sent to these exclusive British public schools. One of the Crown Princes of the Saudi Royal Family was a classmate, as were one of the Russian Mafioso, an Afghani tribal leader's kid, several sons whose dads were the presidents of fortune 100 companies, and the son of a major political figure from one of the banana republics in South America.

These individuals apparently were an important influence for Michael in his chosen profession within the tourism industry. He was able to make very appropriate plans for high-end tourists in some of these countries by calling in frequent favors. That was how the crew saw it anyway - and most of them didn't like it. Michael was careful in public to blow off their criticisms as mere jealousy, but the underground whispers were that Michael's connections were not all as above board or as well chosen as he would like to acknowledge in public. This is not to say that certain Captains and other officers had not availed themselves of favors from Michael when needing certain things done for the ship's safe passage or for more expedient processing of supplies and personal items being sent to the ship. They certainly had!

Michael had known from an early age that he was gay and many of these classmates that he called friends were actually a lot more than just friends. Michael got gifts of Rolex watches, cases of fine champagne and Cuban cigars and expensive jewelry at various times throughout the year. Despite their covert criticisms of Michael, many of the ship's staff members were happy to queue up for their share when these gifts were distributed throughout the crew.

It was widely suspected by many of the staff, including the Doc himself, that some of Michael's former lovers did not want their past homosexual exploits known and so these 'baubles', as Michael called them, appeared and they kept him mostly quiet.

The Doc smiled now as he noted the expensive Rolex and thick gold bracelet that adorned Michael's wrists as he sat in the sick bay wringing his hands. But the situation was obviously getting to Michael. 'Time to get him to open up about Mrs. Brightman, or whatever else is on his mind,' the Doc thought.

"So Mrs. Brightman's on your case, huh? Yes, I can imagine that. But why is this making you so anxious, Michael? You have dealt with her for years. You know what she's like and she seems to worship the ground you walk on…"

"Yes, Doc, I can usually keep her under control," Michael quickly interjected. "But my friend Vasilov called again and said that she actually did cheat him out of a fair bit of money. He was inferring that I was responsible for this, because I made the contact. He is not a guy you want as an enemy. I have known him since school back in the UK… um; well…; we were lovers in school for a while."

The Doc smiled.

"Thought so… So… Are you telling me that this Vasilov guy is threatening you?"

Michael swallowed hard.

"You know that scar on my thigh, the one I had a tattoo put over?"

"Yes," Doc said. "… The one that was very close to your… family… jewels?"

Michael chuckled, in spite of his obvious anxiety.

"That's the one, Doc… Well, one day when we were about seventeen, I became infatuated with an Irish guy who had just joined the school. He was so cute and he just fascinated me. He told me he'd helped his dad, on many occasions, plant bombs for the IRA. Anyway, one thing led to another and he and I started having some real hot sex in the showers down the hall from my room.

"Vasilov caught us in the shower together; I mean really t-o-g-e-t-h-e-r. He took a knife and tried to cut it off. I stepped back just in time and his knife hit my leg. I bled like a stuffed pig and Vasilov fainted."

It was a fairly minimal revenge for that serious injury but Michael took some pleasure in informing the Doc now,

"You're the only other person in the whole world who knows that Vasilov Eranowski fainted at the sight of blood. This is not something that someone who makes his living on being regarded as being the 'fearless, kill all, leave no traces' guy wants people to know."

The grin, too boyish for a forty-something, returned for a while but it quickly vanished as Michael continued,

"Anyway, when he came to, he was repentant, of course. My Irish flame kind of disappeared after this episode, and Vasilov and I were 'a thing' for the next two years. But of course, all things come to an end – especially such intense relationships.

"I hadn't really seen Vasilov again after college until – by coincidence – we were both on a gay cruise several years later. Our rooms were on the same deck on this gorgeous ship. I had just gotten into my best tuxedo with all the trappings and headed down to the inaugural ball, when we bumped into each other. It was an all-gay family cruise… lots of lectures about acceptance, raising children in a non-gay world, sexually transmitted diseases, sex change operations, how to choose a good shrink, etc. There were some crazy parties too. The inaugural ball was the tamest of them all. The fact that there were eighteen hundred gay and lesbian couples, many with children, who chartered the ship, just let us all relax and be ourselves."

Michael was relaxing and opening up now. The Doc felt like he was getting somewhere and actually, he silently hoped that Petra had enough sensitivity not to return with the water he'd asked for and to realize that had just been a convenient ruse to earn some privacy for his nervous patient who would never have opened up with her around.

Michael was on a roll now and he continued,

"Anyway, Vasilov and I became good friends again, not in a sexual way because he was married to a young fellow from Thailand. They had adopted a baby that they were raising, cute baby…"

Michael's eyes became dreamy and moist.

"I wish Alfonse and I had one of those…"

The Doc was sympathetic, but he was also a realist and he had seen the brutal side of Alfonse in his rages. That temper and children would not mix well.

"Some things aren't meant to be, Michael…"

Slightly offended at this implied slur on his lover, Michael did not let Dr. Mayhew continue, but again took up his story.

"Vasilov is in the import-export business. There have been occasions where I have been able to throw him some business. Mrs. Brightman is one of those people."

"Michael…," the Doc interrupted, feeling he may have won Michael's confidence now. "…Has this Vasilov fellow actually threatened you?"

Michael sighed, squirming a little uncomfortably in his seat.

"No, not in so many words… But, remember, I do know how he works, and Doc - it's not pretty. The attempt at cutting my thing off was mild compared to what he does these days. When Alfonse and I were working on a cruise that stopped in St Petersburg every fourteen days, we used to have dinner with Vasilov and his partner from time to time. It gave me a chance to really know him and how he has changed."

The Doc asked,

"You mentioned problems sleeping; do you have any problem getting to sleep? Or is it more a problem that once you get to sleep, you wake and can't get back to sleep?"

Michael responded,

"Both Doc. Getting to sleep is a real problem. There are just so many thoughts swimming round my brain about this and various other things. Then once I am asleep, some of these thoughts come back into my mind and there I am wide awake, counting sheep for hours with no hope of getting back to sleep."

The Doc's ears pricked up, but Michael soon cut him off.

"I can't go into them at the moment, Doc. Just believe me - there are a lot of things going on in my life right now."

The Doc gave Michael some mild sedatives, a tricyclic antidepressant and a muscle relaxer and said,

"These should help let you get to sleep for now, Michael. But we both know they won't get to the root of the problem. You need to work out the problems you're having. You're welcome to come back here and discuss them with either the nurse or myself," Doc added as Petra finally returned.

She knocked more softly upon the door than might have been expected and entered at the Doc's granting of permission. He continued his conclusion of the consultation.

"If these don't take care of it or you need more, come on back in a couple of days and we will get you sorted out."

In fact, Michael didn't return to the sick bay for this complaint for a couple of weeks when he again turned up at the clinic. The Doc had thought about the conversation they had had in the intervening days. It had concerned him, but there was an onboard spate of Norovirus, giving everyone involved diarrhea. As ships' Doc, it was not only his job to treat the victims of the Norovirus, but also to coordinate the medical and public health measures to attempt to diminish the spread of this virus.

A bad outbreak can shut down a ship. It can even signal quarantine of a ship from various ports. No country wants to have several thousand tourists running around a city in the Mediterranean contaminating other tourists and the locals! Being on a ship that is quarantined for such reasons is not very pleasant: thousands of screaming tourists and thousands others that actually *have* the gastrointestinal problems: not a pretty sight.

During a Code Brown, the Doc never got to leave the ship's sick bay, much less get himself a meal. He only had to think of it and it seemed that Nurse Janet, the particular nurse on duty, would bustle in with a wry look on her face, murmuring 'Code Brown' before a very embarrassed an awkward looking passenger. The hunched gait, hands clutching the stomach and the pale and sweaty pallor would have given away the problem anyway.


'CODE BROWN' IS NOT a real code like the official maritime codes that are used for emergencies. The real ones are Code Alpha - a serious medical emergency; Code Bravo - a fire on board; Code Papa - a chemical or other environmental spill and Code Delta - man overboard.

No, 'Code Brown' is a polite way of saying that there is an outbreak of diarrhea significant enough to quarantine an individual crew member or passenger and all of his/her roommates. It activates a series of notifications and actions just like a real emergency, but they are mostly medical and administrative. It is also the polite way of telling the environmental department that a pool needs to be closed down and sanitized so that passengers can return to it without fear of getting sick. This is often the case with the kids' pools. Some parents do not heed the warnings of keeping diaper age kids out of the pools and this age group often forgets that a pool is not a toilet. Seeing the oft repeated situation of a mother carrying a screaming kid from the pool with a stream of brown liquid emanating from their diaper or swim suit is enough to decrease your desire to swim in a public place forever. Of course there are some adults of a certain age that unfortunately do this also and sometimes do not even realize that they are doing it. This happens with urination too – just some of the reasons that the pools on board ships are very highly chlorinated.

The USPH is an agency that serves a great purpose in viewing and inspecting all the ships to determine if they meet a set guideline of standards that are supposed to protect the public from bad food. They are allowed to inspect any ship that lands in a US port. The results of their inspections are published regularly in journals and popular magazines. These results can have great bearing on whether someone goes on cruise ship one or two. A bad mark from the USPH can be the death knell for a cruise company.

The inspections are to determine if the food is kept sanitary, if the preparation is done correctly and if old food is discarded. There are hundreds of other guidelines that have to be met: dishwashing temperature, kinds of soap used on the dishes, temperature that food is kept at, how it is thawed out, whether hand inspections are done for food handlers, whether the ones who get diarrhea (code brown) are treated in a timely fashion and isolated appropriately, and on and on.

The fact that there are these inspections (always unannounced) keeps a company on its feet. There are mock inspections weekly and 'deep cleaning' before every US port to get ready for a potential real inspection. This can take up many man hours of many employees. The coveted 'one hundred per cent' is the reward. This means that the government could find nothing wrong with the ship.

This organization monitors how many 'Code Browns' a ship gets per cruise in both crew and passengers. If it reaches a certain percentage of the ship's population, the ship is quarantined before being allowed to discharge passengers in a US port. Most first world countries abide by the same restriction. Who wants to have several thousand tourists running around a city in the Mediterranean contaminating other tourists and the locals! Being on a ship that is quarantined for such reasons is not very pleasant: thousands of screaming tourists and thousands others that actually *have* the gastrointestinal problems: not a pretty sight.

A ship's management is therefore very cognizant of the GI logs and the ability to quarantine an individual. Unfortunately, it is not possible to lock a passenger's cabin from the outside - especially if the passenger does not want to stay quarantined.

Crew members are a little easier to keep in one place. On most ships crew with the dreaded Montezuma's revenge or some such other exotic bacterial problem stay put and do what they are told. Some get terribly bored in the three days of isolation with only food and phone to keep them company but their continued employment can depend upon their compliance with the quarantine order.

Then there are the other crew members on some ships that feign the diagnosis of diarrhea as a way of getting out of work for three days. A Doc can usually tell if someone is faking by fairly simple means. Once, he had worked with another doctor who had a very objective technique to sort out the fakes; he would do both a finger rectal exam and a proctoscope (large bore metal examination tube that goes into the rectum) for suspected or claimed diarrhea cases. When this Doc was on duty, there were few who tried to feign diarrhea to get out of work!

This most recent Norovirus outbreak had kept the Doc too busy to check on Michael in person. He also figured that it would be an invasion of the man's privacy. But when Michael turned up in sick bay again, the Doc sat him down, determined to get the story out of him if he could, during the examination.

Michael's vital signs were fine except for his pulse, which was again tachycardic. Much more readily this time, the tour director started on another long explanation of the things going on in his life. The Doc listened for a while, not hearing much different from the last time except that particular episode with Mrs. Brightman seemed to have been resolved to everyone's satisfaction. She got the couch and paid for it; Michael's friend Vasilov went back to whatever it was that he normally did.

The Doc listened to Michael's lungs and heart and except for the tachycardia, did not hear anything unusual. He had Petra do a cardiogram, the only cardiac evaluation equipment that the Doc had on board the ship, and Michael's test was essentially normal.

The Doc said,

"Michael, since we are in a decent port tomorrow, let's get a few blood tests done and a stress ECG on you. Come to the clinic in the morning. Skip breakfast – just this once – will you? The nurse – it will be Kelly, the Yank," he grinned. "You like her - will draw the blood and send you on shore to the hospital to run the heart test. Bring your tennis shoes, as you will have to go on a treadmill for about ten minutes."

Michael agreed stating,

"That's fine, Doc. I rather wondered about my cholesterol, anyway. I am still having problems sleeping."

Then came more honest and frank disclosures than the Doc had been expecting from Michael, given their earlier, more reticent, consultation; as the Doc listened, he pondered wryly what it was about doctors that made people speak so openly. Sometimes he was told far more than he ever wanted to know. This was just one of those times!

"There was this friend... Gustav," Michael started in. "I have known him for years... he's from Germany. We were very discrete in our relationship. It was a very deep relationship and his wife and family never knew..."

The Doc kept his face impassive. Sure that hadn't been quite the turn that Alan had expected, but it took all sorts to make a world go round, and Michael carried on his story unabated:

"… He came from a very wealthy family. His father is the Minister of Finance and head of an important bank. This was before I ever met Alfonse. I told Alfonse all about it…"

The Doc nodded, his face straight. If Michael had wanted some reaction he could kick against, he was disappointed. The Doc gave him no excuse to stop in his tracks.

"Alfonse and I have an 'open relationship' and occasionally go out with other guys - just occasionally. If we do, we always tell the other, so I wasn't being unfaithful when I started seeing Gustav again… occasionally… a few years ago."

Again he looked up. Again the Doc nodded.

Michael continued,

"About two years ago, Vasilov walked in on Gustav and I at my summer house in Mallorca. He never gave me any notice that he was arriving and it was a very uncomfortable situation for Gustav and for me. We were literally caught with our pants down, as you Americans put it. It kind of brought back old memories about the time he walked in on me in the showers in college… when he cut me."

The Doc winced slightly but Michael brushed off the concern.

"We have both grown up a lot since then, but it still was obviously on his mind. Vasilov happened to mention something about the incident in Mallorca to one of his associates and…"

All the old anxiety behaviors from the previous consultation returned as he continued,

"This associate has been blackmailing Gustav and I ever since. It is not a lot of money, and Alfonse and I can deal with it financially… it's not a problem… just to keep the peace for Gustav."

It sure sounded like a problem to the Doc but 'each to their own' he figured. No response from him was required anyway. Michael was on a roll now –

"As you know, Doc - it is also no big deal for me if people know that I'm gay. I'm so far out of the closet, I'm positively open plan," Michael joked, but he soon grew somber once more:

"…but for Gustav it *is* a big deal. Gustav's family are suspicious and have come to me asking questions that make me uneasy. I got a call from his partner in the bank that asked where I was going to be on such and such a date, what sports I do, what kind of car I drive, etc…"

At this point, it was obvious that Michael's anxiety level was extremely high and it all did seem rather worrying.

The Doc asked,

"Look, Michael - even if Gustav's family was to find out about the relationship, I'm sure that the worst they would do is chastise him... maybe get him break off the relationship. I can see that wouldn't be a great thing for you and Gustav, but you shouldn't get too worked up about it.

"I'm sure if I took your blood pressure now, it would be sky high. So let's just get these tests done and go from there, shall we? As far as the thing with Gustav's family goes, remember you are on a small island in the Caribbean and not living in Germany, Russia, or South Africa. I doubt if they are going to send the 'goon squad' here to get to you. You've been watching too many movies, Michael. Relax.

"I do have to ask one question, though, while I'm ordering blood tests; when was your last HIV test? Rest assured, I'm not inferring that you are promiscuous like some staff on the ship, Michael. I just think it is always a good idea to have one every six months with your chosen lifestyle."

Michael wasn't offended. He knew that Doc was one of the good guys. He even smiled.

"Thanks, Doc; I had one a few months ago at one of the gay bars that do them free' I have them on a regular basis and I'm negative. Thanks for listening to me, too – about... all this. I know you hear a lot on this ship and have to try and keep us all healthy."

He rubbed his temples, still worried but a bit easier in his mind.

"I'll try to relax and not think about Gustav's family. They really are quite the case, though. They didn't get that rich through hard work, you know. They were well connected during the war and were suppliers of some of the fancy chemicals that Hitler used. Gustav told me a bit about it, but obviously he's not proud of that part of his family history..."

Michael broke off there, figuring he had taken up enough of the Doc's time.

"I'll see the nurse in the morning. Thanks again, Doc."

The Doc nodded as the nurse again interjected to let the Doc know he was in demand.

"They're queuing up, Doc. The usual..."

Now, the reason that Michael had probably found the time to come see the Doc today was that, apart from the staff, the ship was almost empty. They had moored at a 'friendly island' the previous night and the stir-crazy passengers had swarmed off the ship in droves. They had been out all evening and then all day again today to sample the local delicacies and get their share of sun, sea and sand.

Now they were all returning, with the usual wounds and complaints. The stops on the 'friendly islands' often produced a lot of coral scratches, which got infected very quickly and usually ended up bringing many patients into the clinic. The sea urchins with their beautiful, thin spines often ended up in people's legs and feet when they touched them. Today was no different.

"Get it out… Get it oouuuttttt!" screamed Philip, a twenty-something with the pain threshold of a three year old.

He was sitting on the treatment bench in the sick bay and waving his right leg wildly in the air. From this position, the Doc surmised that Philip had inadvertently trodden on a sea urchin.

"Yes, yes, okay. Try and calm down, Philip. We're going to help you now."

"It's *agony*, Doc! Will I lose my foot?"

The Doc stifled his amusement.

"No, but the feet may not go in the same direction for a while," he muttered, quietly.

Philip was drunk – again.

Louder, the Doc was professional and comforting.

"It will all be feeling much better pretty soon, Philip. Nurse – can you get me the meat tenderizer, please?"

Philip let out an almighty scream.

"Whaaattttt!…Y-you..gonna… *hit me*?!"

The Doc sighed.

"No, Philip! Hush… please. *Liquid* tenderizer. It will take the sting out of the sea urchin spike you got. Just trust me, huh? I *have* done this before, you know…"

"I know, Doc. Sorry, Doc."

Philip was chastened and he quieted down considerably, although he emitted a small whimper and sniffle every time the ship's doctor went near his foot. Eventually, though, his foot was cleaned up.

The Doc had learned long ago that trying to remove the fine sea anemone spines was futile. They invariably broke and all you'd succeeded in doing then was creating a wound through which infection could enter.

No, the Doc had found, through experience and scientific research, that the best treatment is to put vinegar and meat tenderizer on the wound and then to keep it clean. The whole thing usually resolved itself without any more pain and no lasting scars.

The crew was also arriving back on board, some of them joining the queue of passengers waiting to see the Doc. The ship having been in port overnight meant that there was bound to be some of the crew that had paid a visit to the 'friendly professionals' who worked in the bar that was just outside the port. These 'ladies of the night' were endemic in many ports. Often the main bar was just outside the gates to the port property where the ship would dock. In this case, many of the Caribbean professionals were very good 'lap dancers'. Accordingly, the bar girls would be scantily dressed with no panties. They would walk up to the customer and murmur sweet nothings then ask for the customer to buy them a drink and they cozy up onto the lap of the generous guy. For a certain sum, split unevenly between the girl's owner and the girl herself, she would accompany the customer to a 'somewhere more comfortable' outside the bar. In the Caribbean, this usually meant a lean-to or other basic structure behind the bar – primitive, usually, but the ship's crew, for whom being cooped up on board for weeks at a time made orthodox relationships difficult, didn't tend to care about these conditions.

As a physician, Dr. Mayhew always assessed all the potential ways one could get infected from the rampant venereal diseases that infect most 'ladies of the night'. It sure did take the fun out of adventures ashore, sometimes. The Doc would jokingly define his job as the 'venereal disease clinic Doc' at times.

Once he had seen his way through the line of spiked feet and suspicious itchy discharges, the Doc made his way to his cabin. He thought he better get some rest now while he could, before the calls of diarrhea, fevers and generally upset stomachs began to come in. He should have a few hours yet on that, he reasoned. He even found time to go check on Michael's cabin, but, hearing no answer to his knock, the Doc proceeded to his own cabin and lay down for a while.

Philip was the first in the queue for his services after the onshore adventures, which surprised the Doc. How many ailments can one guy pick up from a single brief trip ashore!

Many people seemed to go on a cruise with a sole purpose: to consume as much alcohol as possible, and Philip was a past master at this. This cruise line, like several others, provided as much alcohol as a passenger wanted. Consequently, one could always safely bet on finding Philip in the bar. Tonight was no exception. It seemed that after leaving the Doc, instead of taking his advice to return to his cabin to rest his foot, he had headed to the bar in an effort to drown out the imagined pain.

Usually Philip was a friendly drunk, although he would often fall off his bar stool. Usually he was so drunk that he would basically roll off the stool and not hurt himself. The usual routine was for either the bartender or the Maitre'D to call the Doc to come and check him out "just in case". Usually he was okay, although he would come up with the strangest hallucinations when he was really drunk. This particular night, Philip was now roaring drunk and claimed to have seen elephants dancing on the stage. Either this was some strange flashback to something he had seen on his trip ashore or it may have also been him pulling our leg - which he was also known to do.

Anyway, the Doc, with the help of the Maitre'D soon helped Philip up to his cabin where it was hoped he would sleep off his pain and the excess alcohol. The Doc hoped he himself could then enjoy a peaceful night's sleep.

No such luck!

On this same trip, there were a number of people who had eaten at a shore-side restaurant, oblivious to the fact that hygiene measures were not the same in some developing nations as they are with the strict regulations of public health departments in England, France, US and Canada. Unfortunately, a number of them had contracted the Khymer's Curse - otherwise known as Tourista, Montezuma's revenge, Aztec Two Step, Delhi Belly, Moroccan Mash and similarly expressive terms. One of the passengers had had the diarrhea quite severely and had been kept in the clinics' observation room with intravenous fluids to hydrate him earlier in the day. His gastrointestinal tract was extremely irritated and he had evacuated pretty well everything - or so he thought.

He was resting on his bed back in his cabin when suddenly; however, he had another episode of diarrhea. He was so embarrassed that he had a total absence of rational thought and a complete loss of composure. He jumped up off the bed, gathered up the bed sheets and threw them off his balcony outside of his cabin thinking that they would land in the sea and his cabin steward would not have to deal with them or know what had happened to him.

As it happened, poor Philip's cabin was two decks under the cabin of our friend with the tourista and he just happened to be out on his balcony when the diarrhea soaked sheets came sailing down. The sheets landed smack bang on top of Philip.

"What the... gerrofamee... fggnnn... argghhckkk...!"

Philip started yelling, cursing and swinging his arms in an attempt to get free of whatever it was that assailed him in the dark, ending up with the soiled sheets in a tangled pile at his feet.

When the cabin steward answered Philip's call, he saw him still standing near the sheets, splattered with the diarrhea and almost in tears. Philip's tearful and panic-stricken response to the stewards' inquisitive look was,

"I think I just beat the shit out of a ghost."

Philip's new nickname forever after with the crew was "Ghostbuster".

That night, though, the Doc did his best to tend to the diarrhea epidemic - on-shore version - and fortunately only a few cases of true Norovirus. As to Philip - a victim of his own excesses - he would have to sleep off his indulgence to feel any better.

# CHAPTER FIVE

*December 6, 2009: The Atlantic Ocean*

ALAN, NOW ON HIS post-retirement cruise, chuckled, thinking of the headache poor Philip had suffered the following morning, as he made his way from his cabin after a great night's sleep. His own head was a little fuzzy after one too many whiskeys, but it had been worth it. It had relaxed him, helping him to forget about things he couldn't change, so far back in his past.

With the start of their first full day a sea, life on the ship became much more active – the casino opened for business! Alan knew that two things made major money for the cruise line: liquor and gambling. So, it was in their best interests to get both of them available as soon as possible. Alan always envied the position of the gaming director; whatever he wanted for his department, he got. Not so for the medical department that did not earn money for the cruise line.

He thought back to his other cruises, and always thought it interesting that the Disney Cruise Line opted to *not* have gambling on their ships. Granted, it was not the sort of thing that meshed well with their squeaky clean image, but after all – business was business. So, the fact that they decided not to have it said a lot for the company's image and ethics.

Alan remembered one time being asked to fill in for another physician who was unable to show up for his contract on Disney. Since he had some extra time, and needed the money, Alan said sure he would do it. It was only a four day cruise anyway. He arrived, signed in and made his way to the Staff Captain to report for duty. The Staff Captain was cordial and gave Alan all the essential facts of being an officer on his ship. He then said,

"Oh by the way Doc, you'll have to shave off your beard. We have a very strict rule about clean-shaven faces here on Disney."

Alan looked stunned and responded with,

"Sorry, sir; I have had this beard ever since medical school and am not about to shave it off to fill in for another Doc for four days. I have not unpacked, so I guess you can find another doctor for the cruise. Nice meeting you."

And Alan started walking away.

"Hold on, Doc," said the Staff Captain, worried he was about to lose the only medic he was likely to get in time to ship out promptly. "You know we are not allowed to sail without a doctor and we are to sail in one hour. Maybe - if you agreed *not* to be presented at the monkey line (the presentation of officers to the passengers on stage the first or second night) - we could sort of bend the rules this time. In other words, just do your job and don't advertise your beard. OK?"

"Fine with me, sir."

Alan hadn't thought of becoming a bearded poster boy, anyway.

And so went the four days on Disney. Needless to say, Alan never wanted to ship out on a Disney ship again! Of course as a crew member, one is *never* allowed to be in the casino. Crew members are never allowed to gamble on board - although gambling does occur in the rooms of certain crew members. When on shore, one can often see the Asian crew members making a bee-line for the onshore casinos to spend their hard-earned money. There are rather seedy and functional casinos often placed right near the internet centers and other amenities needed by crew members with only a limited time ashore.

Alan felt he was a responsible gambler; it was something he'd learned from his aunt. For each day of a vacation, he set aside a certain amount of money for gambling entertainment. If he lost it in the first hour he was in the casino – well, so be it; he left. He also set himself a deadline as to how *long* he'd stay in the casino, if he was doing well. He'd been in enough casinos - to know the one irrefutable rule about casinos: the house *always* wins! So long as you can keep the people gambling, eventually, they'll dump all their money into the casino's bank. As a result, Alan always set himself an appointed hour at which – no matter how his luck was going – he got up and left the casino.

As a result, Alan often managed to get out of the casino ahead. Sometimes, it was only a few dollars; other times, he walked away with a tidy sum.

On this, his first cruise as a passenger, Alan headed on up to the casino that first morning after he'd chowed down on a hearty breakfast. He found a Blackjack table with an attractive young lady as dealer. Hey, if he had to be there for a few hours, he might as well have something nice to look at.

Getting his chips, Alan put down fifty to start and waited for his cards.

This gave him a chance to take in the room. It was a pretty place – several nice roulette wheels, the blackjack tables, and then row after row of colorful slot machines. Alan had to laugh; the machines still had the big arms from which they'd gotten that nickname: the one-armed bandit, and those spinning wheels.

Alan knew the truth. These days, the machines all had computer chips; the arm and wheels were just for show. He found it funny to see all the different themes on the machines. Some were generic: a treasure hunt or pretty girls. Others had a tie-in to some TV show or movie; he'd seen a "Gilligan's Island" machine as he'd come in. And then there were the amounts. Years ago, there were quarter and dollar machines and the occasional nickel machine. These days, there was a whole line of *one*-cent slot machines all along one wall! So, getting a thousand credits on one of those was not that big a deal.

As Angelina (as indicated by her nametag) dealt, the casino manager, Sven (again - nametag) strolled by, a big smiled painted across his face. Ah yes, the weird world of the casino and its workers. Alan just could not imagine living in such a world, with its surveillance cameras and security people, the undercover staff to keep an eye on everything and all the other "cloak and dagger" types of activity. These days, it seemed casinos had more security than a nuclear weapons lab! Sven was clearly of Nordic extraction, probably Swedish.

As it was early in the day, Alan was able to chat with him for a while as the casino slowly filled up.

Sven was a well educated fellow, better educated than he needed to be for his job, in fact. He had a degree in computer science, but preferred the life on the ship to work in the computer industry. Alan could identify with that!

Divorced twice and not in the least bit interested in marrying again, Sven had a girlfriend, Ingrid, who was much older than him, and it was clear that *she* didn't agree with his stance on a future marriage between them.

"Ack, ya, I think she thinks she has a good find," he said. "I'm thinking she is thinking she probably wouldn't find anyone else."

"Well, there's nothing wrong with settling down, Sven," Alan replied. "So long as it's with the right person; I was lucky enough to do that myself. A true soul mate!.. She uh... just took a little finding," Alan chuckled.

"Ya, but I'm thinking that she's a bit too... anxious," Sven said. "She lives off the ship, in Denmark, but comes on board at every opportunity – and smothers me! She has got her hooks in very deep, and is trying to make herself indispensable."

Alan laughed.

"I was at sea once under a Captain once who had a similar problem...

only problem was that his girlfriend on board didn't know that there was *already* a wife… until she paid a surprise visit at one of the ports!"

"Owch!" exclaimed Sven, almost able to feel the repercussions of that encounter.

"Did he live to tell the tale?" asked Sven, morbidly fascinated with the Romeo's plight.

"Oh yes… and he got his divorce… but not everyone on board lived…," Alan jested, seeing he had an appreciative audience. "…Even though I *was* a *great* Doc, of course!"

Sven was hooked now, lazily spinning the roulette wheel at the adjacent table as the young croupier dashed off with a sudden bout of sea sickness as the waves got a little choppy. Sven carried on talking to Alan sitting just to his right side, with scant attention paid to which bets were laid. He was sure a punter would yell if they were done out of their winnings.

"S-so someone died…?"

"Several people… not all of them from natural causes," Alan replied with relish before realizing that he also had the ears of three more people who had gathered at his table. His endemic caution kicked in. Some of these things were best not shared with people already trapped on board an ocean-going cruise ship. Best not to spread panic among the passengers – and besides, some of the things that Alan suspected had not even been proven… yet.

"Ah… p'raps that's um… best left to another time, maybe…?"

There was an audible sigh of deflated expectation from around the table. Alan hid his chuckle. It seemed he'd been right to stop there before he said something libelous.

"You should write a book," said Sven.

Again Alan gave a little chuckle.

"Perhaps I will…"

Over the course of the morning, Alan learned that Ingrid had lent Sven money for a restaurant in Stockholm that they had started together. He worked at the place when he was off the ship and she "looked after" the operations the rest of the time, when she wasn't dogging him on the ship, or off on her own adventures. It seemed that Ingrid was a race car enthusiast and would follow various races all around the world; that's where they met.

"Ack, she nearly kills me one time; came on ship and sees me with other woman. I thinks I about to die right there!"

"How did you survive?" Alan said. "Introduce the young lady as your cousin?"

Sven smiled and grabbed a pen and paper.

"Ack, that is such good idea! I must writes that one down."

Alan laughed.

"Happy to be of help. But, come on; what did you do to prevent a ship-board homicide?"

"I pretend to have heart attacking; it got me out of room and to sick bay, and earned me big sympathy from my girl."

"I see. Well, whatever works. I hope the lady doesn't completely smother the life out of you…"

Sven nodded, and finally moved on to chat with some other patrons, as Alan continued to play. He looked down at his chips; huh, not bad – he looked to be ahead a decent amount. Of course, his other rule about gambling was to never count his winnings while he was sitting at the table. Huh, didn't Kenny Rogers write a song with a line about that?

Anyway, Sven's story had gotten Alan thinking. His concentration was broken so he decided it was time to get away from the table before he blew his system – and his money! Alan tossed Angelina a fifty dollar chip as a tip and made his way to the cashier's cage to cash out.

Settling down in one of the armchairs in the lounge area with a coffee, Alan remembered back to the romances he'd seen over the years on the cruise ships. He'd even had a few of his own. He smiled again now, thinking of Jo Ann whom he had had the great good fortune to meet on board one cruise to the Caribbean and with whom he had shared so much of his life.

Alan's attention was forcibly dragged back to the present by a struggle to the very edge of his right peripheral vision. He turned his head to see a red-faced toddler being deposited into the chair beside Alan as he kicked and screamed and yelled.

"I… don't… wannaaaaaaa…!"

A young man in his early thirties, presumably the boy's Dad, was trying to adopt an air of calm authority, while he felt all eyes upon him.

"Jamie… stop… James!…"

Finally the man had gotten the boy seated in the chair. He crouched down to be at 'Jamie's' eye level as the boy glared at him with barely concealed rage.

"Now…," continued the young man. "I put you in time out because you weren't listening to me. You were running around the deck area and it's slippery. You could have fallen. You also could have tripped someone else…"

The boy, realizing he wasn't going to be allowed up, softened his body language and started to listen.

"K… n-no running on the deck," he meekly parroted.

'A run on the deck'… fresh air. What a good idea!' Alan thought to himself, hurriedly getting to his feet and hastening out to the promenade deck.

He stopped to inhale the salty tang of the air, a smile on his face.

'Well, maybe not a 'run'. Maybe more of a leisurely stroll… Jamie's dad had a point, after all!'

When he got out on deck, Alan headed toward the bow. Alan had to grin at this point; doing this always reminded him of that scene from the movie "Titanic". Of course, these days, what with security and concerns about passenger safety, you could no longer get all the way out to the tip of the bow.

'My, how shipping had changed,' he thought. It went back centuries, millennia, in fact. The shipping of human cargo was always part of that; much of it was about commerce rather than cruises. It was, at one time, in the holds of old schooners that people were treated as commodities - slaves. Alan thought it was funny that some modern ships had a similar feel to them.

It was when more than explorers and merchants decided to travel larger distances that the ships and accommodations became a bit more like the homes of the people who were using the newfound travel mode. In the steerage class of travel on ships like the *Luciana* or *Queen Mary*, the rooms were small, cramped and poorly lit. This resembled the accommodations one would see in the ghettos of Dublin or London or Berlin.

Then, if you moved up a few notches in class structure on these "Grande Dames" of the sea, the cabins would have brocaded curtains, multiple room suites and rooms for the servants. There were dining rooms of ultra elegance, much like the fine restaurants of Europe and New York and Boston. The quality of service and accoutrements provided in the suites was in every way superb.

Alan could remember his grandmother describing sea journeys like that from London to the US. It must have been a grand time for all concerned, and it was actually his Grandmother who had started him off writing the notebooks of his travels and the people he met along the way. Knowing the history of sea travel, Alan knew that, following the tragedy of the *Titanic*, sea travel got quite the black-eye for a while. Whoever had said there was no such thing as bad publicity clearly did not know what they were talking about!

But then, jet forward some fifty years or so, and the popularity of sea travel returned, and not necessarily for business or necessity of travel, but for pure tourism and hedonism. The key to it was the availability of ships with cabins that the average Joe could afford. For many, being able to go to sea in a cruise liner was (and still is) a great experience - even if they had an inside room without all the accoutrements of the grand deluxe class.

Even with this said, one had to forgo much in creature comforts in "tourist class" to be able to be on the ship to enjoy the other amenities. Where else in the world would someone spend good money for a room half the size of the typical bedroom in a home, with a bathroom the size of a broom closet? And then there was the hallway to the room; it'd be the length of a few football fields and you better not forget the number of your cabin, because the doors all looked the same in tourist class.

On the other hand, in 'upper class' it was a different story altogether. A suite of rooms in some of the modern cruise ships could have more square footage than some very fancy homes and condos. Their private patios, balconies and Jacuzzis were elegantly designed to give the utmost of privacy to the occupants and some areas even had private elevators to whisk the residents to their suite of five, six or more rooms. Some of them even had separate quarters for the servants, nannies, adults and children.

These suites were also known for having the ultimate in technological gadgetry, so that one could view full-screen movies, communicate with one's home office in the privacy of the en-suite office at sea and allow the kids to play the latest in virtual reality video games without disturbing a romantic evening the parents might want to have in one of the living rooms.

Granted, the price differential between the tourist class and upper class on most ships could be significant. Buying a last minute ticket on *Carnival, Celebrity,* or *Royal Caribbean Cruise Line* on the internet for a seven-day Caribbean cruise out of Miami might only cost a couple hundred dollars per person or even less. For the same destinations and departure city, a suite on *Crystal, Regency, Cunard or Silver Seas Cruise Lines* might make the average person's mortgage payment look paltry. Alan could remember seeing suites on some of these ships go for as *little* as twenty-five thousand to over a hundred and eighty thousand per person per week!

Alan also thought about the crews on these ships; they could vary from a single nationality to a very heavily multi nationality crew. One ship he'd sailed on had had seventy-eight different nationalities among its fifteen hundred crew members, and they got along better than the United Nations! Another had had only eight nationalities. Unfortunately, the Human Resources Department for that cruise line did not plan ahead well and hired large factions of traditional enemies! So, that meant there were Arabs and Jews, Pakistanis and Indians, Chechens and Russians and so on. Alan had spent half of his time on that contract suturing stab wounds from the opposing factions — especially those working in the kitchen where there were readily available weapons to settle 'old scores of my forefathers'.

At least there'd been no deaths.

There it was again, that memory rippling through his mind. Yeah, there had been a death – a murder, Alan thought - and he still wondered about it. After all, the murderer had never been discovered and in fact, the authorities at the time hadn't considered Michael's death to be a murder. But now, Sven had talked about faking a heart attack. There were ways to induce heart attacks as well as fake them. What about Michael; had he really just had a bad heart and… died, or was there something more to his death?

Yes, his death had been ruled a massive MI (Myocardial Infarction), and he had a history of heart trouble, but it still gnawed at Alan. Something just wasn't right about that whole sorry episode! He shook his head; oh, why was he obsessing about it? Michael was dead and buried; why not let the past stay buried? After all, he was on vacation – he was here for fun!

Alan shook his head; enough with the wondering; it was time to wander and look for some fun! Thoughts of Michael were becoming an obsession for him.

So, once out in the bow section, Alan found what he had always called the "Kiddie Corner". As with many cruise ships, this one had several swimming pools; each had a specific designation. The main ones (usually mid ship) were generic - for everyone. Back in the stern was often one for adults only so they could swim in peace! And then there was this one; to get in here officially, you actually *had* to have a kid with you. It made Alan smile to see all the little ones at play. Goodness, it seemed like only yesterday that Alexa was a little toddler. Where did the years go? You blink and a decade had slipped away. Alan made a mental note: must "blink" less around Alexa, then maybe she wouldn't age so fast.

The pool area was quite nice: a wide open deck with many lounge chairs. Some were properly proportioned for the smaller members of the ship's company. One little "lady" was very intent on having a proper English tea party. She had her little tea service and took the pot over to the pool to fill it. Oh, Alan hoped she wasn't planning on actually drinking that!

He watched as the little blonde cherub carefully poured a cup for her mother and father, and then for herself. She was very precise in everything she did; she even raised her pinky as she lifted the cup to her lips, and promptly poured the water into her lap! As she was decked out in a little canary yellow bikini, it didn't matter.

"Do you like your tea, Mum, Dad?" She said, with the most delightful English accent.

Her Mum nodded.

"Yes, Janey, it's perfect."

A tea set: such a simple little thing, and yet it packed a lot of memories for Alan. It was Christmas, more years ago than he cared to think about, and his Dad had given Alexa one as a present. He always did that for any little kid. As he said,

"Kids love to have a tea set; they love pouring the water back and forth."

Jo Ann had agreed that it was the perfect gift, although she did get tired of having to wipe up the spilled water.

Alan blinked very fast; he was about to generate some "spilled water" himself. Goodness, he had to get his mind on something happier, before he started weeping uncontrollably!

Alan moved to the railing and took a long deep breath, holding it in his lungs a long time. Oh, that salt air was like pure nectar for his soul.

Alan slowly shook his head and turned to look out over the rolling white waves. Little Janey was certainly much better behaved that other child, Jamie, he'd seen earlier. Oh, and then there had been that other tiny terror and the lovely lady that had been his mother. Wow! Alan hadn't thought about *them* in a *long* time. What was it with him and all this reminiscing today!

Alan had truly enjoyed their times together as a young man. If things had been different, they may have been his family, instead of Jo Ann and Alexa! Alan shook his head. Everything happened for a reason and he was sure that two very good reasons were Jo Ann and Alexa. Any other family was unthinkable to him. Still, Alan's mind was cast back to an earlier romance on board a ship very much like this...

# CHAPTER SIX

*July 11, 1984: The Gulf of Mexico*

CHRISTINA HER NAME HAD been – a real Costa Rican beauty. She was tall, with a slender figure and blonde hair right down to her butt – oh and what a bubble butt! Alan noticed that, even though the rest of her body was draped in a tearful looking toddler.

Jesus, the boy's name was – and often from that date for the next few weeks Alan was heard to exclaim 'Jesus!' with his eyes cast heavenwards at yet another of the of the boy's escapades. 'Never has a child been so inappropriately named', thought Alan.

As soon as Christina stood Jesus down on the floor in the clinic, he rushed to the dressings trolley and proceeded to strew medical and first aid supplies all over the sick bay floor.

"Yahooooooo… ha ha choo!" the little boy exclaimed as his joyous skid across the linoleum, helped by a dressing pad beneath each foot, was halted by an almighty sneeze which sent a jet of bright yellow mucus from his nose right down to his chin.

"Well, he has a cold, but it doesn't seem to be bothering him too much now," Alan said, tensely smiling around gritted teeth.

As Alan bent to retrieve the dressings from the floor and thus avoid the boy breaking a leg or maybe worse, the Doc let out a startled "Oof!" as he was struck forcibly on the back of the neck by the metal kidney bowl that Jesus was now wielding.

Christina gave her son an adoring smile, ruffling his hair.

"My poor baby – can you give him something, Doctor?"

Under his breath, Alan muttered,

"How about a spank...?"

Luckily or unluckily, Christina didn't seem to hear the muttered comment. She was too busy tickling Jesus to get him to drop the very sharp scissors he had seized from the dressings tray on a countertop that the Doc had thought too high for children to reach. It *would* have been too high for Jesus to reach except that while the Doc was recovering his senses, Jesus had yanked open a drawer and was now standing on it to reach all the alluring things that had been placed purposefully out of the reach of children.

"He is very advanced. Can you believe he's only two?"

"No," said the Doc, rather weakly.

Who would have guessed that such a young child could wreak such havoc in just a few minutes? However, during the examination which the Doc managed to carry out, but which took three times as long as it normally would, as the Doc had to practically pry the stethoscope and otoscope from the surprisingly strong toddler, the Doc was beginning to wonder if the term 'very advanced' was nothing more than maternal boasting. Sure, Jesus was incredibly active and his agility at evading his mother's gentle embraces and the Doc's increasingly firmer holds was impressive. But throughout the fifteen minute consultation, Alan was struck by the fact that he never once heard Jesus utter a coherent word, just a series of grunts and cries and angry exclamations.

The only thing that helped the Doc keep his cool under the extreme pressure that Jesus was exerting over his patience was the fact that - within the first few seconds of the consultation – Alan realized this was the girl he had been looking for. At least, she sure looked like her! And it seemed that she liked the look of the Doc too. She kept batting those beautiful long eyelashes at him and he was sure she was bending forward on purpose just so he could see down her top. Oh yes, Christina was an out and out flirt, but right now, looking at *that* body – he didn't care! It just made it all the more easy for him that she was throwing herself at him.

"Would you... oh, maybe can't... with... *him*...," Alan blabbed, confused, words tumbling over each other.

Christina was ahead of him in this game. Some might say she was in a different league altogether, but the Doc was immune to all doubts right now.

"I could join you for dinner," Christina offered freely, but with an edge of coyness which Alan found charming.

"Yes!... Oh yes!" the Doc jumped on her words, grinning like the fool he was usually not. All thoughts of Angelina disappeared. She had been flavor of the month until she threw Alan over for one of the younger cabin crew.

"Th-that's what I was going to say… but…"

Alan's hand gestured ineffectually at the boy who was now unraveling the whole roll of paper towels from the dispenser on the wall and wrapping himself in it. The Doc, with the shred of cognizance he had left, only just stopped himself wishing that Jesus would mummify himself in the paper roll and thus be quieted down, when he realized that this may be a little difficult for him to explain to a police inquiry.

"My parents… they will look after him…," Christine saved the Doc from further unholy thoughts towards the little Jesus.

Immediately, a smile spread subconsciously across Alan's face.

"He… his father…?"

"Is dead," Christina declared as if this was of no consequence to her.

The smile threatened to split Alan's face in two!

"In that case… no… I mean… would you like to join me for dinner?… At my table?… They give me a table… Doc's perks… Very private…"

"I'd love to!" Christina enthusiastically agreed.

So the pair made arrangements to meet up that evening at seven, in the little cocktail bar situated beside the restaurant. Alan looked forward to it all afternoon, even writing in his notebook diary the date and time he met Christina, accompanying the entry with the words 'Today I fell in love'. However, up in his cabin, preparing for the evening meal – and hopefully entertainment – Alan got cold feet. Christina was too forward. He wasn't ready.

Alan remembered another siren he had encountered years back. She had come onto him in much the same way-batting the eyelashes, showing beautiful parts of her body, etc, etc. She was an intelligent girl, which always attracted Alan, and a good conversationalist. She too had a kid.

This one was a bit different from Jesus, in that her daughter was well behaved. 'The little angel' showed Alan her pictures and some of her crafts that she had made, expressly for him on the spot. Alan had had a lovely dinner with this siren, who then invited him back to her place: a lovely apartment, very tastefully appointed and quite large. They talked, and then he was invited to use one of the spare rooms to 'get yourself ready for bed'. He remembered the wording so precisely! He did so, and donned the soft cotton bathrobe that was provided. She came to lead him into her boudoir. He dutifully followed, like a dog on a leash. His heart nearly stopped when he arrived and found that there were three single beds in her 'boudoir'. One was hers, one for her brother (already sleeping), and the one she gestured for Alan to 'have a good night's sleep' in.

Alan made numerous verbal protests, not worrying about waking the sleeping brother, and tried, in vain, to physically subtly seduce her. He left early in the morning. Nothing had happened. With this flash in his brain, he tried to convince himself that Christina wasn't his type.

But, what was his type? Alan didn't really know. He was much better at describing his ideal woman in his diary than he was at actually meeting her, much less having a conversation with someone he found attractive. He sighed, because unless he got talking to some ladies, how was he ever going to find out what his type was! With a deep breath, Alan made a few final adjustments to his uniform tux and, satisfied that this was the best he could do, he walked purposefully toward the elevator and entered it with a small group.

Once in the elevator, Alan had that familiar feeling that he had developed severe B.O. or that fleas were jumping about his collar. The elevator was spacious and airy, and it felt so to Alan, standing tall and proud and comfortable in his smart officers' uniform. But a glance to the other side of the elevator disclosed three women and a man closely huddled together, obviously staying away from Alan, although visibly uncomfortable with their close contact, so not all together. All six eyes were trained on Alan with a look of respect, wariness and morbid fascination that before he became a ship's doctor, Alan had imagined was only reserved for Royalty. Now he realized that all the ship's officers drew such looks.

"Good evening," Alan bade the onlookers, touching his temple in a dignified salute as the elevator doors opened and allowed him to step out onto the floor of the restaurant bar. Alan only hoped that the trio in the elevator recovered from their stupor in time to also vacate the elevator at the restaurant level or else it would surely be summoned back up to the cabins and then it would take ages to return to the restaurant. They might miss the hors d'ouvres!

However, Alan didn't waste much time thinking about that. He had a dinner date and one that certainly was not shy about making eye contact with him – nor close bodily contact! No sooner had he stepped into the bar than Christina (to whom the idea of being fashionably late for a date had never occurred) walked over to the Doc and placed her hand on his chest and caressed his crisp white dress shirt, bringing her body close so he could enjoy the full force of her low cut red evening dress, her heady perfume and her sultry voice as she breathed, almost against his mouth.

"OOoo, Alan! So handsome!"

Alan blushed as red as Christina's dress, he was sure.

"You too... uh... I mean..."

Christina giggled girlishly and it broke the tension a little, allowing Alan to relax and give himself a bit of a silent talking-to.

"You look beautiful… everything… OK?… With Jesus…?" Alan dragged the words he knew were polite from his mouth.

"He's fine. Sleeping like a baby…," Christina effortlessly waved away the doctor's concern.

This was Christina's time and she intended to make the most of it. She took a quick look around to be sure she was garnering the looks she wished. She was. She knew that at least half a dozen women on the nearby tables would have given their eye teeth to be in her position, as the dinner date of the handsome Doc. Alan was pretty happy with the arrangement, too!

"This… the vacation… it's for my parents' Ruby wedding anniversary…"

"Ah…," responded the Doc.

"Daddy paid," Christina inelegantly dropped into the conversation.

'So she's come from money, then,' Alan realized. Bringing your adult daughter and her devil child offspring on such an expensive cruise with you was usually considered to be above and beyond the call of regular parental duty, he was sure.

But, away from the distraction of Jesus, Alan was thrilled to realize that Christina was as intelligent and charming a dinner companion as she was beautiful. Over the first two courses, Alan found out that Christina's family was from Costa Rica. Her father owned a couple of big factories that made jeans and other high end clothes for export to the US and Europe: 'a sweat shop' Alan unkindly but probably accurately presumed.

Knowledge of how her father's millions had been made did not put Alan off Christina in the least. He was never one to visit the sins of the fathers on the offspring… although, quite relaxed after his second glass of good red wine, the idea did temporarily flit across his brain of exactly what someone as beautiful and charming as the lovely Christina could have done in a past life to be visited upon by the devil child, Jesus.

"You were very good with him earlier… Jesus I mean…," Christina interrupted Alan's thoughts.

He grinned at her nervously as a flush that was due to more than red wine warmed his face. It was like she could read his mind. 'Jesus, I've never felt like this before,' Alan thought before mentally slapping his forehead. Jesus was popping up everywhere. How on earth that child got that name he would never comprehend.

Alan smiled weakly.

"Um… thanks… Doctors' training, I guess… Is he… *always*… like that…?" Alan asked cautiously.

"He's full of energy, always. A real live wire!" Christina gushed with loving praise about her son.

"He um… d-doesn't talk much…," Alan again ventured cautiously.

The maternal counter was quick.

"He doesn't need to. He makes his feelings known without words."

'Yeah, you can say that again,' thought Alan ruefully, rubbing his sore neck.

But pretty soon after that, Alan realized that Jesus could do no wrong in Christina's eyes and he saw no reason to spoil the chance of a lovely evening with a beautiful woman by giving an unasked for 'organ recital' on the probable diagnosis of ADHD, maybe even an Autistic Spectrum Disorder, that the Doc had quickly reached with regards to the young Jesus.

"Sooo…," he quickly changed the subject. "You work for your father..?" he picked up on something Christina had said earlier.

"Uh-huh. Human resources. I hire. I fire. Dad has twelve hundred employees. They all know to keep on my good side… or else…"

Christina gave a wicked grin that sent all the right kinds of shivers through Alan. 'It's a pity she didn't exert the same kind of control over her son', he thought to himself. But he said nothing of that, of course – and besides – Alan was falling for this girl – hook, line and sinker.

He was very relieved to find out that Christina was a widow, although that of course left no ex-husband with which Jesus could be left should their relationship progress as far as romantic breaks in exotic cities, which Alan was already hoping it would.

It seemed that Christina's marriage had only lasted one year to a very wealthy Columbian tycoon whom she said was also involved in the clothing business, "among other activities", which Alan did not want to venture into. She was loyal to her husband in as much as she swore he was an honest businessman, but after further discussions of the houses he had purchased for her at various resorts, the fast cars, jewelry, clothes, etc. that he had provided for her, Alan thought that seemed like an awful lot of money he'd made in clothing…

"He died of a heart attack… and now all I have left is Jesus… and… and tonight," she whispered seductively against Alan's mouth before moving in for a kiss.

# CHAPTER SEVEN

*December 6, 2009: The Atlantic Ocean*

ALAN CHUCKLED TO HIMSELF, remembering that first date with Christina so many years ago. Oh it hadn't ended there, of course, but he wouldn't let himself think of that now. That would seem like a betrayal of Jo Ann.

… So, what to do now? Fortunately, the ship - like those on other cruise lines - always printed up what could be called a "daily planner": a listing of all of the activities for the day, along with the times of the respective items.

Alan had left the one provided in his room slot back in his room. He stepped up to the passenger services desk and snatched one up from a pile neatly placed on their desk. A friendly smile from the cute Asian front office clerk belied the probable boredom she had with the multitude of passengers that asked stupid questions and had impossible requests. Ah, just as he thought - a trivia contest was going to start soon in the main lounge. Yeah, that'd be just the ticket for getting his mind off of unhappy thoughts.

Alan knew that trivia was a game often played on the longer cruises, and the games usually had quite the loyal following of daily participants. Back in the day, he'd even run some of the games and there were always a group of questions that had to be answered by individuals or teams. The inducement to cruisers was that some kind of prize was given out, and then they officially had bragging rights on the ship, until they were upstaged by a cleverer group.

As trivial as it seemed, it was almost impossible to consider that one of these cruisers would actually miss out on one of these games. Alan wondered what the subject of the contest was going to be and then got his answer as the pretty, perky cruise director came bouncing into view.

"I hope you all have your thinking caps on!" She chirped.

Oh yeah, a cruise director to the nth degree!

"We're going to test your knowledge of animated TV theme songs today," she added. "And the winner gets this lovely gold-painted plastic ship on a stick."

Alan looked up as she pulled the little trinket from her bag. Yeah, a typical prize. He smiled; it didn't matter, he still thought it was cute, and he knew that the people around him shared that sentiment; he could read it on their faces.

So, pretty little Tiffany got out her CD player and set it on the grand piano of the lounge. The place was a nicely decorated club with a distinctly nautical theme. The piano sat near the outer wall, which was glass from floor to ceiling, and had long white curtains. Around the piano, in a series of semi-circles and arcs, were the tables and chairs, each circle sort of separated from the others by decorations of ship's rigging.

Alan picked up his paper and pencil and got ready to write. Tiffany proceeded to play a series of brief clips from twenty different theme songs. Alan watched her at work; she seemed genuinely happy to be here. He smiled; yeah, he could remember being on shore and wanting so much to be at sea...

"So, everyone ready to add up their scores?" Tiffany said.

Alan snapped back to the present. He looked down; huh, he'd not being paying attention; he'd only written down half a dozen names. Oh, well, maybe he'd have better luck tomorrow with the American history trivia quiz.

A pretty little lady came in first and got her prize. Afterwards, Tiffany came over to chat with Alan.

"I saw you sort of... drift off there, sir. Not one for trivia are you?"

Alan smiled at her.

"On the contrary; I'm usually very good at it. It's just... well; I've had other things on my mind lately."

Tiffany seemed very adept at picking up subtle signals from people. Alan could understand that, that's what made for good cruise ship staff members - feeling empathy for the clients and making them feel at ease. He thought back to Michael, who had been very good at that – and it had gotten him out of trouble on more than one occasion by knowing when to make a quick exit!

Alan's eyes locked on Tiffany's eyes, and saw her gaze slip down to his hand - his *left* hand. Ah, she was good! Now, if she followed the standard protocol for innocent banter, she'd ask a very neutral and innocuous question.

"So, what brings you on board our little slice of heaven?"

Alan grinned. Yeah, she was *very* good! She's asking him a question, thus throwing the conversation into his lap and encouraging him to open up. He rubbed his thumb across the gold band on his left ring finger.

"Oh... I'm not sure. Trying to forget, or maybe trying to remember. A good portion of my life was spent on ships like this."

"Ah... I had a feeling you were 'family'," she said brightly.

"What gave me away?" Alan said, and laughed.

She laughed with him for a moment, then said,

"To be honest; I'm not sure. I guess there's just something about people who've work- ... *served* on a cruise ship that... sets them apart from the... regular passengers. So... your wife is... gone...?"

"Yes. Ah, she was a good woman. Oh, but look at me, taking you away from your duties! Please, don't let me keep you..."

Tiffany reached out and patted Alan's arm. Oh, the 'human contact' bit: very nice. Alan knew that the simple sensation of touch was so very important to human health; it was something he'd been sorely lacking for quite a while. He actually felt a slight tingle in his spine and felt his face grow warm as he noticed goose-bumps breaking out on his arm. Oh, he hoped he wasn't blushing too much now.

"It's quite all right; I've got some free time," she said.

"Thank you. Ah, Jo was one of the unusual ladies in my life; she tolerated me being away. For most of the ladies in my life, they never accepted the fact that, for me, there was a special lure that the sea had. I'd heard about it as a child, when my grandmother told me about men going off to sea for years at a time. But, I never thought it would be me."

"Let me guess; you served on a ship, and then tried 'civilian life', and the... sea pulled you back, right?" Tiffany said.

Alan laughed.

"Oh, you're good, little lady! Yeah, I was standing in an office tower waiting on an interview for a position as Director of Emergency Medicine for a multi-state group in Seattle. God, it was a beautiful summer's day, and I made the mistake of gazing out the window. There, only a few steps away on the Seattle water-front, were the unmistakable features of a cruise ship at the passenger pier."

"Ah, and one look at the... 'lovely lady' was all it took, eh?"

Alan nodded.

"Yeah. The Human Resources Director droned on and on with the usual litany of interview questions, and the entire time I was thinking of that ship sitting only a few blocks away. The thought of being 'stranded' on shore and commuting to work on a freeway made me think of the 'commute' I normally had on a ship: from my room to the medical center."

"Oh, I know what you mean," Tiffany said. "To be here, on this ship, and the sea, the people, the fun! I can't imagine doing anything else?"

"This your first tour?" Alan said.

"Fourth; I keep coming back!" She said with a laugh.

"I know that look," he replied. "The sea has a special magnetism that keeps people doing just that."

"You're right, and it's certainly not the ports, because some of them are not all that interesting."

"Nor the salaries, that are just about the same as flipping hamburgers at McDonalds!"

They both laughed.

"And it's not the extensive administrative work that's required on a ship! Ugh, major boring," Alan added.

Tiffany laughed louder, then looked around, leaned in toward him and whispered,

"And it truly is not the screaming brats that disturb just about every aspect of the daily routine!"

Alan grinned; oh yeah, he well remembered some of those kinds of kids.

"Yeah, it was the camaraderie that formed between the crewmembers. It was the friends I made on the brief visits with the passengers. It's funny, but some of those people were a mere 'flash in the pan', and others - well, some of them I still stay in touch with."

"Perhaps… I'll be one of those," Tiffany said, getting to her feet.

She offered him her hand. He rose, his hand shaking for a moment as he was reluctant to take hers. And then, he gave in to proper etiquette and gave it a gentle shake.

"Who knows? Perhaps… you shall."

With that, they parted. Alan stood there, watching her go. My-my, quite the fine figure of a woman! She had a very nice… wiggle, as she walked. So, he would have to wait and see what - if anything - might develop between them. He blinked, and realized he was holding his breath. Oh, for Pete's sake, he needed to get a grip; he was acting like a teenager!

Sitting back down, he gazed out the window. Ah, what a view: the peace and quiet found in fleeting moments out on the sea. Ah, that beautiful setting, the vastness and variability of the sea. One of the best lessons Alan ever got from a crew member - a lowly boson's assistant who tended the main drive - was respect for the sea. Somehow, those open waters engendered respect from all who visited, saw, or worked on it.

That was undoubtedly the reason that the sea commanded bits and pieces of his life over his long tenure as a ship's doctor, and continued to do so as a fill-in ship's doctor and now passenger.

Putting his feet up, Alan stretched out on the lounge chair, put his head back, and just tried to relax. Ah, he had a feeling that this was going to be a sweet cruise. He felt so completely calm; he found it hard to stay awake! In fact, he fell asleep there, and awoke just about the time the sun was melting into the Atlantic.

Getting to his feet, he yawned and stretched, and tried to get the old blood flowing again. Oh, he was stiff. These chairs were not exactly built for long-term comfort. His stomach grumbled; time to head down to dinner. In the old days, he'd get dressed up for a meal. Now, on his own and… alone - he saw no point.

A loud clang behind him caught his attention, and he turned to see a crewmember trying to mop up something. Alan grinned. Ah, a new member of the crew; he could spot one a mile away. But, such matters were no longer his concern. So, it was off to dinner for him.

From the ship's map, which he had a copy of folded up and tucked in his back pocket, it was easy enough to find an elevator to the dining room.

Stepping into the room, he looked around. This wasn't quite the huge sort of hall he was used to eating in; the ceiling was much lower. The center section was slightly raised, almost like the dais or stage of a conference hall. Huh, no handicap access for those tables! But, that was okay; ringing the raised area were many tables at ground level; their windows looked out over the black waters of the Atlantic.

The place was certainly richly appointed: lovely linen tablecloths, fine china and glassware and the wait staff were decked out in their finest. Of course, Alan knew that it was always a good idea to see the preparation and storage of what was going into his stomach. If he could see it being prepared and he was satisfied that the storage prior to cooking was adequate, the utensils were clean and the food cooked sufficiently, then he was much more confident about the meal not negatively impacting upon his digestive system. Obviously, with current security concerns and health issues, passengers were not allowed to visit the galley. Since they were on a 4 star ship, Alan relaxed and assumed all the accoutrements in the kitchen were up to snuff.

As Alan was alone, there was always the question of where to seat him. Now, he knew that the custom was to stick small groups at the big tables, so the single people would feel less lonely. After all, lots of singles came on cruises for the chance to 'link up'. In Alan's case, he didn't care one way or the other: each type of seating had its pluses and minuses. But on reflection, at a big table, he had the chance to remain silent and out of the conversation, if he chose, so, he opted for that.

He ended up a medium-sized table, with seating for six, and all the others were alone on the cruise. There were four men and two women, but it was soon clear that two of the men were… not competition; they were… single, but together. Oh well, more power to them; Alan was never one to judge. The ladies on his right and left were Jennifer and Christina. Alan caught his breath at the coincidence so soon after thoughts of another Christina from his past, but he soon relaxed. They were "Jenny" and "Tina", as they chirped at him. *His* Christina had always wanted to be addressed by her full name, never have it shortened. It was one of the things she insisted upon. It was one thing he didn't mind – quite liked, in fact – in contrast to other things she insisted upon, which had driven Alan half-crazy. No disciplining her son… no criticizing her son… He squirmed as he even recalled how Jesus was often right there in the bed with them!

No, that relationship was never built to last! Alan's attention was brought back to the present with a faux pas dropped by one of the guys at the table.

It turned out that while Jenny and Tina were single, they were sisters, in their mid-twenties and fresh out of college. Alan had to grin. Oh, there was a time when certain male members of the crew positively *lived* for the chance to get at such lovely ladies. Two for the price of one!

Alan had to bite the inside of his cheek to keep from laughing out loud. He'd met another Christina, and thankfully, this one didn't have a screaming "devil child" hanging on her. And yet, he wasn't the same man who'd linked up with that Christina years ago; a lot of water had gone under his bridge. So, could he find the courage to pursue this one in the same way as the first?

"We're going to go work in developing countries," Jenny said.

Tina nodded.

"Yes, we want to help people to develop new farming and sanitation techniques."

Alan gave his order to the waiter, and then gave the ladies his full attention.

"Ah, that's very good of you. In some countries I've visited, I've had to wonder if the meal I was eating was served on plates washed in sewer water and if the cockroaches were brushed off just before the food was served!"

"Ah yes, cleanliness can be an issue," Tina admitted. "Do you know how hard it is for most people just to get clean drinking water?"

"Oh yes!" Alan replied. "And in regards to getting raw ingredients that were fresh and clean, sometimes the roadside vendors were often a better deal than the so-called fancy restaurants. After all, with most of them, I could see how things were being prepared and not have it hidden behind the fancy tablecloths! I remember one situation where I was told that the place to go for the best meal was a small café down the street from the ever popular tourist restaurant. To get to the place, I had to go in the alley behind this well known, well advertised tourist place. What I saw made my stomach do contortions! The cooks at the popular eatery were wearing such dirty clothes and never even thought of washing their hands after using the outside bathroom! When I arrived at the little café I'd been recommended, what a contrast! The owner politely ushered me in to see his spotless stainless steel kitchen before he seated me. I was so relieved, and had a great meal."

Suddenly, everyone at the table was looking at their own plates. Alan bit his lip.

"Ah, of course, this being a cruise ship in one of the top of the line cruise lines, the quality of food isn't an issue. Cruises and cruise lines are well known for the large amounts of high quality food that they provide to their passengers in the most sanitary of conditions. There are regular inspections of the stored food, the preparation and the timing of its presentation to the passengers. If anywhere, a cruise ship of this caliber is *not* a place that one has to be concerned about the cleanliness of the food. There is even a limit for the length of time that food is allowed to be on the serving line. After that time, the food is automatically taken off and destroyed. It is really a waste of good food that could feed many hungry people, but rules are rules and cruise ships must follow them. Thankfully, a good chef can calculate well how much food will be consumed in a given time, and minimize the food wastage on a cruise ship."

Jenny gave a heavy sigh.

"Yes, isn't it a pity that so much food is wasted here, when it could help those less fortunate in so many countries?" she bemoaned.

Alan smiled. It seemed that Jenny, not Tina, was more on his wavelength. She was pretty, too. He warmed to his appreciative audience and became even more eloquent on a topic he felt very passionate about.

"Yes, I can well remember some of the cruises I've worked on that made stops in areas of the developing world. It was always such a contrast: people throwing tons of food away and coming to my dispensary for something to settle their upset stomachs, and then there were often people on shore who did die hungry. Unfortunately, most governments don't allow cruise ships to offload food items. We crew did, from time to time, occasionally bring some items in our shore bags when we knew someone on shore and that they would not report the ship for bringing them some food."

Jenny almost applauded Alan but he was on his soapbox now, on a subject close to his heart so he soon continued,

"The cost to society of starvation was, and is, a real problem, and had been for centuries. Famines occur due to droughts, fires, pestilence and of course ethnic cleansing and war in general."

Daniel (one of the gay men) seemed less than interested in this conversation.

"That's not usually a subject that's brought up on cruise ships though, is it?" he said with a derisive snort.

Jenny and Tina ignored him, and were now intently interested in Alan. He wasn't sure if it was that fact that he agreed with them, or that he'd let the cat out of the bag about him being both a doctor and former cruise ship employee.

"So, doctor, what are your plans for tomorrow?" Jenny asked, a big smile on her face.

Alan felt a bit warm, suddenly; had someone turned off the air conditioning? The ladies were quite attractive, curvy, without being too thin or too plump, and decked out in some lovely sun dresses. They were low cut and quite short, yet still adequately conservative - at least by today's standards.

Alan licked his lips and cleared his throat before speaking; he didn't want his voice to squeak like someone who'd inhaled some helium!

"Ah, well… in reviewing the ship's itinerary, I see that we'll be at this cruise line's private island tomorrow. After so many years on the 'behind the scenes' side of such playful activities, I'm looking forward to being on the 'good… fun side'."

"Oh, are you going to go to the… clothing-optional beach?" Tina teased, a big grin on her face.

Jenny frowned at her.

"Tina, don't embarrass the good doctor!"

Tina painted a little pout on her lip.

"Oh, was I a… badddddd girl?"

Tina giggled, and winked at Alan. Oh, this was going to be a long meal! Alan decided to try and change the subject.

"You know, during the day on the private island, the ship typically feeds most of the cruisers during the eight hours that the ship is moored off shore. That means that the crew has to bring enough food and cooking supplies to feed about twenty-five hundred passengers and a goodly portion of the one thousand five hundred crewmembers! No small task."

Tina's brow wrinkled.

"And, is all of that food actually eaten by all of the people?"

Alan nodded.

"Yes, for the most part; it never ceased to amaze me how most cruise passengers take the 'all you can eat' dining so literally. I learned a long time ago that you really didn't need to eat *everything* on a buffet. There are many more meals and other food venues around. Most cruise ships provide food somewhere on the ship twenty-four hours a day."

"Yes, I love the pizza oven they have up on the Promenade Deck," the rather rotund Daniel said.

"There you go," Alan replied. "Oh, when I think of all the passengers who came to the medical center with stomach aches. No sooner had I settled their stomachs than it was a virtual certainty that they'd be back at the buffets the next night to eat again. They were definitely *not* bears needing to hibernate, but many took on the appearance of one after a couple of weeks on a cruise!" he grinned, feeling rather proud of himself at being able to elicit some smiles from his table-mates at the inference.

The girls laughed, even as the waiter brought their next course - a small green salad.

"Only in America can you have a situation where it's actually hard to go hungry," Tina said.

Alan chewed, swallowed and wiped his lips with his napkin.

"Yes, usually, just the opposite happens and people complained of eating too much, gaining weight, seeing their blood sugars go sky high with their diabetes way out of control, and so on and…"

Alan's voice trailed off, his fork halfway to his mouth. He was doing it himself now – giving organ recitals! With a little blush and a mumbled apology, Alan resumed his meal.

He didn't know whether to laugh or cringe when Daniel, obviously prompted by Alan's warnings, popped out his little medical kit, opened a shirt button by his navel and injected himself with his insulin. 'Such a convenient little device, that pen syringe!' Alan thought.

That thought awakened another memory in his mind…

# CHAPTER EIGHT

*July 12, 1984: Cozumel, Mexico*

THE DOC WAS REQUIRED to be present that evening at the midnight buffet so he hadn't had enough time to do more than knock on Michael's door and again receive no answer before he had to go cover the buffet. He hadn't minded that duty; the buffet was a downright *orgy* of culinary delights! Many people were used to seeing ice sculptures and there were some really spectacular ones; but this feast featured cheese, chocolate and other tasty treats carved and arranged into beautiful works of art. It was almost a shame to eat them.

Yet, that was exactly what they did. Dr. Zetisman regularly indulged in a true mountain of chocolate; he seemed to have a real fondness for dark chocolate. Now that, in and of itself, was not unusual; many people liked lots of chocolate. What stuck in Alan's mind was that Dr. Zetisman had said he was diabetic. Here again, breaking from one's proper diet and medication on a cruise was not that unusual; Alan had treated plenty of diabetics who did just that. The old adage about people leaving their brains and medicines on shore when they got onboard a cruise ship was not far from the truth. Many times, the Doc needed to fill prescriptions for passengers' medicine for blood pressure, epilepsy, diabetes, COPD, etc. But this guy really seemed to be going for it and he laughed off all of the Doc's concerned advice.

He just patted the metal case he carried, not unlike a glasses case, and said,

"I have my insulin, Doc. If I'm gonna get injected with a horse needle every day I may as well enjoy myself too!"

Such scant attention to one's own health made the Doc cringe, especially in one who proclaimed himself a retired doctor, but the man did seem to remain healthy. He was often seen taking out the syringe to which he would attach a needle so large that it had the ladies swooning away and then disappearing, presumably to inject himself in private. The Doc often thought he did this for effect. Most diabetics he knew were pretty discrete about their necessary medication and they didn't use needles quite as large as that. Perhaps Dr. Zetisman just liked to make the ladies faint! He did seem to take rather a perverse pleasure in the discomfort his syringe caused, especially in the dining room.

Chuckling at that thought, Alan grew somber as a senior cabin crew member hurried across to him and whispered in his ear.

"You're needed in one of the staff cabins, Doc."

Still wanting to keep an eye on the chocolate-gorging 'diabetic', the Doc groaned, suspecting this would be some drunken, over-indulged twenty-something on his first trip out.

"What is it? I'm meant to be on duty here and only called to an emergency…"

"I uh… think you'll consider this an emergency, Doc," the young man said without any attempt at humor.

For the first time, Alan took his eyes off the passenger he was so concerned about and looked into the young man's face. It was ashen.

The Doc got up and hurried out to where he was told the emergency was: the cabin of Michael, the late tour director.

To say 'late' is accurate, since not only was Michael frequently unpunctual; it now appeared to even the couple of medically inexperienced cabin staff guarding the cabin door as the Doc arrived, that Michael was, in fact – dead.

Down on his knees on the floor and checking for vital signs, the Doc knew already that it was useless. Michael had been dead a while – a few hours at least. Rigormortis was already setting in. Doc gave a heavy-hearted sigh and sat back on his heels. To lose a patient was always terribly hard. To lose a crew member – and one so much before his time – was devastating. It hit the Doc especially hard because of all the innermost concerns of Michael that the Doc had been party to so recently. It seemed that all the worry, and the indulgent lifestyle, had finally caught up with him. All the indications were that Michael had died of a heart attack.

Part of Alan wasn't at all surprised. Part of him was deeply shocked.

As he looked around Michael's cabin, he saw obvious signs that Michael had thrashed around before he'd died. The bed clothes were strewn all around and the photos he kept by his bed were scattered, some smashed. The large silver gilt framed photograph of Alfonse, which usually took pride of place among the display, was missing. There were also cuts or more likely scratches on Michael's face and neck, which hinted at but did not confirm a struggle.

"Hmmm – a lovers' tiff, maybe…?" mused Alan aloud but more or less to himself.

The young cabin crew did not want to comment. Alan supposed it didn't matter. Michael was dead and nothing could change that. It was a heart attack, not foul play, he told himself. But if Alfonse had been the one to provoke this fatal heart attack, the Doc pitied him. Even to an apparent hard heart like Alfonse's, guilt could be a terrible thing.

As if reading his mind, Toby, popping his head around the door from his guard position espoused in a voice which the Doc realized for the first time was rather camp,

"Alfonse will be devastated. He loved Michael, you know – he was always much kinder to Michael…"

There was more than a hint of jealousy in the young man's voice.

The Doc nodded.

"Well, this will be for the authorities on shore, now… thank God we're due to stop on shore tomorrow. Unscheduled stops tend to panic the passengers and I don't want to have news of this getting out. You hear me?"

Toby nodded emphatically.

"'Course not, Doc. I would never gossip about Michael…"

Inside his head, the Doc groaned. Was Michael's love life even more complex than he had disclosed to the Doc? Had there been some sort of a fight, or Michael killed in a jealous rage – by Alfonse's hand or…

Alan pushed that thought away. His job was to preserve life where he could, declare life extinct where he couldn't. Michael had just joined the ranks of the dinosaurs. Anything else about how the death was to be explained would be left to authorities on shore at their next port of call.

The Doc got up, issuing instructions to close off the cabin and to touch nothing, while he went to his sick bay to call ahead to the port authorities, notifying them of a death on board. Even though he thought Michael had died of natural causes, he knew that the other, more disturbing possibility of foul play would have to be rule out. Everything pointed to a heart attack, though. Alan noted down a few details in the trusty notebook that went everywhere with him, knowing that those investigating Michael's death would probably ask about these things later.

Of course, at the next port, Officials came aboard and investigated everything. Although everyone cooperated fully with the investigation, and there was in no way any hint of a cover-up, everyone hoped that the investigators would see nothing suspicious in Michael's death, although almost immediately there were rumors of such. Even when Alan tried to point out that the autopsy had confirmed his suspicions of a heart attack, the conspiracy theorists reminded him that Michael's cabin had been in considerable disarray and that Michael had a complex past, peopled by shady characters.

"Heart attacks can be induced…" Alan had been told, more than once; but, of course, Alan knew that.

However, all the staff knew that if foul play was suspected, the ship could be held in port for days or weeks. So, since the staff had no more than suspicions, they felt it better for the local, rather obviously inept, officials to think it a natural death. They had no grounds on which to pursue claims of murder.

Even so, the authorities would not release the body from the next port for nearly a week. The weekend was not the time that any official was willing to go and have to look at a body in the funeral home.

Michael's partner, Alfonse, later complied with his wishes to be cremated and his ashes scattered at sea… eventually. The body had to be sent back intact to then be cremated and then brought back to sea. It was a long, drawn out process that the Doc didn't see the conclusion of, as he gratefully took a short amount of compassionate leave.

The picture of Michael lying there, eyes wide open, a hand to his chest, among the debris of his personal possessions, would never leave the Doc as long as he lived, he was sure.

# CHAPTER NINE

*December 7, 2009: Paradise Island*

ALAN SHOOK HIMSELF, TRYING to rid himself of the image of Michael lying there – dead. It had been a tense time as they had entered port and made arrangements for Michael's body to be taken discreetly off the ship. Actually, 'discreetly' was made virtually impossible as the exit was accompanied by the weeping and wailing of Alfonse, the distraught lover.

With difficulty, Alan made himself recall happier events of the many passengers he had seen in his long and happy career as a ship's doctor, but it was a struggle. Oh, he well remembered, on one occasion, he had attended to a Mrs. Goldenburger, who had a small injury to her toe, or as she called it, her tootsie. Mrs. Goldenburger was not slim. Her four-foot four-inch stature was accompanied by approximately three hundred and sixty pounds. (The ship's clinic's scales didn't go any higher, and the Doc didn't feel it was necessary to take her to the meat locker to weigh her on the big scales.)

Mrs. Goldenburger came from the Bronx in New York and was accompanied by her daughter who had flown in from Israel. She had indulged in far too many sweets and with her poor circulations - due to her diabetes - her toe was in bad shape. She'd almost had to go home early from the cruise to have a partial amputation of the toe.

It was just those thoughts, and newly emerging realizations of what must have happened on that cruise ship so long ago, that kept Alan tossing and turning all night. More than once, Alan got up and read his old notebook of memoirs kept at that time. Yes, it was there in black and white. While never confirmed, Alan had always had his suspicions that there was more to Michael's death than the investigation uncovered. Maybe the doubting Thomases had been right and Michael's shady past had caught up with him.

The next morning on board his retirement cruise, Alan slept late. He had decided, even after his large evening meal, to partake of the midnight buffet on *this* cruise ship, which he thought was better than going back to his lonely cabin and thinking of what he now suspected to be a murder, even if there were macabre parallels with this activity and the night of Michael's death when he recalled that he had been in attendance at another midnight buffet!

But Alan's attempts to forget Michael and his possible murder were all to no avail.

"Heart attacks can be induced…"

The words rang in Alan's ears and continued to reverberate in his memory. Prompted by the sight of that neat little insulin injector which Daniel had used at dinner the previous evening, Alan had realized something - that an over-sized 'insulin' needle could well have been what was used to kill Michael! A large quantity of air, or some potassium injected into the blood stream, could easily provoke what appeared to be a heart attack and not be detected post mortem.

The man wielding the syringe in the cruise all those years ago was quite unlike the discrete Daniel. No – on the contrary, Dr. Zetisman was careful to have his giant syringe seen but to never been observed actually injecting himself with it; he used deference to the delicate sensibilities of the ladies who would not like to see the injections as a feigned excuse but that was hard to believe now, given how much he liked to wave the syringe around. In itself, that was quite enough to have some ladies – and men – swooning! Dr. Zetisman also never came to the clinic to register as a diabetic, which was customary procedure for long cruises, but Alan presumed that was because the man, as a supposed doctor, was comfortable with medicating himself and reluctant to place his care in the hands of another doctor. Doctors are, after all, notoriously bad patients; but also, he seemed to eat those high sugar foods with such abandon. The more Alan thought about it, the more suspicious he became.

Alan's mind racing, he was left with two options: lie in his cabin bed sweating and worrying about what may be a twenty-five year old murder, or calm himself down and do some rational thinking, and then he might actually be able to come up with a plan of how to proceed!

'And besides,' Alan told himself firmly. '*If* Michael was murdered – there were more people than this guy with his syringe who could have killed him. Plenty of people with motives! After all, what could Dr. Zetisman's motive for Michael's murder possibly have been?'

In the end, Alan's logical mind took over and he decided to seek some company. His best thinking was always done subconsciously when he had stopped struggling to grasp an elusive thought. As always on a cruise ship, company – and food – was not difficult for Alan to find.

The midnight buffet had been quite filling and Alan had stayed until well after two in the morning. So, a late morning was not only appropriate, but downright called for. As this was to be their day on the cruise line's private island, Alan decided to dress casual; he went with the bathing suit under his shorts and favorite t-shirt: the old Black Dog Bakery shirt that Jo Ann had picked up for him on one of their summer vacations down on Cape Cod.

After that massive midnight meal, Alan frankly didn't feel very hungry. But, he knew that a few hours of sun and fun would leave him famished. So, he went to the dining hall for breakfast and then headed down to the transport area, as the ship was anchored offshore at the island. For the private island days, the ships would usually utilize local contractors who would provide a tender boat that would transport several hundred passengers at a time. The regular tender boats were an extra on these private island days.

The sun shone brightly that day and the sea was very calm, which was nice; the little boat wasn't rocking and rolling as the passengers moved down the narrow metal mesh gangplank to board it. Alan sat down on one of the benches up by the bow. Ah, the light breeze blowing felt so nice, except for the fact that it wafted in the smell of diesel fuel mixed with the seawater. Even after all his years serving on these ships, Alan still hated the smell of diesel fuel!

Sitting next to Alan was the couple he'd dubbed the 'Royal Pair'. Their names were as noble as anyone could get. He came from a family that had owned many land holdings throughout England for centuries. At the midnight buffet the night before, he'd told Alan that his family was so ancient that they'd fought with William at Hastings and their family name was in the Doomsday Book - whatever that meant. Alan was a bit dubious about that, but decided to humor the man. After all, he had no proof that the man's family wasn't that old, so why question it?

Again, a much more disturbing thought came to Alan, of the night before – or of twenty-five years ago, to be more precise. Michael's murder. But - he'd no proof it was a murder at all, so why rock the boat then – or now?

Alan tried to focus once more on what the 'Royal Pair' were telling him. He'd inherited his title and kept the family farms not only alive, but, because of his business acumen, he was able to develop a very lucrative farming business with several spin-offs that were also very profitable: so much so that four-month trips on expensive cruise liners were not a problem. Ah, to be such a man of leisure!

As that old "Dragnet" TV series would say, we'll change his name to protect his privacy. Alan called him the Duke of Gloucester or simply Duke. His first wife was apparently not compatible with the regal lifestyle, and he'd divorced her. The second wife had been his executive assistant, and she was now the current Duchess of Gloucester. She most certainly lent herself to playing the part better than the first one had. She was a striking tall blonde with features an artist would enjoy painting. She was charming and dressed impeccably, befitting her regal title.

As soon as he found out that Alan had been a doctor, the Duke gave him a complete organ recital – a rundown of his recent medical maladies. Just prior to the cruise, he'd had multiple coronary bypasses and was on a raft of medications that would keep most pharmacies busy. Fortunately, the Royal Couple had a couple of suitcases dedicated only to medications so the medical center did not have to do all the supplying like they do for some passengers that 'forget' all their meds.

When they came on board, a visit to the medical center was on top of the list of "to do's". When the Duchess first described her list of medical problems to him, and the obvious interactions she was having between the nineteen different meds that she was taking, Alan wanted to recommend that she get a new doctor, but instead indicated that she should see the ship's doctor and he may work with her to 'hone down the number of medications' and help her stay healthy. If he had been the ship's doc, that's what he would have done. Alan had been practicing up to two weeks ago. He still had his finger on the pulse, so to speak.

Some physicians will prescribe a medication - or even a series of medications - to deal with a chronic problem: anything from diabetes to multiple sclerosis to lupus. Then, as the patient complains of other troubles, the doctor will merely treat the symptoms and not look for an underlying problem. The end result can be more med's on top of the older ones, just to deal with something that could have been more easily addressed a different way. Sometimes, it's the interaction of the medications themselves (iatrogenesis) that actually causes the problems, and if the doctor would just check on the side-effects and how the drugs interact with each other, they'd see that removing one or changing a couple of them would address the problem.

As a result of Alan rendering his opinion on their health issues, the Duke and Duchess now considered his word to be law, and then regularly pestered him with still more questions. He didn't mind; they sprinkled the questions in among tales of some of their many adventures.

Sitting there on the transport boat, waiting to pull away from the ship, the Duke launched into a tale about a journey to India.

"One of our little side adventures involved riding an elephant," he said. "Now, since the Duchess here didn't want to offend anyone, she wore a long skirt. The only problem was, her elephant had come right out of the river and was still rather damp. The manout convinced her that she would feel safer and enjoy the ride more if she rode the elephant bareback - right behind its ears."

"The *what* did…?" Alan asked, his brow wrinkling.

"Oh, that's what they call the elephant herder," Duchess explained, proud to be able to educate the doctor on something.

Alan nodded.

"Ah, I see; interesting title. Please, continue."

"Well, elephants are wonderful to ride, but one does quickly note how warm they are, how rough their hide is, how prickly the hairs are and what a thorough massage one gets from riding on the neck," the Duke said. "The Duchess enjoyed the ride and continued all the way up the hill instead of taking the minivan."

She blushed as the Duke roared with laughter, slapping his thigh and having a coughing fit which thankfully resolved itself without Alan having to intervene.

Alan smiled. In getting to know the Duke and Duchess, he realized that they were unpretentious, interesting people who were very nice to spend time with. He was a relatively gregarious people mixer, while she was generally quieter, but had her own interesting stories to tell.

Once they reached the little island, the boat pulled into a small, secluded inlet - obviously man-made - and a wide ramp was lowered by hydraulics across the entire bow. Alan gave the Duke and Duchess a little nod and a wave and made his way off to the island. Even though he'd enjoyed their company, his mind was whirling with a million thoughts as past and present collided together. He wanted time to be alone and to think.

Yes, this was your classic private island. Stepping off onto the firm sandy soil, Alan looked around him, savoring the beautiful scenery as he slowly walked along. Off to the right was a little clutch of shops; all the usual things: t-shirts, swimming suits, sun dresses, souvenirs and so on. On the left was the shack you had to pass through to get back on the ship.

There was a time when getting on and off was as easy as one-two-three. These days, after 9/11, even returning from a private island required a security check! So, that little building housed the x-ray machine and metal detectors.

Alan sniffed; his mouth watered. Ah, the smell of corn cooking over an open flame. Yeah, like any good cruise line, there was food aplenty to be found. As he wanted to get some swimming in first, he decided to forgo a meal for now.

All around him, the descending hoards moved off either to the little store-shacks or went straight ahead toward the main beach areas. Alan walked along with the latter group. The broad and sandy path was surprisingly firm; he noticed a very thin older woman in an electric scooter was able to keep up with her family, and not get stuck. For those needing a true wheelchair-type vehicle but didn't have one with the power of hers, there were these futuristic looking contraptions that had gigantic wheels and a seat. It would get even the heavyweights through the sand to enjoy the activities.

In only a few minutes, they reached a crossroads with a small building (one of the many restrooms) and a signpost with a number of small arrow-shaped signs on it. Here again, Alan knew the drill; there was the general beach, the adults-only beach, and the clothing-optional beach. There were also a number of excursions available here. People could go scuba diving, parasailing, windsurfing and so on.

All Alan wanted to do was relax on the beach and get in a bit of snorkeling. He briefly considered going to the adults-only section, but he actually liked the idea of being around families. As they say, a baby's smile and a child's laugh are two very powerful things; either was capable of melting the hardest of hearts.

So, Alan took the path to the left and soon saw where that delicious smell was coming from. The ship's cooking staff had a huge bar-b-q grill set up next to a pavilion that could easily seat a hundred, and they were passing out the burgers, hot dogs, roasted corn, etc. as fast as the people could snatch them up. Alan had to grin, as he looked over the pavilion; bikini-clad bottoms of every size, shape and color lined the benches! Some of those bottoms were a little too... expansive for a bikini, and would have been better served by something a bit more... modest.

Beyond that was a small building where people were renting fins, masks and so on. As Alan had his own snorkeling gear, he skipped that and headed for the small protected cove. Grabbing a lounge chair, he dumped his stuff there and pulled out the good old bottle of Factor 50+ sunscreen. Yeah, he was going to lotion-up for the second time; no sense taking a chance at burning.

"Alan!" came the familiar voice of Tina.

Looking around, he saw Jenny and Tina, each decked out in what basically amounted to three little cloth cocktail napkins and some dental floss. Good God, talk about industrial strength suspension!

They bounded up to him, all smiles and giggles, and tossed their towels on the lounge chairs on either side of him.

"Hello, ladies," he said, trying to sound confident, but doubting he was pulling it off.

Jenny spun around, showing off her incredibly firm body.

"Like my suit? It's new - two hundred and twenty dollars."

Alan's eyebrows shot up.

"My goodness; on a cost per square inch basis, it's probably more precious than gold!"

The ladies giggled as they sat down and he looked around at the people in the nearby chairs, trying to keep his eyes discreetly off his two lovely companions. Some were the usual types: families, teenagers, young couples and so on. Ah, and then there were the "May to December" couples: usually an older gentleman with a much younger lady. He wondered how on earth they could be together. It all came down to one word, he was sure: money.

"Checking out the competition, Alan?" Tina said, taking a seat next to him.

"Who, me?"

Jenny started to spread the suntan lotion across her firm thighs.

"Tina, the dear Doctor doesn't have to worry about competition! Would you... put the lotion on my back?"

Alan cleared his throat and gave her a nod. Moving to his lounge chair, she sat close to him. She had a very firm, yet supple back.

"No problem, Jenny. As for me, Tina, I was... looking at the... company. I was never one to be too cynical about May-December romances, but it seems to me that beautiful young ladies don't fall in love with *poor* old men all that often!"

The ladies giggled, and Jenny looked over her shoulder at him.

"Yes, you're right; we can be so very... naughty, can't we?"

With that, she moved around and promptly lay across his lap! Alan hadn't even had a chance to think about where on earth her response had come from!

"Do you mind?" she asked with feigned innocence, wiggling that incredibly firm and adorable bottom of hers.

Alan's jaw dropped.

"Huh?" He squeaked.

She grinned up at him.

"Some lotion; would you put some on? I don't want to... burn down there."

Tina frowned, stood and bent toward them. Smack! Her hand slapped Jenny's right bottom cheek, leaving quite a large red handprint.

"Jenny, don't embarrass our new friend!"

"Ouch!" Jenny yelped, and climbed off of his lap.

Alan managed a small grin; her cheeks (on her face) were as red as that handprint.

"Ah... sorry."

"It's okay," he said weakly, his mouth dry.

"So… is it true the cruise ship provides… escorts to their 'high rollers'?" Jenny said.

Alan rubbed the back of his neck self-consciously.

"Well… I know that many cruise lines try to… appease their best clients in many different ways, but I've never heard of one actually hiring an… escort for one of the passengers on a routine basis."

Jenny and Tina continued to cover themselves with lotion; even as they stayed in rapt attention.

"Now, that's not to say that escorts, in the *classic* sense of the word, don't exist on ships," Alan said. "But, the pickings for them are generally not too good… That makes sense. After all, there are usually enough singles that are more than willing to… jump into bed with the opposite, or same sex at the drop of a hat, no fees required."

Jenny grinned.

"You sound like you know a lot about that, Alan…"

Alan felt his face grow warm. Oh man, he just knew he was blushing up a sea of red.

"So, Alan, tell us about some of the… shenanigans that go on aboard these ships…? I bet there are some juicy goings-on, huh?" Tina asked with relish.

'Oh, if only you knew the half of it!' thought Alan wryly to himself.

"Well… I can't say too much…"

"Oh please!" the ladies begged, almost together.

Alan gave a little laugh.

"I do remember one memorable incident. This young man that the crew suspected was 'selling his wares' to the old ladies on board, came in to the sickbay. He had been noted leaving from various passenger suites at all hours of the night, a bit disheveled, to say the least. He complained of a 'personal problem', and just had to see me."

"What was it?" Jenny asked, eagerly hanging on Alan's every word.

"It seemed he was with this woman the night before and she kind of *clamped* down on him, with something other than her self!"

The ladies, clearly perplexed, sat there with open mouths.

"What did he mean?" Tina said.

Trying to hold back a very large smile and laugh, Alan said,

"The woman had an artificial hand and it generally functioned quite well. Mark the words: *fairly* well. She was playing with his… instrument, and all of sudden she clamped down on it and couldn't let go. Guess she had some kind of pirate's claw or something."

The ladies burst out in renewed giggles.

"Oh, that's priceless!" Jenny chirped.

"Was there any serious... damage?" Tina said.

Alan shook his head.

"Naw, a rather bruised organ with a few superficial scratches was all. What really upset him was that he had to... decrease his... activity for a few days so that it could heal."

"Oh, he had to cancel a big... 'date'?" Jenny asked.

"Yeah. I just thought it would heal faster if he'd... rest it."

"How do you keep a straight face when they come to you with things like that?" Tina asked.

"Well... I don't... didn't... not after he left. I'm afraid the nurse and I had a good laugh about it. She promised me that the information would go no further, but we both knew differently. It confirmed everyone's suspicions about him and his chosen profession. It also gave the gossip mill some great grist for the rest of the cruise," Alan grinned, actually liking having two attractive ladies in such rapt attention at his stories. He really should write a book!

Jenny got a sly look about her.

"Did he ever come back to your clinic?... I'm not sure if I'd *dare* – but I mean, if he was making a good living that way..."

Alan grinned.

"Oh, you're sharp, Jenny. As a matter of fact, we were not all that surprised to see him back in the sick bay the very next day. He came into the office and I noticed that he was walking rather stiffly. Turned out, he met up with this guy friend on the ship, and they went back to his cabin and... 'played' around for a bit. It was kind of rough, but he apparently liked that."

"Oooooo, do tell!" Jenny said, a wide grin cutting across her face. "What, S and M, B and D, what?"

Alan's throat went dry; goodness, he couldn't believe such things coming from this lovely young lady's mouth. For that matter, he couldn't believe he was telling this wild tale. How did they even *know* about that stuff! Yet, for some reason, he enjoyed talking to these two. Alan laughed to himself; they probably knew about as much of it as he himself did – just what the letters stood for!

"Ah well – sort of... it was a... carrot, and it was... still up there. Stuck. I wasn't quite sure if I wanted to be sick, surprised or gratified that the gigolo had gotten his just reward. My poor nurse was scandalized. Sweet little thing she was... English..."

That was it, both girls burst out in total hysterical laughter. It was several minutes before they could compose themselves enough to ask what he did about it.

"Well, I had the nurse prepare the exam table, and what equipment we had available on board; then we tried to… get it out."

"Any luck?" Tina asked.

"We made a good college try at getting the 'foreign object' out," Alan said.

"Wasn't he just dying of embarrassment at having to see you about this?" asked Jenny.

"Hmm – no, not really," chuckled Alan. "Which is good, of course. I mean – he *had* to see me. But looking back, maybe I was lucky he didn't blame me!"

"*Blame* you!" the girls squealed together.

"Yeah," chuckled the Doc, continuing. "I remember it like it was yesterday, but then again – you wouldn't really forget that kind of thing, would you?"

Alan gave a little sigh. Recently, he'd been remembering an awful lot that he hadn't wanted to. He slipped back into his story of the hapless gigolo, even attempting to feign the man's pain, embarrassed voice as he admitted his little difficulty.

"Doc, you remember that you wanted me to cool it with my instrument yesterday? Well I followed your instructions and cancelled my date. I met this Mexican guy, Miguel, here on the ship a few days ago and he told me that his partner was really drunk, and he wanted to have some fun. We went back to my room and played around for a bit. He was kind of rough, but that can be fun, sometimes. I didn't think it would be a problem when he suggested playing with a carrot. Problem is, Doc, ugh, the carrot is… um… still up there. Honest, we both tried to get it out."

Alan watched the girls' reactions as he continued his story, knowing they would love the response his nurse had given to Alan through the side of her mouth as she pulled on her surgical gloves:

"I am going to enjoy this one, that S.O.B. gigolo, deserves it!"

Embellishing his story a little, for the benefit of the girls' entertainment, as they were lapping up every single detail, Alan continued with relish,

"First, I had my nurse sit in a chair. Then I had the patient, Tom, bend over her lap to get the most abdominal flexion possible, as we attempted to extract the carrot. We thought maybe a little lesson in humiliation - being bent over a woman's knee like a naughty child - might get through his thick head! Of course, what my nurse *really* wanted to do was give him a good, sound spanking. Actually though, considering the fact that Tom was a professional gigolo, he probably would have enjoyed that!"

The girls howled with laughter, making Alan chuckle too. Perhaps they were more innocent than they looked! Still smiling, Alan continued,

"At any rate, all our efforts proved fruitless. - 'I'm afraid, Tom, that we'll need to send you to a proctologist on shore today and let him get it out. He'll have better tools than we do and will be able to do it under general anesthesia. I don't want to hurt you. I'll write the referral and the nurse will set up the appointment...'"

"I gave him another shot to ease the pain and spasms and told him not to eat or drink anything until he saw the proctologist."

Alan dramatically recreated the scene of Tom getting to his feet slowly and saying,

'Anything you say, Doc, just get someone to get that blasted thing out of me.'

"In due course, he was sent onshore, and was seen and treated. The proctologist later told me that he had some difficulty removing the twelve inch, rather broad carrot from his rectum. He had significant bruising, but fortunately, no perforations. We did not see Tom in the infirmary for the rest of the cruise. Funny that..."

The girls were almost crying with laughter. It sure was funny!

Eventually, Jenny calmed down enough to offer some sympathy.

"Poor guy, how embarrassing!... But once word got round about that I bet he didn't know whether to die of shame or put his prices up!"

Alan chuckled, nodding.

"Oh, Alan, thank you for that," Tina said. "That story was priceless!"

"Glad I could be of entertainment value to you," he said. "I was an escort too, you know – quite a few times..."

"You were *what*?!"

The girls' eyes were almost popping out of their heads. Alan didn't quite know whether to be offended or flattered but he thought he better explain, before they choked.

"In those situations, the term meant crewmembers that were lucky enough or assigned to accompany the shore tours. If it was an interesting port and an interesting tour, it was a well sought after assignment. If it was one of the 'cultural experiences' tours with hoards of passengers, it became an assignment of herding cats, and for those tours the crew drew straws to see who was unlucky enough to have to go on it. I got a few of those, I can tell you... but... later..."

Alan was conscious of the sun being over the yard arm and he hadn't even been near achieving the solitude he had looked for in taking this private island excursion. He politely made his excuses.

"Now, if you'll excuse me, ladies? I'm going to hit the water..."

Both ladies were stretched out on their respective lounge chairs still laughing over his story so Alan thought he was safe to hit the water and achieve the solitude he sought right now. They looked like they were there for the rest of the day.

'Probably wouldn't want to ruin their chances of a good tan,' he hoped.

"Well, have fun – and maybe you can tell us some more of your doctor exploits at dinner or something," Tina said, slipping her sunglasses on.

"Oh yes, that would be wonderful!" agreed Jenny, turning onto her stomach and flashing that tight bubble butt in its tight pink Lycra bikini.

Relief made Alan give a little louder chuckle than he had intended.

"Ah – well maybe I should charge you for that…! These stories won't be free once they're in my book, you know!"

With that, he set off at a stroll down the beach. As he was well "lotioned up", and feeling quite like a greased pig at a county fair, Alan entered the water and slipped on his mask, fins and snorkel. Now, if this cruise line was like others, they'd have planted some nice things out in the water to make snorkeling interesting.

He was right. About a hundred feet offshore was a sunken "ship" and an airplane. Alan dived down and pulled out his underwater camera. Yeah, a picture would be awesome and something to show the family when he got home. Prove to Alexa and the boys he'd done his best to have a good time! Actually, Alan realized he *was* really having a rather good time!

The plane had been placed in the water in such a way as to maximize safety, of course: wings well supported and the cockpit blocked off to prevent daredevils from trying to sit in it. Diving down, he held the camera in front of him and aimed it at the plane – and froze.

A small model plane. Now, why did that thought arc through his mind at this moment. No, wait, not a thought – a memory – a memory of a model plane! A pain stabbed him in the chest, and he realized that he was running out of air; he had to surface – and quickly.

Kicking his legs, he rose to the surface, burst forth, and sucked in air. Whew, that was close. He almost… suffocated. Death, dying – murder – these words resounded in his head once more, as did the image (again) of Michael lying dead in his cabin. But, what connection could a model plane have to that? Alan didn't know; or, at least he didn't remember – yet. Time would tell whether or not he sorted these memories out. For now, he'd turn his attentions back to having some fun. So, submerging once more, Alan got some nice pictures of the plane, and then headed back to shore.

After a brief nap in the sun, he awoke starving and alone and made his way to the "food court". As with all cruises, there was more food than could ever be eaten, so he was able to chow down to his heart's content. He had to wonder, did the Duke and Duchess care for American burgers? He made a mental note to ask them the next time they sat down together for a fancy meal in the dining room.

He also caught sight of Jenny and Tina, off playing volleyball with a number of the twenty-something set. Ah, perhaps they'd finally found someone their own age to play with? Alan felt both happy and sad at the prospect of them moving on. In fact, he was a little mad with himself as he realized he was… jealous!

After he'd eaten his fill, Alan slowly meandered back to the little pier and was surprised to not see one of the tenders there. He knew the drill; at this time of day, most people were anxious to get back on the ship. They'd usually had enough of sunbathing and were yearning to get back to gambling, so extra boats were assigned to the island. So, where were they?

Alan moved around to the side of the small building and casually strolled over to the shoreline. This area was not generally a place for the passengers to go; the shore was a mass of huge boulders and the buildings here housed equipment and crew.

Alan looked off into the water and squinted. Yeah, there were the tenders, all of them, but not one was near the ship or coming this way. All his years of experience on a cruise ship told Alan that something was up!

"Excuse me, sir, would you please move back to the main pavilion?" a woman requested in a polite but efficient tone.

Alan turned, and found himself facing Tiffany again.

"Oh, hello, there," Alan said. "Is something wrong?"

Her mouth contorted itself into a variety of silly shapes, even as she sort of wiggled in place. Alan almost smiled; if he didn't know better, he'd have thought she was a naughty girl reluctant to confess her "crime" to her father. She was acting exactly as Alexa had in just such a situation. He sighed. Oh God, did *that* make him feel old; seeing this lovely young woman in the same category as his own daughter!

"Well… I guess I can tell you; as you're… 'family', after all," Tiffany conceded.

This was the first time that she'd ever heard of anything like this happening on board a cruise ship and she was very stressed about it.

"We've had a… mishap on board."

Alan turned his head slightly, so he could still see the activity out of the corner of his eye and talk to Tiffany.

"Someone's fallen overboard, haven't they?"

The signs were all there: all the tenders in a search pattern; high level crew attentive on shore, the searching, and radios going constantly. Alan knew he must be right.

Tiffany nodded, biting her lip.

"Yes, one of the Romanian cabin crew; they're looking for him now. Please… keep this confidential…?"

"Of course; I know how it is - nothing to spoil the passengers' fun." Alan snorted, thinking of the contortions they'd had to go through to conceal Michael's death from all the passengers until they reached the nearest port, while most if the crew were so distraught about it that they could hardly function. Alan wasn't about to share that macabre tale with Tiffany, especially at this time, of course!

"Oh, I can well remember some of the similar events on ships I served on. In fact… we even lost a passenger once…"

Just as Alan was about to offer some light-hearted relief to lighten Tiffany's mood, a real life event lifted her despondency – and in the best way possible…

Full of smiles, waving his arms, a young male crew member arrived beside them, out of breath.

"Crisis averted. All safe and sound," he announced, puffing and panting.

'About as fit as Michael was', Alan though with a twinge of guilt at his disloyalty.

"Really?" asked Tiffany, hardly daring to hope.

"Yep… back in his cabin with a couple of friends to look after him… they'll get a shrink to see him in the next port… but basically, the story goes that he got caught on the 'clothing optional' deck ogling the passengers. When the security staff found him there, he took a swan dive off that 14th deck right into the Caribbean! Pretty good diver, eh?"

"Ooooo naughty boy!" teased Alan, knowing that the 'clothing optional' deck was strictly out of bounds to crew members but partly admiring his gumption to do so and then marveling at his diving ability, to have survived a 140+ foot dive.

Tiffany grinned.

"He wasn't much good as cabin crew, anyway. He had some problem with his knees or something… either that or he was bone idle. He was upgraded to taking care of the passengers' cabins, where he probably thought he belonged all along. Oh well, it looks like his tour of duty ends tomorrow, anyway. I will have to fill out his papers firing him tonight."

Alan nodded.

"Yep and it seems like my beach visit ends now. I'm going to go freshen up for dinner. It's been quite a day!"

All these memories swirled in Alan's head as he stood in line to be checked over before boarding the ship once more: the crew in their cabins, the cabin crew upgrading to a passenger cabin. He thought also about the illicit drugs that a few of them took – not least of all, Michael. He shook his head; why was he obsessing about such things? He was on vacation; he should be having some fun in the present and not dwelling on the past.

But, back in his cabin, resting up on his bed, Alan found his thoughts again wandering back into the past and how much fun those excursions from the cruise ship onto dry land had been. Some were even better – or at least more memorable – than others. Strangely, it had been the early Trivia quiz as much as the jumping overboard of the Romanian cabin crew member that had Alan thinking of past times. In an effort to drag his musings away from the sad death at sea, Alan's thoughts alighted on a disappearance which had been not as temporary as the one today where the crew member was rescued from the sea...

# CHAPTER TEN

*July 13, 1984: Costa Rica*

THE DOC, WHO WAS usually happier with a deck beneath his feet, now actually found he was quite excited about his upcoming medium-term shore excursion, even though it had been precipitated by Alan's distress after Michael's death. Things were going well with Christina, despite the constant irritation that Jesus caused and he had managed to secure a temporary replacement on compassionate grounds so that he might manage ten days on shore. After all, finding Michael's body was bad enough. But then he had heard inconclusive reports back from the autopsy as regards to whether it was the natural death the Doc had originally thought it to be. Maybe the onboard rumors of a murder actually had some substance to them, but with the official investigation closed and Alan and the rest of the crew busy with their regular duties, what could they do? None of these thoughts were conducive to good mental health.

These days, Alan would probably be diagnosed with Post-Traumatic Stress Disorder and put into counseling whether he wanted to be or not. But back then, once the initial inquiries were over and the diagnosis of heart attack was confirmed by the local authorities, the ship was once more on its way and Alan was lucky to get a few days off to 'recuperate'. He was glad of that time which he knew he could spend with Christina – and, if it couldn't be helped – Jesus.

Now, things in the administration of cruise liners don't always work so quickly, so Alan was surprised when it was agreed that he could be relieved on this very tour. And then of course, there was Christina... he wasn't sure he wanted to be relieved of her company. So he was thrilled when she told him she would like to spend what time she could with him in those two weeks.

"I can go on a cruise any time I wish, Alan," she said in that dreamy voice of hers which made it seem not at all like she was bragging.

Christina had been surrounded by wealth all her life and she took it for granted that she could do what she wanted when she wanted. Right now she wanted to spend time with Alan.

"Look – I have a vacation home we can go to. It is nearby the next port and then we can take Daddy's company jet and rejoin the ship in the next port… we can have the best of both worlds. Sometimes here… sometimes there…"

'Best of both worlds'? Alan thought he was in heaven!

So, it was arranged and now here he was, getting ready to meet Dr. Virginia Schaefer. Alan thought with a little wry chuckle how glad he'd been that a temporary doctor was found to replace him. He usually had to do that himself, as well as orient the new doctor and bring him or her up to speed with any patients with outstanding medical conditions before escaping ashore.

This time, though, Alan knew within minutes of a telephone conversation with Dr. Virginia Schaefer to arrange the good doctor's arrival date that a mistake of judgment had been made by the corporate recruiting office. This was a doctor he would never have selected due to her brash "I am the greatest thing that ever walked the earth" attitude, but the promise of two weeks with Christina prevented him from saying a word to corporate.

They had made it a rush job, so instead of the week's orientation that was customary and allowed a good, conscientious doctor like Alan to hand over with complete peace of mind, this time, Alan had been afforded all of ninety minutes. Dr. Schaefer had made it clear that was all he was getting as she was not receiving any extra pay for the orientation.

"MMmmm… in less than two hours it will be just you and me… a-and Jesus, of course," the Doc told Christina, grinning contentedly, extricating himself from her embrace in his bed and fastening his shirt buttons. He quickly slicked back his hair with his hands.

"Oh but do you *have* to go?" Christina begged a bit like a petulant child, although Alan found it flattering when she did it to him.

"You, madam… you have me for the next two weeks. I'm sure you'll live another couple of hours without me so I can sort things with the new Doc and introduce her to the staff captain and the captain as well as sign her into all the appropriate logs she will need to handle for the next two weeks… Besides… you've survived the past thirty-five years without me…"

Christina's eyes flashed with a passionate fire as she picked up the bedside clock and launched it at Alan's crotch.

"Ackkk – you swine! You know I am not that old!"

Laughing, Alan caught the clock before it could hit the crown jewels.

'Christ, no – but I am well past that!' thought Alan ruefully.

As he bent to kiss the quickly forgiving Christina, he thought again how lucky he was to have a girl like her interested in him. Now if only she'd take his advice on a few techniques to use with that brat of hers…

But with that thought, and reluctantly leaving Christina reclining on his bed in only her very attractive black silk underwear, Alan put on his professional 'doctor face' and strode on over to the sickbay to meet Dr. Schaefer. He just hoped this would work out better than some other replacement staff had done.

If, for instance, an engineer, line officer, hotel manager, chef, doctor, or cruise director got sick, (or severely homesick) so they could not do their job, and that position was vacant, the company was obliged to quickly find a replacement to meet international shipping rules and company standards. Once, an Austrian chef had a nervous breakdown because his staff (mostly from Honduras) preferred to make soups in the manner the previous French chef had taught them. When he forced them to do it his way, the managers kept getting complaints from the passengers about how awful the soup (and other food items) were and that they wanted the old chef back.

In this case, the company often had backups, or called an agency to find a replacement. At great expense to the company, they would fly this fellow (or gal) to the nearest port and even helicopter them to the ship. Generally, they did not have time to do much more than throw a bag together and get on a plane, let alone go and get a physical. Consequently, it was the Doc's job to do a physical on them as soon as possible upon arriving - and as far as the company was concerned, to make sure they passed.

A communications engineer was once sent aboard to fill a vacant spot in one of these emergency situations. The ship was making its ten day cruise off Antarctica. No ports. And having a communications officer was rather essential. They found this German fellow (Hans Reichbaum) and brought him from his hideaway in Thailand to Ushuaia, Argentina. From there, he was helicoptered to the ship in Half Moon Bay, Antarctica. The sick guy and he traded seats on the helicopter.

Hans claimed to be sixty-two years old. One could add at least ten years to that. His liver was one of the largest the Doc had ever palpated and as hard as a rock with multiple masses. Alcohol and chronic hepatitis had obviously been Hans' friends for a very long time. Add to this his atrial fibrillation (heart arrhythmia) that was not being covered by Warfarin (blood thinner) to prevent a potential stroke or pulmonary embolism, and you had the short list of the major medical issues that Hans had. He was also a borderline diabetic, among other metabolic diagnoses. It was the Doc's job to keep him alive and functional (basically a full-time job) until they reached a port and could send another replacement.

Thinking about all those physicals Alan did over the years made him remember how much he valued his health. He needed this break with Christina. It's one thing to be healthy and enjoy the fruits of being healthy at home, but what about using that God-given health and venturing out into the wide world, and staying healthy while he was there too? It's easy to stay healthy traveling to the city next door and staying in an upscale hotel, eating in fine restaurants that will cater to your specific diet, exercising in the tame hotel gym and shopping in well ventilated malls. Ah, but change that venue a bit, by any number of parameters and you'll put your body at greater risk of significant health trouble.

As a ship's physician, Alan was used to being on call 24/7 and being called at all hours of the night. Since medical school, he had learned to function on very little sleep. Having to complete needless and endless paperwork for the corporate office with unreasonable deadlines was the persistent 'sleep thief'. Alan almost preferred the 4am call for the heart attack victim to the 'week end tally of medications used and validation of same' paperwork.

Start with multiple flights on a regular basis, like the business road warrior. The frequency with which a ship's crew travels puts them at great risk for a host of psychological and medical issues.

To stay healthy on the road, business and crew travelers have to be able to accept their unique style of life and work with it, learning to enjoy the unique advantages they have. For a ship's crew, it is important that the person not be at war with the sea. What is truly important is to make peace with it, and enjoy the time away from their home base to the fullest.

From his travels, Alan had learned that home is much more than a place in a certain city, a house or apartment building. It is a state of being and a state of abundant living. Any individual who is going to be traveling a lot needed to learn that any destination can be one's home for a time. Alan always remembered a saying his mother had told him. He didn't remember the exact words, but it talked about how you can never *truly* know your home unless you leave it, explore far and wide, and then return.

It was with these thoughts that the Doc entered the waiting room, where there was already a line of people waiting to see the new Doc – 'see' her being the operative word; few of them had genuine maladies requiring medical attention. Since the average age on many of the cruises is older, it was not unusual to hear organ recitals in the chatter, but this one particularly entertained the Doc as he walked down the corridor to greet Dr. Schaeffer.

"My arms have gotten so weak I can hardly lift this cup of coffee," said one elderly passenger.

"Yes, I know," said a regular to the clinic, Mrs. Philips. "My cataracts are so bad I can hardly even *see* my coffee." "I couldn't even punch out the chad at election time back in Florida, my hands are so crippled," volunteered the first lady.

Not to be outdone, Mrs. Philips responded with,

"I can't turn my head because of the arthritis in my neck," to which Dr. Zetisman nodded weakly in agreement.

"My blood pressure pills make me so dizzy!" exclaimed a new guest whom Alan had seen just the day before with blood pressure that nearly got her disembarked from the ship.

"I guess that's the price we pay for getting old."

"Well, count your blessings," said Mr. Philips cheerfully. "Thank God we can all still drive," to which the Doc and his nurse cringed.

The nurse this particular day was Susan. She was still firmly back in the granola generation but she was a total sweetheart. Her hobbies including making baskets and polishing the wood of her log cabin on shore that took eight years to build from the ground up. She was a good nurse who knew what she was doing and was willing to do her fair share of the job, always looking to help. The Doc knew that even with the inimitable Dr. Schaefer, his various, sometimes sensitive, elderly patients were in safe hands with Susan around.

That thought made him feel much better as he met the temporary doctor who was, after all, to afford him a brief onshore respite with the luscious Christina. The Doc was sure his patients wouldn't begrudge him that, even though they didn't know the trauma that he had just been through!

Dr. Schaefer was a very large, not terribly gentle individual. She had worked on very large ships of the non-luxury class and was therefore not accustomed to schmoozing the type of wealthy passengers who regularly spent thousands of dollars a day on the Gold Cruise Line.

She desperately wanted to get aboard a luxury cruise liner with the "fabulous food I would love to eat for weeks". That should have been the red flag! Unfortunately she had a cousin in the head office that had gotten her the job in the first place.

"I'm sure everything will be fine, Dr. Mayhew. I have done this ship's doctoring before, you know…"

The Doc didn't like the sound of that at all.

"Well, we do have some quite complex characters... long term cruisers with extensive medical histories."

Dr. Schaefer was insistent. She wanted to get the Doc out of the sick bay and off the ship so she could claim her territory for herself.

"I will read the files... you *do* keep proper medical records, I presume...?"

"Of course..."

The Doc was affronted and his disgruntled pause gave Dr. Schaefer just the window of opportunity that she needed to guide Alan out of the sick bay.

"But... but..." the Doc blustered.

But Christina was waiting for him outside the sick bay door and she was not one to be kept waiting either. As Dr. Schaefer bundled him out of the sick bay like a harassed Mama glad to be handing over a troublesome child to a sitter, Christina was there ready to scoop him up, taking Alan by the arm and escorting him toward the little crowd of people waiting to disembark.

Among them was John Silver. He was an interesting character: a business man from Boston, USA. John owned several computer chip companies and had done extremely well for himself in the eighties and nineties. So much so that John, at a mere thirty-six years of age, was very comfortably retired with many millions in the bank. Even if the market dipped, John was never going to have to look back.

Beside him was John's traveling companion, Miguel. Miguel was a twenty-three year old, very well built, bronzed, Mexican. One could usually find Miguel in the gym working on making his already bulging muscles look more defined or basking in the sun to bronze his skin even more. Miguel had recently refused the advances of Alfonse, who after being apparently grief-stricken at his lover Michael's death for... ah... almost three days... was now firmly rebounding amongst any gay crew and passengers he could find.

Miguel was educated and spoke with only a slight Hispanic accent. He had been schooled in the US. The obvious rumor around the ship was that he and John were married, but no rings were ever seen and there was no overt public display of affection, although John was quite an adventurous guy. They were otherwise an inseparable pair at dinners, cocktail parties, and land tours.

In fact, this particular day, they stood together but at a socially acceptable distance. They exchanged smiles, and comments which betrayed some familiarity with each other's sense of humor.

The Doc didn't really take much notice, though. He only had eyes for Christina. Relationships between passengers and crew were strongly discouraged in those days so they decided to play it cool until they were off the ship. Jesus had been forewarned that they were all three to be spending the next few days together, so had had more advance warning of this fact than the Doc had had that the child would be joining them on their little vacation away from Christina's vacation. At least the Doc need have no fear that Jesus would tell tales on him back on the ship later, as the Doc, even after almost a week, had still yet to hear a signal clear word come from that child's mouth.

As soon as the gangplank was down, John Silver bustled off with Miguel on his customary chore. Whenever they would arrive in a port, one of the first places he would head was the Post Office. He was so regular about this that several crew members would hand him their letters rather than giving them to the ship's agent. They knew that their letters would get to the Post Office at least a day before the agent if they handed them to John.

Post offices in port towns are not always right in the immediate vicinity of the port. Sometimes they would be a quite a trek but John Silver always seemed to manage it on his trusty mountain bike. One could only wonder at the need for such regular trips and where the money he seemed to return with each time had come from. No-one knew what services John performed but they did seem to be rather lucrative for him.

Anyway, Alan didn't care about that now; he had two whole weeks to share with Christina… and Jesus. 'Must stop forgetting Jesus', Alan chided himself as the devil child attempted to push him over the harbor side into the water.

"Ha ha ha! Such a darling child – so exuberant!" Alan said with a forced smile.

Christina was sure that her son and her new boyfriend were getting on famously so she smiled too as she picked up Jesus onto her hip and slipped her free hand into Alan's as soon as they were out of sight of the ship and most of the people leaving it. Things were going well and she didn't want to get Alan into trouble and blow her chances with him.

"My plane… is waiting," she said in that sultry voice of hers, and it made Alan's knees weak.

It seemed like she was smuggling him off to some secret location to have her wicked way with  him – which, in effect, she was – but Alan had no intention of complaining about this 'kidnapping' in which he was a very willing participant.

It was obvious that indeed, Christina, or maybe her father, did have rather influential connections as a car was waiting for them to take them to a nearby small airfield and in less than ten minutes the trio was boarding a small private airplane at a little private airstrip. As soon as he saw the plane, Jesus let out a high-pitched wail that was positively ear-splitting and began a rocking movement that appeared ineffective as a self-comforting gesture.

"This… is why we go on cruises," said Christina, apparently not finding the screaming right into her ear as painful as Alan feared it might be.

It was certainly grating on his nerves!

"Should I… I brought my bag… force of habit… goes everywhere with me… Does he… *need* something?" Alan asked, resisting the temptation to cover his ears against the terrible noise, since Christina seemed quite used to it.

"No!" she declared with uncharacteristic steel that Alan would never have supposed was in her.

For a brief moment he found that a turn-on and then he realized he had messed up – again. He wilted.

"S-sorry… I was only… concerned…"

"After the plane – he will be fine," Christina was adamant.

Indeed, Christina knew her son well – at least this particular idiosyncrasy. Thankfully the plane ride was short. Just maybe ten minutes, throughout which the high-pitched wail never faltered or even altered pitch, it seemed to Alan. But at touch down, as soon as the doors were opened and they emerged from the plane, even though the plane's engines were still going, Jesus sensed the journey was over and his wailing stopped. He bit his mother none too gently on the shoulder and she, laughing, took that as a sign to let him down.

"He knows his way from here…," she said, seemingly delighted at Jesus' return to 'normality'.

'What a pity!' thought Alan to himself.

The pair of young lovers strolled arm in arm after Jesus, through a beautiful avenue of trees, up to the holiday villa (one of many, Alan later found out) of Christina's family. Staff scurried behind at a discreet distance with the couples' bags and Jesus scurried ahead to be scooped up, screeching, by a rather rotund but jolly elderly lady dressed all in black apart from a snowy white apron.

"The housekeeper," Christina explained simply.

Alan didn't care. He was here with Christina in a beautiful place and Jesus was out of their hair for now. On board ship he had gotten used to having things done for him so he was happy to leave the luggage carrying to Christina's staff. Every moment he could steal alone with her was precious.

Hand in hand with this beautiful girl, Alan smiled down at her.

"Why don't you… show me around?"

Christina grinned, kissing Alan's lips deeply and pulling him off the main path and through the trees across the grass, kicking off her shoes and carrying them in her free hand which was not tugging Alan along.

"I will show you my most favorite place. The view is beautiful…"

"It certainly is!" declared Alan in a dreamy fashion, gazing into those deep pools that threatened to drown him, otherwise known as Christina's eyes.

This caused her to giggle.

Soon, Alan found himself in a beautiful, quiet courtyard, where the only sounds were birdsong and the tinkling of water from a tiny fountain set in the centre. All around the water feature were stone benches. Sitting on them, one could look out through the large arches cut into the courtyard walls, which afforded them views out to the rolling green hillside beyond. It was really beautiful but Alan only had eyes for Christina.

"I've… never been anywhere… like this," he faltered shyly.

Christina shrugged, quite used to her surroundings and so not so appreciative of them.

"And I have never been anywhere… with anyone like you," she countered, smiling seductively at Alan and causing him to fall a little deeper into those two pools.

The next hour was a blur of kisses and caresses for them both, undisturbed by anything from the outside world, not even thoughts of Jesus.

But eventually, inevitably, the maternal instincts took over and Christina broke away, a hand still caressing Alan's chest where she had opened his shirt… sometime. When had that happened?

"I must go see Jesus. He won't nap without me… and we must eat…"

"I thought I was just eating," Alan quipped.

But he was in the first flush of new romance and anything that Christina wanted or felt she needed to do was okay by him. Again he allowed himself to be tugged along – this time inside to the large, rustic but still beautiful kitchen.

Inside was the elderly lady that had rescued them from Jesus for a brief respite, whom Christina now introduced as Lucia.

"She keeps house," she explained.

"And she does that very well. It is beautiful," Alan complimented.

Lucia smiled enigmatically and gave a little nod of appreciation in Alan's direction, getting up from her seat beside Jesus to give way to Christina. Alan was surprised to find that Lucia, and now Christina, were feeding Jesus. Actually physically feeding him. The meal appeared to be a simple cheese and ham sandwich, but Christina was now busily engaged in tearing off bite-sized pieces and popping them into the open, soggy mouth of Jesus.

'Those gannets again', Alan thought to himself.

Out loud, he couldn't stop himself from saying,

"Jesus… doesn't feed himself?… Even simple things…?"

The silent glare which that comment drew from both women was enough to silence him.

"He likes it if we do it," Christina explained frostily.

"I'm sure he does, but…," Alan attempted to offer some doctorly advice.

"He likes it," Christina again stated firmly, indicating that this was the end of the discussion as far as she was concerned.

'Was that a smug smile from Jesus?' Alan wondered as he morosely munched on his own sandwich, efficiently prepared by Lucia.

"Now is his playtime," Christina told Alan of Jesus; a door on the other side of the kitchen was opened and out flew Jesus like a caged bird that had just been set free.

Alan peered out into this courtyard, quite different from the one in which he and Christina had just passed such a pleasant hour. If theirs was the Garden of Eden, this was a barren wasteland. The gravel path had been scuffed up to reveal many patches of dirt and the once grassed area in the middle was torn up into dry, cracked earth baking in the sun. All around, hanging baskets festooned the walls, but most of their flowers had been pulled out and trampled.

'By Jesus', Alan surmised as the human tornado raced around the courtyard with a long stick he had found, prodding the baskets and hitting them so that earth and leaves flew every which way.

"I bet he's great at piñata!" Alan quipped, just for something to say.

He relaxed as that comment made Christina laugh.

"He is!… So energetic!" she gushed.

Inwardly, Alan groaned. Could Christina really not see that this behavior, even for a young toddler like Jesus, was not… normal!

Alan was quickly getting the idea that anything that Jesus did was wonderful and awe-inspiring to Christina while each behavior just exhibited increasingly worrying symptoms to Alan. But Christina had had Jesus for over two years now – and he had known her… how long? In ways it seemed like forever, but Alan knew he was a newcomer on the scene and anything he had to say about Jesus and the help and guidance he undoubtedly needed would fall on deaf ears. Why waste his time, his breath and spoil the fun that he knew he and Christina could have together by pushing the issue too early?

At least Lucia would take care of Jesus. She was out there now, in the little courtyard which was obviously Jesus' kingdom, watching over him like an adoring mother hen as he wreaked yet more carnage on the flowers, the grass, the walls, etc., tossing around the play equipment obviously put there for his use.

Alan, having finished his simple but delicious lunch which made a welcome, fresh change from all the rich food he was tempted with on board ship, went behind Christina, giving her a gentle shoulder massage and bending to kiss her neck.

"Why don't you show me where I'll be staying? I've been here a couple of hours and not seen my room yet," he teased seductively.

Giggling, Christina got up. Jesus raced in. How he saw – or maybe sensed – that his mother was about to leave him, Alan was to marvel at many times during their relationship. But here he was, clinging to Christina's leg like his life depended upon it. Alan frowned, feeling puzzled at the peculiar light that went on behind Christina's eyes at this neediness. She... *liked* the boy like this!

"Come on, up you come, little man!" she cooed, hoisting Jesus to her hip. Alan knew *his* 'little man' was going to have to wait for attention.

He trailed after Christina as she carried Jesus up to a room that was piled high with every toy imaginable for a child of Jesus' age. And this was just a holiday home!

"Wow! It's like *Toys 'R' Us* in here!" he said, only half joking.

Christina gave a little smile.

"He has to have all his toys in each of our houses. It saves on transporting them."

"Yes, well I suppose it would..." Alan trailed off, thinking 'oh, how the other half live!'

Jesus was now once more screaming, this time to be let down to play with his toys. Christina grinned at Alan.

"He will settle soon with me. You should go..."

Alan gave a deflated sigh, wishing, not for the first time, that they had left Jesus back on board with Christina's parents. Even if they had only taken day trips alone off the ship they would have had more fun together, he knew. Rather tensely, he said,

"Where should I go? I only know where the kitchen is."

Jesus was now realizing that naptime was approaching and he wasn't at all keen on this idea. He set up the thin wail that had accompanied them throughout their whole, thankfully short, plane journey here. Christina grew tense, but with Alan, not the screaming brat in her arms as Alan now thought unkindly of Jesus.

"You are a grown man. Entertain yourself for an hour, can't you?"

"An *hour*?!" Alan's voice also became high-pitched.

Again, Christina's glare silenced him.

"I... suppose so," he muttered darkly, turning on his heels and stalking back out to the courtyard where he had so recently been so happy with Christina.

This time, as he sat on the bench and looked out to the magnificent countryside beyond, Alan was not so easily relaxed. Thoughts of Christina… of Jesus… and his own helplessness and frustration, swam in his brain. He was sure he could help Jesus, and so help Christina. But she wouldn't let him. That boy obviously had problems, probably some form of autism and maybe some Attention Deficit Disorder also, but the misguided, smothering love of his mother was preventing him from getting help; as a physician as much as a neglected lover, that drove Alan crazy. He furiously jotted down all these mixed up thoughts in his trusty notebook, his faithful companion throughout his travels.

Eventually, even the scenery bored him and he went in search of his bags. He found them in a pretty, all-white room upstairs. At least that caused him to smile, as he presumed from the décor and the fripperies which adorned the room, that he had been bunked in with Christina. He decided he had to do something to occupy himself and, being stuck for company and without any other distractions, Alan took a recent medical journal out of his bag and settled down in the boudoir chair which was nicely positioned in the corner of the room to give it light from two windows. He began reading.

Glancing at his watch when eventually Christina pushed open the door and entered the room, Alan realized that she had actually been engaged doing he knew not what, pandering to Jesus, for a little over ninety minutes.

Christina pouted like a petulant child, seeing Alan reading.

"You don't want to play with me?" she said from under hooded lids.

Alan jumped up, all retorts he might have imagined in her absence now gone. She was here. The medical journal was rightfully discarded.

"I… was waiting for you… that's all."

Christina was already peeling the clothes from him, her ravishing eyes locked on his.

"We have an hour… maybe a little more," she told him with an urgency born of lustful need as much as the practicality of fitting any fun into Jesus' naptime.

'So he doesn't sleep long, either,' Alan thought ruefully but he had the sense to keep that to himself and just return the favor; Christina was undressing him; it was only fair that he should take off her clothes too.

Once naked, the pair fell onto the bed, Christina on top. That figured! She appeared an expert lover and she led Alan on down the path to ecstasy, touching, caressing, licking and kissing what seemed every inch of his body. He was on fire as he pushed her over gently and mounted her. Grinning down at her, he took her nipples into his mouth, sucking each one and gently tugging it, loving the little mews of pleasure which this brought out in her. His hand lay on her flat belly, toying with her navel.

"You… are… beautiful… You… are… mine now," Alan rasped as he subconsciously wrested his lover from her son, Jesus, and all the other cares of the world.

"MMmm… yes…," sighed Christina, arching. "Take me, Alan… I want to be… yours…"

Alan didn't need a second invitation. He entered her quickly pulling her legs up either side of him and firmly kneading her luscious bottom. His thrusts were deep and powerful and he made sure Christina enjoyed his efforts. He sure did, crying out in ecstasy as he climaxed, but quickly softening as he felt Christina's hand muffling his mouth.

"Shh… Jesus… he will hear!" Christina hissed urgently.

Alan groaned, flopping on to Christina and rolling off onto his back, somewhat… deflated.

"How do you manage?… I mean… since Jesus' father, am I the first?…"

"I manage," said Christina tersely, tugging her clothes back on.

'Well, that told *me*!' thought Alan wryly.

His breath recovered now, he propped himself up on his elbow, reaching out with his right hand to caress Christina's slender back as she sat on the side of the bed.

"You have the most beautiful spine I've ever seen."

"MMmm – thank you, Doctor," teased Christina, giggling as she leaned back to give Alan one more gentle kiss.

Well, there might have been more than one kiss, but at that moment, Jesus could be heard crying. Clearly he felt naptime should be over and he wanted up.

"Is he still in a crib?" Alan asked, trying not to make his question sound weighted.

"Of course; I don't want him to fall out, do I?… Most often he is with me… here… if not, he is in his crib."

Alan swallowed hard. Jesus shared his mother's bed?

"And… when he… *calls*… you always go straight to him?… Immediately?…"

Christina obviously felt that that last question did not deserve to be dignified with an answer. She just stalked out of the room, leaving Alan to hurriedly get dressed. The crying down the hallway stopped like magic. The phrase 'wrapped around her little finger' occurred to Alan and he shook his head, chuckling wryly.

A little while later, Christina and Jesus joined Alan in the kitchen, with Christina laughing lovingly as Jesus bonked Alan on the head with his teddy bear. Thankfully it was quite a soft, plush toy, but sticky with some substance that Alan did not care to think about.

"Such a sweetheart!" beamed Christina.

"That's one way to put it," Alan muttered ruefully, rubbing his head as he went to pour himself some much needed coffee.

"Let's go out. To the market! I love the market… so… *local*." Christina suggested with glee.

That caused Alan to brighten again. If he couldn't be alone with Christina – and clearly he couldn't during Jesus' waking hours - he may as well do something interesting.

One of the most interesting things about being on the road (even when Alan was literally "on the water") was experiencing the vast, rich and unique beauty of planet Earth and the diversity, kindness and energy of his fellow human beings. Whenever he traveled and wanted to really enjoy it, he explored the places and the people he encountered on the journey; he needed to find things that brought him back to that place with joyous anticipation. That meant getting off the "beaten path", as they say; not sticking to the usual tourist stops, and experiencing the country as it truly is.

One of the best places to do that was at a local market. Alan had found that the local market was not only the best place to sample local food, but was also where one could interact with the locals. It was often the best place to purchase the innumerable gifts that one was obliged to provide to fellow crew on a regular basis.

There was this culture of what Alan called 'trinket trading' among the crew. It was kind of a way of bringing a bit of the local culture back aboard the otherwise sterile environment of the crew quarters. It was also a way of providing the crew that seldom had a chance to disembark (kitchen staff and some of the cleaning staff) a way of getting the necessary gifts that they wanted to have to bring back or send to their families back home. In any event, over the years, Alan got quite adept at purchasing these gifts and knowing what kind were enjoyed and what type were recycled to other crew down the line. The local market was seldom the place to purchase the bigger ticket items that were traded between the officers, Alan's nursing staff, close friends and his room steward, but it was also a place to take pictures of real people and not just the tourist sites.

Christina obviously knew this place very well and he recognized an opportunity to sample some of the local color with her, so he quickly tidied himself up and met Christina in the hallway.

She was carrying Jesus so they were obviously taking him with them. Alan's unspoken question must have been clear in his face, as Christina said,

"I don't leave him with anyone but my parents. He loves Lucia but…"

"Has he got… a stroller?" Alan asked, wondering how on earth Christina was going to fare in carrying him all the way round the market.

"He doesn't like them, so I…"

With a disappointed sigh, Alan waved away her explanation. He didn't want to hear any more excuses for Jesus' peculiar behavior and the way he was treated… spoiled.

So the disparate trio set off to the local market. In this world of instant communications, televised wars and disasters, it is far too easy to think of an entire country, event or situation as a three-minute news flash. By actually putting his feet on the ground in one of these countries, Alan always got a much better idea about what life was actually like in that country, especially in a local market, and an appreciation for how easy his life was, back on his own home turf.

Even in those countries where there is poverty, a lack of amenities, political unrest, endemic diseases, poor food preparation facilities and so on, there is still life! - Life as designed by a higher being, but modified intensely by his creations!

Alan had seen a special vitality, some hope and an energy that was only human in its ingenuity. He distinctly remembered being summarily impressed by the peace and tranquility of a Sadu (a holy man) he witnessed sitting in a very busy train station in India. Flies were landing on the sores (impetigo) on his face and on the meager food he had been given by some passerby. Soon after, he arose from his meditative state and had a distinct smile on his face as he consumed the food that the flies had left in his cup. Hope, energy and life; they are the tripod that supports humanity.

Another time, Alan asked some adults why the children in a small, poor village he had visited seemed so happy. From his point of view, they had nothing; they were living in the worst possible conditions, rummaging through the trash on a daily basis to obtain their daily sustenance. They told him that they always strove to teach their children that life was a gift and they should enjoy every moment; those words made Alan weep inside, but gave him a new appreciation for life, love and the world at large.

From many of these experiences, he had truly begun to see the level of interdependence between "the traveler" (himself) and the world's ecosystem. He knew that he needed to learn to understand what the ecosystem had done to benefit him, and for him to do his utmost to work with the other parts of it so that he could survive and thrive, and for the system in which he was working not to fail. Alan snapped out of this philosophic reverie with two feet firmly planted on the soil and put a smile on his face as he took a look around the bustling marketplace that Christina now guided him to.

"It's wonderful! Good idea to come here," smiled Alan as he strolled around the market with Christina.

He had initially tried draping his arm around Christina's shoulders as they walked. But Jesus had sharply bitten his hand, drawing blood and causing Alan to yelp loudly in pain and think very negative thoughts about this little boy.

'Oh if he was *my* son...!'

"What do you do... when he... bites like that?" Alan asked with a pained expression on his face as he rubbed his sore hand and considered the bacteria that had just been transferred to his skin and the antibiotics he was going to be forced to take because of a human bite. (Human bites are one of the worst for getting infected, second only to those of cats, which never have their teeth brushed.)

Again, Christina looked at Alan like he'd sprouted another head.

"*Do?*... Nothing... He has to be allowed to express himself... he didn't want you to hold me... he is... very... possessive."

"Yes, I can see that," responded Alan ruefully.

He gave up. Jesus was obviously not disciplined in any way. What Jesus wanted, Jesus got – lucky boy! Alan contented himself with sampling and purchasing a few of the local delicacies that were all around in the marketplace. Occasionally, he managed to sneak a hand to Christina's tight little bottom where Jesus could not reach to do much about it. This marketplace also afforded Alan a chance to take some great digital photos with his pocket camera. A few of the happy pair (Christina and Jesus, of course) were also taken amidst the color of the local market.

As Christina checked out the fresh fruits – and Jesus demanded (and got) anything that popped into his head, Alan's gaze drifted off to the surroundings beyond the market.

The market sat in the center of a large park area; each stall was set up on a portion of the large tiled deck and all around it was a lovely green park of grass and trees. Something off to one side caught his attention and he stopped, stepped away from Christina and stared intently at it.

There, sitting smack in the middle of an open space was a huge round stone. He cocked his head; it looked like a giant cannonball at least five to six feet in diameter. Was it some sort of war memorial or something? There didn't seem to be a plaque on it – of course, it could be on the other side.

Alan pointed off at it.

"Christina, what is that?"

She turned, with Jesus still in her arms, and looked where he was pointing.

"What? Oh that, that's a *bola*; ah, you would call it – a ball."

Alan rolled his eyes.

"Well, I can see that! I mean, what is it, what's it for?"

"No one knows."

"Really? There's no record of where it came from?"

Christina shook her head.

"No, they've always been here. There's an exhibit on them over at the museum. Some say they've existed for a thousand years, some say longer. Some say the Gods left them; others – aliens."

Alan snorted.

"Yeah, right, aliens. Wait, *they*? What, you mean there are more?"

Now Alan really *was* fascinated.

"Yes, there are many, all over the countryside. Some are tiny, but many are as big as that one."

"Wow. You say there's an exhibit at the museum? Could we go have a look?"

Christina nodded and wiped her brow with the back of her free hand. Her skin glistened in the midday sun, the beads of sweat catching the light ever so delicately.

'My God, she even makes *sweat* look sexy!' thought Alan, chuckling to himself. 'Or did they call it 'perspiration' when women did it?... Bah, sexism!

"I don't see why not. It is getting rather stifling out here in the sun, and I'm sure Jesus would welcome the chance to cool off for a while.

'Yes, maybe he'd even fall asleep again and give us a moment's peace!' Alan thought.

With that, they headed out of the market and strolled over to the boulder. Christina stood off to one side while Alan slowly walked around it and took several photos.

"Fascinating; it appears to be perfectly round! And yet, you say it's a thousand years old?"

Christina nodded.

"At least; some say they're even older than that. Come on - the museum is just across the square."

A short time later, they stepped inside the museum, and Alan let out a sigh of relief. Oh, air conditioning, what a fabulous boon to humanity! Christina had been intent on continuing to carry Jesus, but Alan talked her into renting a stroller. For one thing, it had a nice basket on the back where she could put the little bags of fruit and such that she'd bought at the market that Alan was gallantly carrying.

Of course, Jesus kicked and screamed and stiffened his body. No way was he going to ride in a stroller without a fight – so Alan gave him one!

"Ohhh now – what a silly fuss for a big boy like you!" he mocked in a sing-song voice, firmly pushing the little boy, who was never the less, fiercely strong, back in the stroller. Alan was squatted down in front of Jesus, carefully keeping the 'family jewels' out of the way of flailing legs.

Alan smiled a forced grin, making it look like he was tickling Jesus as he again and again firmly restrained the flying limbs.

"He is playing with you!" the doting mother smiled.

"Yes, how delightful!" Alan managed to say through gritted teeth as, after a few minutes, he felt Jesus give up the struggle.

Alan warmed to Jesus - just a little. It hadn't taken a lot of effort to get him to sit still in the stroller – albeit with a mutinous scowl on his face. Perhaps this may give him an 'in' to discuss disciplining Jesus with Christina. He sure hoped so, because he found himself deeply attracted to this boy's mother.

After that, they started to stroll about the exhibits. Many of them were about the Mayan and other civilizations that existed throughout the area. Alan wasn't interested in them; he'd seen all that before. Instead, he made a beeline for the exhibits on the *bolas*!

Christina had been right; archeologists had first attributed them to the Chorotega Indians and they were built anywhere from 1100 to 1400 years ago. The thing was - there were no records from the Chorotega that mentioned them!

Alan read a display case about the stones.

"Incredible; some are much as thirty tons and they're perfect spheres! Their diameter and circumference are within two millimeters: incredible again!"

Christina giggled.

"Yes, you see what I mean? That's why some say they are the gifts of the Gods."

Alan's brow wrinkled.

"But, what are they for? Why make a big round ball and leave it out in the middle of nowhere? Unless… wait, do they line up on stars or constellations?"

"Ah, *si* – yes, there was a scientist many years ago who discovered that. Come, it is over here."

Christina pushed the stroller across the wide and long room to a massive display against the far wall. There was not a sound from the little boy. Alan smiled. Yes, little Jesus was falling asleep. At last, he and Christina could have some 'quality time' of their own for a while.

The room was quite large and long and many display cases and artifacts were scattered throughout it. Right at the center was a tall and imposing totem pole carved from stone!

Alan paused for a moment to look it over. Wow, what a structure! Granted, it was nothing by comparison to the pyramids, Stonehenge or any other massive ancient structure, but the details, the intricate images and the hieroglyphics made it a true thing of beauty. Tearing himself away, he strode off to catch up with Christina, yet immediately slowed in his pace; he rather liked the view of her walking away. Oh, her pert little bottom had quite the delightful wiggle as she walked; it was like Jello on springs or something!

He was almost disappointed when they reached the display and they stopped so he could look it over.

Christina pointed at the picture of a man, which was hanging over the main case.

"That's Ivar Zapp; he's the man who studied the bolas back in early 80s," Christina explained

Alan stepped up next to her, his right hand coming to rest at her waist – and then sliding down to cup that most adorable behind. He enjoyed tracing his fingertips gently over the fabric of her snugly flattering shorts. And Jesus was no longer awake to protest. Alan smiled when Christina did not pull away, and he turned his attention to the display as he continued his discreet caresses – and she let him!

'Note to self – bring Jesus to museums more often' he thought.

Aloud, Alan said,

"I see; the local legends spoke of the stones having something to do with the stars."

Christina turned toward him, and pointed at a display on the left.

"Yes, so he mapped their positions against the locations of ancient stars."

Alan scanned the display, and his eyebrows shot up as he let out a long slow whistle.

"Wow, and found they created sightlines that lined up with Stonehenge, the pyramids of Egypt, and Easter Island! Again, incredible; no wonder people think they were left by the Gods. Ah, I see; others say this area was the true site of Atlantis. Well, that doesn't make too much sense. Atlantis was supposed to be IN the sea."

Christina laughed.

"Yes, now we have people running all over the countryside looking for the ruins of Atlantis! Oh no, Jesus, where is he?"

Alan quickly looked down at the stroller; it was empty, and Christina had such a look of fear on her face.

"Now-now, don't worry; he can't have gone far!"

He spun around and scanned the room.

'Yeah, considering how you carry him almost everywhere, I doubt he has the strength to walk very far at all!' Alan thought.

Christina screamed, and pointed. Alan followed the line of her arm, and saw the little monster.

It seemed that Jesus was a whole lot more physically capable than his mother gave him credit for. He was making a pretty good attempt at climbing the totem pole!

"Baby, come down," Christina called out, fearfully.

Alan thought it was more a time for actions, rather than words; he sprinted toward the pole, even as half a dozen of the museum staff did likewise. Oh man, this was going to be trouble.

Alan got to the base first and looked up. They were in luck; Jesus wasn't very far up. A moment later, Christina and the staff joined him. They spoke Spanish, in which Alan was pretty fluent, but some spoke the local Indian dialect; he didn't quite get what they were saying, but – for most of it – words were unnecessary; their gestures and tone spoke volumes!

Alan reached up and managed to get a hold of Jesus by his shorts.

"Come down, my boy; it's not safe to be up there!"

"Darling boy, do as the Doc says; this is no time to be playing."

"Waaaaaaa!" the boy screeched.

As much as Alan felt the boy deserved to learn a lesson, he also didn't want him to get hurt. Yet, he seemed bound and determined to continue climbing.

"Jesus, please, you'll get hurt," he said.

Finally, he made the decision: he gave a hard tug on the boy's shorts, and down he came.

Christina screamed.

"Noooo, my boy!"

Plop! Jesus dropped into Alan's arms – and immediately began to wiggle and squirm and complain. Christina darted to Alan and snatched the boy from his arms, quite as if it was Alan who was doing him harm!

"Oh, how could you do such a thing?" she wailed.

Alan grinned. Finally, the woman was dealing with this monstrous child.

"How could you be so rough with my baby?"

Alan's jaw dropped as she looked up at him, fire in her eyes. He turned away; good god, could this brat do nothing wrong?

The staff moved closer and all began to chatter and complain; it was all a jumble to Alan. Christine, for her part, made no apologies.

Finally, when all was said and done, they were asked to leave – and never return! Frankly, Alan couldn't have cared less - at least not about Jesus' 'horrid' injuries. Still, to placate Christina, he checked Jesus over and gave him a clean bill of health. No scratches, no bruises - nothing.

Naturally, Jesus made it clear that this was *not* the case. From the way he cried and carried on, you'd have thought Alan had broken his leg in multiple places! So, of course, Christina babied him, carried him and kept him close for all the rest of the day, and both occasionally shot dark looks in Alan's direction.

So, it was not until much later that day – that night, actually, when Jesus was finally bedded down and had been cuddled to sleep - that Alan and Christina were again able to share an intimate moment. However, Christina had made it very clear that Jesus would be sharing 'her' bed tonight, even if Alan was also there. This was quite the passion killer for Alan, for a while, but as Jesus drifted off to sleep, Alan's natural urges took over. If this was all he was going to get with Christina – and she made it clear that it was common for Jesus to share her bed – regardless of whether she had adult company or not – then he would have to take it.

On the one hand, Christina was quite upset about the 'abuse' that Jesus had suffered that day. Yet, on the other hand, she was definitely in need of consoling. So, Alan managed to 'console' her – three times in fact – before Jesus again awoke and needed comforting.

# CHAPTER ELEVEN

*December 7, 2009: Paradise Island*

ALAN LAUGHED AS HE snapped out of his pleasant daydream of times gone by. A lot had happened in such a short time, and his foggy old brain was having trouble keeping it all straight. So, he'd do what he always did, when faced with confusion: he'd make a list.

As he got up, Alan realized he'd left greasy sunscreen marks on the pristine cream bedcover. A day of fun in the sun had left him slightly scorched and rather dusty and sticky.

'Gee, Jo Ann would have been all over me about that!' he thought to himself, getting up from the bed.

So, first a shower to clean up, some fresh clothes and then he sat down at the little table by the window. He frowned; no he didn't want to be a "shut-in", not on such a beautiful day and ship.

Rooting around in his little travel bag, Alan found his good old journal notebook. Ah, the notes and letters he'd jotted down in this, and similar books, over the years. Sometimes he found these journals a good way to remember names or places, especially for identifying pictures. Other times, he became quite contemplative in his musings and wrote quite interesting notes. At other times there were notes of only the city being visited or the weather or a few scribbles as he had fallen asleep trying to jot down something on the page.

Sometimes, he would do a pen and ink sketch of the scene he was viewing either from the ship or from some scenic spot on shore. It was yet another way of remembering but also a way of practicing the art that his grandmother taught him as a child. She was quite the accomplished artist in her later years. She would do beautiful portrait paintings, miniatures, and then when her hands were quite arthritic, rather modern scenes of the local surroundings. It was in the era of her portrait paintings that she taught Alan how to use color and all, but these days, he usually preferred words.

Grabbing a pen off of the desk now, Alan headed down to one of the lounges once more. He found a nice, little round table off in the corner and started to write.

So, there was Michael's murder, that incident of the man with the syringes that were too big for use in insulin injections and his over-indulgence at the midnight buffet. There was Tiffany. No… no Tiffany was now… Oh how that thought scared him – but there was some reason she had come to mind. Now why did her name ring a bell in his mind right now? Ah, yes; there was that Tiffany *lamp* in Michael's cabin! It had been broken, and there were many shards everywhere across the floor. Alan remembered he'd had some of those attached to his pants' legs as he'd stood up from examining the body.

And then there was the model airplane. Wasn't the subconscious mind a curious thing! He'd never even been aware of that right up to now, until seeing that plane underwater had made him think of that detail from the past. Alan couldn't remember why it was important, any more than the lamp, but he could remember writing it down in his old notebook he kept at the time. He decided to list both of these details now, thinking for sure that they were important. Surely if he put his mind to it he could work out what the police hadn't – who had murdered Michael. After all, the cruise ship was a pretty closed community. Alan didn't think it would be beyond his intelligence – not the Doc's!

There'd been no shortage of suspects at the time, as Alan remembered now. There was the boyfriend… nasty bit of work as Alan remembered him. There were that Russian fellow, and a Mrs. Brightman – was that her name? They'd been connected to Michael because of some shady art deals. Oh, and a long list of boyfriends – as Michael and Alfonse had had an "open" relationship – so, his death could have been connected to a lovers' triangle. Triangle, fie! Given his plethora of companions, it could be a square, pentagon, or multi-sided affair.

Oh - and then there was that 'doctor' who'd been on board at the time of Michael's death! Hadn't he been the one with the syringes? Ah… what was his name? God, he just couldn't think of it now. All these memories swirling in his head had to mean something. Even though he couldn't figure it all out, he knew he needed the pieces to his mental puzzle.

He sat back and smiled. Yeah, that was the way to picture this enigma; it was like a puzzle, but one in which he didn't have a cover picture to guide him. So, in this case, the best thing for him to do was just make the list, put it aside and let the items sort of bang around in his unconscious mind for a while.

Just as Alan had let himself think of something else, the name of the doctor he had been so desperately searching for came back to him: Dr. Zetisman – or Dr. Z as many on board liked to call him. Alan had never graced him with that name, since it sounded too much like a James Bond villain and Alan secretly thought that Dr. Zetisman would actually quite like that. He had seemed to Alan quite the unpleasant character, eager to inflict his groping and touching on anyone who took his fancy – male or female.

The question had been - who was Dr. Z? Let's see; he had an honorary PhD from some school that he had endowed with lots of his ill-gotten money, which was the origin of the 'Dr.' in Dr. Zetisman. Oh, and he was also one of the most obnoxious and disliked individuals on the entire ship!

Dr. Z had the most atrocious table manners imaginable. If you were at the same table as Dr. Z, you could expect to have to make a change of clothes after dinner from the food launched by him from either a fork filled with food he was gesturing with, or from pieces of food emanating from his mouth (which was never closed - even when he was eating.) He was loud, vulgar, and had hands that wandered to the private parts of young attractive females and males of the serving staff.

Apparently, only a few ever took him up on his offers of sexual relations. One would have to have wanted the money pretty badly to have lowered oneself to being intimate with him! Of course, his dietary habits created a rather artistic collage on his clothes. The color combinations were not always correct, but there were certainly extra colors and stains that added to the general impression of this small, hunched backed, loud, obnoxious individual. He would not hesitate to yell at full volume across a room for something or someone he wanted the attention of.

Staff, of course, were obliged to respond to his wild demands for special food, timings for cleaning his suite of cabins, and accommodating his requests for 'things' from on shore. These things were sometimes of a chemical nature and no explanation was ever given as to what they were for.

His background was as a rather notorious lawyer (notorious because of the shady individuals he happily defended and by whom he was rewarded generously from their ill gotten gains when he got them out of jail); one of them had gotten him associated with the business school at a New York College that needed money. He had boasted of being their major fundraiser and apparently did very well for them, and himself, over the years.

Alan remembered that several alumni from the college told him that Dr. Z had taken the title of "Dr." long before the honorary PhD. He had apparently been interested in native Brazilian plants; at one time in his shady past, he was an immigrant to Brazil. Yes, Alan remembered; it had been when the Brazilian Government agreed to take a great number of Eastern European Jewish Prisoners after the war. They had nothing left since their villages had been flattened. They were lucky to be alive and have the good graces of many countries that paid for their transportation, a house, car etc., as long as they agreed to live in areas needing an influx of people, for a set number of years.

The scuttlebutt among the people Alan had talked to was that Dr. Z had come over with this group and gotten himself ahead of the rest by ingenious methods. He apparently had a number of small businesses going at the same time. He'd amassed a lot of items from other prisoners who had asked him to guard things for them when they were leaving the camps. Most people were searched extensively. But Dr. Z had made certain 'arrangements' with the guards and could get away with almost anything in the camp, during the war, and as it was ending.

It was said that Dr. Z had been very friendly with the chemists who had carried out barbaric experiments during the war and some of the other Nazi staff that noted he could get anything done. So, he was often asked to do 'special projects'. Some were said to be the Nazi research that tested all of the potential effects that occurred to the human body when subjected to a variety of toxins and torture!

With all that in his background, was murder such a stretch? Dr. Z had said that when he arrived in Brazil, he had a very interesting array of small businesses. The first, of course, was a pawnbroker business that was started with all of the gold and other objects he was "guarding for others". After that generated sufficient funds, he started a funeral home/embalming service. The latter was supplied, after a few years, with chemicals from another company he owned. He acquired that company from a person he had loaned money to and that had defaulted on the loan.

Alan remembered that Dr. Z had said this was not a major chemical or pharmaceutical company. They manufactured pesticides for commercial and home use - that was it. They used pretty routine chemicals in trying to kill the vermin of the world, the insect/spider type that were ever present in rural Brazil.

Dr. Z had spoken with fascination about learning that the indigenous peoples of the Amazon basin had a variety of native plants that they used to eliminate the variety of insects that destroyed their crops. They also had very effective local toxic ingredients that were put in the poison-tipped arrows used against their enemies. Some of the shamans he had met and worked with in Brazil were very adept at utilizing the indigenous herbs in the treatment of various medical and psychological problems. Although he was never an official student of botany or ethnobiology, Dr. Z became quite efficient at using the various herbs to enhance and often replace the commonly used commercial pesticides.

Alan had to wonder now - with all that knowledge of exotic plants and their poisons, if Dr. Z couldn't have brewed up a noxious concoction to make Michael's death appear to be merely a heart attack. Yet, what would have been his motive? Well, that was yet another question to be answered and he added it now to the quickly growing list he had jotted down.

Dr. Z had talked about how he emigrated from Brazil to the US in the early 1950s. Because of his business savvy, he was readily incorporated into the arms of this financially struggling institution in NYC to which he was introduced. He did well for them, and from that, his legal practice and various other business activities, he was able to take the money he made and take extensive trips around the world on various luxury cruise ships. The Gold Line was one of his regular haunts.

So, what could his connection to Michael be? Alan didn't know yet, but he was going to try and find out. He had his laptop in his cabin. Next chance he got, he'd get to one of the ship's 'hot spots', spend some of his hard earned dollars that quickly disappeared using the ship's email services and get online.

That had been one of the perks of being a ship's doctor: no charge for use of the internet. Many of the numerous reports that the ship's doctor has to send to corporate on a daily basis were done on the internet. If not abused, on some shipping lines, there was time to occasionally use the internet to stay in touch with the real world and one's friends and family back home. There was no use of Skype, Magic Jack or other online communications by voice allowed, but simple emails could sometimes be made. On some of the ships, there was strict monitoring of each email by a full-time group of email monitors (spies), so all crew had to use on-shore internet cafés to make any personal communications.

This was especially true if there was any communication regarding one of the notorious officers with some friend on another ship.

If you were so inclined to tell friends about the escapades of the captain, staff captain with other crew or passengers, you were well advised to do so from an onshore email site. Similarly, if there was something that one wanted to communicate privately to one's superiors in Corporate about a medical condition, a lack of emergency supplies, or needed policy, doing so off the ships was a prudent idea.

Alan remembered treating one of these 'email monitors' (officially called IT Surveillance Technologists) on several occasions, for an ear infection. They got to chatting about this and that, and Alan realized what these crew members really did. Interestingly, they had very short contracts and were shifted from ship to ship; he imagined, in order to diminish the possibility of having time to develop relationships with other crew that might affect their objectivity in their job. This fellow could have written ten books on some of the information he had garnered from surveillance of only a few of the passengers' and crew's emails!

A slight movement off to his left caught Alan's attention and brought it back to the present; he turned to see Tiffany standing there. He looked up at her and smiled.

"Hello again, my dear; how are you - things getting back to normal now?"

Tiffany sighed and took a seat, as he gestured at the chair opposite him.

"Well... slowly but surely they are. The Romanian crew member who survived the swan dive is now refusing to go and see the shrink tomorrow in port, so the Staff Captain has had to post a twenty-four hour guard on his door, and we just have to hope he doesn't try anything else. They will have to physically remove him from the ship tomorrow, and the doctor says he may even have to sedate him. But now I have a new issue to deal with."

Alan sat up straight.

"Oh? ... Nothing serious, I hope."

She shook her head.

"No, we've got... uh... a *dearly departed* on board. You ever have one of those?"

"Yes, a couple over the years. The one that stands out in my mind..."

('Apart from Michael, of course,' thought Alan painfully).

"... was a dear lady and her daughter; ah... Debbie and... Hillary. Yes, I remember; the girl was about fourteen and her father had passed away from cancer. They brought his ashes on board and scattered them out at sea. The captain even gave them a certificate showing the longitude and latitude."

"Oh... that's so sweet," Tiffany said.

"Yes. So, is it a similar case that you're dealing with?" Alan asked.

In answer, Tiffany rose and gestured for Alan to follow her out on deck.

"Ah... not quite. Come have a look and I'll tell you about this... couple."

Intrigued, Alan fell in behind Tiffany and they walked out onto one of the small side decks of the ship. It was a rather secluded spot - the sort of place for a card game by day, and a little... "nocturnal fun" by night! Sitting at one of the glass-top tables, all alone, was a somewhat frumpy middle-aged woman. Her dark walnut-shaped hair was bound in tight curls and she seemed to be staring at a large urn on the table. Alan may not have been a fashion expert, but even he could see that she was no lady. She dressed very well, but a bit more flamboyantly, and definitely on the crude side, to say the least.

Tiffany pointed at her.

"That's Joan, came from Texas. She lost her husband, George, several months ago. He was a high level mechanic in the oil business and he apparently did very well, financially. I helped her get to and from the medical center for a refill of her blood pressure medicine and she mentioned the passing of her dear departed. She said she'd had him cremated, and brought his ashes with her on the cruise."

Alan nodded.

"Ah, so I take it that's… George there, 'facing' her, so to speak?"

"Yeah," Tiffany replied. "She said she had the urn on the coffee table in her cabin. She asked about scattering him overboard, and I said I'd check with the Captain. These days, there are a bunch of forms we have to file before doing that."

Alan's brow wrinkled.

"Really; why, what's the big deal?"

"Oh, it's all these EPA rules and such. Goodness, people are so worried about industrial waste getting into the ocean; we have a ton of red tape to chop through! I get the feeling she's not going to wait. Any thoughts on how I should handle her?"

Before Alan could even form a response, Joan turned the urn over on the table, essentially pouring "him" out on the glass top.

"Eeep!" Tiffany squeaked.

She started to step forward, but Alan held up his hand to stop her.

"Hang on a moment; let her be."

Joan sat there, looking at the ashes while tracing her fingers in them. After a few minutes she started talking to the ashes,

"George, you know that TV you promised me? I bought it with the insurance money!"

She paused for a minute tracing her fingers in the ashes again then said,

"George, remember that car you promised me? Well, I also bought it with the insurance money!"

"Sounds like George made a lot of promises," Alan whispered, chuckling.

Again, she paused for a few minutes and while tracing her fingers in the ashes, said,

"George, you know that diamond necklace you promised me? I bought one very similar in the gift shop today, with the insurance money!"

Tiffany nodded and leaned in close to Alan.

"Oh, I heard about that. The scuttlebutt among the crew is that it was *the* top of the line necklace in the jewelry shop."

"Wow! - Any idea of its cost?" Alan said.

"More than my house!" Tiffany replied. "Somewhere in the neighborhood of $335,000."

Alan let out a long, slow, low whistle.

"Double wow! Boy - if he knew how much she'd spent, he'd drop dead again!"

Finally, still tracing her fingers in the ashes, Joan said,

"George, remember that blow job I promised you? Well here it comes!"

And away went George into the Atlantic.

Tiffany squeaked, Alan snorted, and he mashed his lips closed as tight as he could to keep from bursting out laughing. Tiffany's hands flew to her face, which was turning about three different shades of red. She looked like she was about to explode. She started to double over, and Alan grabbed her about the waist and rushed her back into the lounge.

Once there, they both bolted for the far wall and erupted into all out laughing. Alan held his sides; he was laughing was so hard that he was actually hurting his ribs. Tiffany, practically doubled over, kept her hands over her mouth, giggled and squealed with delight, even as the tears began to flow from her eyes.

"Oh, what a sight, what a story!" she finally managed to say.

Alan, finally calming down, slowly nodded.

"I agree. I'm going to be getting drinks off of that one for quite a while!"

Something popped into his head, and he felt his face flush.

"Ah… sorry about… grabbing you like that. Nothing… ah… personal.

Tiffany grinned like the Cheshire cat straight out of *Alice in Wonderland*.

"I suppose I could be convinced to… overlook it - for a price."

Alan's brow wrinkled.

"Ah… just what are you…"

"How about dinner tomorrow night?" Tiffany said. "I have to do the 'Kiddie Korral' tonight, and the Captain's grand dinner the day after tomorrow."

"My-my, they *do* keep you busy, don't they?" Alan said.

Tiffany nodded.

"Yes; if I'm not being pelted with peas and mashed potatoes, I'm having to be all prim and proper! Tomorrow is one of my few 'ordinary' dinners. So, how about it? I won't even insist you wear a tux."

"Well that's good, 'cause I haven't pressed mine yet!" he joked.

Of course, he did have one with him for the more formal nights.

"Okay, dinner it is."

Bidding her farewell, Alan headed back toward his cabin. It seemed he was going to have a lot on his mind and 'plate' over the next couple of days.

# CHAPTER TWELVE

*July 14, 1984: Costa Rica*

IT WAS REMINISCENT OF times gone by as the story of how Christina's husband had shuffled off this mortal coil. Alan couldn't quite remember how it had come up but he remembered that Christina had been cagey about the details. It had been a heart attack, she said, but considering that Christina had once trained as a nurse before entering the family business for an easier and more lucrative career, she didn't seem knowledgeable on many of the details. Of course, it could just be that it was painful for her to remember and she just didn't want to think about it, but something about it made Alan uneasy.

It didn't make him quite as uneasy as Christina's insistence that Jesus should accompany them to bed every night now, after the brief progress Alan felt he had made in pressing Jesus' independence until the fateful visit to the museum. At first, Alan had thought Christina was joking, but sure enough, that night and many nights after, Christina had moved in for a late night kiss, opening his pants and leading him by a most tender handle to her bed, only to find the reposing body of her young son curled up on the pillow beside Christina's.

The first time, Alan had let out a little cry, backing toward the door. But Christina's hand tightening on his rapidly softening member had made her intentions clear and Alan had little choice but to oblige her. No wonder Christina had become so quiet in her orgasms as from their later whispered pillow talk, it was apparent that Jesus had shared Christina's bed almost all his life, and that his parents and later lovers of Christina had made what fun they could in the rest of the bed. Alan even grew a little used to it as

Christina assured him that Jesus rarely woke at night if he sensed her close by, until Alan opened his eyes after one particularly strong climax to find two deep brown pools so like Christina's staring at him. After a moment of bliss, the frown gave it away. Jesus was sitting up, glaring at Alan in unmistakable disapproval of the closeness with his mother!

Alan had also had his work cut out for him in keeping his temper and holding back on the advice on his brief sojourn with Christina and Jesus. Several times a day, Alan watched Christina give in to her son's tantrums and angry outbursts. Yet never once did he hear Jesus, almost three, say anything approaching a coherent word. It was all very worrying for Alan, obviously not for Christina, and he couldn't understand why she, as a former nurse, was not seeking a medical opinion on this.

But Alan tried to be philosophical about this. He had met Christina on a cruise ship and in less than a week now, they were destined to rejoin a cruise ship. Alan would stay there, whereas Christina, after the cruise was ended, would be on her way. As it happened, Christina was keener than Alan had dared hope and she joined him for quite a few subsequent cruises, but at that point he didn't know that and he saw no need to 'rock the boat' by sharing his views on how to parent the infant Jesus – especially when he had no children of his own! Alan didn't exactly have girls queuing up to be with him – only a few to be with Doc, the ship's doctor – and scaring away Christina with advice she clearly would not welcome, was the last thing he wanted to do.

Christina was able to show Alan around the local area, where the great opulence of her family villa sat beside some areas of real poverty. It reminded Alan of some of the less salubrious stopovers that Alan had had from his many cruise tours of duty.

Ships stop at the most unlikely places sometimes. Russia and former Russian Republics are just some of those places. Just going to shore there can be an interesting experience, even without a tour or any specific goal.

Going to the bathroom, Alan found was just one of those bizarre experiences. He recalled that on his first visit to Russia he was advised by one of the other crew members to take an umbrella. Alan looked at him rather strangely as it was summer and not a cloud in the sky. He disregarded the advice without much thought and wandered around a bit seeing whatever was to be seen in this rather industrial, non-enlightened part of the new Russia. Seeing what was left over from the old communist regime was interesting, but made Alan doubly glad that he did not have to live there.

Naturally, after wandering for a while, Alan's bladder gave signals that it was time for him to find a restroom. He had looked up the proper word and asked in a train station for the bathroom. No real problem finding one, but that was really where the adventure began!

Alan entered a cavernous room that contained numerous squat holes around its perimeter. He always found these interesting and wondered who had feet the size of the porcelain foot outlines that are used in them and who had the sense of humor to design them for men anyway. How can one reasonably think that a male could perform either bodily function without soiling or soaking his pants — unless of course he was an acrobat or contortionist – was utterly beyond Alan, no matter how many times he had to use these primitive facilities.

In this room, there was a mixture of the sexes, and no one seemed concerned or as embarrassed as Alan was. There were no dividers between the holes — no screening anywhere. Finally, Alan got up the nerve to go, having needed to go '#2' for several hours.

Squatting on his hole, Alan noticed a number of people leaving with some rapidity and others opening umbrellas. The advice from his crew member had been forgotten and at first Alan thought those leaving were doing so because of some train leaving or because they needed to get to work. Those opening umbrellas he rationalized were making an ingenious attempt to garner some privacy. Alan found all of this rather amusing until he also noticed a rather portly female enter the room with a hose. This woman looked like every picture you can imagine of the Stalin follower from the 'old era" - sporting a sort of plain cloth button down jacket, a cap with a hammer and sickle on it and ill-fitting pants the same color as the drab jacket.

Soon after the woman entered, it was obvious what the purpose of her hose was. She aimed it in the direction of the holes along the periphery of the room. It obviously did not matter that there was an assortment of men and women in various stages of undress in their compromised positions over their private holes.

Some were afforded the protection of their umbrellas; the rest of us were unceremoniously washed down with her hose, as was the floor around us.

The warm weather fortunately dried Alan off before he had to return to the ship, but that was one bathroom he would never forget! He thought of it now as he strolled around the village hand in hand with Christina. He had worked out a system now where by if he held Christina's hand on the side away from the hip on which she invariably carried her son, and walked so that their arms were outstretched a little, Jesus couldn't reach him to kick, bite or scratch him and the child usually forgot to scream at him after a couple of minutes. So, a truce of sorts was reached.

Christina wanted to know what Alan was chuckling about to himself of course, so he was forced to recount the adventure in the Russian restroom twice as they strolled along the quiet main street of the pretty rural village.

"Oh goodness!... Thank heavens for the cruise ship bathrooms, huh?" she grinned.

It always amazed Alan that, even living in luxury like she did, Christina saw Alan's life on board ship as so exotic. He guessed the grass was always greener on the other side!

"Ohh, you'd be surprised! Cruise ships aren't always much better; to the uninitiated they can be death traps!" Alan joked.

"Oh go on! You're being silly!" a laughing Christina chided him.

Alan was laughing too, carefree now he had her attention and she was relaxed.

"Well, of course, we've made great strides in preventing the spread of diseases on ships," he began as if he was giving an informative lecture to a trainee doctor on his first cruise, teasing her lightly.

"But of course, we, like most public places, have the occasional outbreaks of the Norwalk virus or other gastro-intestinal problems. Ships have done a good job of using wipe-downs and separating potential contaminants. Then you have those hand wash dispensers that all passengers are encouraged to use before all food lines, restaurants and whenever they come back on board the ship after excursions. But going to the bathroom on a ship can be mighty frustrating."

"Yes, but at least you don't need to take an umbrella with you!" quipped Christina.

Alan's tummy flipped, seeing yet again how her eyes sparkled when she laughed.

"Have you ever tried to start off a new toilet roll? Turning it around and around, trying to find the end that it is glued down then you finally get a two inch strip. Of course, that's no good to anyone, so you give it a pull and that gives you a five foot strip. So, some cruise lines abandon toilet rolls for those 'handy' little dispenser things hat give you toilet paper less than one ply thick, one square at a time."

Christina laughed heartily like she had been in just that position! Buoyed up, Alan continued his musings.

"Oh yeah, and cruise liners are built for luxury, of course, so they love to try to make things easier – except making things easier sometimes makes them an awful lot more difficult!... You ever been in one of those auto toilets...?"

"Yesssss!" said Christina, giggling. "The ones where you have to fake it to make it work?"

"That's the one!" grinned Alan. "Sometimes they just go off randomly while you are still on it. How dare you take longer than your allotted time! Of course, to make them work on a ship, they have to have quite a bit of suction. If someone is extremely large around the middle and sits on such a toilet whilst it's flushing itself, they can end up with a rather large suction bruise on their rear end!... Oh and the auto hand washers! They decide how much you are to get – they give you a certain amount of water - never enough... and you're stuck there like a raccoon washing your hands and you have to pull them out and pretend that you are a new set of hands just to get clean!"

Christina snuggled to Alan's side, walking along, laughing.

"Oh but what about the hand dryers?" she joined in the talk from her vast experience of being a passenger on cruise ships.

"They never dry you enough... and that's even if you are lucky enough to get the electronic ones!... I've seen plenty of those automatic paper rolls that so generously give you one piece and then make you wait several minutes for the next piece."

Nodding, Christina made a disgusted face, laughing.

"Yes! – But you can see why people don't bother sometimes, can't you!"

The doctor in Alan surfaced and he added,

"And then, of course, passengers go through the door using the handle that is full of germs from the people who didn't even wash their hands in the first place! … Now at least, many places will provide a receptacle near the door so you can open the door with a paper and leave it inside."

"Yes, Doctor," Christina mocked, giving Alan a playful little push then putting up her face for a kiss.

# CHAPTER THIRTEEN

*December 8, 2009: The Atlantic Ocean*

THE NEXT DAY ON Alan's first cruise as a passenger, the ship was forced to stay at sea; there would be no ports of call. The seas had turned rough and there was no way the tenders could safely ferry people from ship to shore. Now, Alan knew from experience what that meant: lots of activities on the ship. The cruise director always had plenty of things lined up to keep people busy.

After breakfast, Alan headed up to the Promenade Deck and was promptly proven right. A couple of cooks were already giving lessons and another of the staff was entertaining some kids by carving ice sculptures. Alan decided to pass on both. The activity he wanted was the one called wine tasting! On some of the less expensive cruise ships, it was a way to get people to learn about fine wines. Of course, the true goal was to subtly pressure them into wanting to *order* the wines for dinner.

'Oh yeah,' Alan thought, 'plunk down more money for a single glass than a whole bottle? I don't think so!'

He made his way into the main lounge and saw that everything was ready for the wine tasting. A long low table had been set up right in front of the bar and the sommelier was standing next to it. About a dozen bottles were arranged on the tables, along with many plastic wine glasses. The sommelier had brought a nice variety: everything from a Merlot to a nicely chilled Pinot Grigio.

Taking a seat among the many retirees and young people, Alan had to grin. A twenty-something woman had just asked to sample the '*cabaret savings-on*! Oh, the wine steward truly had his work cut out for him educating this crowd!

Alan remembered that on the 'all inclusive' cruise lines, they included most beverages, except for the *very* expensive reserve wines. Oh, now with those, the passenger could add $200-400 per bottle to his on board account! The Wine Tasting on those cruises was also an educational activity. Not all people with money know about wines, especially the newly wealthy.

Sitting there, watching the steward talk about the proper storage of wines, Alan suddenly realized that the Duke and Duchess were on the other side of the room. Getting up as quietly as he could, he slipped over to sit by them.

"Come for a little taste of the grape?" the Duke asked.

Alan nodded, and gave the Duchess a polite little smile.

"Yes, it's a good way to sample the wines the ship has to offer without spending too much money on wines I don't like."

The Duchess leaned in and whispered,

"Is it true that sometimes the sommelier plays a joke on the audience by switching wines and then going on at great length about the fruit, vegetable and legs of the wine?"

"Ah... well, I've *heard* of it happening. But, usually, to preserve his job, he won't do that. In truth, what he *will* do is spend an hour or so giving people the real story about certain selected wines. These are usually the wines chosen for the next formal dinner!"

She slowly nodded.

"Ah... I see, trying to drum up a bit of business, eh?" she chuckled.

The Duke scanned the assembled crowd.

"Now, it's my experience that most people are properly reserved in wine tasting."

"Yes, dear," the Duchess said. "But, that is usually in a more... appropriate setting - not where they serve wine in disposable cups!"

Alan nodded.

"Yes, and most people also know to not drink - and I mean alcohol - before attending. I had a passenger once, a Mr. Philip Johansen, who was of quite a different mindset about wine tasting."

The Duchess gave a light giggle.

"Showed up... ah, after already having downed... what, one to two bottles of wine or spirits?"

"That's putting it... politely," Alan replied. "He was very used to a high alcohol intake, and I was often called to make sure he had not overdone it. 'Blotto-ed', 'smashed', and/or 'highly inebriated' were the usual descriptions of his status."

"He wouldn't listen to any advice regarding the value of… moderation?" The Duke said.

Alan shook his head.

"No, he was on a cruise, which he kept extending, and he was going to do whatever he wanted to, regardless of any advice I could give. In one session I had with him, I told him his liver was a good bit larger than it should be for his 'tender' age of fifty-one. We both knew what was causing it."

"And he told you to bug off, eh?" the Duke chuckled. "I know that name. Mr. Johansen was the financial manager for a very large retirement fund of a Fortune 500 company. Am I right?"

Alan gave a small laugh, and nodded.

"Small world, huh? Yes, he said that while he did drink a bit, he could handle it just like he handled 12.4 billion dollars in assets. He informed me that his managed funds had done very well over the years and that the drinking obviously had not affected his performance. Then he asked how many billion dollars I had, and he was sure that I only drank in moderation."

"I do hope you… put him in his place, Doctor," the Duchess said.

"Well… I don't know how successful I was at that. But, I did say that while I didn't have billions, not even millions, and I did only drink in moderation and none at all while I was on duty. I also did my best to prevent a variety of chronic conditions that would statistically 'take me down' if I were to continue them."

The Duke grinned.

"Touché - well played, Doctor. And how did it end for the enthusiastic inebriant?"

"Well, he let me do some blood tests, but he only wanted me to tell him the results if he needed to update his will! It seemed he didn't want a certain gay nephew to get any of his money."

The Duke did a double take.

"He actually let you draw a sample of his blood? I'm surprised. From what I'd heard of Mr. Johansen, he was a powerful individual who was able to get some things done that would amaze you."

Alan nodded.

"Yes, so I'd heard about him. The rumor on our ship was that he was displeased with the way he was served a meal in his cabin one day. A cabin steward came to see me later that day, and he said Mr. Johansen had caused him bodily harm by lashing out with some cutlery on the dinner tray."

The Duchess let out a little squeak.

"Oh, was it serious?"

"It did require suturing. And then he also had the poor waiter dismissed and disembarked at the very next port of call."

"Oh, shocking!" The Duchess said. "Well, I hope his test results came back horrid!"

"Not... exactly. Several days later, the chemistry panel came back from the port agent. As I suspected, he had some chronic changes in his liver enzymes, indicating early cirrhosis. So, I advised him to cut back on the drinking and boost his water intake."

The Duke chuckled.

"Ah, just how much water would he have to drink to... offset his level of consumption?"

"Oh... about two gallons of water per day, in addition to all the other liquids that he was drinking," Alan said. "That would help... a bit."

The Duchess couldn't help but smirk.

"Oh, I bet he was so thankful for your input!"

"Well... he did thank me for letting him know that he didn't have to put *arsenic* in his nephew's martini - *yet*. Mr. Johansen's attitude was that he'd try to increase his water, if a toilet was nearby; if not, he'd just stick to Bourbon."

After that, Alan settled in to enjoy the wine tasting. He did notice that some of his fellow passengers seemed less than enthusiastic about it, and wondered what was wrong. Then, it came to him: seasickness.

Now, the larger cruise ships prided themselves on excellent stabilizers that kept the ship 'on the straight and narrow', as they say. Often, there was little, if any, rocking motion and the whole issue of getting seasick was... well, a *non*-issue!

Ah, but take people totally unprepared for being on a ship, throw in more rich food and alcohol than they can possibly imagine, and then mix briskly with even a slight motion and you had the perfect recipe for a re-creation of the projectile vomiting scene from *The Exorcist*.

Alan knew from long experience that being nauseated and feeling like you're going to vomit most everything that you've eaten for the last *year* in the next five minutes is not a pleasant feeling. On one of his first cruises, he had 'worshipped at the porcelain altar' for nearly an hour after eating some very rich desserts, and would not have been at all surprised to see his *shoes* come out of his mouth! Today he felt fine as usual, even with moderate motion of the ship.

After a brief bit of wine tasting, Alan made his way out on deck. This time, he decided to head aft. The wind was very brisk this day and the Captain had headed the ship into the wind in an effort to decrease the rocking. Needless to say, the stern was much more sheltered.

Strolling down that way, he passed the adults-only pool, then the rock climbing wall and finally came to the miniature golf course.

"Alan - how you doing?" Jenny called out to him.

He looked around; there were the "Two Ladies", decked out in shorts and snug little t-shirts. Jenny was just as attractive as he'd thought earlier.

"Doing good, ladies. Jenny, Tina, what you up to this fine day?"

"Trying to keep my breakfast down!" Jenny said with a self-conscious grin.

Alan grinned. She did look a bit 'green around the gills'.

"Oh yes, that uneasy feeling is quite familiar," Alan said sympathetically.

"What - and you a ship's doctor?" Tina said. "I'd have thought you were 'immune' to such things."

Alan slowly nodded, even as he gestured at the golf course. The ladies nodded back and then they grabbed clubs and balls. They got to the first hole and Jenny bent down to tee up. Oh, those shorts could best be described as 'cheeky' and she seemed a bit red down there. Huh, it seemed she'd overdone her fun in the sun.

"Yes, I'm pretty much used to the ship's movements," Alan said. "These days, you could say that I get *land*–sick!"

"Well, for me, right after we ate, the room started to get a bit warmer than it was a few moments ago," Jenny said. "Then came an uneasy feeling from somewhere behind my eyes, and then a feeling of weakness."

She took her shot; the ball went careening through the windmill and came to a brief rest near the hole. Then the wind caught it, and it blew back to almost the tee! They all laughed.

"It would appear golfing is a sport *ill*-suited to shipboard playing," Alan said.

"Well, so long as we all have the same… 'handicap', it's okay," Tina said.

Tina lined up to take her shot and Jenny stepped over to the side.

"Right now, I'm trying to fight down nausea," Jenny said. "I just hope it's not followed by vomiting."

Alan nodded.

"Yeah, that would be good. Sea sickness can be a bit of a never-ending cycle of the nausea and vomiting. Has the revulsion to food, the feeling weak and the longing for the whole world to go away and let you die in peace started yet?" Alan teased, knowing that would be a fairly accurate description of most sea sickness cases.

Jenny laughed, tried to sit, and immediately jumped to her feet.

"Ouch! Ah… no, I'm not quite that bad."

After Tina took her shot and had her ball blown almost clear off of the course, Alan lined up to take his shot.

"Ah… Jenny, you okay?"

She blushed and Tina giggled.

"No, she 'cooked' out in the sun a little too long. 'Toasted' her little 'caboose' worse than our Dad ever did," Tina said.

Jenny punched Tina's arm.

"Christina, don't tell him that!"

Alan snorted, trying to keep from laughing out loud. Jenny's face was now bright red.

"So, you say you don't suffer from seasickness now," Jenny said, clearly trying to change the subject. "What about in the past?"

Alan shot, his ball ricocheting off the windmill, back toward the tee and then the wind caught it. A big gust came up, and next thing he knew, the ball was almost in the cup!

"Whoa, aren't you the lucky dog!" Tina said.

"Thank you," Alan said, and then turned to Jenny. "I will have to admit that I occasionally felt 'uneasy' on some of my early cruises when the seas were really terrible and there was a strong smell of grease or diesel fuel in the air."

Jenny crinkled her nose.

"Ewww… not a good combination in any situation."

They continued on with the game, the wind making some of their shots *quite* interesting.

"So, I bet you got called in whenever a passenger was sick and wanted an 'instant cure' for their seasickness," Tina said, as she sunk her ball in the third hole.

Alan nodded.

"Oh yeah. When on a cruise ship, people tend to want to continue eating their *ten* meals a day. Anything that interferes with that *has* to go! Often, I was called to some of the larger suites that are placed in the very aft part of the ship. Of course they get a lot of motion there and giving a shot with that motion can be a real challenge!"

Tina couldn't help chuckling, and Alan didn't make it any better when he continued,

"… Then there were also those members of the crew that didn't realize that they were susceptible to seasickness before signing on."

"Oh… yeah, I bet a lot of them suffer from that," Jenny said.

"Yeah, but usually get over it quickly. There were a lot of times I had to sort out the real from the imagined with crew members who decided that they didn't want to go to work that day!"

The little course only had six holes and by the last one, Jenny was looking *quite* green.

"Oh… Alan, what's the common drug of choice for sea sickness?"

Alan pressed his lips together to keep from laughing.

"Feeling a bit... out of sorts, are we? Well, Meclazine is what most ships give out. It's usually handed out at the reception desk and in the medical department, and entirely without charge."

"Oh... that's good," Jenny said, letting out quite the audible sigh.

"I've never heard of that one," Tina said. "Are there others?"

"Oh sure; there are several other drugs that are also given for the condition. In fact, every ship's doctor has his favorite combination that he uses to treat seasick people. I often found my own combinations that worked best for different sorts of people and dependent upon what other medications they were taking."

Tina, going for a *quadruple* bogey as she tried - yet again - to sink her final shot against the wind, stopped to look at him.

"Really?"

"Definitely. I used to give one med to younger people, one for older. I had yet another for mild cases; one for more serious ones; one for people that had to still be functional at their job and another for those that could sleep it off. And there was always a variety of other options. If the passenger was very sick, and of a younger age, up to about fifty, I'd give them an injection of Reglan and Phenergan; those two have has been a favorite 'cocktail' of mine for years. For those that are really sick and have been vomiting for quite a while, giving them an intravenous liter of saline is often enough to calm things down and it rehydrates them at the same time."

Jenny gave him a weak smile. All these medical details had been a little hard to stomach, but now she saw some hope of relief.

"Oh... a shot to give relief? Yes! Could you do that for me, my dear doctor?"

Alan laughed and teed up for his final shot.

"Well... unfortunately, I'm not the ship's doctor. I'm ... retired, I guess... although I haven't quite gotten used to that idea yet. Why don't you go on down to the sick bay when we're done here?"

Jenny nodded.

"Yeah, I just might do that. Ah... just how quick does that stuff work?"

"It usually works on several body systems that cause the nausea and it quickly alleviates the problem," Alan assured her. "Now, it does make you sleepy, so it's not the sort of thing you give to someone that needs to keep active."

Alan shot, and managed to get a hole in one! It seemed that the pinball game hole was good for him.

"Oh... I wouldn't mind sleeping the day away," Jenny said.

"Not me!" Tina said. "I'm feeling a bit queasy, but I'd like to stay active today."

"Well, then simple Meclazine or Reglan can work fine for you," Alan said. "Got special plans for today?"

She smiled at him.

"No, but I was hoping!"

Jenny managed a small grin.

"Gee, now who's being the bad girl?"

Alan grinned as he retrieved his ball. Bending over, he caught a glimpse of the girls out of the corner of his eye. They were checking him out! Huh, so, it seemed he wasn't too old, after all!

Now, Alan wasn't one of your 'treat 'em mean an' keep 'em keen' brigade – far from it! But this appreciation from not one but two ladies left him just a little bit confused. His years with Jo Ann, which had taken up his adult life since his early thirties, were ended now, but he still felt a little bit like he was missing his left arm. As the game ended, he excused himself.

"Well, ladies – I think you had a good idea – a little ah… rest before… before more food, I guess!" he grinned.

Jenny perked up considerably and appeared set to follow Alan. He went red then white then almost as green as Jenny had been earlier! Thinking quick to correct the impression – and false hope – he had inadvertently given her, he pointed to one of the loungers. Now, reclining out on deck in the heavy seas was not an appealing option, but the cruise line had been thoughtful enough to provide some loungers in a kind of glassed in sun room. From there, one was totally protected from the elements but could recline in comfort and look out to the ocean beyond. Alan figured that with their stomachs feeling delicate as they were, the ladies would not wish to join him there.

His gamble paid off as Jen-Tina politely wished him a relaxing time and staggered off a little unsteadily to lie down in their cabins – Alan hoped after having visited the sick bay for some medication to help their 'sea legs' along a little.

Alan laid down on his lounger for a little while, just soaking up the sheer pleasure of being alone with his thoughts. He chuckled to himself, musing how a cruise which had been aimed at helping him forget was actually helping him remember so much! In fact, there was so much coming flooding into his mind about times long gone by - and what he now saw as an unsolved murder. Alan thought he had better head to his cabin and 'get it down on paper', so to speak; for now, of course, it was all going to be stored safely on his laptop: all the snippets and clues that had seemed insignificant at he time but which were now gathering in importance in his mind now.

Back in his cabin, Alan sat at his desk and turned on his laptop and pondered where to begin again – okay; he would begin with his return to the ship from his sojourn with Christina, and Jesus, and Michael's sad demise.

That had been when Alan first thought something was suspicious about the tour director's death. Initially, the report was a heart attack, and the local authorities had closed the case. Yet, Alan had remembered a needle track on Michael's arm. At the time, he'd dismissed it as simply a sign of recreational drug use, but now he noticed a couple of items in the old notebook he'd brought with him as he had been thinking of writing up his memoirs into a novel on this retirement cruise. First, there was the size of the needle – rather large – larger than normal for a simple "recreational" use; and second, there'd been a slight bruising around the injection site – he'd even made a sketch of it in his notebook.

A short time later, Alan had a bunch of rambling notes, and he paused to look them over. Oh yeah, this was a true jumble! OK; step one was complete: he'd written everything he could think of. Now came step two: trying to organize this mess. So, he set to work cutting and pasting the bullet points he'd created and got them into a rough timeline and sets of related items. That bruise: had it merely been caused by Michael thrashing about – he did have several on his body – or was it something else? It was a very light bruise, so it'd occurred close to his time of death. What if someone had… struck him there, thrusting a syringe into his arm? It could have produced the same sort of bruise.

Alan smiled. Yeah, *now* it was looking like something he could understand and build on. Sitting back in his chair, he nearly fell over when there came a rapping on his door.

'Who could that be?' he wondered.

Setting the chair back with all its feet on the floor, he stood up, and crossed to the door. He opened it, and was mildly surprised but nevertheless pleased to see Jenny standing there. A young lady coming to his cabin? There was a time when this was a favorite fantasy of his - although that usually involved a cheerleader and football player costumes!

"Hello there, Jenny. What brings you to my cabin; still got a touch of the *mal de mer*?"

Her brow wrinkled in obvious confusion.

"Wow, I didn't know you spoke Latin. What's that mean, anyway?"

Alan laughed.

"It's French, my dear little lady; it's a fancy way of asking if you're seasick."

She smiled.

"Oh… my, aren't you the smarty? No, I'm fine now. Well, ah… other than my… sunburn."

Alan smirked, even as her face took on a very slight pinkish hue. He gestured for her to enter.

"Please, come on in."

Alan chuckled as he thought how different things had been before he retired as a ship's doctor. Then, he didn't have patients enter his cabin – but for the delectable Jenny, he'd have made an exception any time!

"I thought you'd never ask!" she said with a huge grin as she stepped into the cabin.

Alan watched her enter. My-my, she did have a delightful wiggle.

"Wow, you've got yourself quite the nice place here! A lot better than the little shoe box of a cabin they stuck Tina and me in. It doesn't even have a window."

"Porthole, Jen; on a ship, they call them portholes," Alan said, stepping over to his collection of tiny liquor bottles. "Can I offer you some refreshment, or would that upset your stomach?"

Jenny laughed as she moved to the large windows and looked out. She bent forward slightly and her brief little shorts rode up just a bit, putting a small expanse of rather red skin on display. Clearly she was quite sore, as she'd not gone with her usual snug shorts.

"A blast of booze upset *my* stomach? Not in this lifetime! You got *Southern*?"

Alan nodded and held up the miniature bottle.

"Right here."

"Great, then make it a *Southern* and *Coke*; that's my fav'."

Alan fixed her drink and then got a *Jack* and *Coke* for himself. Stepping up behind her, he tapped her gently on her bare shoulder blade. She was in a tube top – and showing plenty of well-tanned skin! Turning to face him, she took the drink, and lifted it before him. She was standing *quite* close to him, and her body language made it clear that she did not mind.

"Cheers!"

He nodded and raised his glass. Well then, two could play at this game; Alan didn't mind either!

"To your health!" he responded with a grin and a slight clink of their glasses.

Alan took a sip, and she downed her drink in one gulp! His jaw dropped and Jen giggled.

"Yeah, I got no problem holding my liquor."

"Ah... so it would seem. My goodness, Jenny; maybe you should go easy on that. We are expecting more rough seas ahead."

She laughed.

"Good God, you sound like my Dad. What, am I being a bad girl again?"

Alan groaned.

"Oh... don't say that; I feel old enough as it is!"

Jenny moved to the bottles and fixed herself another drink.

"I'm sorry; I didn't intend to make you feel... old – because you're not!"

Alan took another sip.

"Thank you, my dear, but I *am* quite a lot older than you."

She stepped closer to him and ran her hand across his chest, her eyes looking up at him suggestively from under her eyelashes. Deep brown pools of mischief, they were: a guy could drown in those if he wasn't careful!... And Alan found his ring of protective carefulness which had surrounded him for many years - even way before Jo Ann's death – chip, just a little as she chided him.

"No, you are not! Alan, I've known plenty of men in my time. Oh, wait, that came out wrong. I don't mean I've... ah, *known* a lot of men; I've just um... known them. A lot of young men are actually quite old - and some old ones are the youngest I've ever known."

Alan could feel his chest tightening; his heart was speeding up and he heard the blood pounding in his ears. Of course, he could also tell that the blood was... surging 'South of the Border'.

"Ah, thank you; that does make me feel... better."

Jen grinned, emptied her glass down her throat and stepped even closer to him. Her right calf slipped between his legs and she started to rub him up – most definitely – the right way!

"Yes, I can tell!"

Alan rather tentatively snaked his right arm around to embrace her, even as he felt his face grow warmer. He hoped he wasn't blushing too much.

"Yes, bad; you are so *very* bad," he whispered, his eyes drifting down from those beautiful eyes to her luscious lips.

Her lips met his, and he tasted her sweetness. Oh, it had been a long while since he'd felt such a delightful sensation. Her arms wrapped about his strong, muscular torso and she brought her left leg up to wrap about him.

That proved a mistake – or a very smart ploy. Jenny lost her balance and bumped him; Alan lost his balance and they tumbled back onto the bed, their bodies still entwined. They both laughed as Alan found himself with her lying on top of him.

Again they kissed, this time longer and deeper, their tongues 'sword fighting' back and forth from one mouth to the other. Jen tugged her top off, freeing her ample and supple breasts. No bra. She grabbed Alan's left hand and planted it firmly against them. His hand instinctively seemed to know just what to do, caressing the full breast then tweaking out the deep pink nipple, rolling it back and forth between his fingers. Meanwhile, his right hand slid down to cup her firm bottom. He squeezed and kneaded it; she broke their 'lip lock', tilted her head back and cried out, pained.

"Oh God, that stings!"

Alan whipped his hand away like it had been burned.

"Oh, sorry, I forgot myself!"

Embarrassed at having hurt her, he made to get up but Jenny held him tight against her. She laughed as she reached back to rub.

"Oh… that was… intense."

She didn't seem upset.

"Huh?" he responded, confused.

"It… that is… the… sensation, the… pain, when mixed with the… pleasure of what we're… doing; it really set off the 'fireworks' in my head and… ah, nether regions."

Alan smirked.

"I see."

He reached up with his left hand to grab the back of her head, pulled her close, and planted a huge kiss on her lips. At the same time, his right hand again grabbed her red and tender bottom firmly. Jen practically screamed into his mouth – a blending of pleasure and pain. She groaned, and thrust her bottom back into his hand as her hands unbuttoned his shirt.

"Moreeeeeee," she moaned, her voice husky with sex.

Alan flicked his wrist slightly, giving her still covered bottom a mild spank. Jenny's head snapped back and her whole body stiffened for a moment. Then she just about melted across his body and started to grab at both their shorts. He helped her, and in a moment they were both naked and rolling about on the bed.

Smack slap spank! His hand struck stinging slaps again and again at her tender bottom, even as her hands slid across his body. She kissed the side of his head, her tongue tickling his ear.

"Moreeee… harderrr, pleaseeeeee," she groaned.

Alan's head spun. He didn't know if it was the liquor, the loveliness of the lady or the heat of the moment; he was hungry for the intimacy of being with a woman again. He did as she asked – as she *begged* – spanking her bottom with a firm open palm between hungry kisses, and he felt himself growing… firm.

Jenny covered his face and chest with kisses, even as her cries became louder and more intense: pleasure and pain blending into one. She spread her legs and eased herself down onto him with a deep guttural moan. Alan's back arched; he'd not felt this sensation in far too long! Oh, to be… connected with a woman; it sent his brain into overdrive.

"Ohhhh God!" he cried out.

They kept at it, Jenny bouncing on him like a jockey on a race horse and his hand... 'encouraging' her toward the finishing post they both sought. All at once, she threw back her head and cried out, even as he exploded into her. She collapsed down next to him and they lay there, entangled in each other's body.

They stayed like that, caressing and kissing each other for a while. Finally, Jenny propped herself up on her elbow and smiled down at him.

"Well, that was the most... incredible time I've had in a while."

Reaching back with her left hand, she rubbed her bottom as she looked over her shoulder at herself. She smiled coyly at the pinkness.

"I have to say, I never expected a... ah, smack on the ass... to have *that* effect on me!"

Alan grinned, kissed her and then sat up.

"Well, as a doctor, I can tell you that there are a number of nerves connecting the gluteus maximus and the... genitals. So, sometimes a little... 'stimulation' can have a very... interesting reaction."

"It sure did! Of course, now I have to wonder how I'm going to sit for dinner tonight."

She laughed; Alan laughed, looked around the room, and pointed at the top of the dresser.

"Well, I do have some good moisturizing cream over there. You want to... you want me to put some on you before you get dressed?"

She got up, allowing Alan his first good look at her back view. Yes, her adorable little bottom was quite red. Was it mostly sunburn, or had he contributed? Getting the jar, she handed it to him and promptly lay down across his lap! She looked over her shoulder at him and batted her eyes.

"Please, sir, would you put it on?"

Alan smirked as he opened the jar.

"Oh, you most definitely are *quite* bad!"

Slowly, gently, he spread the cream across her round and supple buttocks. Jenny gripped the sheets and winced in pain, but still the remembrance of a delicious pain that Alan had induced so unexpectedly earlier.

"Oh... yes! Of course, now you... ahhh... know how to... oh boy... deal with me," she gasped between grunts and groans.

"Yes, well... we shall have to see about that in future, won't we?"

They laughed again and Alan finished greasing her up and massaging in the soothing cream. When he was done, he gave her bottom a playful pat and she gave a yelp, before laughing at him, her eyes sparkling as they met his. Getting to their feet, they got dressed.

"Now, not a word of this to Tina, okay?" Jenny said. "She... wouldn't understand."

Alan grinned.

"What part?"

Jenny wagged a finger at him.

"Oh… now who's the naughty one? She wouldn't understand *any* of it."

"OK, not a word. My lips… are… sealed," he teased between kisses.

A last kiss - and Jenny left. Alan sat back on the bed and tried to think about what had just happened. It had been a while since he'd been with a woman; well, a woman other than his beloved Jo Ann. He thought back to one of the more special ladies in his life. Yes, it had been a number of years ago, but his time with Christina had indeed been special too, though not without its… problems…

# CHAPTER FOURTEEN

*July 15, 1984: Costa Rica*

THE DAYS WITH CHRISTINA at her private villa seemed to fly by. However, there was tension as Jesus' behavior was truly intolerable to Alan. The little boy made it quite clear, without ever saying a word that made sense, that Alan was an interloper, taking *his* rightful place with Christina. Now, *that* Alan could have found cute – amusing even – were it not for the aggressive, sometimes downright violent way that Jesus let his feelings be known.

Alan tried – he really tried – to keep his mouth shut and just enjoy the ride with Christina. But as Jesus' outbursts became more frequent and more destructive and so Alan was getting less and less quality time with Christina – he just had to say something. He thought he was being helpful in suggesting an assessment at a very good clinic he could recommend: one specializing in children with behavioral difficulties. Inwardly, Alan was thinking that Jesus was probably autistic, but a child psychologist was needed to make that diagnosis.

The suggestion was met with a frosty reception from Christina. And so it was that they decided to head back to the ship a day earlier than planned. Alan *had* rested and relaxed. Now, with things strained between he and Christina, the sex which had been so magical at the beginning was starting to feel like painting by numbers. They knew each others' buttons and they pressed them, but certainly Alan's mind was elsewhere, preoccupied with concerns which it seemed would always come between the two.

Increasingly, Alan's thoughts turned back to his patients on board the cruise ship and he started to feel a little guilty at leaving them to the not so tender mercies of Dr. Schaeffer. So, he phoned ahead and made arrangements and the trio took the little private jet, once more to the 'musical' accompaniment of Jesus' non-stop screams, and rejoined the cruise ship at the next port, a little way along the coast.


THE FIRST THING THAT Alan did, after dumping his bags back in his cabin, was to hurry along to the sick bay to catch up on what had been happening in his absence. He found himself rather relieved when Dr. Schaeffer wasn't there but when Susan, one of the best nurses he ever worked with, was.

"So, Susan – what's up? Have you missed me?" he probed, good humored.

"Ohhh *Doc!... So* much to tell you!" she began. "That Dr. Schaeffer – she's certainly not *you* is she!"

The Doc chuckled.

"Well – no… last time I looked, I wasn't a woman," he joked.

With a twinkle in her eyes, Susan quipped,

"Last time *Dr. Schaeffer* looked, I'm not so sure *she* was either!"

Laughing, Alan took a seat at his desk.

"Ah well, it sounds like you had some fun in my absence – you had better fill me in!"

"Ohhhh Doc! You sure you want to know?"

Alan grinned ruefully.

"Hit me with your worst, Susan – just how many pieces am I gonna be picking up here?"

"Hmmm – maybe a few," she admitted carefully. "Dr. Schaeffer… ah… well… when she heard you were coming back… she tried to get another ten days to sort out the 'problems of a few of the crew members.'"

"*What* 'problems'?" Alan asked, frowning.

Susan shrugged.

"Well… um… you know we had a bit of a problem with the laundry staff…aches… pains… not sleeping well… loss of appetite… just not feeling good…?"

"Home sickness, yeah!" Alan interjected.

Susan nodded.

"It seems Dr. Schaeffer thought there was more to it than that. Ordered a raft of onshore tests – pretty expensive ones…"

There was practically steam coming out of Alan's ears as he knew *he* was the one who was going to have to justify the budget overruns that month, even if his substitute had made them.

"But I'd been through all possibilities… done a ton of tests already… They… were… *homesick!*"

Again Susan nodded.

"I know that. *You* know that. But when the acting physician at the time tells the cruise authorities these tests are needed – what choice have they got?"

Alan nodded as he gave a little sigh.

"True… so now we have them worried they are ill as well as being homesick?"

"Yeah – pretty much," Susan agreed ruefully.

"Oh well, it's not my money she wasted…"

"No – but it will be *you* – and *me* – that still have to listen to the boyfriend/girlfriend issues. If she'd delved a bit deeper she'd have found those out – but delving isn't exactly Dr. Schaeffer's style!" Susan said, somewhat bitterly. "Oh and you'll love it when you see the meds she ordered!"

The Doc groaned.

"Well – no time like the present. You'd better show me…"

Susan led the way to the well stocked drugs cabinet. The Doc looked it over, bemused by bottle after bottle.

"*What*… are *these* for!… I never use these!"

With a sigh and a defeated gesture with her hands, Susan continued,

"Your guess is as good as mine. Maybe she wanted them for herself…?"

Alan groaned, glad Dr. Schaeffer would be off the ship at the next port and apart from the handover meeting he wouldn't have to have any more to do with her. Of course, she wouldn't be the first doctor to 'self-medicate' and Alan was sure she wouldn't be the last, but he despised that.

There was occasionally a doctor who utilized a rather liberal interpretation of 'physician, heal thyself'. Sometimes the ordering of 'special' medicines by a new doctor was just a means of the doctor getting medications he or she was used to using aboard. Sometimes it was for other reasons. Often, the practice on some ships of lax ordering resulted in a plethora of drugs from various countries. Looking at the pharmacy of some ship sick bays was like looking at a sampling of an international pharmacy. Often many of these drugs had no known equivalents and were discarded after the doc ordering them had left the ship.

Some were alcoholics and some addicted to various narcotic medications. For this reason, and because some of the nurses also had the same addictions, at the beginning of every cruise, and every doctor/nurse changeover, there was a counting (with a security guard present) of all narcotic medications. Alan had to admit, this was truly one of the most boring duties he had to do - counting pills. He would never have made it as a pharmacist!

Trying to change the topic, he asked Susan,

"So – apart from the good Dr. Schaeffer, how have things been?… They…

settle down… after Michael?" he asked of the incidents surrounding the tour director's death.

Susan gave the Doc a look he didn't quite understand for a second, until she continued.

"Ahh that's… old news now, Doc… there's been… a disappearance!"

That stopped Alan in his tracks; amazed, he stared at Susan with a slack-jawed expression.

"A… a *what?*"

Susan nodded.

"Well – put it this way… you weren't the only one not to board the ship again that day of the excursion… so, unless he catches up with the ship later…"

"Unlikely," admitted the Doc, knowing what arrangements it had taken to get him back on board. "So who are we talking about here?"

"John Silver," said Susan.

Alan was surprised, and felt slightly sick. He remembered how he had been talking to John as they had disembarked together just two short weeks ago. But he tried to stay reasonable. They weren't necessarily talking about anything bad – not like a death, like Michael. Alan was intrigued now.

"So… you say he disappeared? What happened exactly?"

Susan settled down in the seat on the opposite side of the Doc's desk, enjoying being able to fill him in on the details.

"Well, most of what is known has come from that security guard, Amil…"

Alan nodded. Amil, a Nepalese citizen and retired Ghurka from the Nepalese army, seemed a pretty straight up guy to him. Like most of these guys, Amil seemed steadfast and honest - a brave guy. His version was probably quite accurate.

"Yeah," Susan continued. "Amil said that John of course went to the Post Office as usual… and then he disappeared. No-one has seen him since."

"No-one? You sure?" queried the Doc. "Miguel…?"

"… is distraught," said Susan, sadly. "Actually, the only person probably more upset than Miguel is the Staff Captain…"

The Doc groaned.

"Not another love triangle…?"

Susan shrugged her shoulders.

"Who knows?... But he seems more upset than you'd expect for mere friends or out of official concern…"

The Doc pondered this possibility of a 'ménage à trois' between John, Miguel and the Staff Captain.

It was true that the Staff Captain was often seen in the company of

Miguel and John, and that the Staff Captain and Miguel were often seen trekking off in the evening to town, not returning until the early hours of the morning on the days that they had overnights in town.

As the doctor, Alan was privileged to the fact that Miguel did have a few 'extra marital' relationships in a few of the ports and he would dutifully come into the clinic to get checked out and to get his shots of Penicillin and the like before he would go back to his partner. The Doc would give him the usual lecture on sexually transmitted diseases and how they needed to be avoided with proper protection and avoidance. He doubted that those lectures were ever heeded, but hopefully the supply of condoms handed out was used.

In ship clinics, there is always a box of condoms available for the crew to help themselves to. The box containing the free condoms was discreetly placed around a corner, so crew could get them without having to ask for them. Alan did remember one ship where the policy was that they had to ask the nurse for condoms. Unfortunately, she was a bit of a hard-nosed brutish type who gleefully lectured the men making such requests and tried to propose to the female crew who wanted to get protection.

Unfortunately, the staff on that ship had two unwanted pregnancies and a higher rate of venereal disease than most cruise ships: no surprise to the Doc. By the time he left, he had convinced the captain to allow free retrieval of condoms by the crew in a discrete box.

It was usually the nurses' duty to separate the long rolls of condoms that were then placed separately into the box. Occasionally, when Alan was in the clinic late, he would check the box before retiring and make sure it was refilled – to decrease his future work, of course.

Sometimes condoms were provided to passengers too, especially the newlyweds.

Thinking of that brought Alan's mind back to John Silver, and why he may have gone missing. Miguel was a frequent user of these free condoms, so it was obvious that John was not his only sexual partner.

Alan doubted whether John had, unlike Michael, agreed to an 'open' relationship. Maybe John had found out about Miguel's illicit wanderings and had had enough. The Doc doubted that John was one to put up with infidelity. He seemed too confident in himself, somehow, so maybe he had finally left Miguel, and the lack of an explanation was his way of getting revenge on his unfaithful lover.

But Miguel was pretty much one of the good guys. He had trained as a nurse in Mexico and once when there had been a nasty outbreak of gastroenteritis from a party that was well attended on shore at a 'fancy' restaurant, Miguel was kind enough to lend a helping hand one afternoon, filling in for the nurse for several hours while she grabbed some much needed sleep. She was exhausted trying to refill IV lines. They had to give fluids to rehydrate these people who had very severe vomiting and diarrhea. Miguel had obviously been well trained and his help was welcome by both the Doc and his nurse.

Alan was keen to find out what Susan knew about John Silver's disappearance. Although he thought it had a perfectly simple explanation that he just didn't know yet, coming so soon after the tour director's death, it unnerved him. So, he pressed her for details.

"The first I learned of it, Doc, was when Miguel came to the clinic in the afternoon and was obviously quite upset.

"I asked him, 'what's going on, Miguel?' and checked his blood pressure. It was much higher than normal. That's when he told me 'John is gone. He left for the Post Office this morning on his bike, and no-one has seen him since'.

"Of course, I asked him if John might have planned on going sightseeing after and just not returned yet. Miguel admitted that is what he'd thought at first but when he didn't show up for Trivia, he said that's when he knew something was wrong."

Alan chuckled.

"Yeah – the serious business of trivia, huh?"

Also chuckling, Susan nodded as she continued,

"Well, it seems that they had earned over fifty points this cruise and if they get only ten more, they would have got the grand prize, which were embroidered jackets. Of course, they didn't really need them, but they thought they'd be great trophies to be able to show off to Linky who you know is always complaining that they are such an uneducated pair. They wanted to show her that they could win at trivia... and of course that meant that she would have lost..."

Alan laughed out loud, despite the serious reason for the recounting of this tale.

"The lengths people go to for bragging rights over trivia!"

"I wanted to try to reassure Miguel, of course," said Susan. "So I said, 'Come on Miguel; he probably knew that you could handle the Trivia and just got involved in something interesting on shore.' We didn't sail until the next afternoon anyway, so there seemed no urgency about returning to the ship. Dr Schafer gave him some pills for his high blood pressure and offered a mild tranquilizer – Ativan, I think - but he refused them. He didn't want John to see him all doped up when he got back, he said."

"Except he *didn't* get back...?" asked the Doc with a frown.

Susan shook her head silently in agreement.

# CHAPTER FIFTEEN

*December 8, 2009: St. Croix*

ALAN MANAGED TO AVOID the 'double team of 'Jen-Tina' (as he was starting to think of them), for the rest of the day as he tapped away on his laptop. He was feeling a little… awkward… about his encounter with Jenny, although he had enjoyed it immensely. So, he busied himself, adding details of John's disappearance to his notes on Michael's murder. After all, at this stage, Alan wasn't sure they were connected but he did have to admit that a murder *and* a disappearance on the same cruise was a bit of a coincidence… especially given that John, Miguel and Michael had all been… of the same… sexual persuasion - and all of them knew each other… perhaps intimately.

Miguel was obviously the recipient of any funds that might be in the estate of John Silver should he reach an untimely demise. Therefore, when John disappeared, it was obviously the talk of the ship as to what might have happened and whether Miguel would inherit.

Of course, when it was clear that John was indeed not returning to the ship and all attempts to trace him on dry land failed, the authorities were called in and almost all officers and hotel management were questioned. The Doc sighed once more at his luck as he had returned to the ship just in time to act as a translator for the local officials. Those of the crew who spoke Spanish were asked to help translate for some of the other officers who had a better command of Scandinavian languages than Spanish!

Lying back now, thinking on all the years that had passed and how many of the events on that cruise were left unanswered, Alan chuckled to himself as he thought how different *this* cruise was. He'd been sent on this trip by his daughter and two grandsons under strict instructions to try to relax and forget all the pain of losing Jo Ann, and now his thoughts were very firmly fixed on the living.

If Alan didn't know better, he'd think of Jenny and Tina as "cougars", but (as he understood the term) that really referred to older women who tended to pursue men. As he recalled, there was even another term - "Tadpoling" - which was older women chasing younger men.

Huh, was there a term for ladies who could be considered young "cougars"? Maybe just 'healthy young women'?

Ah, wouldn't you know it; they come up with such great things when *he's* too old to enjoy them! But *was* he?... Alan had certainly enjoyed his time together with Jenny, but right now, he needed to be away from all those complications of Jenny's young, sexy body. The question now was - what should he do to entertain himself so he could stop dwelling in the past – at least for a while?

The thing about working on a cruise ship for so many years was that you tended to get to do just about all of the excursions. It was sort of like living in Orlando, Florida, right outside the main gate of Disney World: after a few years, the magic of the place kind of faded.

So, Alan wandered about the ship: just sort of meandering about, with no particular place in mind. He thought about his last trip with Jo Ann: she'd loved the cruise around Italy; it had been like a second honeymoon.

A sudden shout of glee brought Alan back to reality, and he stopped and looked around. He was down in the entertainment area, right outside the video arcade. Alan grinned; oh, did he remember playing some of those old classics, years ago. In his day, he'd been quite the *Pac-Man* expert and a pretty decent *Asteroid* shooter. He paused at the door and looked in; the place was a large open room, and the air conditioning was blasting out rather hard.

The thin carpeting was decorated to look like a huge pinball game and all manner of games lined the walls. Of course, there were *no* pinball games. For them to work, they had to remain level – and, unfortunately, level was not a word you normally associated with a cruise ship!

Hey, why the hell not; why not have a bit of fun? Alan stepped into the room; it was fairly crowded, so he couldn't take his pick of games. Ah, but there was a nice one: *Time Crisis*! Now there was a game of which he'd truly been the master. Alan grinned as he stepped up to the unit. Jo Ann had always found it odd that a doctor -someone dedicated to healing - should be so good at such a violent game. He explained that it was a great stress relief for him.

Rooting around in his pocket, Alan got some quarters out and slipped them into the slot - and they promptly came right back out. Oops, he needed tokens. He rolled his eyes; sheesh, these new-fangled machines!

So it was back to the front door to exchange a couple of dollars for a pile of tokens. Ah, now he was ready for... combat! Returning to the machine, he slipped a couple of tokens in, picked up the gun and prepared himself to take out the bad guys.

It had been a while since he'd indulged in such... frivolity; his reflexes were a bit rusty and he didn't remember some of the sneakier villains, but he eventually hit his stride. Before he knew it, he was facing the chief bad guy and taking him out! The "girl" (the kidnapped princess) was in "his" arms and the helicopter was evacuating them from the smoldering ruins of the island fortress.

Suddenly, Alan heard applause behind him. Lowering his virtual weapon, he turned to look around; bunch of kids was watching him - had obviously been watching him for a long time! Alan put his initials in the game's Leader Board and gave them a little bow.

"That was awesome, mister!" a girl said.

"I've never seen anyone beat that game," an awe-struck boy said.

A lanky teen gave Alan a grin.

"Not bad, dude."

"Ah... thank you, thank you," Alan said, and then made his way out of the arcade.

He felt so embarrassed: a bunch of kids cheering him on for playing a silly game. Yet, as he walked down the hallway, he still grinned. Yeah, he wasn't quite so old, was he? He might have a touch of gray in the beard, but he wasn't over the hill yet.

That evening, Alan strolled into the dining hall and took a seat at a nearly empty table. Looking around, it was clear that the rough seas had resulted in many people deciding to pass on a full meal. As for him, he was well able to take it all in stride. Sitting there, he chatted with his fellow dinner companions about their activities on the ship today, but he withheld the tidbit about him playing a video game or having a delightful time with a beautiful girl.

Right about the time dessert was being served, Alan had the distinct impression he was being watched. Trying to act very casual, he waited until the waitress was pouring the coffee; he used her as a block and gave a quick glance around. There, at a nearby table were a couple of kids pointing at him.

Now, why would they be staring at him? Naw, he was imagining things. He turned his attentions to his dinner guests, who were, once more, the Duke and Duchess.

"So, what did you two manage to partake of today?" Alan asked cheerfully.

"I enjoyed the pool," the Duchess said.

"I took in a bit of fun at the casino," the Duke added.

"Any luck?" Alan said.

He shook his head.

"No, I never seem to do all that well with games of chance."

Alan grinned.

"Well, you know what they say about being unlucky at cards, don't you?"

The Duke gave him a blank look, even as the Duchess gave a rather *un*-ladylike snort.

"Huh, what; there's a saying about that?" he said.

The Duchess smirked.

"Yes, dear; I'll explain it later," she said. "And what of you, dear doctor; how was your day?"

Alan gave them a rundown of his activities. Well, he did rather gloss over the video game bit.

"Now, my dear old mother - she was always the lucky one when it came to gambling," he said, trying to change the subject.

"Oh, she always won?" the Duke asked.

"Well... not... always, but certainly more than seemed reasonable!" Alan replied.

The Duchess nodded.

"Ah, now, you see, I've always suspected that the casinos are actually rigged. Every once in a while, they let some dear little gray-haired old lady win a *huge* pot, and that brings in still more suckers - ah... gamblers."

Alan laughed.

"To be honest, I sometimes thought that was the case with her; her luck just seemed *too* incredible to believe. One time, she was sitting reading the Sunday paper and she checked the lottery numbers against her tickets. Well, lo and behold, she'd gotten six of the numbers!"

"Wow, and how much did that mean she'd won?" The Duke said.

"About seventy thousand dollars."

"Wow!" his two dinner companions exclaimed, just about at the same time.

"Yes. She was so excited, she jumped to her feet, grabbed her keys and raced out the front door," Alan said. "It was then that she realized she was still in her nighty."

They all laughed.

"Not exactly appropriate for going to collect her winnings, eh?" the Duke chuckled.

Alan shook his head.

"No, not at all. So, she ran back inside, got dressed and raced out again.

And promptly realized she'd forgotten to put on any *underwear*! So, back in she went and tried again. Finally, all properly dressed, she drove over to my brother's house - he lived nearby - and had him check the numbers, just to be sure she wasn't seeing things."

"And had she been right?" the Duchess asked, hoping that was the case.

"Oh yes, there was no mistake. So, needless to say, she was then able to save a good chunk of money, go on a vacation to France and give everyone a wonderful Christmas," Alan replied.

"I also remember an incident when both my sister and I were quite small. We were driving to meet my Dad who was flying to Montana from where he was working. We were all headed for a camping holiday in the Canadian Rockies. We had to stop for gas and a few items at a drug store and gas station in Nevada.

"My mother had some loose change from the purchases. She wanted to teach us children that gambling was not a good thing to do. She took the change and showed us how you could easily lose the money in a one armed bandit-slot machine. Much to her chagrin, the few cents produced a mountain of nickels, all over the floor, which we gleefully picked up."

The assorted company around the table laughed as Alan continued,

"Later, we were shown the other side of gambling when we were accosted by some beggars who voluntarily told us their tale of woe while begging food money. My mother jumped on the occasion to reinforce her lesson on gambling."

"And did it put you off?" inquired the Duchess.

"Not really – but I always make sure I have money left in my pocket for the next meal!" Alan teased.

The rest of the meal, they chatted more about life, luck and the fortunes (and failures) of both. It was funny - thinking of gambling always made Alan think of Jo Ann. Not that she was a big gambler; far from it, in fact. She truly didn't care for it. No, it was that she tolerated his gambling as one of his little… indulgences. It was one of her most endearing qualities. He had to wonder, would he find such a lady again? For that matter, did he want to?

### December 9, 2009: St. Croix

THE NEXT MORNING, ALAN awoke to find the seas a good deal calmer than the day before. He sat up in bed and looked out of his cabin's window. The blue-green waters of the Atlantic stretched before him and he could just see a little peninsula of land coming into view on the right. He stepped out onto his balcony and took a breath of good fresh sea air. Ah, they were arriving in St. Croix.

On this day, there was no ambiguity as to what he had planned; he was going to go on one of his most favorite kinds of excursions. Today, he was going to meet the dolphins.

For Alan, the first time he'd done this had truly opened his eyes to the power and majesty of these gentle creatures. It wasn't just getting to interact with the dolphins that excited and impressed him; there were two key elements that he'd noticed right from the get-go. First, there were those eyes. For many creatures, Alan would look at them and their eyes were without expression, like a doll's eyes. With the dolphins - oh, he looked at those eyes and could see that there was a real mind, a real soul behind it.

That was an awe-inspiring event. And then there were the reactions of the other people, particularly the children. Alan didn't know what he enjoyed more - interacting with the dolphins or seeing how other people reacted to these gentle sea creatures.

So, getting up, he showered, shaved and headed down to breakfast. As he was early, he had to stand in line and wait for the doors to open. Standing there, he again got that feeling - the feeling that he was being watched. Alan tried to act very casual about it and slowly turned around in his spot so that he could look over the people around him.

Huh, just families waiting to get in to the dining hall. That made sense; families with small children were generally up early, while singles and couples tended to sleep in. After all, they were the ones who stayed up late to party (in *every* sense of the word!).

A little whisper caught his attention and he looked around. Then he had to look down; two little boys were staring and pointing at him! He cast his eyes downward; was his zipper down or something? No, everything seemed fine. So, what were they going on about?

Finally, one of the boys - clearly at the urging of his friend or brother - came over to Alan.

"Ah… excuse me, mister, but… are you… *the one?*"

Alan's brow wrinkled. "I'm not sure I understand. 'The one'? The one what?"

Had these boys seen *The Matrix* once too often? Even if they had, how could they mistake Alan for that Reeves fellow?

"Are you… him, the one who beat the *Time Crisis* game?" the boy asked, looking up at Alan in awe.

Alan smiled.

"Oh… that; yes, I'm the one."

"Wow…" the boy replied slowly. "So, are you going to play it again?"

"Ah… well, I don't know. We'll have to see about me doing that."

The boy nodded like some little bobble-head toy.

"Oh, okay. Thanks, mister."

And with that, he scampered off back to his family. Alan couldn't help but roll his eyes. Great, just great; he was now a video game hero to some of the little boys on the ship. How would Tiffany and the others react to that?

Finally, the doors opened and they were admitted in for breakfast. Alan was never so grateful for the chance to sit down and sort of disappear into a crowd. Yet, that feeling persisted and every time he looked around, there were the children whispering and pointing. Goodness, some adult was going to accuse him of being a stalker or a pedophile or something!

After eating, Alan made his way to the elevator and down to the gangway deck. As the ship was able to come into port and dock at the pier, it was a simple matter to disembark out the gangplank and pick up the bus to the dolphin cove.

Of course, this being an excursion which children loved, the bus was just about overflowing with them and still more were pointing and whispering. Alan was a bit surprised; these were *not* the same two boys. What, had word of his… accomplishment spread throughout the ship? Oh well, he decided to put it out of his mind and enjoy the day.

The island of St. Croix was quite the lush, green tropical paradise. There weren't many vehicles around, but there certainly were plenty of people. Yeah, this was a place dependent on tourism. As the bus made its way through the center of town, there were banks, gift shops, jewelry stores and a host of other tourist-oriented businesses.

Alan smiled. Ah, he remembered wandering among some of those businesses and the whole downtown area with Jo Ann. She did love to shop, but always looked for deals!

His mind was also cast back to some of the on-shore excursions he had taken while he was a ship's doctor, some of them for the sake of the many medical emergencies that occurred on a regular basis! There was one particular time that Alan remembered. The ship he was with made its scheduled stop in Grenada every week for several months and every time Alan would get a chance to go ashore, a rather diminutive local fellow who called himself "Big Guy" was there waiting for the ship, ostensibly waiting to 'guide' someone, get beer money, learn some gossip from the ships and get hard to find candies and pop etc. that crew would have in their backpacks and give over to him. Over time, the Doc learned a great deal about the life of the average Grenadian through the eyes of Big Guy. He met Big Guy's family, kids and friends and found the whole experience quite an eye-opener.

Big Guy was not 'big'. In fact, he was rather diminutive which is probably why he took the name. It was an education for the doctor to learn how one survives on street smarts, some education and a good knowledge of the local plants and herbs that served as the family's medicine for the most part.

A short time later, Alan's thoughts were pulled from Big Guy and the past to the present as the bus pulled into a small and well-worn asphalt parking lot surrounded by some lovely old palm trees. The pavement had a light dusting of clean white sand and Alan had to smirk as he watched some of the people walking across it. Those who were barefoot were finding the asphalt to be just a bit too hot to suit their thin skin.

The local, a big burly man with a thick Jamaican accent (now *there* was a difference!) and a head full of dreadlocks, led them along a narrow and winding dirt trail. Here there were many beautiful palms, pines and other trees; they all gave ample shade to the path.

Alan inhaled deeply. Oh, the smell of pine mixed with saltwater and seaweed. Some people thought of it as foul, but for him, it was like coming home.

Eventually, the path wrapped around a small, secluded cove and met up with a short wooden pier. Their guide stepped out onto the creaky boards and turned to face them.

"Now, if y'all will step down to the water's edge, I'll summon our friends."

Alan bit his lip to keep from laughing. A man on St. Croix who looked like he belonged in Jamaica and yet he spoke with the thickest southern US accent he'd ever heard. Boy, talk about an international cross-section of humanity all rolled into one person!

A number of people - those barefoot or in water shoes - stepped into the water right away; Alan and the others less well prepared slipped off their shoes and soon joined them. As if on cue, a series of fins appeared in the waters just offshore. Several people in the group jumped, clearly unsure as to whether these were the dolphins or sharks!

"Don't worry, folks," Alan said. "Those are dolphins."

The guide cocked his head and looked at Alan. "Y'all knows your stuff, *sah*. How'd you know?"

Alan pointed out into the water, even as the fins drew closer to shore.

"The tails; with sharks, the tails stick up - like the dorsal fin - but with dolphins, it doesn't; it's horizontal. Or, I guess you could say it's flat."

The man laughed a deep baritone laugh.

"Ya, man, y'all is right. So, everyone come on down closer and remember everything I's told you on the drive up here."

A moment later, the dolphins rose out of the inky water and were greeted by squeals of delight from children and adults alike. The grin on Alan's face went just about ear-to-ear. The sparkle is the eyes of those children - oh, it was worth the price of going on this excursion. Heck, it was worth the cost of the cruise!

Getting down on his knees, Alan put out his hands and gently patted a dolphin. Oh, that soft and warm skin, so unlike the touch of a fish. Yeah, and there it was again, that glint of intelligence in the eyes. This was a great way to spend the day!

GETTING BACK TO THE dock after the dolphin encounter, Alan decided to take lunch at one of the little beachside snack shacks. It had been a few years, but he always loved getting a taste of the local beer. The place he chose was delightful: tasty, clean looking food, a nice tiled deck area surrounding the small building and a deck covering of palm leaves. They didn't block out all of the sunlight but they gave enough shade to make the area quite comfortable, and given the especially wonderful view (of the lovely ladies on the beach), Alan was happy to have an excuse to stay a while.

He didn't happen to see "Jen-Tina" at all; he wasn't sure whether he was happy about that or not, but he did see a family he recognized from the ship. Tilting his head back, he closed his eyes and sighed. It'd been a while since he'd done that.

"Janey!" the man called out to the little girl.

Alan looked down just in time to see a man (the girl's father) get up from the towel he'd been lying on. It was obvious that the little girl had just dumped a pail of water right over his head and now he was 'chasing' her around the beach. It was equally obvious that he wasn't running nearly as fast as he could.

Little Janey squealed with laughter as he caught her, dropped to one knee and plopped her over it.

"Ah, now you're going to get it," he scolded, his tone very playful as he proceeded to 'spank' her little canary yellow bikini-clad bottom.

Alan grinned. Ah yes, the carefree days of playing with a beloved child. Seems like only yesterday he was doing that with Alexa and the boys and then he blinked, and she was going off to college. Now her boys were shooting up like weeds, practically overnight. He made a mental note: less blinking around his kids in future.

A while later, as the shadows of the little food stands were stretching across the beach, Alan figured it was time to head back to the ship. Little Janey and her parents had made the same decision; her dad had her slung over his shoulder and she was out cold! It seemed someone was going to be in bed early tonight.

But not Alan - *he* had a prior engagement! He smiled as he recalled his arranging the dinner date with Tiffany!

'My goodness; I'm becoming quite the Tadpole!' he chuckled to himself.

Once back on board, Alan got a shower, changed into a nice outfit and headed down to the dining hall. As he expected, Tiffany was there at the door, decked out in a very pretty opal colored dress. It seemed to shimmer and glisten like sunlight on the ocean; it hugged every curve of her supple frame and was revealing yet tasteful.

"My dear doctor, how very good of you to be punctual," she said, her lips seeming to caress the words.

"I - what the devil are they staring at?" Alan asked.

Tiffany pointed behind him and Alan turned to look. Once again, a rather large contingent of children was whispering and pointing at Alan. He sighed and rolled his eyes as he turned to face her.

"Sorry; that's my doing. It seems I've become the hero of children on this ship by-"

Tiffany's jaw dropped for a moment.

"No, don't tell me... you-you're the one who beat my score on *Time Crisis*?"

Now it was Alan's jaw that dropped. They stood there a moment, slack-jawed and staring at each other and then burst into laughter.

"Well, it would seem we have a common... hobby," Alan said.

Tiffany gestured toward the dining hall.

"Great! Shall we discuss... tactics - over soup and salad?"

Suddenly, her brow became deeply furrowed as she gazed off at something. Alan looked at her, a little concerned.

"Tiffany, is something wrong?"

She lowered her head and turned slightly away from him.

"There's a man over there, and he... seems to be... listening in on our conversation!"

Alan started to look around, and she smacked his arm, chuckling at how blatant men could be.

"Don't look!"

He gave a little jump at her smack. It wasn't hard - merely surprising.

"Well, how can I know what's going on if I don't look?"

She rolled her eyes.

"Sheesh, don't you know how to look without looking like you're looking?"

Alan chewed his lip as he tried to decipher what she'd just said.

"Man, I wish you came with a translator!"

"Just... try to be... subtle."

"OK-OK, let me see what I can do."

Alan stretched, rubbed the back of his neck and turned slowly around as he yawned. All around were many people, but nothing seemed out of the ordinary. Wait, there was a man signing to a woman next to him. While Alan couldn't understand what they were 'saying', he at least recognized what they were doing. He turned back to face Tiffany and lowered his arms.

"Ah... do you mean the deaf man over there?"

Alan sort of 'pointed' with his eyes and Tiffany clearly followed his gesture. She nodded.

"Yes, he's the one," she said. "How do you know he's deaf?"

"He's using sign language," Alan replied. "My uncle was deaf and he and my aunt used it. I never learned much of it but I can at least recognize it when I see it. So maybe he can read lips."

Tiffany slowly nodded.

"Ah... that must be it. It just... threw me when he seemed to... understand what we were talking about."

"How could you tell he understood?"

"The way he was gesturing; it was as if he was playing the video game."

Alan laughed.

"So, it would appear you and I have a rival for the title of *Time Crisis* champion, eh? Huh, a lip reader ... I remember shipping out with someone else who could do that once, several years ago."

# CHAPTER SIXTEEN

*July 16, 1984: The Cayman Islands*

OFTEN ON THE SHIP there were deaf or nearly deaf passengers. Mr. Sponecki was an elderly gentleman who had suffered from serious hearing problems for a number of years. He had been a regular passenger on the ship so the Doc knew him well. Most of their communication was with the use of pen and paper, but it appeared that he did also lip read a little.

Mr. Sponecki spent a good deal of his time in the Observation Lounge. Everyone knew he was deaf. He would sit next to people and they took no heed of him as he would be reading and obviously not listening.

Now, in one of the ports just before he disembarked, the Doc had been able to have him fitted for a set of new digital hearing aids that allowed him significantly better hearing. He had given up wearing the other hearing aids for which he had been fitted, as they really did no good whatsoever. When he came back to the ship after a month's absence, the Doc tested his hearing with the equipment he had on board. According to those tests, his ability to hear had improved significantly and he was now able to comprehend what he was hearing. That was the cruise on which Michael died.

Often it does take a person a while to be able to comprehend speech after years of not being able to hear, but after his exam this cruise, the Doc noted,

"Your hearing is a lot better with the hearing aids considering the years of damage. Your family must be really pleased that you can hear again."

Mr. Sponecki replied, chuckling,

"Oh, I haven't told my family yet. I just sit around and listen to the conversations. I've changed my will three times!"

Alan just roared with laughter.

Mr. Sponecki also had some very interesting comments about what he had heard in the Observation Lounge after Michael's sad demise and he picked one of the consultations with the Doc upon his return after the sojourn with Christina to share these tidbits.

Apparently a Mrs. Clapham had been making some disparaging comments about the gay tour director and inferring that the ship would be much better off 'if Michael were kicked off or knocked off.' That just made Alan fume. How could people always see the bad side in people, never the good?

"Hmmm… Mrs. Clapham, you say? That name's not familiar to me."

Mr. Sponecki laughed.

"Well, Doc; it's not like you have to get to know everyone on this blessed boat. Maybe she's healthy in body if not in spirit!"

Now it was Alan's turn to laugh.

"Ship, my dear sir; it's called a ship."

"Well, whatever you call it, it's very full of very noisy people!"

"Well, Mr. Sponecki, I'd say that's partially due to the change in your… perception."

He nodded.

"Yes, it is odd to suddenly be surrounded by sound after so many years of silence. Oh, and please, call me Bruno."

"Very well, then you must call me Alan. That Doc stuff gets a bit stuffy after a while."

"Oh, you want stuffy?" Bruno said. "There's this fellow on the ship, walks around with such airs about him. Ah… Al… Alfred… Alfonse! He seems quite the arrogant fellow, and always talking about his connections to the Russian underworld."

Alan grinned and slowly nodded. That was just like Michael's lover. If he wasn't strutting around the gym showing off his physique he was strutting around the deck showing off his shady connections to the underworld… and even those he only got through Michael! It wouldn't have surprised the Doc if he hadn't annoyed one of them enough to take it out on Michael – practically the only way to get to Alfonse. He was halted in that disturbing line of thought by returning his focus to Mr. Sponecki.

"Ah, yes; some people are like that," Alan said. "Oh, the number of times I've overheard some smooth-talking fellow tell a lovely lady that he was a CIA agent or something, just to get her in bed; I can't begin to count."

Bruno, snorted, gasped and broke out in a fit of laughter. It took a moment for him to collect himself and be able to speak.

"I just heard a fellow use that exact line out on the Promenade Deck!"

Alan pressed his lips together as hard as he could, trying vainly to keep from exploding into laughter. Instead, the laughter came out his nose so hard and so fast that he just about sounded like a train whistle!

"Oh man! These Casanovas never change."

"Yes; well, this fellow seemed quite intense. He was in one of the ship's cafes, talking on a ship to shore phone. This Alfonse was talking to someone and I don't mean chat; they were really talking. After being deaf - oh, excuse me, *hearing impaired* for so long - I'm very good at reading lips."

"Ah, so that's where you learned of his claim about the Russian mob?"

"Yes; from his side of the conversation I gleaned that he was none to keen about his family learning about something to do with Michael and he – or the other guy - was desperate to get something back from him."

Alan laughed.

"That's a whole lot of 'somethings' there, Bruno."

Bruno smiled.

"Well, when you're reading lips, sometimes some things get… lost in translation, shall we say?"

Alan slowly nodded.

"Ah… I see what you mean. Huh, I wonder what could have made him so upset - and who was he talking to?"

Bruno shrugged.

"That I cannot say. But, from the color his face was taking on, Alfonse was pretty angry. Here I was thinking that he and Michael were… ah, friends. In my day, such things were never spoken of – openly - but I was also never one to judge which side of a man's 'bread' he chose to… 'butter'. But where does such rage come from?"

Alan sadly shook his head. He was focused more on how this might relate to the now deceased Michael and what could it be that Alfonse so desperately needed to get back from him?

"I don't know, Bruno, but it does seem that some people tend to focus on the negative all the time."

When one reads great tomes on being good in one's life and doing the right thing with all the people and things around you, most of the sages over the years will encourage a non-judgmental attitude, especially toward other human beings. The theory goes that if you are not perfect, how on earth can you have the right to judge other people? In theory this is very righteous and we should all follow these suggestions. At the one extreme we have the people who criticize everything and everyone - usually complaining about several things at the same time. Psychologists recognize this as a person who is unhappy with his or her own life and have to criticize others to feel better about him- or herself. It seemed to the Doc on some cruises that an inordinate amount of these serial complainers seemed to vacation aboard ship!

Complainers come in all shapes, sizes and nationalities on a ship. One could argue that since someone is paying over $1200/day per person, that one has the right to complain a bit if things aren't the way they would want it to be, but the Doc did tend to think there were limits! Some of the things some passengers complained about were simply ridiculous, in his opinion, and he dreaded being stuck on the 'Complainers' Table' for dinner.

One complainer had developed a reputation of complaining so much that no one would sit with her at dinner tables, in the card room or anywhere else. It got so bad that there were edicts sent out assigning various petty officers to the job of sitting with Passenger X. Besides the fact that this American woman was a complainer, she decided to take a title "Lady" much to the chagrin of other passengers who actually had titles rightfully given by the Queen.

'Lady Ruth' would complain about the food: it would be too hot or not hot enough; there would be too much or not enough; no variety or too much to choose from. She complained the air conditioning was not working (when all agreed that it was) or that it was working too well; other times the water pressure was not to her liking, or was too hot or not hot enough. One particularly uncalled for incident came when, after she had torn open the wrapped laundry, she complained that there were little pieces of paper seen on the floor. The laundry was carefully wrapped in three layers of tissue paper and sealed with three sticky seals normally and brought to her, usually the same day it was set out in a laundry bag. One day she sent a formal complaint as there were only two layers of tissue paper and only one sticky seal.

"What are they doing, trying to get cheap on this 6 star ship?" she bellowed.

That turned into a whole tirade of complaints she had apparently stored up between all the other complaints she actually voiced, with shore tours too short - only two things seen; the room steward was not picking up her personal things from the floor, but in the same breath she also complained that the steward was hiding things! There was not enough variety on the TV, but she wanted more old films, fewer of the new disgusting films.

Lady Ruth had perhaps one understandable complaint the whole of her trip; there was no price list of the spa treatments in her room. She used the rather expensive spa on a regular basis (where one is talking of the prices for a routine 50 minute massages being $380, body wraps $430, foot or hand massage $160, etc.)

Like most of the serial complainers found on board ship, Lady Ruth had no real basis for other comments on life so this constant barrage of petty fault finding was at least one way that she could get people to be around her (even if against her) and was a way of feeling some control - as in reality she had none (even though the firing of the manager of one rather illustrious 5 star hotel was suspected to be because of her.) The concept of people being happy and enjoying life had never breezed past the thought processes of Lady Ruth. At dinner tables where the unlucky had her holding court, comments about trying to see the pleasant side of things rushed by her like a seagull who just found a sandwich on a park bench when its owner looked the other way.

Sitting at dinner with Dorothy was an experience in what a real complainer can be like. Dorothy was a very well dressed, socially proper English lady in her late seventies. She was traveling alone. (Even her friends said that they could only stand her in small doses). Dorothy spoke the Queen's English impeccable, but oh was it biting! The meat was not done to her liking; the water was too cold; the wine was not at the right temperature; they didn't have the vintage of champagne that she normally liked. She even asked if the chef had something against her so that she ended up with terrible food (on a cruise line that was renowned for its 6 star cuisine).

When the barrage of gripes about the food and the chef ceased, she started in again on the temperature of the restaurant, how slow the service was (it wasn't), how surly the waiter was (although the poor guy was most polite), and anything else she could find to complain about.

That particular meal, the Doc tried a number of times to change the subject. He was successful in changing it to the interesting port that they had just visited - the Yacht Club in Panama that had been used by the Americans during the reign of the US in the Canal Zone.

Previously, one was not even allowed to set foot in Panama if you were transiting the canal. With the turn over to the Republic of Panama, these rules were eliminated to allow for tourism to occur. Consequently, a trip from the cruise liner was designed to allow the passengers to go to this quaint yacht club and from there to the surrounding rainforest for nature walks, visit the old instillations of the canal and the like. Basically, it was a nice opportunity to see from the ground what previously was only possible from afar. But not according to Dorothy; this was the "biggest waste of time", "such an untidy forest", "funny looking native people dressed in less than proper dress" and the like.

Eventually, the Doc gave up and let others at the table respond to the barrage of attacks that occurred when the topic of world politics was brought up.

Thankfully, that allowed the Doc a chance to zone out a little and reflect upon how one will occasionally meet other people who will go through life saying that everything is perfect - usually those who have taken the proper dosage of Lithium or another antipsychotic! But the Doc had been privileged to meet in India some people (sadus) who go through life actually accepting their lot and feeling that the world is a beautiful place. When one looks at their lot in life, it is amazing that they can be happy with their lot, but at the same time one must respect their strong belief in religion that gives them the power to accept the rags they wear, the boxes they sleep under and the meager portions of food people give them in their cups to eat.

But most of us go on doing what we do. We sit in a café or in some other place watching people (in most of Europe and South America and now most Starbucks cafes) and not only watch the world go by, but also comment about the interesting creatures that we often see passing by - other humans.

Sure. We're interesting creatures. We dress in funny costumes; we walk in unusual manners; we have outrageous decorations that we adorn ourselves with; we talk with strange communications one to one and verbally into devices that make others miles away also listen to our verbal diarrhea; we listen to music from a variety of devices as we ambulate being totally unaware of the world around us.

As other humans observing this mass of humanity, we often are judgmental of others as they pass. Perhaps monkeys in the zoo do the same thing when they stand there watching people watching them.

We need to be able to accept all this humanity and what it stands for without making a judgment about it, but it is hard not to make some comment about the funny hat that someone is wearing, some funny accent someone is grating out, etc.

In contrast, Alan always tried to see the good in everything, and the good in being back on ship, apart from returning to a job that he loved, was that, curiously, Alan and Christina had more time together, it seemed. Jesus could now be looked after by his doting grandparents, who seemed no more inclined to discipline the boy than Christina herself did, which meant she was free to join Alan outside of his surgery hours, the multitude of meetings, and the inevitable emergency which always happened at the wrong time. As Alan had been a ship's doctor for a few years now and Christina was a seasoned cruise traveler, that left the pair plenty of time to forgo the onboard entertainment and make their own fun inside Christina's cabin, or his when they felt more daring. The Doc found that although he was concerned that such staff-passenger romances were frowned upon by the authorities, he was able to justify it as this was more than just a fleeting 'jump into the sack' affair. He was quite smitten with Christina and she seemed equally keen on him!

After he was filled in on the events during his absence and had received news of yet another mystery onboard this ship with John's disappearance, Alan found himself hurrying back to Christina to share his news with her.

She was an intelligent woman as well as a beautiful one, although Alan had to admit, if only to himself, that it had been her physical charms which had first attracted his attention. She would no doubt offer some useful insight as to what might have happened to John.

Alan hurried to her cabin, straightening his hair and checking his breath. He tried the door handle, intending to let himself in, as was his custom now, but he found she was not in her cabin. Alan was far from disappointed. Instead, a secret smile spread over his face and he made his way to his own cabin. Quickly, he opened the door and stepped inside, demanding in mock sternness,

"Just *what* is the meaning of this – stealing my cabin key and letting yourself in!"

He could barely hide his grin. There, naked on his bed except for a crisp white sheet which covered just her bottom, Christina laid sprawled out on her tummy. She had clearly recently awoken from a nap and she still had a dreamy quality about her sleepy smile.

Alan sat himself on the bed beside her as she turned slightly to kiss him. His right hand cupped one of her breasts, lightly kneading it as his left hand snuck under the barely-there cover and caressed her supple, shapely legs and pert little bottom.

"Mmmm I think someone's been a naughty girl, sleeping in *my* bed, he teased, firmly kneading a buttock.

"Ooooo – Goldilocks earned a spanking?" Christina teased right back, kissing him hungrily and giggling against his mouth as Alan stripped off his jacket, shirt and tie. There was also a strong reaction inside Alan's pants.

"You sure did!" he growled, playfully, pulling her over his lap.

He raised his hand high, grinning at her.

"Now – are you sorry for letting yourself into my cabin and sleeping in my bed when I wasn't here?"

"Nope!" Christina declared defiantly, grinning.

She yelped, giggling as Alan's palm landed sharply on her bottom and rose again; a large red handprint was now 'branded' across her creamy white flesh. She watched him, grinning gleefully.

"And are you sorry you didn't wait for me before falling asleep?"

"Uhh… no!" Christina again giggled, with barely any pretence at hesitation.

More playful questions followed from Alan, only to be met with giggles and delightfully flippant answers – so his hand landed again and again on Christina's upturned little bottom. It grew rosy and warm and her laughter increased with her squirms until they were both pretty hot! Finally, Christina got up to kneel astride Alan's lap, facing him. He cupped the butt he'd just reddened, firmly kneading it as he feasted on her pert, ample breasts, lightly tugging the nipples in his teeth. Christina lowered herself onto him, breathing increasingly harder as he continued to pay attention to her breasts and bottom but as his mind was more and more drawn to his own groin.

Christina was an expert lover but Alan was no novice in the bedroom, either, despite what Captain Halvorsen and some of the other crew members might believe; he was just choosy. He soon laid her back gently on the bed and made love to her right through the first sitting of dinner. Hours later, he lay beside Christina on his side, propped up on his elbow. He smiled at his lover beside him in the bed as he traced his fingertips down her slender back to caress her still pink bottom again and again. She had soon turned over when her tender butt had hit the bed!

"You have the most beautiful spine... quite the prettiest I've ever seen," Alan told her, half dreamily, half teasing.

Christina laughed.

"Is that your idea of a compliment?"

Eyes sparkling with mirth, Alan patted the shapely bottom he had warmed earlier.

"Is that your idea of a polite answer?" he quickly countered with a tease.

The two collapsed into a giggling heap, cuddling until Alan could no longer ignore the grumbling of his hungry stomach. He kissed Christina gently on the lips.

"You've got me famished, woman!... Take me to dinner before I have to throw you over my shoulder and go slay a dinosaur!"

Alan and Christina dressed quickly after he massaged some soothing cream onto her tender buttocks and shared post-coital teases and giggles, and then they went down to dinner, hand in hand, much to the amazement of some of the crew who thought that Alan would never dare return any of the admiration which he undoubtedly drew from many passengers. Alan was a good looking guy and he kept himself fit, but they had all thought he was too shy to ever follow up with someone as beautiful and... forward, as Christina. Alan chuckled to himself, knowing exactly what they were thinking.

# CHAPTER SEVENTEEN

*December 9, 2009: The Caribbean Sea*

ALAN COULDN'T HELP HIS mind wandering back and making a comparison between Tiffany now and Christina then. Not with Jo Ann. Jo Ann was beyond comparison, as far as he was concerned, but there were certain similarities between Tiffany and Christina. Both were classically very attractive; both were intelligent; both had an easy charm which helped the shy Alan to relax.

Alan and Tiffany now got seated in the dining hall, in a rather intimate little table off to one side. He scanned the area with an experienced eye. Yeah, he well remembered this type of table; they were often set aside for a couple to have a modicum of privacy while dining. Too often, a meal in the center of the dining room could turn into a shouting match as you tried to hear over the bedlam of the area. The acoustics of the center of the room were far from ideal for intimate dining, but ideal for those wanted to show off their finery or to show others that they were dining with officers.

Alan, ever trying to be the proper gentleman, held Tiffany's chair for her and then took his own seat. He very much enjoyed his meal with Tiffany. He did spot Jen-Tina looking over at him and if he wasn't very much mistaken those were pretty jealous daggers of looks being thrown in his direction. But then he scolded himself for his pride. What on earth would those beautiful young women have to be jealous about over him! No, he was simply enjoying some pleasant company with a nice lady. Nothing to be jealous over, nothing to feel guilty about!... Guilty? Where had 'guilty' come from! His brief interlude with Jenny had been wonderful, but also just a fling. It wasn't as if they were a committed couple. No, they were merely two ships passing in the night. Alan did have to smirk, though – he noticed that Jen was sitting rather... tenderly, shall we say?

He pushed thoughts of her away, not able to deal with it right now. Instead, now he and Tiffany were alone... well, alone at a table in a room full of people – Alan decided to open up to her a little, but in a way that he could handle without feeling bad.

"You... over... the thing... you know... with the... ah... ashes...?"

Tiffany gave a little chuckle.

"Oh yeah. It's a case of *having* to be, isn't it?"

Alan nodded, giving a little resigned smirk.

"You can say that again. What you can't change you have to accept..."

'Wow - that was philosophical!' Alan thought to himself.

"Talking of which... I've been hearing that you have more than *one* claim to fame – *Doc*!"

Alan squirmed in his seat, turning a little red.

"Ah... what do you mean...?"

Tiffany chuckled and patted Alan's hand as it lay on the table.

"*Relax*!... It's not really about you, anyway... Just... well, in the staff lounge... I should warn you that Sven is a bit of a motor mouth... "

"Ugh!" exclaimed Alan, taking his hand from the table and rubbing his temple with it. "...And I suppose that telling him there had been a murder on board a ship I was Doc on was a bit too much of a temptation for him to keep quiet?"

"Ahhh, Alan – your talents extend to mind-reading as well as *Time Crisis*!" she teased him gently, even giving him a sassy little wink.

Alan gave a playful little groan.

"Well – unfortunately not quickly enough to realize that Sven might share my... ah... *news*!" he declared ruefully.

He realized his hand must be back on the table again when Tiffany patted it. He wondered how it was that the room had suddenly grown warm again; were they in for a storm?

"Aww look, if it makes you feel any better – there were only a couple of us there when he mentioned it. My colleague didn't believe him anyway and it was obvious after that, that Sven wasn't sure whether you'd been teasing him, either..."

Alan felt a little better.

"So...," he ventured.

Tiffany grinned.

"So... I thought I'd ask you about it and test out whether it was true!"

Tiffany grinned.

A smile spread across Alan's face at her audacity.

"Whhyyyy… yoouuuu… baddddd girl!"

Tiffany laughed happily.

"Yep… sneaky, huh? But now I know it's true – you may as well tell me the details… Come on – spill!… After all, after Joan and the… ah… *ashes*… we're partners in crime, aren't we?" she wheedled playfully.

Chuckling, Alan shook his head like one might at a child pushing their luck. That realization made Alan feel old once again.

"Weeellll… I wouldn't exactly call what Joan did a *crime*… more a service…"

"But… like you said at the time, Alan… the authorities probably wouldn't agree," Tiffany pointed out to him.

He nodded with a sigh, realizing she was correct in that summing up of the situation.

"So…," she continued. "You didn't let on about that… and you know I can keep my mouth shut… so, I'm interested. What is it about a murder…?"

Alan thought about what had happened to Michael and what he knew already – not much, he had to admit. He felt slightly foolish.

"Well… I don't even know if it *was* a murder…."

"Yeah you do," Tiffany interrupted him. "I know you, Alan… already. You wouldn't say it was a murder if you thought it wasn't."

Alan was flattered a Tiffany's assessment of him but it made him slightly hot under the collar.

"Th-thanks…"

"So go on – tell me what happened… and this…"

She looked around the dining hall. There was no-one within earshot but she whispered anyway, partly to show Alan that he could trust her to be discreet. She also turned her head to avoid even the most skilful lip-reader!

"… this murder… Sven said it's… unsolved?"

Alan nodded.

"So far, yes… The authorities just thought it was a heart attack…"

"But heart attacks can be… induced. How exciting!" squealed Tiffany, thrilled.

Alan winced, screwing up his eyes. He gave her a quick medical précis of what he had found that day in Michael's cabin.

"Um… s-sorry," apologized Tiffany, lowering her voice once more.

Her next response was much more measured, having to wait until after the first course of their meal was served. As she spread her snowy white napkin on her lap, Tiffany asked,

"So then you thought it was natural causes and now you don't?"

"Uh-huh. That's about the size of it. Just little things... they keep coming back to me... they don't add up... if it was natural causes... but they do if it's a murder," Alan said slowly, trying to choose his words carefully, and trying not to induce any more attention-grabbing squeals from Tiffany. He was glad it was the slightly more sensible Tiffany he was talking to and not Jenny or Tina. Again, Alan gave a self-conscious squirm – all these women he seemed to be hanging out with!

To get his mind off that uncomfortable thought and the image in his mind of Jo Ann looking down at him and wielding a meat cleaver at his head, Alan filled Tiffany in on what he had remembered so far and why he now suspected that Michael's death had been deliberate.

"There was – unfortunately – no shortage of suspects," Alan admitted. "He was into some pretty dodgy dealings and his love life... well, a tarantula would have been proud of *that* web!" he chuckled.

Tiffany gave Alan a knowing smile.

"But you liked him, didn't you?"

Surprised at the astute deduction, Alan looked keenly into Tiffany's eyes through his own narrowed ones, but slowly he nodded.

"Yeah... I did. Michael had a way about him... he was... easy to like..."

Again his hand was patted and again the room grew warm. But now Tiffany was in practical mode.

"OK – so... Michael was murdered... supposedly... and I'm sure you've made a list of likely suspects...?"

Again Alan nodded.

"It's on my laptop in my cabin..."

Tiffany sipped her wine.

"I love a mystery, Alan... and I hate an unsolved crime... The authorities... it's not right that they dismissed this as natural causes if it wasn't. I don't care if twenty-five years have passed..."

Alan grinned. Oh how like Jo Ann she was with that steely determination! No wonder he liked her! Now that he had seen the similarity between Tiffany and his late beloved wife, Alan ironically felt better about liking Tiffany, so when she said, "After dinner – how about we go on up to your cabin and go over your notes so far?" he readily agreed.

After that, the slight tension seemed to be broken between the two co-conspirators and would-be sleuths. The conversation flowed freely with the wine and the good food, and Alan found himself remembering a few more details which he thought may or may not be significant about Michael's murder. Tiffany was proving herself an able assistant already as she slipped a pen out from her purse and turned to a blank page in the back of her diary, jotting down the gist of what Alan told her now.

"I liked Michael… although I disapproved of some of his choices, of course. But there were plenty of others who didn't like him at all, for all sorts of reasons: some good, some bad and some downright stupid…"

Just then, he saw two familiar faces sit down at the adjacent table but he couldn't quite place them. Tiffany, obviously seeing his confused expression, turned to see what he was looking at. She smiled and waved at the couple.

"Hello, Nick; hi, Heidi, how are you two this fine evening?"

They returned her greeting, even as the waiter appeared to get their drink orders. It was then that Alan remembered them; Dr. Fillem, the dentist, and his new young wife. He hadn't gotten their first names on that first encounter up by the pool and hadn't seen them since. Nick looked a bit tired and then Alan remembered: the poor man had probably suffered a stroke recently. Alan slowly shook his head; maybe a cruise was not best for the man just now.

"What kept you two?" he asked. "First seating is nearly half done with dinner."

He hoped the delay had been nothing to do with health issues. He was soon reassured.

"Oh, Nick was having a real hot streak of luck in the casino," Heidi chuckled. "And he just didn't want to leave until the dice turned cold."

Alan slowly nodded. He knew how that was.

"Yes, I've had such runs of luck."

"So, I take it that your presence here means that his luck finally *did* run out?" Tiffany said.

"Yes," Nick replied, smiling as he scanned the menu. "Fortunately, I had the good sense to leave before losing too much of my winnings."

Heidi gave a little harrumph.

"Well, if he'd stopped a few minutes sooner - as I said he should have - he'd have won even more!"

"Now-now, Heidi," Tiffany said, trying to be diplomatic. "You must allow your man his… indulgences."

Alan smiled, and gave her a wink.

"Well put, my dear."

A moment later, the waiter returned with the appetizers for Nick and Heidi.

"So, Alan, you're quite the video game aficionado, eh?" Tiffany said.

He slowly nodded. Ah, smart girl; she was changing the subject, now that they were no longer alone.

"Well… I was, and now I am… again," he said, trying not to stammer.

"Oh, your… career was… interrupted?"

Alan laughed, a forced laugh; he really didn't want to bring up Jo Ann now.

"Oh… you know how it is; the carefree days of youth give way to the needs of adult life."

Tiffany gave him a warm smile.

"Oh, of course; how silly of me not to realize. You being a doctor and all, and having a family to care for; I imagine silly video games were the furthest thing from your mind."

Alan grinned. "Well… not the furthest. Oh, I went through quite a few game systems over the years. I had the Nintendo, Super Nintendo and a bunch of others. Well… technically, they were my daughter's systems."

"Ah, but you got as much use out of them as the kids did, right?" Tiffany said.

"I tried. But, well… Jo, she… she thought them a waste of time. And, with me away on ships so often, she did want as much of my time as she could."

Tiffany's brow wrinkled. "Jo?" Her eyes darted back and forth. "Oh, Jo Ann, your wife!"

Nick grinned and leaned toward their table.

"Why you sly dog," he chortled. "Off on a little getaway from the wifey?"

Alan's face must have betrayed his discomfort, as Tiffany suddenly had a very pained and concerned look to her.

"Ah… Doctor, now let's not jump to conclusions," she said quickly.

Heidi's brow wrinkled; it was clear she knew something was amiss, but wasn't quite sure what. A moment later the tension was eased by the waiter bringing them their next course.

Tiffany leaned over the table slightly and Alan couldn't help but get a tantalizing glimpse down her dress. Oh, she was… quite nice!

Dr. Fillem realized what must have happened.

"I'm sorry. She… was a good woman?"

Alan nodded, even as he felt his throat tighten.

"One in a million; I met her… more years ago than I care to admit."

"Was it love at first sight?" Tiffany asked, gently, being a sucker for a good love story.

Alan laughed.

"Far from it; she thought I was a world-class geek and I thought she was a New York… ah, she-devil. We met on a ship actually."

"Oh, you the ship's doctor, and she… what, a passenger?" Tiffany asked.

"No, she was working on the ship; she and her theatre group had been hired to do a series of shows. As it happened, they needed some extra help backstage."

"Oh, why were they shorthanded?"

"A touch of the flu was going around and my sickbay was just about full of people coughing and hacking their guts up."

Alan gave a little gasp.

"Oh, I'm sorry; I don't suppose that's polite dinner conversation now, is it?"

Tiffany giggled.

"Oh, it's quite all right. You must remember, I often dine with the children's group and that can get quite... interesting. If the boys aren't complaining about cooties from the girls then the girls are whining about the boys picking their noses!"

Alan laughed, long and loud.

"Ah, now you're making me think of my daughter when she was young."

"You have a daughter?"

"Yes, we – I... have Alexa – and she has two boys of her own now. Jo and I, we... had a good life together."

"After you got through the... difficult, ah... 'opening scene', shall we say?"

Alan nodded.

"Yes. She *was* impressed that I was so interested in the theatre. So, that was the first step."

"And what changed things for you?"

"Oh... there were a lot of little things - her laugh, her playful attitude. It's funny, but it was an illness that brought us together, and I don't just mean the cast members getting sick. It was later, while we were ashore between cruises."

Tiffany cocked her head at him.

"Oh, what... she got sick?"

"No, quite the contrary - *I* got sick!"

"Awww, and she got to play nursemaid to you - is that it?"

Alan nodded, chuckling wryly.

"Yeah; you know what they say - doctors make the worst patients. So, I wasn't really inclined to be the good, co-operative patient. But, she got me to the doctor, got me my meds and even bought some groceries to tide me over for the week."

"And that's when you started dating?" Tiffany asked, hanging on every word.

"Well… sort of," Alan replied, slowly. "She felt sorry for me - being alone - and invited me to a 'Fall Party' she was having."

"A *what* party?"

"Ah… she didn't want to call it a 'Halloween Party'; some of her friends were Jehovah's Witnesses, and they would have been offended."

"Ah… now it becomes clear," Tiffany chuckled. "So you went - and that did it?"

"For her - yes, but I didn't know it at the time," Alan replied.

"Okay, now I'm *really* confused," giggled Tiffany.

Alan laughed.

"I arrived first - very early; I hadn't yet learned about the rule about being 'fashionably late' to things and I brought her a little gift."

"Oh… how sweet!" Heidi said from the next table. "Oh, sorry, didn't mean to eaves' drop, but it all sounded so interesting."

Tiffany laughed.

"Seems you're becoming quite the storyteller, Alan. So, what did you give her?"

"A little pin with a hologram of the comedy and tragedy masks," he said. "I'd picked it up at an arts and crafts fair."

"Oh… I bet it must have been lovely."

Alan smiled softly, as he remembered Jo Ann's reaction.

"She thought so, and asked why I was giving it to her. I told her it was a thank-you for helping me when I was sick."

Both Tiffany and Heidi smiled and nodded; Nick looked quite confused.

"Ah… so that's when your relationship changed," Tiffany said.

"And why she knew it, but you didn't," Heidi added.

Alan nodded.

"Yes, exactly."

Nick's wrinkled brow became even more wrinkled as he slowly shook his head.

"I still don't get it."

Heidi and Tiffany laughed long and hard (although Tiffany did try to control her chortling, unfortunately with no success).

"It's okay, my dear doctor Nick," Alan said. "Women - they have their own system of codes and signals for all kinds of things."

Nick grinned and slowly nodded.

"Ah, yes; that is one thing my father did teach me. He always said that there was a veil of absolute secrecy drawn across the mysteries of the feminine world and not even the Chinese water torture could shake the details loose."

"Yes, like the whole issue of them going to the bathroom in groups!" Alan said. "I could never get a straight answer from Jo as to why they do that."

Tiffany grinned.

"It's then that we talk about all of the men in our lives."

"Oh, Tiff', you've violated the Code of Secrecy," Heidi said. "Fifty lashes for you."

Tiffany hung her head in obvious mock shame.

"Sorry, milady."

Alan grinned.

"Don't worry; Nick and I won't say a word… Well… after that, we started dating. But the life of a cruise doctor did prove tough at times, as I was away on different ships and she was now land-bound. But… we managed. We had a nice little place out on Cape Cod. My family had been going there since I was a kid and it was a place near and dear to my heart."

Nick slowly nodded.

"I know that area, ah… let me think. Oh, *Jaws* was filmed off the coast, on one of the islands, and that bastard Teddy Kennedy killed that girl…"

Heidi rolled her eyes in exasperation.

"Oh boy, here he goes again! Darling, there's no proof that he did any such thing."

Nick snorted.

"That's only because old Joe - his rich, old goat of a father - paid everyone off! I knew Teddy when he was a little crook in Massachusetts, and now-"

"And now he's a big one in Washington," Heidi said quickly.

Nick crinkled his face into a foul expression.

"Hmmm… so, it would seem you've heard that before, eh?"

He laughed, Heidi laughed, and then Tiffany and Alan joined them.

"I know the Cape area; I spent a summer with my grandparents at Martha's Vineyard," Tiffany said. "It was August, and they were having a festival known as Grand Illumination Night."

"Oh… sounds special," Heidi said.

"Yes, it's a very old tradition; goes back over a century," Tiffany replied. "The little cottages there hang Japanese lanterns on their porches. According to my grandparents, they started doing it as a celebration of the end of summer and then the town fathers asked them to move it to earlier in the summer."

Heidi's brow wrinkled.

"Why would they - oh… tourism, right? They wanted to attract more people to it."

Tiffany nodded.

"You got it! Well, I'd never seen anything like it. I don't know what to compare it to - except maybe a parade where the floats stand still and the people move."

"Wow… it must be a beautiful sight," Heidi said. "Huh, we'll have to make plans to get up there one of these summers and see it."

"Is it only in August?" Nick said.

"Yes, it's tradition," Tiffany replied.

"Too bad; that's normally when we go to the south of France," he said.

"Well, maybe we could make an exception, dear one," Heidi said.

"Well, we'll see," Nick said. "Huh, sounds to me as if working on a cruise ship is a little like being in the military."

Alan and Tiffany both laughed.

"You know, I never thought of it like that," Alan replied. "But, you've got a point. The drill sergeant of a Staff Captain with his weekly safety drills, the reams of computer and paper reports, the uniform requirements for each type of function, etc., etc. and I missed a lot of holidays with the family. Yes – very like the military! That's why some call it the Merchant Marines. From the shape some of the officers and crew maintain physically, it's definitely not *the* Marines."

Nick slowly nodded.

"Yes… as a matter of fact, I remember reading about the whaling ships of old. They'd be gone for two, three years at a stretch. Then the men would come home, be with the wife and family - usually get the wife 'with child', as they said back then - and then they'd be off for more whaling."

"Ah, I know about that," Alan said. "I learned about it while growing up. They used to say that the children were born a 'Cape Horn' voyage apart."

Heidi gave the two men a blank look.

"What's a… Cape Horn?"

"Southern tip of South America," Alan explained. "The whaling ships would sail around it getting from New England to the whaling grounds of the Pacific Oceans. The journey generally took between two to three years to complete."

"And that's why the whaling families had children spaced that many years apart," Nick said.

For a good portion of the rest of the meal, Nick and Alan swapped stories about sailing, whaling and the sea in general. Alan and Tiffany relaxed with coffee and dessert while Nick and Heidi enjoyed their main course. Alan looked at her, casually sipping her tea.

"Ah… this has been a wonderful meal, Tiffany; I thank you for this."

She smiled as she set her cup down.

"You're most welcome, Alan. I've truly enjoyed myself too. But, it seems we're now unable to… speak about… what we were talking about before."

Alan's eyes darted over to look at Nick and Heidi for a moment.

"Ah… yes, I see what you mean. Well, as we're nearly done, how about we pop off to my cabin? I'll boot up my laptop and I can show you all the details I've assembled on… what we were talking about."

Tiffany reached across the small table to touch his hand gently as her eyes met his.

"Sounds like a great idea to me! Night, you two," she said, rising and giving Nick and Heidi a wave.

Alan also got to his feet, they exchanged goodbyes and he offered Tiffany his arm. Wrapping her slender arm about his, they left the dining hall and headed for the elevator. They weren't alone in there, so Alan felt he couldn't talk directly about Michael's murder, but the man was still on his mind. As he thought more about it he just grew angrier at the prejudice and hatred that Michael and Alfonse faced, and he had to get one incident off his chest…

# CHAPTER EIGHTEEN

*July 17, 1984: Jamaica*

ONE PARTICULAR DAY, A steward had called the Doc to an 'incident' between a passenger and member of staff. Fearing a fight, Alan hurried down to the sun lounge, to find an elderly passenger in quite a surprising position with Alfonse, grieving lover of Michael, the late tour director. Now, Alan had always seen Alfonse as gay and not at all interested in the ladies, and anyway, at seventy-five, he considered Lady Merrill rather too old for him. So it was with some surprise that the Doc, upon his approach, thought the two were holding hands.

This notion was soon corrected. As soon as the Doc was close enough for Lady Merrill to be aware of his approach, she screamed at him,

"Get him off me! This… this *fairy* has got my tickets and my hand stuck! Get his dirty hand off of me, Doctor!"

Alfonse just quietly fumed, his free hand clenching and unclenching in anger by his side. The hand to which Lady Merrill had referred was tightly held in a vice-like grip, together with what appeared to be some pieces of paper and a white lace handkerchief.

Alan was intrigued but he didn't have to wait long for the irate Lady Merrill to scream something of an explanation for the situation.

"He has my tickets… and my hand!"

The Doc realized then what must have happened. Mrs. Sarah Merrill, better known as Lady Merrill, was a frequent passenger on Gold Cruise Lines. Unlike one of the other older women who called herself Lady, she actually had been married to a Lord for six months. Mrs. Merrill, at one time in ancient history when she was young and beautiful, had pretended to have gotten pregnant by a young Welsh nobleman, who was then forced to marry her. When her real character came to light and the baby did not, the marriage was annulled. The title which she was given while they were married stuck for another fifty years.

Lady Merrill gave everyone of the crew a bad time but was particularly vehement toward 'fairies' and 'foreigners' as she called them. Alfonse was never going to be on her Christmas card list.

Lady Merrill had a false hand on the left. All the crew had 'potential stories' for how it happened and some of the stories were quite intricate. The real story that she did tell the Doc once when she needed to have the mechanism readjusted in a port was all to revealing of her and the society she kept at one point in her life. She apparently, at that time, was one of the wives of a Tunisian Tribesman. This was husband number six. She was found stealing something from one of the other wives and had her hand amputated. This episode was modified numerous times by her great ability to confabulate, but the medical records that the Doc had on her did indicate a "traumatic removal of left hand and wrist and replacement with a mechanical hand device". She had a state-of-the-art device that not only looked pretty real but functioned fairly well too. Most of the time.

Once or twice, it had to be modified and upgraded by some orthotists at the University of Southern California when she visited Los Angeles. They did a nice job and tweaked it so that it did not squeak when she bent the little finger even though many of the crew wanted the Doc to make sure that remained for comic relief. It still did it occasionally and sometimes got caught in the flexed position. The fellow at South Florida Orthotic service was not as expert as his compatriot on the other coast.

It was apparent that at a most unfortunate time for poor Alfonse and Lady Merrill, the device had seized up again. As the Doc was using a device the Orthotist from USC had given him to release the tension, Alfonse began to explain how they had become trapped together.

Lady Merrill had been married an incredible thirteen times by this tour. One day, researching the records, a disgruntled crew member who had felt the rough edge of Lady Merrill's tongue one time too many had found out that husband number eight had in fact been an English Earl. She had been married to him for only three months before he died, but she kept the title and played it for all it was worth. She was from Texas, and far from anyone else's definition of a lady, but she registered as Lady Merrill for everything she did in life some twenty-some years after this marriage. She had been married five times more after that. Unfortunately her husbands had all died except for the first one whom she had divorced.

Lady Merrill was currently on the look-out for husband number fourteen and a number of the single gentlemen on the cruise did everything in their power *not* to have to sit with her. She was truly a 'black widow' and although charming to many people, was a real handful to deal with.

Lady Merrill also utilized a walker, or Zimmer frame, as the English would call it. However, the walker was not in evidence this cruise. The Doc had wondered about this, but he wasn't overly surprised when she responded in a tone of voice that would have made you think that she was in her thirties instead of her seventies,

"Oh I am in love again. We are both deaf, but he does say sweet nothings to me all the time. It is just so exciting that he would be interested in an old lady like me. He is so charming".

Her new beau was an eighty-eight year old British fellow, Bert Ranowski. He dressed abominably, usually walked looking toward Mother Earth due to his kyphosis, and seldom had something intelligent to say. Bert had made his fortune running a garbage collection business in one of the industrial towns of the midlands of England. The British of good upbringing would classify him as 'lower class' and his accent, when he spoke, was not the Queen's English, or even close. Definitely not someone you would bring home to introduce to mother if you were a respectable girl.

However, despite Lady Merrill's obvious prejudices, the Doc had something of a soft spot for the elderly woman who was so full of life. It was cute to see these two old characters holding hands ninety-nine percent of the time, even in between courses of meals. No wonder she did not use her walker, she had to hang onto him and a walker was not in the romantic plan for husband number fourteen.

That was how she had come to be in her current predicament with Alfonse. It was a big surprise when she had called the tour desk to book a tour. She would not normally speak with 'poofs' directly, but later, Alfonse told the Doc that the conversation went pretty much as follows:

"This is Lady Merrill and I want two tickets to go on the Athenry Gardens tour tomorrow. You two should know about gardens, shouldn't you? Well - get me the tickets and send them up to my room so I can be sure you fairies don't mess this up. It is very important to me that Bert and I get a chance to be in the romantic gardens together."

Even though he assured her that would be attended to and her tickets duly sent up to her, Alfonse said that she arrived about fifteen minutes later wanting her tickets. He said,

"Here are your tickets, Lady Merrill. I think you will enjoy the gardens. Make sure that this time of the year you visit the Petunias. They have a big floral display of them in various …."

As Alfonse described it, he was rudely cut off when she grabbed the tickets with her orthotic hand: "the grab of the pirate" he called it. Unfortunately, this was one of those times when the hand malfunctioned and thus the Doc had had to be called to fix it. Thankfully, there was no lasting damage to either party and the three, including the Doc, were soon able to go their separate ways. Of course, that unfortunate, but amusing, incident went right into the Doc's notebook. He didn't want to forget a second of that incident!

# CHAPTER NINETEEN

*December 9, 2009: The Caribbean Sea*

ONCE ALAN AND TIFFANY returned to his cabin, Alan sat at the desk and booted up his computer. His eyes reluctantly drifted away from Tiffany but he could hear her moving about the cabin.

"Wow, nice; you got yourself a good-sized suite, didn't you?"

"Huh, what? Oh, the room; yes. Well, I figured, what with this being my big vacation, I'd go with a fancy place," he replied, smiling.

"Oh, don't apologize," Tiffany said. "You've every right to enjoy yourself. Oh, that's so cute!"

Alan turned around in his seat and saw that she was looking at the bed. He was surprised at first, but then saw what she was pointing at. His cabin steward had folded his towels into the shape of a bunny rabbit, and put his sunglasses on it.

He laughed.

"Oh, that… ah, what's the name of my steward? Trudy, that's it! She does that with my towels all the time."

Tiffany nodded, and crossed over to him.

"Yes, they're trained to do that; they can do a whole bunch of different animals."

Alan turned around to face his computer as he heard it play its little musical refrain to signify that it was nearly done booting up.

"I remember. As I recall, one ship I sailed on even had a class where the passengers could learn how to do it too."

Stepping closer to Alan, right behind him, Tiffany rested her slender hands on his shoulders.

"We don't have that here – normally; we use it as a 'rough sea day' alternative activity, but we do have a book in the main gift shop that shows you how to do them. So, what you got there?"

Alan opened the *Word* document on his computer, and began to slowly scroll through it as he pointed at the different items.

"OK, Michael *appeared* to die of a heart attack, but he had a needle track in his arm. Now, at the time, I chalked it up to drug use, which is something he tended to… indulge in far too much."

"But you don't now?"

"Well… I've been thinking about it more and more and I realized something – Michael was more the smoker and… inhaler. Any time he came into the sickbay for treatment for anything, he seemed a bit… skittish about getting a shot."

Tiffany, her reflection clear in the laptop's screen, slowly nodded.

"Good point."

"Then there was a model plane, which had hung in his cabin."

Tiffany's brow wrinkled as she brought her face down next to his. Oh, did she smell nice!

"What was special about that?"

"For the longest time, I didn't know, but I remember something now – it was pulled down and it's propeller broken on the floor. I had to wonder, it was hanging way up at the ceiling. So, someone had to really strain to reach for it. Why?"

Tiffany moved to sit on the edge of the table, so that they could truly talk face to face.

"Well… that might not mean anything. Maybe Michael had taken it down for some reason. Any idea what happened to it?"

Alan shrugged.

"I'm not sure; it's so long ago. I kind of find myself swamped with thoughts of some details and struggling to recall others."

Tiffany pointed at the screen.

"And what's this mean: 'Shady Russians'?"

"Michael was involved with a Mrs. Brightman and a Vasilov Eranowski in some… questionable deals regarding Russian antiques," Alan said. "The scuttlebutt around the ship was that she'd cheated Vasilov on a number of those deals, and both were pretty pissed at Michael as the go-between."

"Ah, I see," Tiffany replied, putting the information together in her head.

Alan smiled at her.

"Then there were the gifts from some of the... friends he made on cruises. Some said they were bribes, others that they were blackmail!"

Tiffany's eye grew large and her jaw dropped for a moment.

"Bribes, blackmail? Goodness, what sort of man was he?"

Alan laughed.

"A nicer guy than I'm making him sound!... But he moved in high circles... with men who wanted their... orientation... kept as quiet as possible."

"Ah, now I understand," Tiffany said, sadly nodding her head.

Alan continued,

"Then there were Alfonse and Gustav; they were the two main men in Michael's life."

Tiffany's eyebrows slid up into her bangs.

"The *two* men main in his life?"

"Michael and Alfonse had an... open relationship," Alan explained.

"Was that what they both believed, or was it just Michael's view?"

Tiffany was a little skeptical that 'open' relationships were ever really consensual and weren't just one partner's pathetic attempt to keep hold of a straying partner, but it seemed in Michael's case she was wrong – at least in Alan's estimation.

"Oh no, they both felt that way. Now, here's a real twist to the story – Gustav was an associate of Vasilov's, and it was said that Michael was blackmailing both of them!"

Tiffany rolled her eyes.

"Goodness, Michael's life had more twists in it that a TV soap opera

"So..."

She traced her elegant forefinger down the screen, taking in the list of 'suspects'.

"That puts this Vasilov... Gustav... and even Alfonse in the frame, I guess."

Tiffany had pulled up a chair and sat beside Alan at the desk. She was so close that Alan could smell her perfume. If he turned his head just slightly to the left he would be able to see right down Tiffany's dress.

'Mustn't do that... keep eyes forward... don't turn head,' Alan told himself sternly.

"Isn't it a pity that some people *still* have to hide their sexuality because of such prejudice? You'd hardly believe this is the 21st century!... Well, 20th *then*, I guess, but it's still crazy!"

Tiffany was showing herself to have a keen sense of injustice, and a dislike of it; that impressed Alan. He nodded somberly. He couldn't agree more.

"Yes, very sad..."

"And that... Lady Merrill? From what you told me, she hated Michael... and his 'kind'. Couldn't she have done it? Killed him, I mean?... and you said he had scratches?... Couldn't that have been the artificial hand?"

Alan frowned, considering the thought for a moment but then finally dismissing it.

"She *could* have, but that would have probably entailed touching him... I doubt she would have done that."

"Hmm fair point," admitted Tiffany and returned her gaze to the screen.

Alan laughed then at a little shout from Tiffany:

"Hey, what's this? 'Tiffany'? How am *I* connected to this little mystery?"

"No, my dear, not you," he chuckled. "A tiffany lamp was in Michael's cabin – broken. Again, at the time, I thought nothing of it."

"What's changed?" Tiffany asked, quickly on to the significance of this.

"Well, I remembered all those bit of different colored glass. I ah... was reminded of them when I saw a collection of brightly colored ah... swimsuits back on the private island."

Tiffany smirked.

"I see. So, all those... suits awakened a memory, eh? How important was it?"

"I'm not sure. But, I remember something happening later on the ship having to do with broken glass. If I remember correctly, the doctor that took over for me while I was away said something about someone coming in with a deep cut. Again, at the time, I thought nothing of it; mainly because she'd wasted so much time and money on a bunch of unnecessary tests for staff that didn't need anything more than a listening ear!"

"Ah, so maybe the person with the cut got it from the lamp, eh?"

Alan nodded.

"Maybe – and..."

"Heeyyyy!... *Maybe* Gustav... or Vasilov... or... oh, I don't know... Maybe Alfonse... *they* broke the lamp... getting back... ah... whatever it was that they needed to get back?"

"Good thinking," praised Alan, already pleased that he had involved Tiffany in solving this twenty-five year old mystery... a *murder* mystery, he was now convinced. He typed in a note to that effect on his ever-growing 'Michael Murder Mystery' file, before continuing,

"Then there was the supposedly diabetic man – Dr. Z. - who seemed far too taken with sweets and who had needles far too large for insulin injections!"

Tiffany gasped.

"Oh, I saw something about that in a movie once; a suspense thriller, ah... *Wiccans' Lair*. The killer injected air into the victim's bloodstream and it caused him to have a heart attack!"

"There you go… it's a definite possibility, huh?"

Tiffany let out a long slow whistle.

"Well, you've certainly got yourself a fully-fledged mystery here: plenty of clues and suspects. So, shall I be 'Daphne' to your 'Freddy' and we see about solving this murder?"

Alan laughed and patted her thigh. Oh, it was quite soft and supple, and so nicely encased in her silky gown. He pulled his hand back, a little unsure about her reaction to his touch. Pausing a moment, he looked into her warm gentle eyes and read her body language. There was no hesitancy there: no negative reaction, stiffening or recoiling.

"Can you afford the time to help me? After all, you have your ship's duties to attend to. I wouldn't want to get you in trouble for neglecting them!"

Tiffany smiled; ah, such a warm and delicate smile. She had the most sparkling teeth, undoubtedly the result of a number of visits to the ship spa and their Super Tooth Whitening Program.

"Don't you worry; I can always get some of my friends on the staff to cover for me; I've done it for *them* often enough! Just tell me what you want me to do! I'm yours to command."

Tiffany found all of this *very* exciting.

Alan let out a little squeak of surprise and Tiffany gave a little shudder.

"I-I…" he stammered.

"Oh, I'm sorry! That came out totally wrong," she said quickly.

Alan rose to his feet and patted her upper arms. He was getting that familiar warm feeling again and he was slowly coming to the realization that it was… Tiffany! *She* was the cause of his… overheating! He had to get a little distance… get some perspective on this.

"It's all right, Tiffany; we're both tired from a long day. Ah… how about… we… call it a day?"

She smiled, even as her eyes drifted to the shelf behind him. She wasn't to be gotten rid of so easily!

"Good idea. But how about a nightcap first? I could use a little drink."

Alan turned around and looked at his little collection of liquor bottles. She wanted to stay; his resolve was weakening too.

"Sure, why not?" he said, his voice a little hoarse.

With that, he mixed them up a couple of drinks and they sat down on the couch to relax. Alan needed to calm down and regain his composure before he made a total fool of himself, he was sure.

*'Think of something neutral to say!'* his head screamed at him.

"So, I imagine you spend a lot of your time on your feet, eh, Tiffany? And tomorrow, you have to face off with the kids, right?"

She seemed to sense Alan's predicament and she responded accordingly, nodding and replying,

"Oh, I don't mind the kids too much. Some of them can be a bit trying, but a lot of them are a true delight. To see the joy sparkling in a child's eyes makes my job – and all its pains – totally worthwhile."

Alan smiled. Oh, the twinkle in her eyes spoke volumes. Here was a truly lucky woman, someone who delighted in her work – just like he did.

"I know that feeling only too well; being a doctor and helping people is all I've ever wanted to do ever since I was a little kid, when my friends were talking about being firemen, policeman, astronauts and the like. That's part of the reason I've become so focused on Michael's death, I guess; I really want to know the truth of what happened to him now, and who was responsible!"

Tiffany leaned forward, once more putting her delightful 'twins' on display, and patted Alan's thigh. It was a very friendly pat.

"I could see that caring nature in you, Alan, from the moment we met; it's part of your charm."

He smiled and cupped her small chin in his hand, then looked into those eyes of hers.

"Oh, and what's the other part? I'm sure it's not my youth!"

She smirked.

"Well… it's your brains. I have to admit, I find intelligent men ever so sexy!"

"I see. So, if I rattle off something like $E=MC^2$, that'll get your attention?"

Tiffany laughed, then tilted her head back and let out a mock cry of ecstasy.

"Oh! Oh my, such excitement," she cried.

They both laughed, and she slid just a bit closer. Alan's hand slipped behind her to gently caress her back. He could feel her spine and he laughed to himself. Goodness, could he ever stop being a doctor? He also noticed that she was not wearing a bra! He couldn't help but think of Jenny and her tube top. Good grief, he'd not… been with a woman since dear Jo had… departed; and now two women in as many days. Was he lucky, or were they desperate? Now-now, no sense thinking such things about Jenny, and certainly not about Tiffany!

He smiled at her. No, he was going to put such thoughts out of his mind, and just enjoy their time together.

"Well hey; I've got plenty more where that came from, my dear."

Tiffany ran her hand up and down Alan's chest.

"You don't need them, Alan, not with me."

Her voice was low and sultry as she gave the old standby 'eye-eye-mouth' gaze. Alan instinctively responded to this body language. His hand slipped up to caress the back of her head, play with her hair and then he leaned in to kiss her. It was only a gentle kiss, but it felt better than any kiss he'd known since he last kissed Jo.

Tiffany set down her drink, brought her smooth, delicate hands up to cradle his face, and kissed him back – long and deep.

Alan pulled back from her just a bit.

"Are you... sure? I can't make any promises, and I didn't come on this cruise looking for love, whether brief or long-term..."

Tiffany smiled at him, her thumb caressing the pink lipstick stain she had made on his lips.

"Alan, let's not worry about tomorrow; let's just... enjoy this moment... enjoy... tonight..."

With that, they embraced and again kissed. Alan's long arms wrapped about her, pulling her into him, and sliding her up onto his lap; she fit so nicely! Her hands moved across his shoulders and chest and began to unbutton his shirt. Alan – very tentatively – began to unzip her dress. He slid it down just a bit, and then waited for her reaction. Internally, he rolled his eyes at himself.

'For goodness sake – how much more... invitation do you need, you big dummy?' he chided himself.

With that, he slid the soft fabric down, and it fell away to reveal her beautiful, shapely body. Those pert little breasts – braless - heaved upward as she took a deep breath and helped him to slip his shirt off.

Gathering Tiffany into his arms, Alan lifted her up and got easily to his feet. She was feather-light in his arms. Her dress slipped away to reveal her black lace panties and he moved to the bed.

Setting her down, he shed his trousers and underwear. Tiffany smiled up at him, and tugged off her panties. Lying there, naked on his bed, she looked like Botticelli's Venus. As she opened her arms to him he slid into her embrace, his body melding to hers, and then they rolled about on the bed. They both giggled; it seemed they couldn't work out who was going to be on top!

They ended up on their sides, facing each other and Alan's hands ran up and down Tiffany firm, slender body.

She giggled.

"Goodness, you've got more hands than an octopus!"

Alan pulled her close, his arms wrapping about her to caress her back and firm bottom.

"Don't be fresh, young lady!" he chuckled, his mouth on hers, and his cupped hand cracked into her bottom. It sounded loud in the cabin and she giggled mischievously.

With that, he entered her, and she gasped. Their eyes locked, and then their lips. Her ample bosom heaved, and Alan groaned in pleasure; those delicate mounds were like lightning bolts; they send a surge of energy straight to his mind - and his penis!

Alan's hips rocked and pounded into her and she dragged her nails across his back, grabbed his upper arms and tilted her head back.

"Oh... oh God! Yes, Alan, yessss..."

Rolling onto his back, Alan grabbed Tiffany at the waist, and drove himself into her – even as he climaxed. She arched her back, grabbed the hairs on his chest, and cried out a guttural scream of pure pleasure as her eyes rolled back in her head.

TWO HOURS – AND three 'couplings' later, they reclined in bed, wrapped in each other's arms, the soft pillows supporting their heads.

"Well, someone took a double dose of *Viagra* today!" Tiffany said with a grin.

Alan snorted, and reached down to give her shapely bottom a playful smack.

"Oh - sooo bad! Young lady, I'll have you know that was *all* me, no 'artificial stimulants' whatsoever - only a natural one... called *you*."

Tiffany giggled, even as she twirled his chest hairs about her finger.

"I know; I was only teasing you. On some cruises, some of the... older gentlemen go out of their way to let the ladies know that they're... well medicated."

"Ah yes, I've had plenty of patients with that problem," Alan said. "I hope that *that* particular difficulty remains a distant one for me – for as long as possible."

Tiffany rubbed her right calf up and down Alan's legs as she gave him a big smile.

"Oh, I don't think you have anything to worry about, my man."

Alan kissed the top of her head.

"Thank you, my dear; a man likes to hear that. Well, I'd say we've gone where Freddy and Daphne never dared."

Tiffany chuckled.

"Oh, I don't know about that. I mean, how many times did the two of them go off looking for clues all by themselves? What, you actually believe no hanky panky went on between them?"

Alan laughed.

"Tiffany, please, that was a kids' show; hanky panky was strictly not allowed!"
She smirked.

"Well, maybe not on-screen! But... who knows what they were implying, huh?"

Alan shook his head and rolled his eyes.

"Oh, sooo bad! ... You, young lady, are incorrigible!... How did you manage to grow up without being royally smacked daily by your parents?"

Tiffany giggled and batted her eyes at him.

"Because I'm the baby of the family! And you know what they say about the babies."

Alan slowly nodded.

"Ah yes, they do get spoiled," he said, and then sat up straight, a little panicked. "Oh my, look at the time! Ah, do you need to... get back to your... cabin?"

Tiffany sat up, her lovely breasts giving a gentle bounce as she turned to face him.

"Why, sir, are you trying to get rid of me? I see how it is with you rich doctors; three or four quick ones, and it's slam-bam, thank-you-ma'am!"

Alan opened his mouth to deny such a thing; it was furthest from his mind – and then he saw the gleam of delight in her eye and the ear-to-ear grin on her face.

"More sass, eh?"

She laughed.

"Sorry, couldn't resist. You're worried about me getting in trouble with the Staff Captain, right?"

Alan nodded.

"Yeah; in my day, there was the bed check - and the idea of crew 'fraternizing' with passengers was strictly *verboten!*"

Tiffany moved closer, wrapping her arms about him and pressing that warm, luscious flesh of hers into his bare skin. Oh, she felt so very nice!

"Not to worry, sweetie; I won't get in trouble for having a 'sleepover' with you. My job definition allows me to co-ordinate things all over the ship at all hours of the day and night."

Alan wrapped his arm about her and tilted his head so that his face rested against the top of her head. Ah, her scent was like the sweetness of spring!

"Coordinate things, eh? In that case, you're welcome to stay, but I don't know how much sleep you'll get. You have bewitched me, my dear... and you do have the kids to be with tomorrow. Won't you need all your... energy - to keep up with them?"

Tiffany tilted her head to look up at him and gave him a playful grin.

"I'll drink a lot of coffee!"

# CHAPTER TWENTY

*December 10, 2009: The Caribbean Sea*

THE NEXT MORNING, TIFFANY was indeed up with the lark and off to her duties organizing and supervising the children's activities, leaving Alan a little time alone. He chose to spend that time in his cabin, noting down some remembrances and preliminary conclusions concerning Michael's murder. He was amazed that Tiffany could be so bright and bubbly after their late night. Alan himself needed the pot of coffee he ordered to be sent to his cabin, just to get his brain in gear sufficiently to power up his laptop, get out his notebook and begin to put some ideas together.

Even so, Alan's thoughts at first centered on his lost bulging biceps, six pack, etc., and the fitness and vitality of youth. That sent his thoughts toward the gym, and Michael's lover, Alfonse, who seemed to spend most of his time in the gym when he wasn't organizing passenger activities as well as some time when he *should* have been organizing them!

*July 17, 1984: Jamaica*

PHYSICAL FITNESS AND STRENGTH were so important to Alfonse. It seemed odd that he should take a lover like Michael, for whom good living meant rich food and plenty of it, and to whom 'exercise' was such a dirty word that the Doc often threatened him with when checking his cholesterol.

Alfonse was definitely a 'Jock'. On any ship you have a group of individuals that are in charge of sports activities and adventures for the passengers - and sometimes the crew. These fellows and gals are generally in the best shape of any of the crew, save maybe the non-positive dancers from the spectacular reviews. They were the real 'jocks'.

These other jocks were generally very well trained in their favorite sport but were required to participate in many sports to accommodate all of the activities of the ship. Many of these guys are really gung-ho about their own sport. They often tried to squeeze their non-work related sports activities into the short, on shore leave – which is sometimes only a few hours, other times, the better part of a day. Because of this, they often hurt themselves, are real motivated to get back to work, but seldom listen to the suggestions you gave them about getting healthy.

One particular guy, Jim, epitomized this genre of ship employee. Jim was a sky diver, parachutist, free fall stunt artist, and all other associated permutations of what one can do after jumping out of a plane with a nylon bed sheet attached to your back.

The Doc wasn't one to judge this harshly. He too had gone skydiving a couple of times and done static jumps a few times also. These were voluntary, not at the behest of any government military. What had made him do it? Interest? The feeling of flying? Proving to himself that he could do it? The Doc had felt all those things but for him, he had to admit that the over-riding feeling was a trust that all would go well and that he had tempted fate one more time. It was a sort of indirect verification of his invincibility, which was being notched away little by little, day by day, as he got older.

Jim was 45 years old, 5'7" stocky with a bit of extra beer belly, but muscularly strong-particularly upper arms. This was very helpful in helping passengers of extra adiposity, get over the hurdles that occasionally befell some of the adventure tours. The ship offered a variety of 'adventure tours', everything from white water rafting on the Aca River in Costa Rica to ballooning over the Loire Valley in France and literally everything in between.

Jim was bright, knew his trade well. If the Doc was ever going to go skydiving, Jim was definitely the one he wanted to pack his chute. He was supremely responsible, mostly always professing that he could or could not do something that might affect his performance that could endanger one of his passengers, etc. Of course he felt this special responsibility for skydiving in tandem with passengers a bit more than those he was leading in horseback riding or elephant rides, rightfully so in many instances, but for some people, riding an elephant might be just as awe inspiring and intimidating as jumping out of an airplane at twelve thousand feet.

Like many crew on board, Jim was fond of a drink or six, but he would always forgo this pleasure the night before a risky pursuit he was leading. Not that Jim wouldn't be able to function well on that much beer; it was just his honesty in the matter. Furthermore he had a very strict no drug, no alcohol policy on the job.

Alan recalled how Jim had told him that when he was working as a jumpmaster at a sky diving location in Arizona, he would do anywhere from two to eleven jumps per day (in a well oiled machine of an operation), would return to his apartment and drink a few beers, smoke a joint or two, and kick back watching TV. Not exactly the Doc's lifestyle, but he supposed that if he had been tempting death any number of times a day that he too would find a special kind of way to relieve the pent up stress involved.

After Jim reassured the Doc that he would make sure he was sober for an activity on the cruise line and would adhere absolutely to the cruise line's zero tolerance on drugs, the Doc and he became firm friends. Jim made it is special responsibility to make sure that any of the Doc's patients with special problems got gentle care and were still able to enjoy their experience.

Alan recalled now how Jim knew Alfonse well because they had to work together on planning and executing the adventure tours, and didn't like him. However, he had been sure at the time of Michael's death that Alfonse was very much in love with Michael and had even been working at the time that Michael had died. Alan remembered that Jim had stressed that, even way before there were any real suggestions that Michael's death was due to anything but natural causes.

Alan became so engrossed in typing up his thoughts so far on the murder and possible motives and suspects that he didn't leave his cabin all day. Some may see that as a waste of a day on a cruise, but to Alan it was a luxury he'd never had as a ship's doctor. He had to admit to himself that he had the bit between his teeth now and he wanted to solve this mystery. So much so that when Tiffany returned from her day's work, they ate in the cabin as Alan filled her in on his progress and eventually they fell into other's arms and into bed, both exhausted from a hard day's work. And Tiffany had drawn the short straw of children's activities the following day too!

# CHAPTER TWENTY-ONE

*December 11, 2009: Jamaica*

MANY IMAGES SWIRLED AROUND Alan's mind as he slept. When he awoke, he looked around. He was in his cabin, Tiffany wrapped about him once more. He had to wonder, was he truly awake, or was he still dreaming? He was tempted to pinch himself, but he was never one to believe that old wives' tale.

Tiffany, seeming to sense his movement, yawned and stretched, the sheet slipping down to reveal those lovely twin mounds of hers. She looked up at Alan, smiled softly and gave him a kiss.

"Morning, sweetie; how you doing - oh, I see you're doing... well!" she grinned.

"Huh - what?"

He was confused, but then followed the line of her gaze to the little... ah, 'pup tent' down at his groin! He grinned, and then gave a little jump as her hand snaked under the sheet to... get a hold of him.

"I guess someone was having a good dream," she said with a smirk.

"Whoa! Easy there, darlin'; don't mangle the merchandize. I was actually thinking about the case."

Her delicate fingers slid up and down his firm shaft, tickling and teasing him. Her grinning face looked up into his eyes.

"Liar! What, thinking of murder gets you... this hard? I think not. If it does, I better watch my back!"

Alan's arms wrapped about her, as he laughed and pulled her closer to him. Her bare breasts felt wonderful against his chest, bumping his tiny but still sensitive nipples.

"Well… there was this… cheerleader there."

"Me?" she asked hopefully with a big grin on her face as they kissed again.

"Ah… no," he replied, barely above a whisper.

Tiffany threw back her head and feigned hurt.

"Oh, off with another woman, the minute my back is turned!"

"Hey, it was just a dream," Alan shot back. "And besides, I was back with you by sunrise, wasn't I?"

Tiffany laughed.

"I know; I'm only kidding with you."

She shifted and got up on top of him. "Seems a shame to… waste your… effort. Come on, I'll give you something new to dream about!" she teased provocatively, beginning to rock, astride Alan's groin, while her hands continued to stimulate his nipples.

An hour later, they were dressed and heading for the dining hall; both were famished. Sitting down to eat, Alan chewed his lip as he stared off into space.

"Sweetie, what's… on your mind?" Tiffany asked, placing a gentle hand on top of his on the table. "Something… troubling you?"

"No, just thinking about some of the images from my dream… no, not the cheerleader," he chuckled as Tiffany playfully threatened to swat him. "No… I.. ah… I think my subconscious was… sort of… playing with the bits and pieces that we were reviewing last night: trying to make sense of it all."

Tiffany nodded.

"Yes, I've heard of people doing that. I once read a story in *Ripley's Believe it or Not* about a man who was trying to crack a secret code. One night, after a frustrating attempt at solving it, he fell asleep. He had a dream where he saw the first page of the text all solved, and he was able to remember it when he woke up. That actually gave him the key to solving the code."

Alan's brow wrinkled.

"Really? Go on; that's too crazy to be real. Are you serious?"

"Hey, it was in *Ripley's*; if you can't trust them, who can you trust?"

"Huh, good point. So, maybe my brain was trying to work things out regarding Michael?"

"Exactly. So, what do you remember - other than the cheerleader – who *wasn't* me?"

Alan grinned.

"Jealously does not become you, darlin'. Actually, I remember something pointing the way to… Alfonse."

Tiffany slowly shook her head. Men could be so… straightforward, at times!

"Oh, I don't see it being him! Based on all your notes, it seemed that he and Michael were very much in love. Now me, I think… my money is on it being something to do with those Russian antiques. When you're dealing with stolen goods, there are lots of crooked characters and lots of shady deals."

Alan chuckled, having recalled Jim's refusal to believe that too.

"OK, so that makes two of you. Alfonse isn't off my suspect list but he's low down, OK?" he pacified her. "Hmmm – stolen goods a strong motive? That's true too. Ah, but I remember something else – it was Alfonse who made the model plane! That could be a critical clue. I don't know why; I don't know what's important about it, but I just feel it is."

Tiffany nodded thoughtfully.

"Okay, you may be on to something there," she admitted. "But… how can we find out? After all, surely that plane is long gone."

Sadly, Alan was forced to admit that Tiffany might have a good point there, but still there was some hope. Alan – even though he was no longer 'the Doc' – wasn't one to give up easily – especially when murder was involved!

"Huh, let me think… where do we go from here? Michael's things were… boxed up and…" Alan said slowly, trying to remember.

He snapped his fingers and grinned in satisfaction as it came back to him.

"Ah, they were shipped back to his parents! We need to get in touch with them."

"You really think they still have it? They may even be dead for all we know."

Tiffany hardly dared hope that they would have kept it. After all, it was a model plane… probably broken: not a great reminder of their murdered son that they might want to keep hold of.

Alan shrugged.

"Well… it's worth a call – or email."

"Okay, I'll grant you that. Ah, and we should also contact your old cruise line and see if you can find out who it was who came in with that deep glass cut. You think you can get those records?"

"Officially – no. But, I still have some friends at the cruise line; so let me see about calling in some favors."

Tiffany smiled, took a final bite of her eggs and downed the last of her tea. She checked her watch and shook her head regretfully.

"Well, I'm going to have to take off here soon; got the 'Slip and Slide' time with the kids in half and hour, and it takes time to get everything set up."

Alan nodded.

"Oh sure, I understand; you're still a member of the 'working stiff' crowd."

A few minutes later, after a quick peck on the cheek, Tiffany took off, and Alan leisurely finished his breakfast. He kept mulling the different points over in his head; so many suspects, so many small bits of information. Yet, which bits fit together to make the correct picture to solve the case? He rubbed his chin as he sat back in his chair. It was like having a picture puzzle where you didn't have the picture to guide you – and the puzzle pieces were all different shapes and all one color!

Okay, where to begin? He'd been to a reunion party of his old cruise line two years ago. Now, what was that administrator's name? Ah, Bill Wil', that's what they called him – short for Wilkins. Alan chuckled as he remembered that name. Bill Wil's nickname stuck not just because of his surname but because he was a very accommodating fellow who was known for doing anything that was within his power to help anyone; yes, Bill was the very man to contact, Alan knew.

'Bill will take care of it,' was often heard aboard ship.

With that thought making him chuckle happily, Alan left the dining room and returned to his cabin. Pulling out his PDA, he scrolled through his address book until… yes, there it was – Bill's phone number *and* email address. In this case, a phone call was called for. Ah, and he also found the email address for Alfonse that he'd gotten all those years ago. He'd forgotten he had that; Tiffany would be pleased with him! – And that thought pleased Alan greatly! He decided to make the emails first, to give people time to open them. He could call Bill later.

Grabbing his laptop, he headed up to one of the clubs, a WiFi hot spot for the ship and got things set up. He sent an email to Alfonse, even though he wasn't sure the address was still valid, and then he set about doing a search for Michael's parents, to see if they had a phone number listed.

'So, let's see if Google and the online phone book listings can help me,' he said to himself.

Little more than an hour later, Alan had several numbers to try; he'd sent still more emails to some old crew mates and he was now ready to make some phone calls. He checked his email one last time – nothing. Leaving his laptop on, he whipped out his cellphone and checked the display. Yes, he had service!

He made the first call, and was rewarded with word that Bill Wil' was not only still with the company, but he remembered Alan.

"Yes, Alan, it's a pleasure to hear from you. I was sorry to hear about your wife; please accept my sincerest condolences."

"Thank you, Bill; I appreciate that. Look, this is going to sound like something wayyyy out of left field, but I'm trying to get some information on an old case: a patient that was treated for a deep cut."

"Was it a patient you treated while working on one of our ships?"

"Yes, exactly."

"How long ago?"

"About twenty-five years," Alan admitting, woefully, realizing that this was an awful long shot.

"Whoa, talk about ancient history! At least from the corporate standpoint," Bill said with a laugh. "Ah... that's going to take some doing, Alan. Records that old are usually purged. Is it important?"

"Ah... yes; turns out, there could be a potential malpractice suit!" Alan hurriedly bluffed.

After all, he could hardly explain his genuine reason for this request, could he? Bill would think he was nuts, at best. At worst, Alan would unleash a whole tirade of publicity around a murder he had no proof at all for yet. He grew a little hot at Bill's reaction.

"What? After all this time?" Bill said, his voice going up an octave.

Hopefully, instead of being doubtful of Alan's motives, as he feared, Bill was just groaning at the thought of having to trawl back through twenty-five years of records. Alan carried on with his bluff hopefully.

"Oh... you know these lawyers; they're like sharks. All it takes is them 'smelling blood in the water' and they're licking their lips in anticipation of a fat fee. These days, all they have to do is threaten to sue and people run for cover."

Alan relaxed as he heard a chuckle down the phone.

"Yeah-yeah; I know just what you mean. Tell you what - I'll see what I can find out. Can I call you back at this number?"

"Yes, you should be able to; I should get service wherever I am."

"Okay, give me a day or so and I'll see what records I can track down in the archives," Bill promised.

With that, they said their goodbyes and hung up. Alan then tried to the numbers he had for Michael's parents, Edward and Fiona. His efforts proved fruitless: an hour later, and he'd found no trace of them.

Around lunchtime, Alan's stomach was giving him clear signs that he needed to eat. So, he ambled back to the dining room. Tiffany wasn't there, but he did see Nick and Heidi sitting at a medium-sized table. He was about to sit off by himself so he could think about this investigation he was about to embark upon, when they gestured for him to join them.

'Well,' he shrugged, thinking to himself. 'I'll have plenty of thinking time later. Time to be sociable and have some fun!'

"Well, hello, you two," he said happily. "And what are you up to this fine day?"

"Gambling," Nick said, gleefully, like a child indulging in his favorite naughty habit.

"Suntan," Heidi chirped, equally as gleefully.

It seemed the two had reached a very mature decision to give each other some distance to indulge in what they each loved, but which just did not appeal to the other.

'After all, there was quite an age gap between the two. They were bound to like different things,' Alan figured.

Heidi turned her back toward Alan and tugged her snug little top down to reveal a slender, elegant back with no visible tan lines.

"I was up on the *nude* sunbathing deck. Effective, wouldn't you say?"

Alan nodded as she turned back around. He licked his lips, feeling a certain 'movement' under the table. He crossed his legs, grimacing as he bumped his knee. He uncrossed his legs, rubbing his tender knee.

"Quite. Are you sure you didn't… burn?"

She laughed and shook her head.

"Not at all. I get a tan regularly and I make a point of keeping it… even."

She winked, even as the waiter stepped up to take their orders. That let Alan off the hook a little, as he almost felt bound to give Heidi the benefit of his medical experience and warn of all the dangers of excessive tanning. Instead, as the waiter took Heidi's order, Alan turned to her husband.

"And you, Nick - how went your luck at the tables today?" Alan said.

"Very good again; I'm on a real hot streak," Nick said with a grin.

Looking around, he leaned in toward Alan.

"Had a little private game with some high rollers. Oh, did I take them to the cleaners! Now, they're begging for a re-match."

Alan chuckled.

"You going to give it to them?"

Nick sighed as he sat back in his chair.

"Well… I don't know."

He brought his trembling right hand up and rubbed it with his good one.

"I'm… not as young as I used to be."

"None of us are, my friend; none of us are," Alan said, consoling.

"Speak for yourselves, gentlemen!" Heidi snapped, a little tersely, Alan thought. "I intend to fight old age tooth and nail; just like Cher. You don't see her showing her age."

Alan laughed.

"Hey, when you've got her kind of money, you can pay for the surgery needed to maintain that look!"

Heidi looked at Nick.

"Do we still have that kind of money, my love?"

"For at least another few surgeries, my dear," he replied, patting her strong, tanned hand with his rather shaky, pale and blue-veined one.

Alan slowly nodded.

"Well - after that, maybe you'll need to get a painting in the attic."

"Huh?" Heidi said, her face blank – which was quite normal for her.

Nick smirked.

"Ah… I'll explain that later."

He doubted, as all at the table did, that 'The Picture of Dorian Gray' had ever been on Heidi's reading list.

With that, they continued to chat about nothing much in particular. Once lunch was over Alan headed back up to the lounge area, logging on to the WiFi to continue his search for Michael' parents. No sooner had he sat down then he heard two familiar voices. Looking up, he saw 'Jen-Tina' standing over him. Oh dear, he hoped this wasn't going to go badly.

"Ladies - and how are you this fine day?"

Tina gave him a big grin.

"Just fine, Doctor Alan. We haven't seen much of you lately; where you been hiding?"

"Ah… hiding? I haven't been hiding!" Alan quickly dismissed the suggestion which was too close to the truth for comfort. "… just… enjoying the sights and excursions," Alan replied. "You?"

Then he realized he should try and be a little nicer to the ladies; after all, they had only been friendly to him… especially Jenny.

"… Jenny … you're looking very nice today; got a… healthy glow to you."

She smiled at Alan, and gave him a little nod as she slowly turned around in front of him.

"Oh… I've been having a fair share of fun myself, Alan. And, don't worry, I understand about you wanting to… sample all that the ship has to offer. I've been doing the same."

Alan smiled and slowly nodded. He got the message – Jenny wasn't expecting anything more from him than what they had, a bit of pure escapist fun. Either that or she was mightily annoyed at him and trying a double bluff at pretending to brush him off and make him keener to… ah… re-acquaint himself with her. For now, he would take her words at face value and relax, he decided. He had made no promises to Jenny and she had asked none... and Tiffany was taking up and awful lot of his thoughts and attention these days. It wasn't just that she was trying to help him solve Michael's murder he realized, if he was being honest with himself. He knew there was more to it than that... on *both* sides, it seemed.

But Alan's attention was soon distracted from those thoughts by a question from Tina:

"What are you doing inside staring at a computer screen on a day like this?"

Jenny grabbed him by the arm.

"Yeah, come on; come out and have a dip in the pool or soak in the hot tub with us!"

Alan hesitated. Officers and other employees on board ship are not allowed to use the pools, hot tubs, topless deck etc, as many people might believe they do. As an officer, he could sit in uniform with passengers in his deck-chair, but even that would risk him being called up on an offence. So now, on his first cruise after retirement, Alan felt a little uncomfortable about these things, still.

He laughed at himself. He was retired now, so he should stop worrying about that. However, now he wondered even more now just what Jenny was up to. But he was a big boy and he could handle her advances. Nothing was going to happen that he didn't want to happen, so why not go with the flow and have some fun?

"Okay, ladies; sounds like fun. Tell you what; just let me check my mail and I'll zip down to my cabin for a quick change."

"Why bother?" Jenny asked with a wink. "We could go up to the nude sunbathing deck!"

Tina smirked.

"Jenny, didn't you learn your lesson last time?" she said, and then turned to Alan. "You should have seen her after our day on the island. Goodness, I haven't seen her sit that gingerly since she was sixteen. Oh man, did our Dad let her have it then!"

Alan pressed his lips together, trying to keep from laughing. He swallowed hard and cleared his throat a couple times, even as he saw Jenny's face take on a distinctly pinkish hue.

"Really, you don't say? Huh, sounds like she really got... burned. So, let's stick to the regular pool. Give me ten minutes, and I'll meet you there."

Tina nodded.

"Okay, but not a moment more, or we drag you out there!"

With that, they took off, their delightful bikini-clad bottoms bouncing all the way out the door, one in black, the other in pale blue. Alan grinned as he watched them go. Ah, to be young again. Anyway, on to more important business; he opened his email account and checked for messages.

Ah, he had a couple! Opening them, he read through each one quickly. The assistant cruise director from the old ship had written – he had nothing much to say: nothing of importance to Michael's murder. The next two were more of the same. Ah, the musical director had written. It seemed that he remembered Alfonse pulling a double shift, working at the theater the night Michael died.

Alan sat back and chewed his lip. So, it would appear Tiffany was right about Alfonse being innocent. Oh, he hoped she didn't gloat! So, if Alfonse wasn't Michael's killer, which of the other suspects could it be?

Alan shut his computer off, unplugged it and headed back to his cabin. Enough of this for now; the girls were right – he needed a break. He'd link up with Tiffany – in more ways than one (he hoped!) later, and they'd consider their next move.

And so, Alan spent the rest of the afternoon pleasantly swimming in the shady pool. Soaking in the hot tub, and sharing some innocently flirtatious conversation with Jenny and Tina. He smirked to himself when he entered the hot tub. He must have been very attracted to the two lovely ladies, because normally Alan would shun the hot tubs because of the known bacterial counts.

As the ship doctor, one of his duties was always to review the water test results that the nurses would do on the pools, hot tubs, Jacuzzis and other water sources. It was a requirement of the US Public Health and other agencies to monitor the chlorine level and to culture the water (drinking and other) to see what the bacterial levels were and what would grow out. Ice, of course was a no-no. The results from the ice chests and machines were usually fairly high in e.coli bacteria. One needs to scrub down the entire machine regularly to eliminate the growth of bacteria. If this is not done one can spread a great deal of disease. Then, even if one has great ice made, if the scoop that is used to get the ice up is laid on a contaminated surface or handled by someone's contaminated hand, you have a great conduit for more bacteria to be spread to the non suspecting individual.

There were several ships Alan served on that were none too clean, in as much as water was concerned. One drank bottled water and never had ice in a drink on those ships! Hot tubs, if they were not regularly cleaned, highly chlorinated and emptied nightly, had just the right temperature to grow various bacteria. An open wound or sensitive skin could give one a nasty skin infection just from sitting on the edge of the hot tub (where the bacterial counts were usually the highest). Since Alan did not have any open lesions and lounging with these two was so alluring, he submerged blissfully.

He had to smile as he chilled out with a nice iced tea late in the day. Ah, this was such a great idea, taking this cruise. Despite the stress of meeting (and dealing with) all these lovely ladies, and the pressure of this whole murder investigation – he was actually enjoying himself.

Quite abruptly, Alan snapped awake and sat up. He'd dozed off and it was almost sunset. Oh, Tiffany! They were supposed to meet up for dinner! She'd be furious if he was late!

Alan bolted out of the lounge chair, raced to his cabin and jumped into the shower. A quick drag of the old razor across the small part his face that got shaved, a fresh outfit and he managed to get to the dining hall in time to meet up with Tiffany.

Alan just about gasped at the sight of her. Wow, she was in a dazzling red gown that just about put the 'voom' in va-va-va-voom! She grinned at him, enjoying the effect which she was obviously having on him.

"Why, Alan - I do believe you're blushing!"

He swallowed hard, and took a deep breath, attempting to laugh it off.

"Not at all, darlin'; it's your dress, the glow from it is reflecting off my lily-white face."

Tiffany laughed heartily, a genuine, warm laugh, as he offered her his arm. She took it, and in they went to dinner. Once there, they relaxed together, sharing stories of their pasts. They both seemed to appreciate that their relationship was deepening and becoming something which might last beyond this cruise. Tiffany welcomed that, but it scared Alan a little and at first his reminiscences were impersonal, funny stories connected with his past cruises and the people he had met on them. As they both chose the salmon simultaneously, and Tiffany remarked how they were even beginning to think alike, Alan covered his blush with tales of times gone past.

# CHAPTER TWENTY-TWO

*December 11, 2009: Jamaica*

ON ALASKA AND CERTAIN Caribbean cruises, many of the outings for the passengers are on fishing boats to 'catch the big one'. It often happens that the passengers in fact *do* catch a fish or two. Then the question arises as to what to do with it. Do you have it frozen, packed and sent home? This process usually turns an expensive tour into very expensive frozen fish that arrives at your house-hopefully when you do. Sneaking it on the plane as carry on luggage is not generally felt to be a good idea and now with security issues and customs and agricultural issues, not allowed. This also goes for putting it in your suitcase.

One couple was so keen to take the king crab that they had caught in Alaska home that they put it in plastic bags in their suitcases. Unfortunately their suitcases did not follow them to the same airport and a week later the evening gowns and tuxedos had an undoubtedly fishy odor to them when they arrived at their home.

Sending frozen or otherwise prepared water creatures on as extra luggage is really the only way one generally has a chance to get 'it' home. Even then it is 'luck of the draw' and not being well refrigerated the entire way, it carries a strong chance of some spoilage that puts your health at risk.

Tiffany did not seem at all put off the fish on her plate, nor Alan, so he continued, warming to his theme over a glass of wine,

"Generally the ship's doctor doesn't have to deal with this end run issue, but the cleanliness of the catch that is brought on board and sometimes allowed by the Food and Beverage manager to be consumed by the passengers is unfortunately the doctor's issue."

Tiffany nodded.

"Yeah. I guess you get to clean up… literally."

Nodding, Alan continued,

"I can remember one avid fisherman who was so proud of his Halibut catch off the coast of Canada. He brought it back to the ship and got permission to have it served to his friends on board. He even had the proper Canadian Fish and Wildlife papers needed. Unfortunately, this fish was not as healthy as it could have been. This may have been why it got caught in the first place! In any event, I had fifteen of his family and friends to treat for acute gastroenteritis that evening. All had had a piece of his fish."

"Oh dear," Tiffany wryly groaned, and then hurriedly had to explain to the waitress taking their plate.

"No… not *this* fish. This fish was wonderful… This was… *years* ago – right, Alan?"

Then it was Alan's turn to groan. Sometimes, even without meaning to, Tiffany had quite the knack of making him feel old. He just nodded, a slightly pained expression on his face and launched into another anecdote to keep himself from once more contemplating their age gap.

"On many of the cruise ships now, there is a variety of golf offerings to allow passengers to practice their favorite sport while at sea and then take the overpriced golf excursions when they get ashore. I remember Cabo San Lucas, Mexico had golf outings for $1600 a day, plus equipment rental, taxi, tips and the like."

"Wow!… Serious money!" exclaimed Tiffany and Alan relaxed. He had her attention again.

He explained how the Gold Cruise Line where he had been the ship's doctor for many years had its own golf pro that traveled with the guests to the golf outings and tried to train the novice passengers on the ship.

"After one of these outings, Mr. John Philips, a passenger, returned to the ship and presented at the infirmary, in a great deal of pain. It was hard to get the history out of him. I found that he had no allergies to any meds and had a list of his current medicines. Soon after I gave him some Toradol (pain medicine), he told me about two women who were on the course and sliced a shot into the foursome from the ship. Mr Philips related that he collapsed, holding both hands to his crotch.

"One of the women ran down to him, apologizing profusely, explaining that she was a physical therapist and could help ease his pain."

John stoically said, hands still between his legs,

"No, thanks. Just give me a few minutes. I'll be fine,"

Alan then went on to relay how John had told him,

"Taking no heed of my 'no, thank you', this not unattractive woman gently unzipped my pants and started massaging my genitals. Who am I to tell her to stop, especially when my wife was not there? This is confidential; isn't it, Doc? And you don't have to write down all of this down do you?"

The woman carried on, asking,

"Doesn't that feel better?"

He said,

"Well, of course it did, Doc. It took my mind off the pain right away. Unfortunately my thumb is still hurting. Can you please look at it and make sure it is not broke?"

Tiffany roared with laughter.

"Oh, aren't people wonderful, Alan!"

Alan grinned.

"Yeah they sure are… some more than others."

He leaned forward and gently kissed Tiffany's lips, realizing with a start that this was the first time he'd shown affection in a public place to any woman since Jo Ann. The thought startled him and made him go on with his story quickly,

"I assured him that the reason for his sore thumb was confidential and any other activities of the day. After examining his thumb, I found it wasn't fractured, but badly sprained. I gave him a proper splint and medicine and sent him along with a note to his family doctor."

Tiffany couldn't help it. She laughed, despite feeling sympathy for the poor guy.

"And… with all that rubbing… I'm guessing nothing else needed a splint?"

# CHAPTER TWENTY-THREE

*December 12, 2009: Jamaica*

ALAN AND TIFFANY HAD a pleasant dinner that evening, and once their meal had been served so no more wait staff were hovering, they managed to talk about Michael's murder in peace, without interruptions. Alan gave her a rundown of all that he'd learned that day, and she graciously kept the "I told you so's" to a minimum.

"So, what's our next step, Alan?"

"Tomorrow we land in Jamaica. What say we go ashore and just have some fun? Or, do you have to work again with the kids?"

Tiffany nodded.

"I'm afraid so. As you say, I'm a working girl. But what about the case? Surely now that you've got *this* far…"

"Oh, I'm not suggesting we abandon it; just put it aside until we get some answers from the people I've called and written. It's a pretty heavy thing to be thinking about constantly… "

But Tiffany, who had been fortunate enough not to have to ponder the circumstances of Michael's death on and off for the last twenty-five years, had the bit between her teeth now. She thought she saw another way to break into the case and move them forward. 'Them' – the thought made Tiffany smile. She felt very involved with Alan now, and the case.

"What about Michael's parents, any chance of finding them?"

Alan chewed his lip, a little agitated at himself for having drawn a blank there so far.

"Well - I don't know. The search of the internet phone books yielded nothing. So... what else can we try?"

Tiffany sat back and began to play with her hair as she stared off into space.

"Let... me... think."

Silence.

Alan drank some more of his coffee and waved for the waitress to get some more.

Tiffany sat up suddenly, slapping the table and making the crockery clatter.

"Ah, I've got it! The British census!"

Alan's brow wrinkled.

"I... don't follow."

"If his parents are alive, they have to legally be registered in the census - and the records should list their address. There could be a lot of people with the same surname, but at least it'll give you a lead."

Alan slowly nodded.

"Oh... okay, now I get it. Gee, that's sharp, Tiff'; how'd you come up with that?"

She smiled.

"My Dad. He's been working on researching our family genealogy for years. Not so far back, we were all Brits. One way he finds people is to go online to the census for a particular area that he's interested in, and do a name search."

Alan sat back in his chair, and just gazed at her; she was practically glowing, she looked so happy.

"Wow; I've got my own little *Shirley* Holmes!" he exclaimed, chuckling at his little play on words.

Alan loved Sherlock Holmes novels. He had no idea he would one day be writing his own murder mystery novel – much less featuring in it himself as chief investigator!

Tiffany smiled and winked at him.

"Well, in that case, 'Watson', how about toddling off to my... *apartment*... for some... seductive reasoning?" she teased, trying to make her little cabin sound more glamorous than it really was.

Alan laughed.

"Actually, I think in England, they call it a *flat*."

"Whatever they call it, so long as it has a *bed*, that's all I care about!"

Alan grinned and slowly shook his head.

"So bad," he said, barely above a whisper.

"Well, if that's the case, you can... teach me a few lessons!"

With that, laughing, they headed off hand in hand, this time to Tiffany's cabin, and shared yet another night of wild passion. It seemed natural to Alan now and not one image of his late wife popped into his head as he slowly undressed Tiffany and kissed every inch of her body. They eased onto the bed with an easy, unspoken consent and soon found a rhythm with each other, their bodies fitting together perfectly. Again and again they took each other to the heights of ecstasy and satiated their desires.

Several hours later – the timing being something that Alan was *quite* proud of – they again fell asleep in each other's arms, Tiffany's head lying comfortably on Alan's chest and his chin resting on top of her soft, sweet smelling hair.


NEXT MORNING, TIFFANY HAD to dress and leave quickly as soon as they awoke, a little later than she was used to doing; she had a staff meeting to attend, as they were fast approaching port. So, Alan had a quiet breakfast – alone, and was surprised to see Heidi also sitting alone. He hoped that Nick wasn't feeling poorly.

"Hey, Heidi; how you doing this fine day? You look… troubled."

"Oh, hi, Alan. I'm just… thinking."

"Penny for your thoughts," Alan said, trying to sound upbeat.

"Oh… they're not worth that much," she replied, also trying to sound happy – and failing.

"So… what's wrong?"

"It's Nick. He… he didn't come back to the cabin last night, and I'm worried about him!"

Alan's eyebrows shot up. This was potentially serious; the role of a doctor of many years standing came to the forefront of his thoughts. Had Nick had another stroke? Was he lying ill somewhere, undiscovered, on the ship? But he didn't want to take a chance of upsetting Heidi; so he tried to sound calm and collected while he thought what he should do to set about finding the elderly dentist.

"Oh, I'm sure he's fine. After all, we're on a ship; it's not like he can get lost."

Heidi was not in the least bit reassured!

"No, but he could fall overboard! I asked my steward about him, and he didn't know squat."

Alan was growing a little alarmed. The stewards and cabin crew usually knew *everything*… except who commits murder, Alan thought wryly to himself.

"So, when was the last time you saw him?" he tried to be practical and get some information out of Heidi that might help him track down her husband.

"Last night, a little before midnight…" she said in a voice that told of her panic.

Again, Alan tried to be calm and reassuring, which was where his physician training came in very useful.

"Where was that?"

"In the casino; he was playing blackjack."

Alan got to his feet and crossed to her, his arm out to protectively shepherd her. He knew if he was to get any sense out of Heidi and solve the mystery of Nick's whereabouts – for which he was sure there was a perfectly simple explanation – Alan would have to take charge of the situation.

"Okay, let's go talk to the people at the purser's desk. I'm sure they can help."

With that, like a child blindly obeying because that is what was expected of her, Heidi got to her feet and walked with Alan. They headed up to the main deck, and got in the line for the purser's staff. A few minutes later, they were at the counter and explaining the problem. That is, Alan was explaining. Heidi got about two semi-coherent sentences out and then started to blubber.

The staff tried to be consoling, but the more they tried to assure Heidi that everything would be all right, the more she cried. Perhaps Heidi was more astute than he had first thought, mused Alan, concerned; she seemed to realize that Nick being missing on board a ship at sea, in his state of health, for this long, was becoming a serious cause for concern. She was genuinely distraught and Alan began to feel a little ashamed of his early 'trophy wife' assessment of her.

Finally, a lady staffer came around the counter and helped her to sit down. Meanwhile, Alan took the Head Purser, a lady named Charlotte, aside for a quiet word.

"Perhaps you should call one of the medical staff down here; see about giving her a sedative," Alan whispered to her.

Charlotte nodded.

"I agree. What's your take on the situation, Doc… oh, yes, I know you used to be a ship's doctor up until recently. Word travels fast," she smiled in response to Alan's surprised look.

"… So, what - you think hubby is just off bed-hopping for the night, or is this serious?" she asked, according Alan a respect which made him feel flattered, but still helpless.

He had no real clue about what might have happened to delay Nick from his return to the loving arms of Heidi, but he knew it wasn't likely to be another woman. Alan shook his head.

"Oh no, Nick had a stroke recently, and he's in pretty… poor shape. Plus, he's no… raving beauty; I doubt many of the ladies would give him the time of day."

"Well, Heidi obviously did!… And he *is* rich," Charlotte pointed out, trying to avoid the distraught young woman from hearing. "For some women, that's all they care about."

"True," Alan replied. "But… again, I just don't see Nick – ah, Dr. Fillem - being that type."

Charlotte nodded her assent to Alan's point of view as a person to be respected on this.

"All right; I'll alert the security staff and have them institute a Phase One search. We'll also pull the security recordings for last night and see what we can find. Where was he last seen?"

Alan gave her the details that Heidi had imparted to him, and a few minutes later, a nurse arrived. As a crowd was starting to gather, it was decided that they should move the lady out of sight. Taking his arm, Heidi leaned on Alan as they made their way into the back office.

By the time Heidi had been given something to relax her, and the ship's Chief of Security, Stewart Davis, had arrived on the scene. After being given the details, he suggested they head over to the main security office. Alan had to smile; this was like 'old home week' for him, strolling around the 'backstage' area of the ship. Although, he had to admit, the staff area on this particular ship was bigger and more spacious than he remembered from most of his assigned ships. And he wished this trip down memory lane was not being taken in such stressful circumstances.

Along a narrow corridor they went, and reached a snug elevator. From there, they went up to the main deck; Alan estimated that they were not far from the bridge: just a little astern of it.

The security center was very different from the ones that Alan remembered, having been shore-bound for a few years now in the latter part of his medical career. Boy, talk about high-tech! But, in the aftermath of 9/11, every year, new and more technical methods to avoid collections of 2-3000 relatively wealthy passengers from becoming targets of fanatical terrorists were added to the security systems of major cruise liners. Since most of the passengers represented affluent nations, these floating playgrounds served as a poignant reminder to radical and ultra-conservative zealots that some people can have fun and at the same time live responsible lives. Unfortunately that makes them targets.

Consequently, the security systems, security checks made of service personnel, suppliers of goods at major ports and of course the passengers themselves, were all updated regularly to protect the sacrosanct shipping industry. After all, in 2009, a number of spectacular hijackings of supertankers occurred off the Horn of Africa, on the Somalian coast. This ship was equipped with a very extensive video surveillance system headquartered in this fairly large room with several workstations spread throughout it, and the far wall – across from the door – was covered in many tiny video screens.

Video surveillance systems have been on ships (both cruise and cargo) for a long time. The technology has just gotten better. Alan mused that, as crew, one often felt, in fact, one *knew*, that Big Brother was watching. A whole department of full time employees assigned to watching monitors, existed on most cruise ships. There is little that can go unnoticed on a ship's public or crew areas except in the individual cabins. As crew, this was your only refuge. For a passenger, it meant that they could do whatever romantic or kinky thing they wanted out of the eyes of the surveillance people. One could even carry out foul play, just like in a Sherlock Holmes novel. It seemed as though, in this case, someone had.

Heidi sat, her mouth open wide in awe.

"Oh… my… goodness! Can you see everything that goes on on this boat?"

The wonderment at all these screens had distracted her from her distress about her missing husband, much like a child is easily distracted from a scraped knee with a few cuddles.

Stewart grinned as he nodded.

"Just about, ma'am; and, it's a ship."

Heidi slowly scanned the screens.

"Gosh, I'll have to be careful about scratching my butt around here!" she giggled.

Alan grinned. He was glad to see she was feeling a little better. After all, they didn't know that anything bad had happened to Nick. He may turn up any minute now.

"Yes, and picking your nose," he added with a chuckle, patting Heidi's shoulder gently.

Stewart moved to the central workstation and sat down at the controls.

"Okay, let's pull up the records for last night. If you'll watch the center screen, we'll see what we shall see."

As he spoke, the view on the center screen changed from a live feed of the casino to a tape of last night. There were the blackjack tables, and a great many people were seated at them.

Heidi jumped to her feet and pointed.

"Ah, there he is; oh, and there I am. Ugh, look at me in that dress! Could my ass be any bigger?"

"Hmmm... time code is 11:34 pm," Stewart said, ignoring the self-conscious ramblings of what he considered a very shallow young lady. He had a missing passenger on his hands and this was serious. Dr. Fillem needed to be found, whatever he had been up to.

"Okay, let's fast forward and see when he leaves..."

A few buttons were pressed and the image went into 'zip mode', the people beginning to move much faster. By midnight on the tape, Heidi had left, and Nick was still playing. A little before one in the morning, he got up and left with two men.

Stewart froze the tape at about the best possible image of the trio.

"So, Mrs. Fillem, do you recognize those men walking with your husband?"

She nodded.

"Yes, they're the ones that have been playing cards with Nick all week."

"Cards?" Stewart asked, his interest piqued at a possible lead on Dr. Fillem's disappearance.

Alan and Heidi gave him a rundown of the little poker game that Nick had gotten involved in.

"I see. Well, we generally frown on that sort of thing...," Stewart admitted, frowning.

But that wasn't important now. What was important was finding the missing elderly man whom it now appeared may possible have gotten himself into some trouble.

"Okay, let's see where they went after this."

A few more keystrokes, and then the frozen image on the screen was surrounded by a ring of other movies, all from the same time period.

"Okay, these are all the cameras in that area of the ship. So... let's... see."

Alan scanned the movies; so far – nothing. Then Heidi gave a startled cry at seeing her husband on screen again.

"There they are!"

She pointed, wildly gesticulating quite as if she had just found Nick in the flesh, fit and healthy and strolling into the room. Unfortunately, he wasn't. It was a small image of Nick passing across the screen a good few hours ago.

"Hmmm... heading out to the starboard side," Stewart remarked.

"You don't have any cameras out on that open deck that would register any images at night, do you?" Alan asked, hopefully.

Stewart shook his head.

"Sadly, no. It's too dark out there at that time to get any definitive images.

Sometimes we can capture movement, but we do not have the night vision technology that the military does, yet."

"So, it's a dead end?" Heidi asked glumly, desperation once more creeping into her voice.

"Not at all, Mrs. Fillem!" Stewart replied, trying to sound more cheered than he felt. "We'll just switch to the footage from all the cameras on the starboard side that cover the doors. If they went out on deck, they had to come back in at some point."

Even as he spoke, the huge collection of screens again changed. Now there was a whole bank of images playing out before them. The three expectant watchers fell silent as they studied the footage, looking for any sign of the men.

Minutes passed, and still they watched.

"Wait, is that one of them?" Heidi suddenly piped up.

Stewart froze the image and they studied it for a moment.

"Huh, I think… it is, the tall fellow," he said, and then turned to Heidi. "You sure it's the same man your husband was gambling with? Do you know his name?"

Heidi nodded.

"Absolutely! Ah… nope, I can't remember a name. Sorry. Nick wasn't very forthcoming with such things; and, to be honest, I wasn't much interested."

Stewart nodded. 'That figured,' he thought wryly to himself. Out loud he added,

"Okay, so we're on the right track. Let's keep going, and see what else we can find."

He resumed the little 'movie show', and they kept watching. Yet, they never saw Nick or the other man come back in. This was not looking good.

Finally, Stewart rose to his feet, his mastoid (jaw) muscles twitching and clenching in tension. Stewart had been with the British Navy and then with a local constabulary in the North of England. He was not naive, and he had worked with some pretty rough characters in the Navy and in the rough parts of town where the steelworks had once flourished. When he suspected that something more than just making stupid tourists happy and content was at hand, he would demonstrate various clinical signs that Alan had noticed before. It was a signal to Allan that the guy was serious or knew something really was up. He had spasms of the sternocleidomastoid muscles in his neck and had a partial neuropathy of the facial nerve. With his body more worried about its physical well being, he let slip some unguarded words:

"Now, this is damn peculiar! They didn't just jump off the ship in-"

Heidi let out a squeak of surprise.

"Jump!"

Alan stepped closer and patted her on the arm, giving the loose-tongued Chief of Security a glare for his thoughtlessness.

"Now-now, Heidi, stay calm; we don't know what happened to him yet."

A phone rang, and Stewart answered it. He had his emotions and his facial muscles under control again now and he was cool and calm as he efficiently dealt with the call.

"Chief Davis here; talk to me. I see; up on Fiesta Deck, eh? All right, rope the area off and ask the Doc to look it over. He's the closest thing to a pathologist we've got on board. After that, contact the Jamaican authorities and let them know what we've found."

With that, he hung up and sat back down at the controls.

"News, Chief?" Alan said.

He nodded.

"Yes, an overturned deck chair and a… smear of blood have been found on the Fiesta Deck, back near the stern, on the starboard side."

"Blood!" Heidi squealed.

Again Alan glared at the tactless Chief of Security. Weren't these guys trained for these eventualities anymore? Alan recalled all the drills and procedures … not that they'd helped much. The reality was often very different. But at least Alan couldn't recall an incidence of such crass insensibility from the staff of any of the ships where he had served as a doctor. The chief of security on one six star ship Alan served on would have been fired on the spot.

Finally, Stewart appeared to realize his duty to reassure the distraught wife of the missing dentist.

"It isn't much, Mrs. Fillem; so let's not overreact just yet," Stewart said quickly.

He moved back to the console and began typing away, his fingers fairly flying across the keys.

"And… what are you doing now?" asked Alan, peering over Stewart's shoulder, a greater sense of urgency now surrounding their scanning of the images.

"The Fiesta Deck is one deck up from the casino," Stewart explained. "So, I'm pulling up the footage from that deck for the same time. Let's see what we can find out from that."

With that, the screens changed and a series of new images filled them. These proved much easier to study; given the lateness of the hour, and the fact that the Fiesta Deck wasn't exactly a popular spot at that hour, there weren't many people out and about.

Heidi pointed at one screen.

"Hey, I know those two: newlyweds. Now, why are they going out on deck at that hour?"

Alan looked at the screen she was pointing at; a young couple – clearly no more than in their early twenties, were sneaking out one of the doors onto the deck. Alan smirked. Oh yeah, he well remembered doing that with Jo Ann on more than one occasion.

"Ah… they're just going out on deck to… stargaze, Heidi."

Heidi snorted.

"What a waste of time! Sheesh, if I was them, I'd be back in my cabin having… ah, a really good time."

"Look there!" Stewart shouted, pointing at the screen.

Heidi and Alan looked at where he was indicating. Yes, there was the second man – alone. Stewart froze the image, printed out a still and then continued scanning.

An hour later, and they were no closer to an answer; they never saw Nick appear on screen again. Heidi – despite her sedative – was near hysterics by this point.

Alan moved closer to Stewart and whispered,

"I think someone should take her to sickbay. This isn't looking good now, is it? If you let her near the… scene of the… the crime, she'll have a complete meltdown."

Stewart nodded somberly.

"I agree. I'll have the nurse come up and take her down there," he replied, his voice low.

Standing up, he turned to Heidi. "Mrs. Fillem, I'm going to check out the clues up on deck, and then coordinate things with the local authorities."

"Can I come along?"

He shook his head.

"No, I'm afraid not. What with-"

"Why the hell not?" she snapped.

The realization that this was her husband and that it looked pretty serious for him now was getting through the cotton-wool-like protection of the sedative she'd been given.

"Calm yourself, ma'am."

Stewart knew he had to handle this sensitively and he did his best to resume is well-polished manner.

"As I was about to say, with this being an… open investigation, we can't have… civilians gumming up the works. Besides – we don't know what any of this has to do with Dr. Fillem being… missing… right now."

Heidi lowered her head for a moment, sighed, and then looked up at Alan. She trusted him. He was almost like her envoy, she felt.

"Well… could Dr. Mayhew go along? I mean, he *is* a doctor; doesn't that count as an… official?"

Alan and Stewart looked at each other. Alan licked his lips nervously. While he wanted to help, he didn't want to… insert himself where he wasn't wanted, or needed! He'd come on board for a relaxing cruise to get over the death of his beloved wife of many years and already he was involved in investigating one murder; he didn't need a second mystery on his hands – or his mind!

However, the Chief of Security saw that Alan knew what he was doing and that he was adept at handling Heidi. *He* wanted him along, if only for those reasons.

"Well, tell you what, I'll let Alan tag along and… observe."

Alan smiled and nodded weakly. How could he refuse?

"Yes, there you go, Heidi - and then I can give you a full report on what they find, okay?"

She wiped the tears from her pale cheeks, her hands trembling.

"Yes, that would be fine. Thank you, Alan."

A few minutes later, the nurse arrived and she and Heidi left together. At the same time, Stewart and Alan departed for the Fiesta Deck.

As they approached the 'scene of the crime', it was clear that the staff was keeping everyone well back from the area, and that the Jamaican police had arrived with all their regalia. One even had some mini-dreadlocks.

Stewart gestured at Alan.

"Wait here; let me see what they've found out and I'll tell you what I can."

Alan nodded. He knew that it would seem odd to the police if he was to be brought right to the scene of the investigation and Alan had no wish to bring that kind of close scrutiny upon himself.

After years of dealing with officials of various rank, from a variety of third and first world nations, Alan no longer had any intention of being a person of interest. Once, Alan missed a nice tour to some pyramids because the local Egyptian policeman wanted Alan to work for him to solve a local crime. It had very little to do with the ship, other than the fact that the ship was in Port and one of the guests had been drunk and disorderly in the same restaurant where a shooting had occurred three days earlier!

"You got it."

Alan moved to the railing and looked out over the water as Stewart stepped forward to speak with the others. Alan slowly shook his head. What a pity; such a lovely place, with the peace and quiet of the ocean waves lapping up against the sides of the ship, and now it was marred by something like this. While he couldn't hear what was being said, the tone of the conversation and body language of the participants made it clear – something very bad had happened.

Finally, Stewart shook hands with a man – clearly the senior Jamaican police officer (he had the fanciest uniform!), handed him the CCTV still and came back over to Alan. He did not look happy.

"I take it the news is not good," Alan said, very matter-of-factly.

Stewart slowly shook his head.

"No, it's not good at all. Our Doctor found quite a bit of blood here, too much to just be from a small cut or even a gash."

Alan winced.

"You think it's from… Dr. Fillem?"

"Probably. The sickbay reports that no one's come in with any sort of injury, and there's no trail of blood leaving the scene. So…"

Alan sighed.

"So, whoever bled went… over the side."

"Exactly; and as he's the only passenger unaccounted for – QED, it's a virtual certainty that he's dead. Of course, we can't make that official determination yet; the Jamaican authorities want to investigate further."

Alan's brow wrinkled and he rolled his eyes. What doubt could there possibly be? Better to inform Heidi now and let her start coming to terms with what had happened, in his opinion. His verbal reaction showed his exasperation.

"Oh, for goodness sake; what else do they want as proof?"

"Well, as it turns out, they don't really need that picture I gave them."

"Huh, why not?"

"They found a bloody fingerprint at the railing - and it's not Dr. Fillem's."

"How could they know that already?"

"They ran it through the police network using their new Blackberry that some Canadian Police Chief gave them to try and stop some of the drugs heading north. They got a hit almost immediately. It belongs to a man named Kevin Coleman."

"His print's in the system? So, I take it he has a police record?"

"Exactly; he's got one – what's that thing they say in all the police shows? Ah… as long as his arm: embezzlement, theft, money laundering, and so on."

"Is he a passenger?" Alan said.

"I'm having that checked on. But, according to his file, he has a whole string of aliases. The Jamaican police will pull up his file and compare his picture to the one I gave them. I'm not a gambling man, but I'd be willing to bet that they'll match."

"So, what do we tell Heidi?"

"For now… that her husband's missing, feared abducted, and we're looking for a suspect. Until we catch this Coleman fellow and question him, we can't say for sure what's happened to Dr. Fillem."

Alan nodded.

"I understand; official legalities must be followed. Very well, I won't tell her anything more."

Alan and Stewart shook hands, and parted. It was a long slow trudge back down the stairs – Alan did not want to take the elevator this time. He wanted some time to compose himself and think of what he was to say to Heidi. Walking along, he chewed his lip, deep in thought. For some reason, what Stewart had said resonated in his mind. Yet, what was it? Embezzlement… theft. They were common motives for murder… yet there was more… and the wheels were turning in his brain…

An image formed in his mind, an image of a small piece of clear plastic. Yet, it wasn't clear; a series of fine lines were sort of etched across it.

And then it came to him – a fingerprint! Yes, he remembered now; on the window of that stupid model plane he'd found all smashed up in Michael's cabin had been a fingerprint. At the time, it wasn't considered important, because it was most probably Michael's print. So, as it was his model, what could be more expected than to find his print on it?

Yet, as Alan had now also remembered that Alfonse had made the model and hung it high up at the ceiling as a surprise for his lover – why would Michael's print even be on it? It wasn't like he had to clean his own cabin with the cruise liner's daily maid service, nor that Michael was at all agile enough to be able to reach the plane: after all getting into shape was one of the things that Alan had been after Michael about for quite some time. The plane hung up far too high to be easily reached. This was all starting to sound very significant. Alan decided right then and there – he *had* to find Michael's parents and get some answers!

"HOW IN THE WORLD could a fingerprint on a model plane be important?" Tiffany asked as Alan caught up with her in the corridor and filled her in on the morning's awful events, as well as his further thoughts on the twenty-five year old murder.

"Michael's fingerprint was found on *one* window of the plane – *in glue*," Alan said, as they enjoyed a private conversation in a little recess off the main corridor. "I remember quite a few details now. The plane was dusted for prints – along with the remnants of the tiffany lamp - and nothing special was found. There were just a few old smudged prints, and that one pristine, crystal-clear thumb print of Michael's."

Tiffany gave a small tug on her hair as they emerged from the recess and decided to head to lunch.

"Oh, and because Alfonse put it together, you feel Michael's fingerprint being in glue is significant? Couldn't he have just broken the plane and had to fix it?" Tiffany reasoned, level-headed as ever.

"Sure," Alan conceded. "But he could equally well have popped the window off and… hid something inside, and glued the window back. It's worth checking on, at least, don't you think?"

Tiffany nodded.

"So, have you done a search for Michael's parents yet?"

"No, I was… helping with Heidi most of the morning. She… did not do well."

"Took the news pretty hard?"

"Yeah. I tried to be… gentle – even upbeat and hopeful, but…"

"She saw right through that, right?" Tiffany asked, comfortingly rubbing Alan's arm.

"Yeah."

Tiffany shook her head, giving a wry chuckle.

"I'm not surprised, Alan; you *do* sort of wear your heart on your sleeve."

"I do not!" Alan said, very indignant.

Tiffany laughed.

"Oh, come on, sweetie, you do! I've only known you a few days, and I can always tell how you're feeling; it's written right across your face."

Alan brought his hand up and rubbed it up and down his cheek, self-consciously.

"Yeah, Jo Ann always said the same thing. I just… didn't think it was so obvious to others. Huh, I guess that's why I've never been good at poker."

Curiously, he realized he felt totally comfortable talking with Tiffany about Jo Ann.

"No good at bluffing, eh?" she remarked, sympathetically.

"Nope. So, I'll stick to blackjack. Now, tell me – any news on the investigation?"

Tiffany gave him a blank look for a moment, and then blinked her eyes.

"Oh, the current one! Sorry, I thought you were talking about *ours*."

Alan laughed in spite of the tragic circumstances.

"It is strange, isn't it, *two* deaths to be investigated?"

"Yeah. Well, the scuttlebutt 'below decks' is that they found that Coleman guy onshore – he was trying to catch a plane off the island. He'd been on board as some guy named… Stevens or something. Anyway, he was using yet another fake name at the airport. But, as his picture was plastered all over the island, the staff recognized him right away."

"Wow! Anything else…?"

"The Doc confirmed that the blood on the deck and railing was the same type as Dr. Fillem's."

Alan sat back and slowly nodded, swallowing hard.

"Huh, so… Nick's blood, Coleman's fingerprint *in* Nicks' blood, and a picture of him near the scene. Sounds like a pretty solid case."

"Yeah, but don't say anything to anyone yet. This is all just… talk among the crew! You know what that can be like. Rumors travel like wildfire, whether they're true or not. Cruises are great for passengers, but for the crew, sometimes gossip is the only thing that brightens up a boring day of polishing silverware, cooking soup or cleaning up after slobs."

"Oh sure, I understand," Alan said.

He mimed pulling a zipper across his lips.

"It goes in the vault. What about Heidi?"

After he had seen her safely into the hands of the medical staff that were going to give her some more sedation, Alan had not seen Heidi since. Of course, that was the last time she had emerged from her cabin with the appropriate sedation given.

After Heidi awoke from the diazepam sleep, she decided to leave the ship - understandably.

Tiffany explained later,

"She's going ashore and staying there until the case is resolved. It seems she really did love Nick!"

"You sound surprised."

Tiffany shrugged.

"Eh… you know how it is; on a ship you see a lot of those… kinds of marriages that are *so* obviously a complete sham. To see such genuine affection is very touching."

Alan lifted his wine glass.

"To Nick and Heidi!"

Tiffany did likewise.

"And to genuine affection!"

They clinked glasses and drank, sparkling eyes locked together.

Alan lowered his gaze for a moment, and then looked up at Tiffany – rather sheepishly.

"May we… find that as well," he said softly.

He didn't know when it happened – his… moving on… to find happiness elsewhere – but it seemed to have happened. He realized all at once that Tiffany made him very happy – very happy indeed!

Her gentle hand with its delicate fingers and neatly manicured nails edged across the table to gently caress his. She had longed for him to open up to her emotionally as well as physically, and now he had. She smiled at him – and Alan wasn't sure, but the room seemed to brighten just a bit.

"I hope we do too!" Tiffany said earnestly, squeezing Alan's hand.

Walking back to his cabin with Tiffany, though, Alan became sadly aware of there age gap and how many May to December relationships he had seen in all his years. He recalled one such relationship from his many years as ship's doctor. Leon Catzberger.

Leon was only sixty-nine but appeared to be in his eighties at least. His redeeming feature was his beautiful white hair. Reminiscing, he began to tell Tiffany about him on the way back to the cabin, although he caught himself wondering if really he was shooting himself in the foot by mentioning Catzberger and potentially reminding Tiffany how old Alan himself was.

"Alan, Alan… just relax, will you?... I don't think you're old and my memory hasn't failed yet so I can still recall your more than ample… abilities… Besides, isn't that what you're about to go and prove to me again?" she teased mischievously. As they were alone in the elevator, Tiffany took the opportunity to reach out and cup Alan's crotch, kneading it lightly in her warm, delicate hand as she moved in for a deep kiss. Her eyes sparkled up at Alan as they parted slightly but she left her hand right where it was.

"Well… now I come to think of it, Catzberger might have been bent over a cane in public… but… well, his girl did seem to have a smile permanently on her face. Perhaps it wasn't *all* the money he was fond of splashing around."

Tiffany's fingers gripped Alan's privates a little more. Her eyebrow arched. He got her point, but he carried on the teasing, even though his heart was now warmed with her reassurances.

"No tips were allowed on the ships but he didn't care. He was pretty generous. What have I got to give a beautiful young woman?"

Tiffany's eyes narrowed and she frowned, squeezing a little harder. Alan gave a small wince but he continued, laughing now:

"I guess at least I don't wear Pampers."

"Pampers!" Tiffany exclaimed, in utter surprise and mirth, not having expected that at all.

The doors of the elevators opened and they stepped out, laughing.

"Oh yes. He turned quite a few chairs a new shade of brown on his cruise. Urinary and fecal incontinence. If it wasn't that, it was constipation. I saw quite a lot of Mr. Catzberger on his particular cruise…"

Tiffany was biting her lip now, trying not to laugh now as it probably wasn't funny for the poor guy. Although Alan was doing his best to make the whole situation to sound as hysterical as possible!

"Have you seen the TV program 'Little Britain in the USA'?"

Tiffany shook her head, unsure where he was going with this as Alan let them into his cabin.

"There's a guy on there - pretends he needs a wheelchair. But when his caregiver goes off, he's like an athlete, climbing trees, jumping off dive boards. Catzberger was pretty much like that. I never did quite work out how much he really needed the wheelchair and cane he seemed so attached to! But he did take a quantity of pain meds."

Tiffany pulled Alan into the cabin, pushing him back to the door, closing it and smothering his mouth in kisses.

"Enough about Catzberger..."

Teasing still, Alan grinned against her mouth and jokingly went on with his tale, regardless of how keen she now obviously was for different oral activity.

"He was a political fundraiser..."

Tiffany struggled with Alan's belt, getting that and his pants open.

"Right... but now I'm more interested in what *you* can raise!"

Alan gave in, showing quite naturally that although he may think of himself as a more than middle-aged man at times, his body could still do what it needed to, and right now it needed to satisfy Tiffany; which he did – many times – that night. Eventually, feeling young and at peace with himself again, sleep came to Alan. In his dreams, he was young once more the young, fit ship's Doc that he had been in the past...

# CHAPTER TWENTY-FOUR

*July 19, 1984: The Bahamas*

AT 0630 HRS EVERY morning of the Doc's career, his alarm rang. He'd soon got tired of the buzzer and similar alarm clocks, so he purchased a portable, programmable, alarm clock that has a variety of sounds. His favorite 'wake up call' was the 'babbling stream'. Previously it had been the 'north woods' with chirping birds and frog. The only problem was that in rural Indiana, it was too close to the real outside. It was nice because of the usual fact that the windows were closed to make the air conditioning work -but not the most practical method of getting you to wake up. Therefore, the Doc had switched to the babbling stream. After that, he'd launch into his usual routine of a few stretches to wake up his joints and remind them that they had to function in a reasonable fashion for another twenty-four hours.

After a few years of sports and other physical endeavors and accidents having left his body in less than pristine condition, the Doc needed the stretches. Although he hated to admit it, there were times when his neck went into spasm as did his lower back. It was not unusual to wake up with a sore back, but a few stretches and he was usually good to go. Sometimes, though, he would have to move cautiously due to the discomfort. Even so, he still moved and could not really understand some patients who would stay in bed all day because of their back discomfort!

His knees had been through a lot and told him so on a regular basis. Barreling down hills on a pair of fiberglass slats, ski mountaineering, downhill and cross country skiing, ski jumping, mountain climbing, rappelling, etc occupied a good deal of his extracurricular time a number of years ago.

A catalog of simple and complex accidents had left his knees definitely needing a morning stretch, but at some point, the Doc knew, they'd need to be replaced.

Then of course there was his wrist that limits the manner in which he could do some of his stretches. He was a victim to being nice to 'the little old lady' in the airport who asked if Alan could help lift her suitcase off the turnabout. Naturally he agreed unbeknownst was the fact that the suitcase weighed over 290 pounds… on a moving belt… at less than ideal height. The torn triquetrial lunate ligaments in his wrist never fully healed, but years of therapy and NSAIDS brought it under control even though it still needed protection when lifting heavy objects or doing certain stretches.

Rearranging the less than spacious doctor's cabin was necessary if any meaningful stretches were going to be performed. Fortunately on this ship, there were some movable parts to the furnishings, and a central core was created for visual and practical purposes.

Alan always followed his stretches with twenty minutes of meditation, which helped to make up for never getting quite enough sleep. He remembered when he first learned to meditate in medical school; the teacher specifically said that even though the rest was profound, it was not intended to replace proper amounts of sleep. Not that the 'words of wisdom' were not understood, but medical school, internship, residency, and years of practice taught Alan to live on much less sleep that he recommended to all of his patients. So stretching and meditation became an essential part of is morning routine.

There just never seemed to be enough hours in the day/night to accomplish all the things he wanted to do, or felt that he had to do. When he could, and he wasn't interrupted by medical calls, he liked to spend his free moments reading or watching movies on DVD. Usually he then became either engrossed in the movie or mesmerized by the moving images in front of his tired body and watched them until far later into the night than he should, thus not leaving sufficient time to sleep. Thus, for the Doc, his meditation was more often than not used to fill that sleep deficit rather than growing his spiritual being to higher planes of understanding about the ethereal self.

His bed was, of course, the most comfortable place to do the meditation, but the sounds from the neighboring cabin were often a bit distracting for a deep meditation. Mind you, there were sometimes very interesting noises that emanated from that cabin. If it was sex, it was quite unlike any sex Alan had ever had or would wish to have!

His other choice was meditating on the couch, but that meant the very real possibility of having one of the orchids or other plants on the sill fall on his head when the sea was rough. The air conditioner also blew a fair stream of air in that direction, making dressing first a necessary event, so usually Alan made what he could of meditation on the bed, blocking out any untoward noises as much as he could.

Often, the peace of the Doc's daily meditations was disturbed by calls from staff 'just wondering' if they could see him just a little earlier than his regular surgery hours. The office hours for passengers is usually listed on the door and published in the daily bulletins. There are traditionally a couple of hours in the morning and a couple in the afternoon. Then there are usually another couple of hours added to that for crew. Add to this being on call 24/7 and you have the usual clinical schedule for the doctors on board a ship. Add to this people stopping you in the corridors and wanting free advice and treatment for usual and sometimes unusual disorders.

The Doctor is generally required to be in attendance for the Captain's meeting, safety meetings, training sessions for crew (i.e. first aid, stretcher team, etc), Public Health inspections, crew welfare, crew cabin inspections, department meetings, budget meetings, fire, man overboard, emergency drills, etc. In addition to these 'try to stay awake meetings', the Doctor is also required to be in attendance at various social functions such as dinners, presentations, VIP parties, frequent cruisers presentations, etc and one can see how one's 'free time' is rapidly used up.

So when passengers state,

"Oh I see you only work one hour a day."

The hairs on the back of the Doc's neck really started to prickle. They also forget about the multiple times one is called at night for seeing crew or passengers; sometimes for serious things and sometimes for things that could easily wait until the next day.

Usually people called on the Doc outside of surgery hours because the staff members in question had some embarrassing ailment they didn't want anyone else to know about. Figuring that it was better that they did that than not seeking medical attention at all, the Doc usually saw them. As an example, he was perfectly polite when accosted by one rather nervous looking senior officer.

"Doctore I ask you to make me a special appointment to see the dermatologista in the next port."

The Doc was a little surprised at the apparent amount of anxiety but he quickly took the concerned senior officer to the sick bay where he could examine him and talk to him in confidence. There, he got the full story.

"Doctore I found a new spot last night and decided to use the medicine that I was given at the port in Ireland; that doctor knew what he was talking about because he had seen a lot of cases. He gave me some medicine..."

"Uh-huh…hmm-mm," Alan mumbled as he made his examination. "So… you knew about this… when you came on board?"

The officer didn't seem to feel at all badly that he had boarded the ship with a severe case of scabies.

"Yes I did forget to tell you about that visit, but it got better after he saw it and I didn't think there was going to have to be anything else."

The Doc sighed. Skin rashes were a common occurrence on board a ship. You get passengers that bake in the sun and find themselves attacked by an assortment of insects and marine animals and plants. You are living in an air conditioned environment that has a tendency to dry out the skin and consequently also cause rashes. Then there is the crew. They scrub and shine everything on the ship all day. That requires caustic solutions and exposure a variety of liquids on a regular basis. Special creams and gloves are of course provided on the better cruise lines, but getting crew to use them is another story.

Then there are the crew's adventures on shore - with the sea, lakes, and ladies of the night. Even sitting in taxis or public toilet seats can be hazardous to your health—or at least the face saving rationale given to fellow crew members and passengers when the rash can not be covered with the uniform. However, with this officer, this was obviously scabies, so to avoid an outbreak on the entire ship certain quarantine procedures would be needed. Alan quickly had those put in place as the afflicted crew member went to his cabin, hopefully mindful of the further treatment that he needed to see through until the case was cured this time. This also required a whole series of calls to the head of housekeeping, staff captain (because he was losing one of his officers for a few days), and a multitude of forms.

The Doc then hurried on to get breakfast. As he was a little later than usual, he realized that Christina was more likely to be around. The thought made him smile. He then realized that at this time, Christina's parents were more likely to be around to take care of Jesus. The thought made him smile even more and there was quite the spring in his step as he hurried along to the dining room they usually favored.

Christina was there and he was most gratified that she seemed happy to see him.

"Alan!" She squealed, hugging him around the neck and planting a warm kiss on his mouth.

Blushing, looking around self-consciously, Alan gave her an embarrassed smile.

"Ah… yeah… we uh… we need to be careful… with the affection…" he pointed out, knowing how staff-passenger relationships were totally frowned upon.

Thankfully, it didn't dampen Christina's enthusiasm.

"Awww Alaaannn… not to worry, dear one… we shall have breakfast together?"

Alan smiled and nodded.

"That's… what I was hoping. I missed you last night."

Christina gave Jesus an adoring smile.

"I missed you too… Jesus is happy to be back on board now. He understands where we are again… and with Grandma and Grandpa…"

'Thank God for that!' Alan thought to himself. He was more than a little relieved when, with an understanding nod, Jesus' grandfather put an arm around the waist of his wife, who was carrying Jesus, and nodded toward a corner table.

"The boy will like it better," he said simply, but Alan could have sworn it was a generous attempt to give Alan some privacy with Christina. Perhaps he too knew how to get through to the older woman in his life. Like with Christina, for her, what Jesus wanted was what Jesus got.

So, having collected their choice of breakfast of fruit, yogurt and toast with honey, Alan happily escorted Christina to a table a little distance from the rest of her family.

"The bears are going into hibernation again," he joked in Christina's ear, giving a little nod across the room to a woman who must have weighed no less than five hundred pounds. Her girth was such that her husband had to sit opposite her, not beside her at the table, as her ample buttocks together covered almost the whole of three seats. In front of her was a plate piled high with bacon, wieners, eggs and sweet breads, while her rather more slender husband had opted for fresh figs, honey and yogurt, sprinkled with nuts.

Christina giggled at Alan's little quip.

"You are here breakfasting with me and you think of bears?"

"No – I'm here breakfasting with you and I think of sex… but…"

Again Alan chuckled as he nodded toward the mismatched couple.

"Sex between those two?... Wow!"

"Hey that reminds me of a doctor I once new. Young guy…"

Christina's eyes raised practically into her bangs.

"No, not the sex, silly girl! Jees, Christina!... The wieners…"

Again Christina's face registered alarm. Alan sighed. He'd meant to share a story with her by way of getting to delay her dragging him off to bed long enough to allow him to eat. It felt like he'd missed too many meals lately with emergency calls that didn't turn out to be emergencies.

"No, listen… there was a new young MD starting his residency. He wanted to make a bit more money, so he was assigned to the ship medical clinic on a busy holiday weekend to assist me as the senior doctor. One of the ship's dancers who routinely got venereal diseases came in for an exam, complaining of vaginal itching. She was a very beautiful girl...oh not as beautiful as you of course... but no dog either. She had no modesty either, stripping off her clothes, shunning the modesty sheet until the nurse insisted, and hopped up into the stirrups.

The poor young guy was definitely embarrassed when performing pelvic exams so he had unconsciously formed a habit of whistling softly to cover his embarrassment. I suppose it could have been a useful technique... kinda 'whistle a happy tune'... now what movie was that in? Anyway, the young dancer he was performing this exam on suddenly burst out laughing and further embarrassed the junior Doctor.

I'm afraid he forgot all professional decorum and snapped,

"Just what is so funny!"

She replied, "I'm sorry doctor, but the song you were whistling was 'I wish I was an Oscar Meyer Weiner'!"

Laughing heartily, Christina grabbed up Alan's hand, tugging him to his feet and before he could complain, finish his breakfast, or even worry about what his superiors might think, she had pulled him with her out of the dining room and they made their way back down to Alan's cabin until they were later disturbed by something of an emergency call.

At two o'clock in the morning, one never wants to hear the words "short of breath". When it is the last night of a cruise, one usually thinks any visit is either very serious or someone wanting to document something that they can get a free cruise out of the company for.

This time, the Doc found that the rather large woman he had seen at dinner was indeed medically short of breath. While getting her medically sorted out, the following history was revealed by her nurse sister, recently widowed, who was accompanying the lady and her husband on the cruise.

"Evangeline was a nurse too but had to give it up because it was too hard to get around, ya know. She done gone to the hospital two days before wees got on the ship and were admitted there for the short breathing thing. They done a number of tests but ain't got no diagnosis which pissed my sister off so she just signed out of the hospital against their advice."

The Doc groaned.

'And brought her medical problems with her for me to sort out in the middle of the night. How kind!' he ungraciously thought to himself. However, the sister's words pretty much confirmed that.

"She done that the morning that we got on the ship. This being her first cruise and all, she weren't about to miss it. She smokes over three packs of cigarettes a day ya know. I'se been telling her she aint gonna stay well if she do that. She been some short of breath during the week, but with da booze, she didn't really realize it. Booze bill got a bit big when she done seen it today so she stopped ordering dem drinks. Me thinks that that is da reason that she got the problem now, and you'se know I is a nurse."

The Doc nodded, tight lipped as he continued his examination.

"Well, you're correct in one respect," he said, trying to keep the sarcasm from his voice. "The alcohol probably had covered over some of the symptoms of her pneumonia."

The sister, in her position as former nurse, had the good grace to look a little embarrassed. The lady was appropriately treated with nebulization and oxygen and antibiotics and advised not to drink until she was finished with the antibiotics.

'At that will give her a few days of time off for the liver,' Alan thought.

It never ceased to amaze him how blasé people could be about their own health. He saw it all the time on cruise ships: people eating and drinking to epic proportions; people self-medicating rather than paying even small fees to see the Doc – that could include even very rich people too.

The 'problem' of self-medication wasn't just on behalf of themselves, either. The Doc recalled many such incidents where parents refused to have their child seen if it wasn't free – although they probably lived in countries with no free medical care too. Perhaps there was so much on offer on cruises such as the surfeit of food and the free-flowing drink that people grew to resent paying for anything.

The Doc recalled one woman who came to the clinic inquiring,

"How much does it cost to get my kid seen?"

The nurse responded,

"That will be fifty dollars to see the doctor plus the cost of any medicine."

The woman came back with,

"Oy vey! Just to see the doctor? All I wants is to have him look at her ears and get some pills."

The nurse reiterated the company policy about having to have the physician see the passenger before medications could be handed out.

Again this less than gentle voice which the Doc was listening to quite easily from three rooms away said,

"Well I ain't paying that to have her ears looked at; she'll just have to wait. Guess I'll be back if she really starts screaming."

"Guess so," the nurse muttered under her breath and then later that evening the Doc noted the woman shopping for clothes for herself in the boutique. Great parent!

It was a very philosophical but sleepy Doc who crawled back into bed and snuggled to Christina's back, resting his chin on her shoulder, arm around her to cup her luscious breasts. Not for the first time, he was grateful for her beautiful body and thankful that while perhaps not beautiful, his own body at least functioned well and did all that it needed to.

# CHAPTER TWENTY-FIVE

*December 13, 2009: Jamaica*

CRUISE SHIPS TEND TO be like little floating cities; after all, many are bigger than some typical American and Canadian towns. So, people are always talking, and news is always getting around. The next morning, the ship was delayed a few hours in leaving port. The official line was that there was a patch of bad weather off to the west and the cruise line was concerned for the safety of the passengers. While quite a noble sentiment, it was also a complete sham, and just about anyone over the age of ten knew it!

Alan didn't say a word to anyone about Heidi's abrupt departure, or where Dr. Fillem had gone. Here again, the official line was that his health was declining, and he and his wife had elected to go ashore and fly home. Most passengers are familiar with that happening if they have cruised a lot. Unfortunately, that load of… bull only lasted until about noon.

By the time Alan and Tiffany were sitting down to lunch, the *only* subject of conversation in the dining hall was the murder of Dr. Fillem, and the *arrest* of his wife as an accomplice!

'Jen-Tina' just about bolted over to the private table Alan and Tiffany were sitting at to share their views on this juicy bit of gossip.

"Did you hear… did you hear?" Tina squeaked excitedly. "Murder… an actual murder… right here on the ship! Some bitch and her gigolo tossed her husband overboard."

Tiffany sighed, and Alan rolled his eyes – even as he got a rather big eyeful of Jenny's cleavage; she was in her 'nearly-nothing' bikini, and bending *way* over the table next to Tiffany.

"Ah, Tina, that isn't quite the case," Alan said, rather irritated.

He had grown fond of Heidi in just the short time they had known each other and he hated that she was being suspected of anything so heinous, even though she wasn't on board to be offended by it now and her presentation to the world was less than the demure debutante.

Jenny's brow wrinkled.

"Oh? What, you know different?" she asked as she plopped herself down uninvited into the seat opposite Alan.

Alan nodded.

"Yes, I do, as a matter of fact. I happen to have… ah, spoken to a few people who are 'in the know', as they say."

"And-and… come on, what's the scoop?" Tina prompted, her voice full of urgency.

"Well…" Alan said slowly.

He looked at Tiffany, unsure of how much he should say, and she just shrugged. He shrugged back, and then proceeded to give them just a few details on the matter – a sort of 'Cliff Notes' version of the crime and clues. After all, he didn't want to say too much; the ship's rumor mill was already on overdrive. No need to add to it!

When he was done, the girls 'oohing' and 'ahing' through most of it, they bounced off to find a table of their own, or perhaps to find some people with whom to share their 'insider' information. Tiffany turned to watch them go.

She snorted derisorily (and a little jealously, Alan thought) and turned back to face Alan.

"God, if that Jenny wiggles much harder, she's going to shake something loose! Are they for real?"

Alan laughed.

"Isn't that a relative term? I mean, they're real American girls; so, what's that make them?"

"Self-centered airheads with the attention span of a four-year-old?" Tiffany responded rapidly, an eyebrow raised and a slight smile on her face.

"Hey, you're an American girl!"

Tiffany smirked.

"*Au contraire*, my friend; I'm Canadian."

Alan let out a little squeak of surprise.

"Ah! I had no idea."

"Well, the subject's never come up for discussion. I guess we had… *other* things on our minds."

"True," Alan said, grinning, and then scanned the room. "You know, it seems to me that this ship needs something to distract these people.

Otherwise, Nick's... passing - is going to be the one and only subject of conversation until we get back to port!"

Tiffany slowly nodded.

"Yeah, I think you're right. Well, I guess that would be my job, then, eh? What can we do to... entertain them?"

Alan gave a dirty laugh, and Tiffany swatted his arm.

"Behave!... I'm serious – and no 'Alan and Tiffany Home Movie Show' quips!"

"Well, I think you hit the nail right on the head there, Tiff'. I can't help but think of a line from an old movie I saw once: 'Hey, kids, let's put on a show!' Maybe the entertainers could whip something up to get people's minds on other things.

"Well, as it happens, like most cruise ships, you know that we employ some great entertainers: everything from the gala Las Vegas-style girlie show to a sedate pianist in one of the bars, some clowns for the kids, and everything in between," Tiffany replied.

"Excellent! I knew that, as a general rule, a larger ship like this would have the space and resources to put on the big shows. I wasn't sure, but it looked to me as if there were some bits and pieces of some Broadway shows or other musical extravaganzas in the show I saw the first night of the cruise."

Tiffany nodded.

"We've definitely got some people that have worked on Broadway, eh. It's always a challenge, and I'm not just talking about working with the Prima Donna personalities; on a moving stage, to accommodate some of the particulars that are needed in these large stage shows."

Alan grinned.

"Oh yeah, I *well* remember that! From my point of view, as a doctor, the issue is always more urgent and iffy when the show requires the performer to walk down small runways, fold themselves into strange positions and wield an assortment of frou-frou items on the stage. Add to these the non-ergonomic encounters a moving stage offers, and you have the formula for potential ankle injuries, back strains, shoulder dislocations, cuts, and contusions!"

Tiffany nodded, chuckling.

"Spoken like a true doctor! But you're right; in some of the performances, the acrobatics performed would be considered incredible on *any* stage. Consider also the positions achieved by the performers, add a moving stage, and you really have something the audience can applaud for; and something the doctor cringes at."

"And, let me guess, I imagine the entertainers you have here are not the most sober group?" Alan said.

Tiffany laughed at how astute Alan was.

"Right… unfortunately… so they have yet another added risk factor. The dancers and singers are often the ones that sleep a great deal of the day, go to their rehearsals in the afternoon, perform in the evening, and party 'til the wee hours of the morning. They are also the ones that often have their bar bills cut off for exceeding the dollar limit more often than other crew members!"

"Ah, I well remember that too," Alan said. "Often, I got called in to alcohol test some of the entertainers, and it never surprised me to find limits well over the 'very drunk' level on the breathalyzer test. Of course, other drugs were forbidden on all the cruise ships I served on, but they occasionally got used. I remember losing one of our best Calypso Bands from Grenada once, when they were found using various illicit drugs."

Tiffany grinned.

"Well, not much has changed in that department. Add to that the in-fighting that often goes on between a group of Prima Donnas, and other ego-centered individuals, and you've got a recipe for disaster. Fortunately, we've got a Theatre Director who keeps such things under control. I'll get with her and the Captain, and see about arranging some extra shows for today," she promised.

With that, they finished eating and headed out to her office. Alan sat down and looked around. Ah, just like his old offices on the ships he served – a regular cornucopia of little mementoes from previous cruises. Tiffany got on the phone and made some calls.

It soon became clear that one of their entertainers was… 'out of commission'. It seems the girl had over-indulged at dinner the night before, and then spent all night and day vomiting the expensive drinks.

Alan slowly nodded. Oh yeah, there had been plenty such women on some of the ships on which he served. The binge eating and forced vomiting that went on with some of the entertainers who wanted to look inhumanly thin, and the lack of sustainable nutrition often took its toll on their ability just to stand up, never mind perform or eat normally! There had been one young lady with bulimia who maintained her weight at ninety-three pounds. Now, the fact that she was nearly six feet tall meant she was a virtual living skeleton! When her electrolytes went out of balance in a big way, Alan had had to refer her to a shore-side hospital for medical and psychological treatment.

Tiffany hung up the phone and turned to Alan with a big smile.

"Okay, we're all set. They're going to announce a special show in the theatre, some mimes are going to do a sort of roving show across the Fiesta Deck and the clowns are going to come out and do something for the kids, right by the main pool."

Alan smiled.

"That's great! That should help lift the mood a lot."

"Yeah, but we've got two dancers down."

Alan's brow wrinkled.

"Two? I only heard about the one. What-"

Tiffany's face became about seven shades of red as she tugged on her hair, hemmed and hawed, and was finally able to speak.

"Ah… it seems we've got a slight outbreak of a… sexually transmitted disease."

"Oh man, what happened?" Alan said. "Or can't you tell me?"

Tiffany looked around to make sure they weren't going to be overheard, but she trusted Alan.

"No, it's okay. After all, you are a doctor. Seems one of the female dancers has slept with nearly every one of the engine crew and given them all a good case of herpes. She's down in the clinic right now, complaining that her thighs are sore."

Alan slowly nodded.

"Ah, and let me guess, she has to do some complicated splits in her dance routine?"

"You got it. Whenever she gets in those positions, she screams in pain. So, our doctor is saying she needs to change her dance routine, until her herpes has resolved sufficiently."

"I agree," Alan said, as if he was still a practicing doctor.

The habit was hard to break.

"I suspect that some of the tenderness in her legs is also due to the… ah, nightly extracurricular activities she's participated in."

"That's about the size of it," agreed Tiffany. "Oh, and we've also got several comedians on board. So, they're going to spread out across the ship and do some of their stand-up routines."

"Great, sounds like you've really got things covered. So, can you help me with more of the investigation into Michael's murder today?"

Tiffany nodded.

"You got it! Come on, just let me check on a couple of things with the staff, and we can… what, go down to your cabin?"

Alan chewed his lip. As much as he enjoyed going down to his cabin with her, he thought that may not be the most productive way to advance their investigation.

"Hmmm… well, if we want to continue looking for his parents, we need to get online. Let's go to one of the hot spots."

"Sounds like a plan!" Tiffany agreed happily.

She really did want to help.

With that, they headed out, and Alan got a little mini-tour of the various shows getting set up to perform. In one of the smaller venues, a hypnotist was already performing. He was swinging his grandfather's gaudy pocket watch back and forth in front of the audience. The lights were just right, so that the gleam of this watch shone brightly. He accompanied this with the words "Follow the watch!... over and over..."

Alan and Tiffany stood off to the side; she whispered with the staff and Alan looked over the audience as they sat in rapt attention. The man's efforts were working. Alan could see a great number of people entranced by him. All of a sudden, the watch slipped out of his hand and fell onto the stage, smashing into pieces to which he said,

"Shit!"

Alan cringed. Oh well, it did *not* look like he would have a second show; unless he had a spare watch tucked away somewhere. Furthermore, the housekeeping staff was going to be kept quite busy cleaning up the mess left by his unintended hypnotic suggestion.

Tiffany sighed.

"I'll have to stay here and coordinate the next show. Why don't you go ahead, and I'll catch up with you later in the club?"

"Sure; sounds good. I'll see what I can find out and then we'll go from there."

Not long after that, Alan was again in the club, typing away on his laptop. He tried again to find some information on Michael's parents, but his efforts proved fruitless. Maybe Tiffany would know the right sort of search to do. He got out his cellphone, and was about to maker a call when his co-investigator arrived.

"Sorry it took so long; we had to juggle a few acts to get a comedian that had material appropriate for a family audience."

Alan laughed.

"Ah yes, that can be a problem. The good ones have two sets of material – the family-friendly stuff, and then their adults-only jokes for the midnight shows. I was just going to call my old cruise line about those medical records."

"You really think they'll give you some old records? I mean, what could you say to some corporate flunky that he'd put forth that kind of effort?"

Alan gave her a rundown on his claim about a possible malpractice suit.

"Are you serious?" Tiffany said, her face betraying how incredulous she was.

"Well... you got to remember, the US is known for being the 'Land of Law Suits'. It's a sad fact of our times. Touch wood, I've never had a malpractice suit against me in over twenty-five years. It's called practicing good medicine, making sure you follow up on medical cases, and certainly a bit of good old Irish Luck. It didn't always make me popular, my being cautious, I can tell you."

Caught up in a memory, Alan launched into a tale of how just as he was boarding the bus for a wilderness experience shore side trip he was called back to an emergency that the patient really wasn't willing to accept was an emergency.

"Mr. Warren Thomas, it was – a former director of the LA Zoo – he'd not had a chance to 'paint the town red' as they say, but he has sure colored the room and all furniture in it with the sudden onset rectal bleeding. Quite nasty it was, but he was adamant that he not only was joining the excursion that day but that he was reboarding for the rest of the rest of the cruise.

"Surely you didn't let him!" squealed Tiffany, amazed at the naivety of some people about the realities of their own health.

Alan chuckled, patting Tiffany's arm.

"No, dear — I said not until I got the results of the colonoscopy he was he was so adamantly refusing. So that was our shore expedition, for the pair of us, finding a clinic that had the appropriate equipment and physician capable to performing the test. Then it was always a question of finding the appropriate medications and other treatments he needed. My ship's clinic just wasn't equipped for such a procedure."

"Not quite the wilderness adventure you were looking for, eh?" Tiffany chuckled wryly.

Alan's laughter was a little more genuine as he remembered the clinic they had found.

"As it happens, it *was* an adventure – and it got pretty wild!"

"What do you mean?" asked Tiffany, puzzled.

"Well, he bled again later that day while we were at the clinic, resulting in an emergency bowel resection. He stayed alive that way, and he was lucky."

"Yes, lucky you were adamant about him not rejoining the ship," Tiffany said, proud of the ethical doctor she was now so fond of.

"Ah… actually… luckier than that, even…"

Alan went on to explain,

"When we arrived at the clinic we found the staff in a bit of disarray, anxiously watching the clock. It was a Sunday morning, around 10.45 a.m. when we arrived. The staff just seemed to be intent on watching the ward, but quite nervously. It seemed that there was quite a pattern that had built up in this Intensive Care ward of the clinic, whereby patients always died in the same bed and on Sunday morning at 11 a.m., regardless of their medical condition. This puzzled the doctors and staff and some even thought that it had something to do with the supernatural. No-one could solve the mystery as to why the deaths always occurred at 11 AM. The Doc was not superstitious, but he would have insisted that his passenger did not occupy that 'special' bed.

Apparently, a world-wide expert team was convened and they decided to go down to the ward to investigate the cause of the incidents. For a full week they were unable to determine any particular reason for the deaths. This illustrious company of experts was all there as we showed up that particular Sunday a few minutes before 11 a.m."

Alan could see that Tiffany was in rapt attention, wanting to find out the cause of all these mysterious deaths, just as she was with Michael and Dr. Fillem, so he relished the continuation of the story:

"All the doctors and nurses nervously waited outside the ward to see for themselves if the terrible phenomenon would occur again. The oxygen system had been checked, as had the electrical outlets, defibrillation units, monitoring systems, etc. All appeared to be in proper order. Some of the staff members were holding wooden crosses, prayer books and other holy objects to ward off potential evil... Just when the clock struck eleven..."

"Yes!... Yes?..." exclaimed Tiffany, eager for the conclusion.

Alan didn't disappoint, and although it could hardly have been what Tiffany was expecting.

"... Abdullah Mufta, the part-time Sunday sweeper, entered the ward and unplugged the life support system so that he could use the vacuum cleaner."

Tiffany just gasped, wide-eyed in horror at the careless stupidity. Alan had to agree.

"Strange what some people can get away with, isn't it? Especially in some countries, and yet on a number of the cruise ships, there have been deaths, and other medical situations that undoubtedly led to lawyers suing people once the participants got back on shore. I've seen a few situations where there could have been an earlier referral to a local doctor and hospital that probably would have made things better for the final outcome."

Tiffany's thoughts returned to the information that Alan's old friend was hopefully going to get his hands on about Michael's murder

"Oh, so you convinced this Bill guy that you're facing a possible law suit, huh?"

Alan nodded.

"Yeah, it helped that Bill Wilkins was familiar with a ship I almost served on. Actually, I was asked to return to one of the ships I had previously worked on, to do another world cruise. I debated doing it. The income was paltry and the hours were going to be long. Granted, the food would have been great, as it always is, the company fascinating, and the ports of call interesting, even in the small doses that you have available time-wise to enjoy them..."

Tiffany smiled.

"In other words, you talked yourself into doing it again."

"Right. I made the call to the new doctor coordinator, who was a fellow from southern Europe. The company had contracted out the marine operations and given the medical part to this fellow, instead of the old team I had known in Florida. As requested, I sent him a resume and the letter of recommendation from the Captain who wanted me back."

"Oh, and... something went wrong?"

Alan nodded.

"Yeah; the doc was friendly enough, and said he had read the paperwork and was sure I would make a great asset to the company again. Then he asked the fateful questions: 'Are you an American? Are you a resident of the USA?' Of course, my answers to both were yes."

"And that sank you?"

"Yes again. He explained that most of the cruise companies that could, still weren't hiring American doctors, because of the malpractice problem. The insurance companies were charging such outrageous sums that they couldn't afford the insurance."

"Why only American doctors?" Tiffany asked, thinking that was strange.

"Well, if an American wanted to sue an American doctor who's on a ship, they can easily do so in the state they live in. If, on the other hand, the ship has *foreign* registry and *foreign* doctors, then if the passenger or crewmember wants to sue, they have to do it in the country of registry, like the Bahamas, Norway, Greece, and the like. Most other countries don't have such a litigious society with juries that give such outrageous sums for settlements as the US."

Tiffany slowly nodded.

"I get it. The end of the story is: there's no way a good American doctor can work for any cruise lines that cater to Americans any more."

"Right, until the litigation laws of the United States get changed."

"Okay, then; let me see what I can find out about Michael's parents," Tiffany said. "So, where did Michael come from?"

Alan moved from where he was sitting in front of his laptop so that Tiffany could use it, and then he picked up one of the folders that he'd created to keep track of their clues. Flipping through it, he found the biographically information on Michael and handed it to her.

"Here you go; Michael Hamilton, York, England. That's all I could find."

Reading it, she started typing away on the computer keyboard.

"All right-y, let's see what we can find."

Alan stepped up behind her to watch over her shoulders as her dainty little fingers just about flew across the keys. A Google search yielded a web site for public records in that area, and Tiffany went to it.

"Okay, now, what are his parents' names?"

Alan rifled through the file, and found the print out from his first efforts.

"Ah, here they are; Arthur and Fiona."

Tiffany started typing again.

"Good; now we'll see if there are any records for them."

She hit 'Enter', and they waited for the results. The little hourglass seemed to stay for the longest time, and finally came the words: 'No Records Found'.

"Huh, a dead end then?" Alan said.

Tiffany chewed on her fingernail for a moment as she stared at the screen.

"Ah... let me think. Maybe they live in a nearby community. But... how do we figure out what towns are around there?"

Alan snapped his fingers.

"I've got it. Pull up a map of the area around York, and we'll look for city names."

"Good idea!"

A few keystrokes, and they had a map of the York region. Zooming back a few times, they got a good map of the entire area.

Alan grabbed a pen and paper, and jotted down a few names.

"Okay, got them. Huh, looks like York is the only major city in the vicinity. Now, can you search these communities for their records?"

Tiffany started typing.

"Well... let me see what I can find."

At first, nothing was found; the little cities and towns had no records online. But then, in the small town of Scalby were several documents listed. Among them, a death certificate for Michael Hamilton!

"Bingo; I think we have a winner!" Tiffany said, glee in her voice.

Alan bent down closer to her, and read the details. Oh, she *did* smell so very nice.

"Okay, here's a name and address. Huh, I don't see it in comparing it with the other list I drew up. So... does that mean they don't have a phone?"

"Maybe their number is unlisted?"

"Ah, good idea!" Alan said. "So, how are we going to get in touch with them?"

"How-how... how?" Tiffany said slowly and softly.

"Hey, how about we contact some of the locals; the police, the local sweets shop or grocery store? Maybe one of them could help us connect with them."

"Hey, good idea!" Tiffany said. "Here, let me see if I can find the number for the local government office: a town hall or something."

Again her fingers danced across the keyboard, and a few minutes later, they had a phone number for the town hall.

Alan whipped out his phone again.

"Okay, let's make some calls and see what we get this time!"

He dialed, and was soon talking to someone in the town hall. It wasn't hard for Alan to convince them that he was a friend of the Hamilton's – he remembered enough details about Michael to do that. Writing down a series of numbers, he thanked the lady for her help, and hung up.

"Okay, we have a number to call!"

Again he dialed, and waited. A moment later, a woman's voice came on – and Alan just knew it had to be Michael's mother; there was a strong resemblance.

"Dr. Mayhew you say? Mayhew… Mayhew, now, why is that name familiar?"

"Well, Mrs. Hamilton, I knew Michael years ago, on the cruise ship that he served on."

"Ah… yes, now I remember!" she replied. "Yes, Michael spoke of you, Dr. Mayhew; he said you were always a decent fellow towards him."

"Why thank you, ma'am; I always thought of him as a good friend."

"But, why are you calling now, after so many years? Are you in the area and want to… see his final resting place?"

"Oh, no, ma'am; I'm actually on a cruise ship steaming around the Caribbean right now."

"Really? My-my, isn't technology wonderful?"

Alan laughed.

"Yes, it certainly is. Anyway, the reason I'm calling is because I'm trying to rundown some… information that might be among Michael's personal affects. Do you still have all of his… things?"

"Oh… now, I'm not sure," she said slowly. "Let me think. I know we've left his room just as… it was. His father, the big softie, he couldn't bear to change a thing."

"Ah, I see. And, what about his things from the ship; ah… the… last ship he was on? Do you think he might have saved them? Could you ask him?"

"Arthur is out golfing – as usual – I'll have to speak to him when he gets in," Mrs. Hamilton said.

"That'll be fine. I'm very sorry to hear that, ma'am."

"As for Michael's things, I threw out most of them – the things that were… unimportant. After all, why keep his old nametags. eh?"

Alan bit his lip. Oh, this was *not* good!

"Well, the item I was looking for was not that, it was a model plane that Michael… made."

"Model plane? Now that… I don't know; I'll have to check. Why is it important, after all these years?"

Alan looked at Tiffany, lowered the phone and covered the mouthpiece.

"What should I tell her about… you-know-what?"

"Well… I don't know. You may have to be honest with her, if you expect her help. On the other hand… she might think it's a lot of nonsense."

Alan thought about it for a moment, and then made his decision. Fiona was Michael's mother; a mother's love is a very powerful thing. So, putting the phone back up to his face, he told her.

For the next few minutes, there was nothing but total silence from the other end as Alan related all that he'd remembered and learned. Finally, he finished, and waited for her reply.

Silence.

Alan swallowed hard; was she going to hang up? He opened his mouth to ask, and she spoke.

"I always thought that whole heart attack story was nonsense!... So, how can I help you, Doctor?"

"Well, I suspect that something is hidden in that old model. Something which may help us to find out what happened to Michael. If you can find it, and take a look inside, we just may have our answer."

"I see. Well, it may take some time to find it, of course. Give me your number, and I'll call you back when – if – I do get my hands on it. I'll do my best."

Alan gave Mrs. Hamilton his cellphone number; they said their good-byes and he hung up. The smile on Tiffany's face said a lot.

"I take it she's going to help?"

Alan nodded. The intensity of his smile matched hers. The call had gone very well and Mrs. Hamilton hadn't thought he was a nut, dragging up unwelcome memories, as he'd feared.

"Yes, seems she's as intent as we are on solving this mystery."

Tiffany breathed a sigh of relief.

"Well, it's nice to have an ally!"

She looked at her watch and groaned.

"Oh, man, I'm going to have to go; we've got a special play session for the kids in an hour."

"That's fine; it may be a while before Mrs. Hamilton gets back to us, anyway. I'll go ahead and do some more research, see if I can find anything else about our other suspects. Dinner tonight?"

Tiffany got to her feet.

"Sounds like a plan; the research, I mean. As for dinner… afraid not; I have to attend another kiddie café."

Alan grinned.

"Oh, so you'll be wearing your poncho, I take it?"

"I wish. It's worse than feeding time at the zoo! Meet me back here after dinner, about eight? I'll change, and we can go see a show or go dancing."

"Yes, that also sounds like a plan! See you then."

With that, they kissed and went their separate ways. Alan settled himself in a sunny spot where there was Wi-Fi connectivity and set about pursuing one line of inquiry into Michael's death: the room stewards.

# CHAPTER TWENTY-SIX

*July 20, 1984: The Bahamas*

ROOM STEWARDS AND STEWARDESSES are a division of the Hotel department, which is usually the largest employer on the ship. Sometimes the hotel department is split up and has some of its divisions under others. This keeps one from having one person who is all powerful in the scheme of corporate ladders. Sometimes the least competent is advanced. This *does* happen in the hotel department of cruise ships.

Fortunately it does not happen in the Deck and Engine department where the Captain and senior officers are divisioned. Medical also usually comes under Deck and Engine. Only once did it fall under the hotel department, and it was a total disaster. The hotel director thought he was a doctor and tried to manage the department, which he was legally allowed to do in their corporate structure. Ernst, a good solid Aryan German fellow, was friendly on the surface. All the staff questioned his sexual orientation with his longish hair and beautiful jewelry, but the rumor mill never picked up any specific liaisons, so we dubbed him the eunuch.

Ernst was just useless. He would spend hours reviewing reports and never come up with any useful recommendations or changes. He would spend hours looking over the shoulder of various well experienced chefs, housekeepers, and food and beverage directors. Not in a practical way to help them cope with a certain problem or anything, just to intimidate them by being there breathing down their necks.

In any event, besides trying to practice medicine, he would hang out in the medical center. He would have the Doc get him free medicine to 'beautify' his skin, of course charged to our budget. Then he would yell and scream that the medical department was spending too much money and, of course, did not generate money like the casino. Disaster in a uniform – enough said.

Thankfully, he was not in charge on the cruise on which Michael met his sad demise, and the stewarding was running smoothly. So Alan was able to pick up some useful information from the room stewards, making him even more surprised that the investigating team seemed ignorant of some of the details of Michael's life, until he informed them himself.

Room Stewards and stewardesses are one of the biggest portions of the hotel department on the large ships. They clean rooms. On a large ship, that is a lot of rooms. For the passengers, the room stewards can be the passengers' link to all the little extras that make a cruise a memorable adventure and a comfortable one. Most of the small details that people rave over when they enthusiastically gush about any cruises they go on are largely thanks to the room stewards.

The make animal shapes out of towels on the turn down. They place the chocolate in the 'beak' of the towel mouth. They remember where things are and how one likes things placed. On a long cruise they become real buddies. In short, they remember things.

On many ships, they garner big tips too. The Doc remembered one room stewardess from Romania who was given a Christmas tip of $10,000 by a wealthy passenger that thought that she was "so nice — why not?" No doctor ever got a tip like that, even after saving someone's life! Most of the tipping on the larger ships is included or strongly suggested or automatically added to a room account at the rate of ten or fifteen per cent or a fixed dollar amount per day. This is much fairer in that then the whole amount is divided among all the staff in that division.

Then there are the room stewards for the officers. These may not make fancy shapes from the sheet turn down but they provided a high level of service which allowed a ship's officers to live a life of luxury that many people envy.

Ah, but Alan well remembered a passenger who did *not* appreciate all that her cabin steward could do for her! Back on that same cruise where Michael was lost, but before his untimely death, Mrs. Brightman; let's see; what was her first name?

Gail? Abby?

Ah, Abigail; she had been the sourest of bad people and gave new meaning to the term 'Queen Bee'. Most of the staff called her 'Queen B', and left it to the individual to fill in the rest!

Alan got involved with Mrs. Brightman and her cabin stewardess – a lovely young Romanian girl by the name of Mischa – due to an odd series of events. First, the cruise ship had to spend an extra day in port – due to some bad weather heading our way – and, as a result, a number of the crew were given extended leave.

Mischa was among them, and she spent the day ashore, having fun. That evening, she came by the sickbay to see Alan.

"Dear Doctor, I having bad pain, but I not want talk about it, but I must talk."

Alan rubbed his hand over his mouth to hide his smile as he got his equipment ready.

"Now, you mustn't be embarrassed if you have a… female problem, Mischa; I'm a doctor, and my nurse here – Nurse Kelly – is well qualified to examine you."

The girl blushed.

"No, it not… female problem; I just embarrassed about what hurt. I…"

Her voice trailed off as her hands slipped behind her. Slowly, reluctantly, she turned around and lifted her uniform skirt. As she was wearing a thong, the problem immediately became apparent: she had a bee sting or bug bite on her right cheek, and it did *not* look good!

Nurse Kelly took one look, and turned to Alan, slowly nodding her head.

"Ah-huh, allergic reaction; right?"

Alan turned to the medicine cabinet next to him and started rooting around in it.

"Exactly! Mischa, are you allergic to bee stings?"

She turned her head slightly toward him, even as Kelly maneuvered her to the exam table and got her to lie down.

"Yes, Doctor, but I not stung by bee! So, it not be that."

Alan got some cream and a shot ready.

"That may be, but it didn't have to be a bee. Most insects have a similar type of venom; it's usually based on formic acid. So, if you react to bees, you'll probably have the same reaction to fire ants and other critters. Where have you been… sitting lately?"

Mischa's brow wrinkled as she was clearly lost in thought for a moment.

"No places strange. I went ashore with friends, and we went… ah, jeeping? Went up in hills, went swimming, and had picnic; that all we do, I swears!"

Alan handed the cream to Kelly, and she started to apply it to the affected area.

"Oh, I believe you, Mischa; I'm sure it was perfectly innocent. I'm equally sure that somewhere along the line, you got bit!"

He wiped her arm down with alcohol, and gave her the shot. She gave a little jump, and looked back over her shoulder at the... injured area.

"It not leave... scar, will it?"

Kelly giggled as she finished and flipped Mischa's skirt back down.

"Well, I'd wear some more... conservative underwear for a while."

Alan nodded.

"Good point, Kelly. Yes, Mischa, a thong will allow your skirt to cause chaffing. So, regular panties until it heals! Understand?"

Mischa slid off of the table and stood up.

"Yes, Doctor, I do, and thank you. For once, I glad I not have job with lots of sitting!"

The three of them shared a good laugh, and they bid Mischa good-bye. After that, they wrote up the incident, just like any other, and Alan went on with his regular evening. As that evening was to be dinner with Christina, Alan wanted to dress nicely, but he also knew that time was short. So, he hustled down to his cabin – and found that his cabin steward had done a splendid job at straightening up – and got changed as quickly as he could.

Zipping back up the service elevator to the main dining hall, he was able to time his entrance almost perfectly; Christina – monster-child in tow – had just been seated. Alan, positively cringing at the thought of another meal with Jesus, painted a smile on his face and took his seat – next to Christina, but across the table from Jesus – and said a silent prayer that he might behave, just this once.

Yet, it was not to be.

Alan spent a good portion of the evening ducking; Jesus was deadly accurate with his peas, and Christina found all his actions cute.

"My-my, he is an... energetic child, isn't he?" Alan said.

"It's his most endearing quality," Christina replied; she was positively beaming with joy and pride.

At that moment, Alan had a new found appreciation for the cruise staff that dealt with the children on board. How they survived a meal – and kept their sanity – he would never know.

"I can't wait for us to visit your home, Christina," Alan said. "I don't think I've ever been to this area of the world."

"Then I shall simply have to give you the grand tour! We're the opposite then, as I have never been much of anywhere."

"Really? Oh, there are places that are so beautiful and delightful, I could return there a hundred times!"

"Oh?" Christina replied. "Please, tell me about some of them. You tell stories so well; I feel I'm actually in the places you speak about."

"Well… let me think," Alan said slowly. "Ah, now Key West, that is a place with a rich heritage, and is now a very… colorful community."

"Key?" Christina said, confusion written across her face. "Ah, island, yes? That is English word for island, correct?"

Alan nodded.

"Yes, - well, actually, it's the *American* word for island. Don't let the Brits hear you call it an 'English' word!" Alan grinned. "There's a string of such islands that run for the southern tip of Florida out into the Gulf of Mexico; the last one in the chain is called Key West. I've been there three times."

"Oh, what is its great appeal; what is its history?"

"Well, its appeal and history sort of tie together, for me. I'm from Massachusetts and-"

"That state up north," Christina said with a smile. "I remember you telling me that."

"That's right. Well, as it turns out, Key West is very much like my home."

"It's like your Massa-too-chits? How can that be?"

"Long ago, when ships had sails, there was a colony of New England sailors living there. They made their living salvaging cargo chips that would wreck on the reefs offshore. So, over time, the island developed a look and culture very much like what I'm used to."

"I see. Is that the only reason you like it?"

Alan shook his head.

"Oh no; it also has the Hemmingway House, and – as a writer – I sort of have to make a… pilgrimage there."

"Hemmingway? Oh, Ernest Hemmingway?" Christina said. "I love his 'The Old Man and the Sea'!"

"Yes, a good book. My favorite is 'For Whom the Bell Tolls'. Such a writer! So, as a man who… dabbles in writing, seeing his home, his typewriter… they sort of… inspire me."

"So, you're a doctor *and* a writer! My, you are so talented," she replied, batting her eyes at him. "Could I have read anything you've written?"

Alan chewed his lip – and ducked another onslaught of mashed potatoes – and shrugged.

"Ah… not exactly. I keep planning to write a book, but… I…"

Christina giggled.

"Getting from idea to full story isn't easy, eh?"

"Yes! I also love going there for Fantasy Fest."

"Oh, that sounds like fun. Is it something we could go to?"

Alan cast his eyes toward Jesus – building a castle out of his remaining mashed potatoes – and slowly shook his head.

"Ah… it's more of an… adult form of entertainment."

"Oh! Then I won't be able to attend; I simply can't go anywhere without Jesus."

"I see," Alan replied. "Well… I'm sure we can find something else to do."

"Yes; after all, Florida has Disney World! We can take him there."

Alan cringed: *we?* Oh, that did not sound good. Well, that was for the future. For now, he would enjoy Christina's company – and tolerate Jesus'. He just hoped that the coming trip would be more fun than frightful!

After dinner, Alan tried to get closer to Christina, but she had Jesus just about grafted to her hip – and his hands were thick with chocolate from dessert. So, this was an effective 'defense' against Alan getting too close to his mother. As they strolled along the deck, the cool night air had a heavy taste of salt to it, and Jesus started to nod off; his eyes were heavy with sleep.

"It seems someone is getting tired," Alan said. "Shall we put him down for the night and then go see a show?"

Christina shook her head.

"Oh, I can't do that!" she replied. "If he wakes up, and I'm not right there at his side – or at least in the next room – he'd be traumatized. We'll just retire for the night. Goodnight!"

A quick peck on the cheek, and they were gone – Alan barely had a chance to even say anything in reply – and he was alone. Alan felt a bit frustrated, but he also wanted this relationship to work. So, he decided to let it go, and retire himself. After all, they had a trip ahead of them, and a good night's sleep would help.

The next morning, Alan was trying to enjoy a quiet breakfast – and preparing to leave with Christina – when he got a call from Captain Halvorsen. Hustling down to the Purser's Desk, he was ushered inside, and found the captain, Mischa, and "dear" Mrs. Brightman.

"Ah, my dear Doctor, perhaps you can settle this-" Captain Halvorsen started to say.

He never got to finish.

Mrs. Brightman jumped to her feet and pointed at poor Mischa (she was sort of cowering next to the purser's desk, where the captain was seated).

"The only thing that's going to 'settle this' is for her to be dismissed!"

Alan gave a little jump. Good God, what was wrong with this woman?

The captain rose and took a few steps forward, effectively blocking Mrs. Brightman from getting any closer to Mischa.

"Mrs. Brightman, before we do anything, we're going to get the facts. Now, please tell the doctor what you told me - provided you keep it civil!"

She fumed, her face red with anger, and flared her nostrils for a moment. Then, she seemed to calm down a bit, and sat down.

"This… person has been… snooping into my… personal… papers!"

"She stole something from you?" Alan said.

She grumbled and mumbled, and shook her head.

"No, it's not that. Everything's… where it should be. But… things have been moved! Things that I had safely locked away in my briefcase. As I'm the only one with a key to my cabin, it *had* to be that girl!"

With that, she again pointed – in a very accusatory manner – at Mischa. Alan looked at Captain Halvorsen.

"Ah, Captain, why are you asking for my input in this matter?"

"Based on what Mrs. Brightman has told us, the bag in question was only in her room – and unattended – for a brief time last night," Captain Halvorsen said. "Between seven and eight o'clock. Mischa wasn't on duty last night, and she says she was with you during that time. Can you confirm that?"

Alan nodded.

"Absolutely! She came into sickbay complaining of a… bug bite; she had an allergic react-"

"Are you sure of the time?" Mrs. Brightman snapped.

"Well… it was after first sitting. I'm positive it was a little after seven," Alan replied. "I have the incident report down in my office."

Captain Halvorsen frowned.

"You do? Why isn't it in the system?"

"Kelly wrote it up, and then she wanted to leave. Frankly, we were both hungry, and I had a date… ah… appointment to get to. So…"

"So it's still on your desk," Captain Halvorsen said, completing Alan's sentence.

He turned to Mrs. Brightman.

"I'd say this settles the matter, ma'am."

Mrs. Brightman jumped to her feet, indignant.

"No, it does not! It merely means that someone else got into my room; I want to know who!"

"Mrs. Brightman, with all due respect, if nothing's missing, and there's no sign of forced entry, there's not much for me to investigate," the captain said calmly. "If the only evidence is your assertion that 'things have been moved', what am I to do about it?"

She fumed, her face getting redder by the second, and a litany of swear words escaping her lips, under her breath. Yet, she – officially – said nothing.

"Perhaps moving her to another cabin?" Alan suggested.

"We do have a fine suite available, ma'am," Captain Halvorsen said. "I could move you up there – at no cost to you."

Mrs. Brightman ground her teeth and sighed.

"Yes, that would be… fine."

With that, she stormed out of the office. Alan rolled his eyes; oh, some of these passengers could be royal pains. Like poor Mischa's "malady", that pain could be in the ass!

# CHAPTER TWENTY-SEVEN

*December 13, 2009: The Caribbean Sea*

AFTER BIDDING TIFFANY GOOD-BYE, and securing his Wi-Fi access, Alan began sifting through his pile of papers, he looked over his list of suspects in what he now knew was Michael's murder. Now he needed to attack this logically. He just had names. He didn't even know what some of these people looked like; for all he knew they could have been on that fatal cruise of twenty-five years ago. For that matter, even if he did know what they looked like, they could have been in a disguise! Granted, that did sound a bit like an old detective novel, but it was still a possibility. For that matter, just how reliable was his memory? After all, it had been twenty-five years. People change; a man's memories can change. Alan was beginning to lose confidence in his abilities so solve this; but if he didn't, who would? The police weren't interested anymore. Even at the time it was seen as a pretty much open and shut case of natural causes, perhaps precipitated by an argument – but nothing more threatening than that. No, this one was down to Alan... and Tiffany, of course – but right now, she wasn't here, either.

What if he focused on the '*why*', instead of the 'who', for now? Alan chuckled to himself. From what he knew of Fiona, Michael's mother, he was already sure she would have told him that should be 'whom', not 'who'.

So, the possible motives were as follows:

Blackmail over possible exposure regarding the suspect's... orientation.

The Russian antiques, smuggling.

And, a lovers' quarrel; pure blind jealousy.

Now, Alfonse had already been eliminated as a suspect. So, what about

Gustav? Alan checked all the information on him. Huh, it seemed he could have killed Michael for any one – or all three - of these reasons! That meant he bore closer looking at.

In skimming through the notes he had made, Alan found all the information he'd collected on Gustav: family, home, known associates… Alan would start there.

Twelve emails and eight phone calls later, he was no closer to an answer; twenty-five years was a long time for people to remember details about a man's life. So, that night, as he and Tiffany sat and watched a Broadway Revue in the main theater, he wasn't able to tell her much. He did have to grin as they sat there; she had quite the distinct aroma of peanut butter about her. She reported that dinner had been quite a playful time period for some of the younger children.

"The kids were still talking about you, Alan," she said. "The boys, anyway…"

"Oh, wha- Ohhh, the arcade game, yes?"

She nodded, grinning.

"Yes, they were wondering if you were going to make another appearance and try and beat your own record."

Alan laughed, patting her hand.

"Well, we'll see if I can slip that into my itinerary before we reach port."

"Such is the life of a celebrity," Tiffany said with a wink.

After the show, they decided to make an early evening of it and retired to sleep. Well, that is, they went to *bed*; sleep came much later!


## December 13, 2009: Scalby, England

MEANWHILE, BACK IN A little village in England, Fiona Hamilton sat in her old easy chair, the one right by the stone fireplace in the main sitting room. She'd always liked this spot; the small window on her right gave her a lovely view of the rolling countryside beyond the stone wall of their country estate. The sun was setting now, creating a fiery glow in the western sky.

It was late in the day: too late to have Arthur get up in the attic and look for Michael's things tonight; they'd get to it first thing tomorrow. Dear Michael, how long ago it seemed now. Had it really been twenty-five years since he was… laid to rest in the village cemetery?

Fiona blinked; it wasn't proper to weep now. She put her knitting aside, rose stiffly and adjusted her matching sweater and cardigan. The wall on either side of the fireplace held floor to ceiling bookcases. She stepped over to it, searched through a shelf and found the book she was looking for.

She frowned at the bit of dust along the top of the book. She made a mental note to speak to Megan; the girl simply must do better at keeping the place clean. The fact that this album had been untouched for… some time - was *no* excuse!

"Fiona my dear, how was your day?" came Arthur's voice behind her.

She turned and sighed.

"Arthur, I know you enjoy your time on the links, but please – shoes!"

Arthur looked down at his feet.

"Oh, yes; sorry, my dear. Still - had a smashing good game!"

Fiona moved to the chair and sat.

"I take it that means you were only thirty over par instead of your usual forty?"

Arthur gave a grumble – but didn't deny it - as he slipped off his golf shoes and set them aside.

"What's that you have there?" Arthur asked, moving to his easy chair.

His matched hers, a high backed deep buttoned dark brown leather armchair at the other side of the fireplace to hers. Arthur sat and reached for the fireplace poker to stoke up the fire a bit more.

Fiona tugged her cardigan closer around her and opened the book.

"Oh, just our old photo album. I wanted to… reminisce a bit. Ah, thank you, Arthur, dear; the room did have a bit of a chill to it."

Arthur grabbed one of his pipes from the sideboard next to him. Opening his tobacco tin, he started to pack it tightly.

"Isn't that Michael's album? Such a pity he… didn't amount to more."

Fiona played with the string of natural pearls around her neck with her left hand as she caressed a theatre program with the thin fingers of her right.

"He… did all right. Didn't give me any grandchildren, of course… but he was… a good boy."

Arthur gave a harrumph as he lit a match and held it up to his pipe.

"Not much chance of his doing that, the great poof! Why this nauseating stroll down 'Amnesia Lane', Fiona?"

Fiona sighed, and sat forward in her chair a bit. They had been through pretty much the same conversation many times while Michael had been alive, but he was still her baby. Nothing would change that – not even death… and certainly not his… lifestyle choice.

Looking out the window, Fiona could just catch a glimpse of the old oak still standing majestically at the end of the lawn. It tended to shade her garden too much, but she didn't mind. Silhouetted against the dimly lit horizon, she could make out the swing: *his* old swing. It was the one outwardly remaining sign of Michael's presence, and she was not about to get rid of it.

She closed the album and set it aside.

"I got a rather interesting call today," she began carefully.

Arthur snorted, sending a small puff of pipe smoke into the air.

"Has a new delivery come in at M&S, or is the Women's Guild in need of a chair for some new committee?" Arthur mocked – good-naturedly, he felt.

Fiona shook his head sadly.

"Neither. The gentleman was a Dr. Mayhew; an old crew mate of Michael's."

Arthur frowned and bit down hard on the stem of his pipe.

"Michael's old... friend?"

"No... not at all – well not like that. The doctor from the ship on which he served... last."

Arthur gave another harrumph.

"'Served on'? My dear, please; you make it sound as if Michael was nobly serving in Her Majesty's Navy! He was an... entertainer on a pleasure craft."

"Be that as it may, he called with just cause!" Fiona said firmly.

As the fire crackled, and Arthur puffed away on his pipe, Fiona related the gist of her conversation with Dr. Mayhew including the fact that he was looking for a model plane Michael had apparently made. Arthur remained stone-faced, his pipe smoke billowing about his head like the London smog.

"Are you quite sure he's serious?" he asked, when she had finished.

"Quite - and so am I. So, tomorrow *we* shall get down the boxes from the attic and go through them," Fiona said.

Arthur smacked his pipe against the stones of the fireplace – hard.

"We will do *no* such thing! Fiona, this is complete and utter twaddle. Why on earth are you going on about this now, after all these years? Who is he... this... this Dr. Mayhew... to suddenly drag this... episode up again?"

Fiona was furious. Here was a chance to find out what had really happened to cause her son's death and she was going to take it. Nothing Arthur could say was going to stop her.

"Oh yes, we will! According to the doctor, he only recently began to put the pieces together. It doesn't matter how many years ago it was; no matter what – Michael was our *son*! And, by God, we're going to do all we can to help find out what killed him!"

It is said that there is nothing like a woman scorned but a woman flying to the defense of her baby was just as powerful an entity.

Arthur crossed his arms in front of him and lowered his chin onto his chest as he mumbled some sort of protest; yet he said nothing out loud. He knew when he was beaten.

The tiniest hint of a grin crept across Fiona's face. Yes, she knew that gesture; his act of resignation.

She got to her feet, put the album away, and gave a little stretch.

"Well, it's late; I think I shall retire. Coming, Arthur?"

He reached for his tobacco tin.

"I… want another smoke first."

With that, Fiona walked down the richly carpeted hallway to the grand entryway. She could picture Michael now – as a child, sliding down the railing of the spiral staircase. No matter how many times she scolded him about it, or admonished his nanny to properly discipline him, he kept doing it. Moving to the first of those wide low steps, Fiona paused to pat the railing. She would very much like to see him come sailing down it right now: just one more time.

Slowly climbing the stairs, Fiona went down the long hall to the master suite. Along the way were the portraits and other family mementoes. She smiled remembering how Michael had thought it silly to sit for portraits.

"Why not just get nice photos taken of all of us?" he had said.

Oh, that boy had no appreciation for tradition and custom. She supposed that that came with him being… different. The door to his old room – now Arthur's games room – came up on her left, and she paused. Another memory swirled within her mind. Yes, he had thrown the door open and come out like the Queen -ah, like Prince Philip on the balcony of Buckingham Palace; all made-up for the part of the Emcee in the musical *Cabaret*. He had been so proud when he got that role at the school theatre. So had she… but Arthur had found it all very… *difficult*.

Fiona patted the door, and moved on; no sense dwelling on old memories. Coming to the large double doors of their suite, she went in. At least Arthur had been thoughtful enough to not come up here in his shoes!

Fiona changed into her nightgown and prepared for bed, smothering her face and neck in the thick anti-wrinkle cream which cost a fortune and which appeared to be working as well as could be expected for a woman of her age. Getting herself settled down in their large four-poster bed, Fiona looked about the room before switching off the light. Yes, the place hadn't changed in many years: the same furniture in the same places. This was how things should be – neat and orderly, and in accordance with tradition.

It seemed that no sooner had Fiona closed her eyes that her nose twitched, and she awoke. It was morning. Arthur was already up and brewing the morning's tea. One thing that man was good at was preparing a nice pot of Earl Gray - warming the pot first in the traditional English way before putting the tea and tea water in; he had never once spoiled it – not in all the years they'd been together. Sitting up in bed, Fiona looked around, and sighed despondently. He had also left his clothes from the day before all over the floor again! Yet another thing he'd never learned to do – pick up his clothes!

No matter, it was time to rise and greet the day, and deal with the matter at hand. Slipping on her dressing gown and slippers, Fiona headed down the back stairs. They were narrow and wound like a corkscrew, but she liked that they took her straight away into the pantry – and from there the kitchen, and the stairway being narrow she knew she could easily grip the railing if she needed it. One of the exasperating things about old… of getting older - was a poor sense of balance!

Fiona reached the bottom of the stairs and made her way through the pantry, past the cabinets and shelves that lined the walls and held most of their groceries. Hmmm… she'd need Arthur to get to the market later; they were low on a few things, and she had a rather large and important dinner party coming up. Fiona rubbed her hands up and down her arms; the pantry was always a bit chilly this time of year. Opening the door, she stepped into the kitchen, and smiled to see Arthur just sizzling some sausages.

"Good morning, my sweet," he said. "Sleep well did you?"

She moved to the table, sat, and dropped a lump of sugar into her fine bone china cup. Pouring some tea for both of them, she nodded.

"Yes; I didn't even hear you come to bed, or snore during the night."

"I remembered my allergy medicine."

"For a change!" she chuckled, giving him the 'look'.

Arthur brought the food to the table and served them both, and then sat down to eat.

"Now then, I'm off to the links today with Stephen and the boys, so-"

"*After* we're done with our bit of business," Fiona said quickly.

Arthur grumbled as he chewed and swallowed a mouthful of eggs.

"Fiona, you're not still going on about *that*, are you?"

"Arthur, we owe this to Michael; it's the very least we can do!"

"What can you hope to do, after all this time? Isn't it better left… alone?"

"For Michael, Arthur; we do it for Michael," she said simply.

Arthur sighed, but also nodded. With that, they continued eating, and had their usual leisurely breakfast. When they were done, they went upstairs and got dressed; Fiona made sure that Arthur put on his old work clothes. He most certainly was *not* dirtying up his good clothes on such a messy job, even though it was an essential one.

After that, they walked down the hall to the top of the stairs, and then followed the hall as it looped back to the far end of the house. It was there that the old wooden stairs led up to the attic. Oh, it'd been a while since they – or anyone – had been up there. Climbing the creaky steps, Arthur fished the large key out of his pocket and set it in the lock. A twist, a clink, and the old door opened.

Arthur stepped inside and grabbed the thin string dangling above him. Click, and the one little bare light bulb came on.

"Hmmm... now, let me think; where did we put those boxes?"

Fiona stepped up behind him and gestured off to the right.

"I know some of them are over there. That... ah, Al fellow who brought Michael's... who brought Michael back to us; he helped pile some over there."

Arthur nodded, and moved to the stack. The place was quite crowded with all manner of objects and quite dirty. Fiona made a mental note: come the spring cleaning, she really must have Megan, their cleaning girl, give this place a good going over.

The old nursing chair was there; oh, and her own cradle! Such quaint old items. Fiona looked across the large room at the small window in the far wall; one of the panes looked cracked. Yet another little item in need of doing.

Arthur set the first box on the floor and opened it.

"Hmmm, just a bunch of videos in here; I think they're from all the theatre shows he did."

Fiona stepped over to the box and looked in. Picking up some of the cases, she read the titles.

"Yes, that, and videos from the ships he served on. This isn't the right one."

Arthur nodded and slid the second one out. A quick tug, and the string came undone. He flipped the top open, and had a look inside.

"Oh, we may be close, dear. These look to be personal effects from - ah, here it is!"

With a triumphant flourish, he pulled the small object from the box. He may not have been keen to have set out on this trip down memory lane but Arthur was a perfectionist, so once he was set a task he liked to try to fulfill it to the best of his ability. He was still perturbed about the significance, though.

"Hmm, all this fuss over a little toy airplane. So, what are we to do with it?"

Fiona held out her hand, gesturing for him to give the toy plane to her. He did so, and she looked it over, brushing the dust off of the small wings.

"Well, I suppose the easiest thing to do is break it open."

Fiona was fierce, a mother bear fighting for her cub. She couldn't save Michael's life but by God if he had met his end by foul play she would do all she could to see his killer brought to justice. It was left to pedantic Arthur to urge some caution.

"Well… maybe, dear - but *if* there truly is something inside it, we should exercise care."

Fiona was scornful.

"Ah, you just want an excuse to use your new roto-zip on it, isn't that it?" she said.

"Now, now, Fiona, that's the furthest thing from my mind. But, now that you mention it…"

She grinned, amused she had spotted Arthur's intention, but quickly wiped the smile from her face as the seriousness of their task once more crept into her consciousness.

"Very well; have at it."

Arthur took the model back, clicked off the light, and headed down the stairs. Fiona slowly shook her head. Oh, that man of hers and his toys. She closed and locked the door, and followed him.

Down the hall they went, Arthur striding along at quite the good pace. Yes, he was anxious to fiddle with one of his gadgets, but if that was going to get them to the truth about Michael's death more quickly, she didn't mind. By the time Fiona got to the door of his workshop, Arthur was already sitting at the desk. The room was a mishmash of tools and equipment – most of them little used; the thick dust gave testament to that. Yes, this was one area Megan was not allowed in. Women didn't understand these things, Arthur was sure. Michael had rarely been in here either…

Fiona moved to his side and watched as he fitted the roto-zip with one of the large round cutting blades.

"So, that will do the trick?"

Arthur nodded as he switched the device on.

"A quick zip-zip, and we'll see what – if anything – is inside this."

Holding the small model, he brought the 'zip' close to its top, and then slowly moved it around the tail in a complete loop. The tail dropped off, and Arthur turned the model to look in the end.

"Well, by Jove! That doctor fellow may have something here - there *is* something in there… something black, I think… but I can't quite tell if it's part of the model or not."

"Does it look fragile; can you break the model open a bit more to get at it?" Fiona prompted, impatiently.

"Let me just cut the tail off a bit higher; right about where the wings start."

Another zip-zip, and a larger chunk of the plane fell off – the object in it. Arthur picked it up, looked in, and pushed against the object with his pinkie.

Clunk! A small film canister dropped to the table. He picked it up, astonished.

"Some old film negatives!"

Fiona snatched the canister from him.

"Get the car, Arthur; we're going to the film lab to get prints of these."

Arthur rose to his feet, and groaned.

"Fiona, really, do you think that's necessary? I mean, they could be nothing more than pictures of Michael… with his… friend. Do we really want the people at … at *Boots* to… see him like that? Think of the scandal!"

She turned away from Arthur and wrapped her fingers tightly about the canister as if she might squeeze the truth out of it. Unscrewing the cap, she tugged the contents out a bit – it was an old roll of 35mm film negatives.

"We *must* know the truth! Money can buy silence, Arthur; if there's anything… inappropriate on the film, we'll see that it's kept quiet. Now, get the car; we're going – now!"

Arthur knew when he was beaten and Fiona had him on he ropes, he knew.

"Yes, dear."

While Arthur headed out to the garage – after Fiona made him change into decent clothes, of course - Fiona got her purse and checkbook. Stepping out the side door of the house, she walked across the stone paving stones to the edge of the gravel driveway, and waited for Arthur to pull up next to her in the car. She never stepped onto the gravel for fear of ruining her shoes and not even her eagerness get to get the photos developed could change that.

A moment later, Arthur pulled the car up by her, and she hopped in on the front passenger side. He drove down the narrow and winding country road, passing the large homes and cottages that dotted the wealthy area. For all the seclusion of their rural idyll it only took a few minutes to reach the center of town, and then they found a place to park.

"Do you want me to come with you, dear; or shall I… take care of the shopping?" Arthur said.

"So long as it doesn't include a stop in the pub – yes."

"Now, Fiona, I'm shocked you would suggest such a thing," Arthur replied. "It's far too early in the day for me to-"

"For you to go there!" she said sharply, just in case he had other ideas.

She handed him the grocery list.

"Here it is. Now, take care of it and then meet me in Boots the chemist; I'm staying there until the pictures are ready."

With that, they both got out of the car and went their respective ways.

Fiona strode along the wide sidewalk like a woman on a mission but mindful of the importance of good manners in the community in which she had some standing, she gave a courteous nod here and there as she passed several people she was acquainted with. She moved beyond the sweet shop, the petrol station, and finally came to Boots, and strode down the center aisle to the back where the photo lab' was.

"Can I help you?" the young woman behind the counter asked pleasantly enough.

Fiona eyed her up and down. Oh, she was one of those… what were they called, a… Goth? Fiona rolled her eyes. These young people today, no sense of propriety! But as a plus, if there were any… inappropriate images on the film - she would not be upset.

"I have a roll of negatives here; I'd like prints made of them," Fiona said.

The girl had not missed Fiona's derisory glance. She took the canister, popped it open, and had a look. She snorted.

"God, lady; where'd you get this, a museum? Don't you have a memory card with your pictures?"

"It's an old roll, young… lady. Now, can you make the prints, or shall I take my business elsewhere?" Fiona said, anger evident in her voice.

"Yeah, all right - chill, will ya? I'll see what I can do."

The 'Goth Girl' moved to an open doorway behind the counter, and had a few mumbled words with someone in the back. After a brief exchange, she nodded and turned to face Fiona.

"Okay - Abdul says he can handle it; be about a half hour. You want to wait?"

Fiona moved to a chair and sat.

"Yes."

As it turned out, the Abdul fellow was better than his word; Fiona had the pictures in less than twenty minutes. Standing at the counter, she flipped through them, and was confused.

"Is this all?"

The girl nodded.

"Yup; just a bunch of documents. How do you want to pay – cash or credit card?"

Fiona handed over the cash without another word, gathered the prints and film canister, and left. As it happened, Arthur was just returning to the car, his arms laden with the food he'd bought. Fiona quickly joined him, and presented him with the pictures.

"Hmmm… interesting," he said slowly as he flipped through them.

Fiona's eyebrows went up.

"You find them interesting? I thought sure you'd dismiss them with one of your usual 'harrumphs'. Can you make head or tail of them?"

"Yes, they're some sort of financial records; something to do with purchases and sales among a number of people. There are several names here: Vasilov, a Mrs. Brightman, Gustav-"

Fiona snatched them away from Arthur.

"All right, that's enough of discussing them in public! So long as you understand the documents that's sufficient. Come, we'll return home, and call Dr. Mayhew."

Getting in their car, Arthur drove them back to the house. Fiona saw little of the sights along the way; her attention was focused on these odd pictures. Now that she really studied them, she could see what Arthur meant; they were clearly pages from some sort of ledger. Not what she'd thought they would find at all. It appeared that a large number of Russian antiques had been bought and sold over the years, and from what was contained in these documents – the deals had not been legitimate!

'Ohh, Michael, what have you done!' Fiona railed in her head.

Had Michael somehow died because of these deals? How deeply had he been involved? These and other questions swirled in Fiona's mind as they got out of the car. She didn't even look back to see if Arthur had put the car away properly; she was too intent on speaking to the doctor.

Once in the study, she checked the clock – late morning. So, what time was it out in the Caribbean?

"Arthur, what's the time different between here and… oh, Eastern America?"

Silence. Fiona sighed; what was he up to now? She rose and stuck her head out the door of her study. There he was, golf clubs leaning against the wall, and slipping his cleats on. At a time like this!

"Arthur!"

He looked up, a rather sheepish expression on his face. He shrugged. He saw no reason to disturb his usual routine for a son that had been dead to him for more years than he cared to remember – pretty much ever since his… what did they call it – his 'coming out'?

"What? We're done now, and I'd like to get a quick eighteen holes in."

"Oh… very well." Where Michael was concerned, Fiona was very used to doing things on her own. "But do you know the time difference between here and the Caribbean?"

"Hmmm… let me think. I think it's five hours; that is, they're five hours behind us."

Fiona nodded.

"Thank you. And yes, go have fun."

She looked at her watch, just about eleven o'clock: probably too early to bother the doctor. So, what could she do to pass the time? Ah, she had an idea; that assistant from the Women's Guild, she had showed Fiona how to use the scanner attached to her new computer. Dr. Mayhew would probably want these pictures. So she could scan them and then… what's the term? … Attach them to an email? Yes, that was it.

Turning on her computer, Fiona flipped open the top of her printer/scanner, and put the first picture in. She had to slip her glasses on to see the controls clearly, but the scanner button was easy enough to find. Oh, this would be easy!

So, over the course of the next hour or so, Fiona carefully scanned and saved a copy of every photograph they had found inside the little model plane. Long about noon, she was finally finished. She could hear the grandfather clock in the main entryway striking noon, and she checked her watch. Hmmm… the clock was a bit slow. She'd have Arthur adjust it when he got back.

At any rate, it should be late enough to call the doctor now; surely he was up by now! Flipping through her notebook, she found his phone number, picked up the receiver and dialed.

# CHAPTER TWENTY-EIGHT

*July 21, 1984: Nassau*

ALAN WAS, IN FACT, in that pleasant, dream-like state one experiences just before fully awakening, and his thoughts this time were of the past.

His time with Christina was a true emotional rollercoaster; he went from incredible highs to desperate lows! Now, granted that they'd only known each other for a brief time, but he was truly enjoying being with her, and he had to wonder: did they have a future together? The 'deal breaker' was Jesus. Alan wasn't an ogre; he was actually rather fond of the boy, but his behavior – and Christina's total kowtowing to his every whim – made any sort of long term relationship impossible.

So, Alan decided to see where their relationship might be headed. Once they were back on the ship, and he'd tried – without success – to line up some one-on-one time with her, he decided to treat them to a little excursion.

Over breakfast, where Jesus just about wailed through the entire meal, he made a few suggestions.

"Christina, how about we go ashore today? The ship will dock in about an hour, and the island here has an aquarium; Jesus might like to see the fish."

"Well… I don't-"

"Nah…na…fiissssh!" the child howled.

Alan couldn't help but grin; yeah, that settled it – they were going.

So, after they'd eaten and Alan had slipped a little extra tip to the staff for how well they had coped with Jesus littering the floor and table with enough breakfast food to feed two children, it seemed, they headed off to dress.

On a cruise ship, the standard tipping arrangement was to give the staff money at the end of the cruise. Typically, you gave your cabin steward several dollars per person per day, and the same for your waiter/waitress. The Maitre'D got only a dollar or two per person per day, but – of course – he or she got tips from everyone in the dining hall. But, considering the rather sizable mess that Jesus left on – and under – the table, Alan felt it appropriate to give the staff a little extra. Just from a quick glance, it was clear that it was going to take a while to clean up this mess.

Alan went to his cabin and got some nice shorts and a pullover shirt on, plus a hat. He's long ago learned that a hat was vital in this kind of heat! Once he was ready, he headed down in the elevator to the level for the dock, camera in hand. Oh, he was so glad that this island had a deepwater port and they did not have to use the tender to get on and off the ship; he did not relish spending time on one of those with Jesus.

Christina and Jesus were not already there, which did not surprise him. In fact, he had to wait a full thirty minutes before the mother and son arrived.

"I'm so sorry," Christina said. "It… took a while to find just the right outfit for Jesus."

Alan painted a smile on his face. He'd seen the fight to get him dressed, many times. He had often thought it would be easier to let him go naked but of course that would attract stares of the wrong kind and it was good for Jesus to start learning the rules or regular behavior.

"I can just imagine. Shall we?"

He offered his armed to Christina but quickly retracted it as Jesus lunged as if to bite Alan's forearm. Instead, he gestured toward the gangplank, and they headed down it. Christina went first, Jesus just about glued to her hip, and he decked out in khaki shorts and a Sesame Street t-shirt featuring a colorful picture of Big Bird right in the center. Following them, Alan now had a reason to give a genuine smile – the rear view was quite nice. Christina was in a cerise pink bikini top and snug black shortie-shorts that looked as if they'd been spray painted on!

Once on the dock, Alan looked around, and saw the signs for the various excursions. As it happened, the little ferry to the aquarium left right from the same dock, and he could see the aquarium off of a tiny island on the other side of the harbor. It had a huge metal tower – it almost looked like some sort of lighthouse – sitting atop a coral reef standing just off shore of the island.

"Ah, here's the place we need to go," Alan said. "Come on, we can catch the shuttle to the aquarium right here."

Taking Christina by the elbow, he led her to the other end of the dock and they got on the small ferry.

"Oh, isn't this nice!" she exclaimed happily, stepping onto the boat.

Alan stepped on board, and made to sit next to her, but she sat Jesus between them. Alan sighed, and sat – even as Jesus started to fidget.

"Fish; fish!" he whined.

Christina patted his cheek and ruffled his hair.

"Yes, my sweet boy; we'll see them soon."

She turned to Alan.

"Will they leave soon?"

Alan opened his mouth to answer, but the roar of the engine cut him off.

"There's the answer to your question," he said with a smile.

'Thank God we're underway,' he thought. The last thing he wanted was a long wait with Jesus throwing his usual hissy fit.

The engine revved even more, a cloud of black smoke billowed up at the stern and the scent of diesel wafted through the air as water was churned up. The boat pulled away from the dock and began to move across the harbor. Alan held onto his baseball cap; the wind was pretty strong and the sunlight especially bright. Looking around, he could see the small harbor; the docks were crowded with fishing trawlers and sailboats and there were many people out on the water.

"Ugghhhhhh!" Jesus whined.

"Yes, sweetheart," Christina said. "It's from the boat, but it'll be gone soon."

Alan marveled at how well Christina interpreted her son's seemingly unintelligible grunts and whines. He would have been impressed but for the fact that he had the distinct impression that her desire to understand his every sound was holding back his need to develop his oral language skills. But today was definitely not a day to mention that. Alan was getting the idea now that there was never a good time to suggest to Christina that her son may benefit from being handled a different way.

As it turned out, it was not entirely true of Christina to reassure Jesus that they would soon reach their intended destination; the boat had to meander across the harbor to avoid the traffic, so it took a while to get to the small island. Once there, Jesus insisted on being the first one off of the boat. From the looks the crew was giving Alan, it was clear they were glad of his departure – and already dreading the return trip. Alan gave a helpless shrug. At least, he hoped, they'd probably seen him often enough to know that Jesus was not *his* son.

"So, where shall we go first?" Alan asked, making his tone forcibly bright.

Jesus' understanding of language was obviously better than his grasp over the spoken word. As quick as lightning, he pointed at the tower before Christina could do anything more than open her mouth.

"There!" he screamed.

Alan didn't have to wait for Christina to confirm the order; he took her by the elbow and headed off to the left. At least if they went where the boy wanted to they may get some moments of peace, and it did look an interesting place to visit. The pebble walkway was wide and winding and lined with palms and native trees and bushes. It only took a few minutes for them to be approaching the entrance to the tower. It stood about twenty feet offshore and looked a lot like the tower of a submarine. Actually, the more Alan studied it, the more it made him think of the Nautilus submarine from that old Disney movie '20,000 Leagues Under the Sea'; it was made of large metal plates held together by huge rivets. From the base of the tower, a gangway stretched to the shore, right to the end of the path where they were standing.

"So, we just walk right in?" Christina asked, unsure.

Alan nodded. It felt good to have her look to him for direction for once, instead of constantly blocking his efforts to change anything with Jesus.

"Exactly. Come on; I'll show you around."

They walked up the narrow walkway, the high railing giving Alan a good sense of security – Jesus would not be tumbling into the clear blue-green waters here! The hatch stood ajar and Alan nudged it open and they stepped inside.

"Ohhhh…," Jesus said. "Down!"

Alan almost gave an audible sigh of relief. Jesus liked the place.

"All right, my love," Christina replied softly.

She kissed Jesus' cheek softly before she set him down, and immediately he was off. The room was round, and all manner of tanks lined the walls, all full of various kinds of fish. In the center was a corkscrew-like staircase that led both up and down within the tower. Jesus made a beeline for the stairs, and down he went.

Christina sprinted after him.

"Oh, where is he going?"

Alan kept pace with her. He didn't want any repeats of the earlier museum climbing stunt.

"Not to worry; the underwater observation area is down there, and this is the only way in and out. He can't get far."

Down they all went, and Alan was thankfully proven right. Like the upper area, the room was round and there were windows everywhere. In this case, there were no display cases or aquariums. Children and adults stood at the windows and looked out into the sea life that naturally filled the harbor.

Jesus was no exception; he bolted for the nearest window and shoved the two little girls standing there aside.

"Hey!" one of them complained.

"Wait your turn," the other said.

Jesus jumped up and down; he wasn't quite tall enough to see out the window.

"Up!" he whined.

Christina moved quickly to him, picked him up and held him behind the girls, so he could see out but the peace could be kept by not obscuring the other children's views either. Alan stepped up next to them, and they could see fish and crabs moving about, in amongst the seaweeds and kelp.

"Wow," Christina said softly. "I've never seen anything like this. Is that big one a lobster?"

Alan slowly nodded his head.

"Ah… I think so. I'm used to New England lobsters; they have two large claws. These Caribbean types don't."

"OW!" the two girls howled.

Alan looked down; Jesus was using his two 'claws' to yank the girls' hair. Reaching out instinctively, he squeezed Jesus' hands, forcing him to release the hair of the tormented girls. The girls turned, gave Alan a weak smile and a thank-you and darted away.

"Alan! Don't you hurt my baby!"

Christina cradled Jesus protectively to her bosom and stepped away from Alan as the child, assured now of his mother's full attention, promptly burst into a flood of crocodile tears.

"Christina - *he* was the one hurting those *children*! I just had him let go!"

Christina was not to be talked down.

"They were bothering him! They should not have stood there!"

Alan sighed, shook his head and turned away from her. How could he make her see that Jesus had major behavioral and communication problems that she was doing him no favors by ignoring? Rubbing his forehead with his hand, he gathered his thoughts, he realized it was futile. He turned back to face her.

"Christina, we need to talk! Now, I know we've not known each other long, but we've had some good times together…"

"Yes, we have, and I would hope that they could continue," she replied, a little too curtly for Alan's comfort, but he pressed on.

"As do I. Yet, continue - how? Do you see us merely being friends, or do you want… more?"

Christina continued to soothe and comfort Jesus as she moved to a nearby bench and sat down. It was clear that Alan was commanding a little less than half her attention at this moment in time. She faltered, obviously having seen nothing wrong in her defensive stance and not having anticipated this conversation with Alan.

"Well… I don't know – yet. If – if you can understand how things are for me – then more, much more."

Alan sighed, and looked at Jesus. He pretty much knew the answer to his next question, but he had to ask it anyway.

"And, how do I … show you I understand?"

Christina shifted Jesus on his lap so he was facing out – so Alan and he were facing each other.

"By being kinder to Jesus!"

Alan nodded.

"That's as I thought. Christina, I think I love you, and I'm willing to make the commitment to try and make this relationship work. But, I will not bend to Jesus' will; I will not go through him to get to you."

There was a steely glint in Christina's eyes.

"You don't love my son, do you?" she snapped.

Alan was exasperated now. It was true that he was no real fan of Jesus as he was now, but he also knew that this continual pandering to his tantrums and demands was doing the child no favors at all.

"I didn't say that! I know you come with… baggage, and I accept that," Alan replied.

"My son is not a bag!"

Alan groaned, realizing how his metaphor had not translated well into the Costa Rican mind.

"I'm not saying he is! I'm saying that I love you, and I can grow to love Jesus like a son – and treat him like a son. That's the critical point – *treat* him like a son, treat him like a son should be treated, with love and discipline."

Christina just about gasped as she gathered Jesus into her arms.

"You'll not beat my child… monster!"

Alan realized just how much Christina meant to him as he struggled to make himself understood. He fought to keep his voice level and calm, although the pitch of Christina's exclamations was getting higher and so was Jesus' agitation, as a result.

"Christina - discipline does not equal beating; it doesn't even mean to smack or spank, necessarily. It means setting limits for a child and enforcing them with appropriate consequences. You indulge and spoil Jesus, and you do a disservice to him as a result! What will he be like when he grows up?"

Christina rose to her feet with great determination and headed for the stairs.

"A confident man, unafraid to speak his mind, and get what he wants! We are through, Dr Mayhew; good day to you," she said, practically spitting the words at him.

Alan opened his mouth to protest, to apologize, to do something to keep her from going – and then Jesus kicked out at him – and she praised all but praised him for it!

"There, there, baby – Mama will make the nasty man go away."

That was it.

Alan stood there, watching them go and knew it was over; if she could allow her child to do such a thing to a man she *said* she cared about – loved - what future could they have together? Moving to the bench, he sat down, rested his elbows on his knees, and buried his face in his hands. At that moment, he felt a pain so deep in his guts, he hurt in places he didn't even know he had!

He didn't know how long he sat there, but he was starting to feel hungry; so it had to be close – or long after – lunchtime. Getting to his feet, he started to slowly plod up the stairs. He didn't stop at the ground level, but kept on going up, and eventually reached the peak.

The top was small – just a small glass room with a narrow outer deck running around the outside edge of the stairwell – yet the view was incredible. Alan stepped out onto the deck, bent forward slightly, and gripped the cast iron railing. He closed his eyes and just sort of drank in the cool bracing wind; it helped him to feel alive. It was strange; with Christina gone, a feeling of great emptiness was gnawing at him. But, being up here, out in the open, he could feel his mind clearing – just a bit.

Did the pain ease? No, but at least he didn't feel quite so empty and alone. There had been no future for him with Christina with Jesus so often coming between them. And if that was a sample of Christina's philosophy on parenting, Alan felt any future children they may have had would have only increased the nightmare for him.

He looked down; there were a number of families milling about down at the ground level; they were embracing as they went to the outside tanks and fish displays. Yes, *this* was how families should act; this was how they should be.

Right now, all Alan was feeling was pain. Yet, he knew that it would pass. There was that old saying, 'And this too shall pass'. At this moment, that seemed very appropriate. The pain would pass, he would move on and maybe – just maybe – he would look back on this episode and actually see something good as coming out of all this. Had his stomach not been royally grumbling, he would have stayed there and tried to soak up some more... warmth.

Plodding down the metal mesh steps, he could hear his heavy steps echo up and down the tower. It was strange; it seemed to take a long time to reach the ground floor. In addition, the room seemed just a bit darker than he remembered. Christina and Jesus were nowhere in sight. He'd no idea where they had gone but he found, to his surprise, that he didn't much care.

Once Alan stepped out of the door, the sunlight was almost blinding, but he actually welcomed the sting to his eyes; the pain mimicked the pain within him.

He thought about walking around the island and seeing the rest of the aquarium, but he really wasn't up for it. Instead, Alan went down to the dock and waited for the ferry boat to take him back to the ship. He hoped that by returning early he could avoid seeing Christina and Jesus whom, he calculated, would probably spend as long as possible in the greater freedom the island afforded Jesus to run around ('and cause havoc', Alan found himself unkindly adding in his head).

Once the ferry arrived, he stepped on board and took a seat on one of the benches. For most of the trip, he just sat there, head down, and ignored everyone and everything around him. As they neared the main dock, he looked up, and he saw that the boat crew was smiling at him.

Alan wasn't sure what to make of the crew. He had to figure that they'd maybe they'd already seen Christina and Jesus come back without him, and now here he was looking sad and dejected. These guys might be ignorant boat tenders, but they could put two and two together and figure out that they'd broken up.

The captain gave Alan a big smile.

"Senór, there be plenty fishes in the ocean; and you able to do better!"

Alan sighed.

"I… suppose so. It's just… right now… it's tough."

The man, a big burly heavyset Latino stepped closer. Oh, his breath was like whiskey mixed with boat fuel! But he was ready to help a fellow male with woman trouble. He'd had plenty of is own in the past!

"I knows club in town, senór; it have senóritas that make you forget her – even just for a few hours – and they very cheap."

Alan rose to his feet and started toward the gangway, waving the man off, as kindly as he could. But the professional advice came instantly to his lips.

"Thanks, but no thanks; I'm a doctor, I know what sorts of diseases those ladies have!"

"You doctor? Ay, can I ask you? I having pain right here," the man said, pointing at his right side, just about at his belt. "What it can be?"

"Ever have your appendix out?"

He shook his head.

"I no have nothing out, excepting my teeth!" he said, and gave a big smile.

Alan cringed; yeah, he'd had a *lot* of those out!

"Could be your appendix; go into town and see a doctor."

"It important?"

"Been hurting long?"

"'Bout… three days," the captain replied.

"It's important! Left untreated, it could burst and kill you."

Fear filled the man's face.

"Ay, I go doctor now! Gracias, Doctor, many thanks."

Alan gave him a weak smile and moved up onto the dock. As he headed toward the ship, he couldn't help but realize something – he felt a little better. Yeah, his work helped him to get over the pain of his love life. So, that's what he'd do – he'd throw himself into his work, and try to forget.

# CHAPTER TWENTY-NINE

*December 14, 2009: The Caribbean Sea*

ALAN FELT SOMETHING WARM and soft brush his face. He smiled – it was quite nice. Then he frowned; it was a hand, and it was squeezing his nose! Alan opened his eyes and looked around. What was that noise? He lifted his head and paid closer attention to what was going on around him – his phone was ringing!

He sat up; Tiffany, naked and lovely was sprawled partially across him, and had been tugging on his nose.

"Your phone's ringing," she grunted, her face buried in a pillow.

Alan wiped the sleep from his eyes and looked at the clock.

"Seven o'clock in the blessed A.M.? God, this had better be damn important!"

Rolling over, he grabbed his phone, flipped it open and pushed 'Talk'.

"Hello, is this Dr. Mayhew?" came a woman's voice.

Luckily, the distinctiveness of the cultured English tones seared through Alan's sleep-fogged brain.

"Yes. Ah, Mrs. Hamilton?"

"Yes, quite correct. I was calling you back regarding that matter we discussed yesterday."

Alan swung his legs around and sat – naked – on the edge of the bed; she now had his full attention.

"So quickly? Have you… found something?"

"As a matter of fact – yes," Mrs. Hamilton said, rather matter-of-factly. "I shan't bore you with the particulars; suffice it to say, we found a roll of film hidden in that model, and I have prints of all of them right here."

Alan was impressed – and hopeful.

"Really? Do you feel they may be relevant to our investigation?"

"Oh yes, I should say so."

Fiona gave him the particulars on the items, and let him know that she had image files all ready to send to him! By this time, Alan was standing – still nude – next to the bed, and Tiffany was sitting up. Clearly, while she couldn't hear the full conversation, she could glean enough from Alan's end of it to know something big was brewing: the expression on her face said as much.

"My goodness, Mrs. Hamilton, I give you ten out of ten for this; well done!"

"Thank you, Doctor. So, shall I send them along to you?"

"Most definitely; let me give you my email address," he replied.

He did so; they chatted a bit more, and then said their good-byes. Alan promised to contact her the moment he had any news for her.

"So, it sounds like you were right!" Tiffany said as she bounded out of bed.

Alan had to smile; she did wiggle and jiggle ever so nicely when she ran about in the nude!

"Yes. So, let's get up to the club, and I'll see about downloading the pictures."

Tiffany turned to him, and a confused look crossed her face.

"Why the big grin? Oh... checking me out, eh?"

Alan raised his hands in mock surrender.

"Guilty as charged, darlin'; you truly are a sight to behold!"

She laughed.

"Hey, good thing Mrs. Hamilton didn't call last night; she might have... interrupted us."

Alan, also getting dressed, tilted his head back and laughed – long and loud.

"Oh, does that ever remind me of something; a little... incident that happened a few years back."

"Really? Tell me about it."

"Well... okay. It was on one of the larger cruise ships that I worked on," Alan said. "I was confronted by a couple who insisted on being seen together. This was not unusual, of course, and we were often confronted by couples where one had Alzheimer's and the other didn't. In this case Mr. and Mrs... Ah... 'Smith' both appeared to be lucid and quite healthy. One was sixty-seven, the other seventy-two."

"I don't get it; 'seen together'," Tiffany said, her brow wrinkling.

"Oh, I'll get to that. I asked what I could do for them, and the man said, 'Will you watch us have sexual intercourse? I've had a prostate problem for a number of years and I don't think that it's working right. My woman doesn't get satisfied.' Something, huh?"

"You're kidding!"

Alan raised his right hand, as if being sworn to testify in court.

"Hand to God, it's true. I indicated that this was most unusual and that it was not the practice of the ship's doctor to do this. They both pleaded. I performed the usual prostate test and didn't find anything wrong. I then consulted with the nurse who said it would at least provide comic relief for the otherwise busy day. I also contacted the staff captain of the cruise line; you always had to do anything that the passengers wanted, as long as it was within the shipping rules."

Tiffany nodded.

"Ah yes, and the staff captain is the keeper and interpreter of those rules. So, what did he have to say on the matter?"

Tiffany's eyes were already shining with mirth and she could hardly get her words out.

"He found it most amusing and asked if the woman was at all attractive. If so, he'd volunteer to come and watch. She was not at all attractive by my standards. In the end, I told him that I would do this only if one of the nurses was also present."

"Ah yes, a wise move. So… you… did it?"

Alan nodded.

"The nurse and I agreed to meet back after lunch and observe Mr. and Mrs. Smith to… medically evaluate if there was a problem with their… intercourse. They arrived, disrobed with little discomfort about being naked in front of two perfect strangers, and then they… did their thing in the missionary position without any obvious difficulty. Mrs. Smith appeared to have an orgasm and Mr. Smith appeared to ejaculate. I informed them that all appeared normal. They were charged for a regular office visit, and went on their way."

Tiffany snorted, and then burst out laughing.

"You charged them?"

"I had to! I had to account for my time and the nurse's. Of course, I was at a bit of a loss as to *how* to code the visit."

"Ah, good point," Tiffany said. "What *would* that fall under the category of?"

"My nurse came to the rescue; she coded it as anxiety difficulties and charged it to Mr. Smith's shipboard account."

By now, they were both dressed, and both laughing heartily as they gathered their things and headed out of the cabin.

"I take it that's not the end of the story?" Tiffany asked.

Alan shook his head, chuckling.

"Not by a long shot. Much to our surprise, Mr. and Mrs. Smith returned the following day and asked to repeat the previous day's exercise. I indicated that neither the nurse nor I had seen any significant difficulty with their… intercourse - and on examination, no problem with his prostate. They were most insistent and I suggested that they speak to the staff captain.

"Now, phones are all wireless and hands free. Back then, I had one of the old style types with a cord. So, I rang up the staff captain, we put him on the speaker phone, and they pleaded with him that maybe this would be the answer to all of their problems, if the doctor and nurse could see what was going wrong with their intercourse. In the end, he suggested that, if the doctor and nurse agreed, maybe we could try once more, but further than that they would have to seek help off of the ship. As far as my nurse and I were concerned, we both figured that exhibitionism on their part was maybe at the root of the exercise."

Tiffany nodded as they boarded the elevator.

"It sure sounds like it. I had a boyfriend like that once; he kept wanting to… do it out in the woods behind his house."

"Did you?" Alan said.

She blushed.

"Ah… well… I did end up with poison ivy in a rather… sensitive spot. Now, come on, finish your story!"

"All right, all right. So again Mr. and Mrs. Smith went at it, fat flying in all directions as the excess adiposity seemed to meld into one large wave as they had intercourse, again in the missionary position on our hospital observation bed."

Tiffany grimaced.

"Oh, that is not the best image to have in my mind right before breakfast!"

Alan laughed.

"Well, you did ask! As this had been agreed to be the last of their… experiments - Mr. Smith finally confided in me. He asked if there were any other areas of the ship where they could 'practice'. I indicated that their *cabin* might be an appropriate place. He then explained that Mrs. Smith was *not* really his wife but his old high school sweetheart, married to another man. They were all on their fiftieth reunion cruise. They could think of no other way of getting together, so they came up with the doctor's office as a potential… rendezvous site. We fell for it hook, line and sinker, never imagining this was the real reason!"

Tiffany laughed.

"Oh, that is priceless. Well, I've got to give them credit for creative thinking! What's that phrase? Ah, they were truly thinking outside the box."

"Yeah, my daughter competed in the Odyssey of the Mind back in high school, and that's their motto," Alan said.

"My-my, seems that phrase can have a multitude of uses, huh?"

They got off the elevator and headed straight for the club; neither seemed interested in eating just now. They wanted to see what Fiona had sent them over. Once there, Alan booted up his laptop and got online. A few mouse clicks later and he was opening his email.

"Ah, here it is!"

Tiffany came over to stand behind him and bent over his shoulder, her hair cascading across his right cheek ever so nicely.

"Wow, that's a lot of files!"

"Yeah, we need to print them out. Where can we do that?"

"You got a flash drive?"

Alan fished around in his laptop case.

"Yeah, a new one, in fact; two gig of memory on it. You want to put them on your office computer to print them out?"

Tiffany nodded.

"Yeah, that'll be easiest; don't you think?"

Alan slipped the drive into one of the empty USB ports of his computer.

"I agree. Okay, let me save the images to my computer, and then I'll copy them over to the drive."

A few minutes later, they had all the image files saved and Alan handed Tiffany the flash drive. She took it with a grin and turned to dart off to her office.

"Come on; I can't wait to see what these are!"

Alan, desperately trying to gather up his things, called after her,

"Hey, hold on; wait up!"

"See you there!"

He looked over his shoulder just in time to see her zip out of the club. It took a few minutes, but he finally managed to follow.

Although Tiffany went through the 'Authorized Personnel Only' door well ahead of him, Alan was able to follow. The other crewmembers knew him by now and they waved him through.

Once again, they found themselves in Tiffany's office. She worked at printing out the pictures, and Alan took a moment to sit and relax. His stomach grumbled. Huh, they'd need to get to the dining hall after this and eat something. They could study the pictures in a more leisurely fashion while they ate.

Alan pulled them from the printer as them came out, and flipped through them.

"A ledger; antiques, purchases and sales, shipping dates, and a list of customers and their personal information. Hey, Mrs. Brightman; I remember that name only too well."

Tiffany finished printing, grabbed the last couple pictures, and turned to Alan.

"So, it would seem the murder came down to good old fashioned greed, eh?"

Alan slowly nodded.

"That's what all this would suggest, yes… but this is a lot to digest! Come on, I'm about to pass out from hunger."

Tiffany laughed.

"Okay, my man, let's get you fed."

Giving him back his flash drive, she led Alan to the dining hall, and they took their seats at another private table off to the side.

As they ate, Alan started to study the pages in depth. It was clear that Vasilov had been engaged in a lot of illegal activity for some years; Mrs. Brightman was just one of his many clients. Something caught Alan's eye on one page, and he held it out for Tiffany to see.

"Have a look at that entry on the bottom."

She looked at it, and her brow wrinkled.

"Huh, a 'consulting fee' paid to Michael every month. What kind of consulting could he be doing?"

"Could be blackmail," Alan suggested.

"Or, could be a… sort of retainer," Tiffany replied. "Maybe he was paying Michael to steer some clients his way…?"

Alan slowly nodded.

"Yeah, hard to tell what it was for. Hey, look at this! The last picture isn't really a page from a ledger. It looks more like an address book."

He handed the photograph to her, and she scanned it over thoroughly.

"You're right; the home addresses for Mrs. Abigail Brightman and Mrs. Erica Clapham. Huh, they both lived in Sarasota, Florida. Coincidence, huh?... But I wonder why Michael had them listed separately from everyone else?"

Alan drank a bit of his coffee, and then set the mug down.

"Maybe he wanted to check them both out; maybe he suspected that they knew each other or something. That name – Clapham, it's… familiar for some reason."

"Did she know Michael?"

"Ah… I can't remember. Tell you what, after we're done eating, we'll check both of these ladies out and see if we can link either – or both – to Michael."

Tiffany nodded.

"Sounds like a plan!"

Once breakfast was over, Tiffany wanted to continue researching the case, but she had work to do. As she didn't want to – as she put it - 'miss out on the good stuff', she made Alan promise not to do anything until she was done – later in the afternoon.

So, instead, Alan had to content himself with a bit of fun for a while. Returning to his cabin, he slipped on some nice comfy clothes and headed up on deck. He stepped over to the railing and saw that the waves around the ship were just a bit rough. Not badly, but enough that the stabilizers would be needed to keep the ship even and steady.

"Hello there, Alan," came Jenny's voice.

Turning, he saw that 'Jen-Tina' were once more decked out for some fun in the sun.

"Hello, girls. You come to get some sun? You have a good breakfast this morning? Oh, those omelets were incredible!"

Jenny grimaced and rubbed her stomach.

"Oh, don't mention food!"

"Jenny's feeling a bit seasick again today," Tina said. "She thinks the boat's rocking too much."

Alan laughed.

"Too much? Oh, this is nothing. When the waves get rough, as they often do en route to Hawaii from the west coast or in the Tasman Sea around New Zealand, one really feels that you're truly out to sea. Seeing the force seven to ten waves and wind is most impressive, and you can only be grateful that you're not in a small sail or motorboat and having to deal with that weather."

"Ewwww… sounds horrid!" Jenny said.

"Yeah. Of course, when the seas got *real* rough, the requests for seasick medicine and shots would always increase significantly. The overuse and abuse of scopolamine patches also increased."

"Sco-whatta?" Tina said.

"Scopolamine patches. They're a relatively new utilization of a very old drug with a modern application that keeps being taken off the market for safety reasons and then put back on again. They're small diskettes that you put on the skin, usually behind the ear. They came out in the 1980s originally, and it was found that there were way too many side effects and it was taken off the market within a few years."

"Well, then why are you talking about them now?" Tina said.

"After the new millennium, they were brought back, and are still available for purchase."

"Why the patch?" Jenny said. "Why not just take a pill or something?"

"The patch allows the drug in it to be slowly released into the body. It keeps most people from being nauseated when there is excessive motion in the vestibular canals."

"The what-what?" Jenny said.

"Boy, I wish you came with English subtitles!" Tina said.

Alan laughed.

"Sorry, the doctor in me keeps… leaking out. Ah, it's the inner ear - the balance mechanism - that gets affected by the motion of the ship in the rough seas. The drug is very effective in most people by moderating the effect on the eustacean tubes, and keeps the patient from suffering from seasickness. Unfortunately, it makes your mouth very dry, your vision blurry and there are a variety of other side effects. It can't be given to people with glaucoma and certain other conditions without serious side effects. If a person is one of the lucky ones that don't get lots of side effects, I could always be sure of not getting a call from them in the middle of the night for seasickness."

"Gee, I'd like to try one of those patches," Jenny said. "You think they have them on board?"

"Maybe. But, you need to be careful. Unfortunately, some people will have no symptoms from the patches and can forget that they're wearing them. If you touch the patch in addition to wearing it, you can get a double dose of the drug and increase the symptoms. I remember one call to a passenger's cabin to take care of a problem. There weren't any rough seas, and she had no history of any significant medical problems or of taking any particular medications. She was apparently speaking in a very strange manner about the sea monsters coming to get her, and had a strange glassy look in her eyes. She hadn't gone to the bathroom for days, and was complaining that her mouth was very dry no matter what she drank. A quick look behind her ears revealed six scopolamine patches!"

Both Jenny and Tina let out a squeak of surprise.

"Oh my goodness!" Jenny said.

"How could she do that to herself?" Tina added.

"When I first spoke to her, she had forgotten that she had put any on. Later she remembered and told me, 'I put a few on, Doc, so that I was sure not to get seasick.' The treatment for her was easy: take off the patches and drink lots of fluids."

"I think we'll pass on using quite that many," Jenny said.

Tina moved to the railing and looked about.

"So, are you saying that the waves aren't so bad today?"

Alan nodded.

"Oh yeah. When the waves get so high that the crew in the staff quarters, which are usually on Deck Three and Four, are required to put the storm windows in place, you know it's rough."

"Safety windows? What are those?" Jenny said.

"Metal-hinged windows that are used to make sure that the portholes are truly waterproof, if there should be a strong wave that breaks the quadruple pane glass."

Jenny's jaw dropped, and Tina's eyebrows shot up into her bangs.

"Wow, those are some windows!" Tina said. "Boy! - And here I thought our little shoebox of a cabin was tough to live in."

"Have you been in a lot of rough seas?"

Alan nodded. He was enjoying impressing the ladies with his knowledge of the sea.

"Yeah, rough seas can be had in many parts of the world. The astute captain tries to avoid them. He gets better post-cruise reports from the passengers that way; they can then brag that they have been through such-and-such passage without getting sick. And then the cruise line's home office likes that because those people tend to then book more cruises. Sometimes it's difficult to figure out why a captain uses a certain route. I remember one cruise from Sitka, Alaska to Vancouver, Canada. It was the captain's last leg of his three month assignment and he was undoubtedly anxious to pack and get off in good time for his flight back home to Italy. Instead of taking the picturesque, famous, but slow, Inland Passage that goes on the inside of the Queen Charlotte Islands, followed by a beautiful view of fjords and Orcas between Vancouver Island and the mainland of Canada, he chose the sea voyage *outside* of those protective land masses. This meant that the full force of the Pacific Ocean was bashing the ship with nasty swells, just as it has for centuries along that barren western exposed coastline. Needless to say, I was busy during his venture 'Out to Sea'."

"Wow, makes me glad that we stick to the Caribbean," Jenny said.

"Yeah, if the open Pacific is rougher than this, we'd be puking our guts out and hold up in our cabins the whole voyage," Tina said.

"How often have you worked on those Pacific cruises, Alan?" Jenny said.

"Oh, a number of times. Rough sea passages can be had readily between

Australia and New Zealand in the Tasman Sea; in the passage around the bottom tips of South America and Africa; and many other places. The Straits of Magellan are particularly rough at certain times of the year. Trying to get from east to west through the straits can be nearly impossible! You girls know the story of *Mutiny on the Bounty…?*"

"Isn't that an old movie with Mel Gibson and what's-his-name?" Jenny said.

Alan grimaced. *Old* movie? Oh man, did *he* feel old now! The Gibson version of that story was like the third incarnation. As far as Alan was concerned, no-one was better than Clark Gable and Charles Laughton. But, that was another matter: best to stick to the subject at hand and not confuse the girls.

"Yes, that's the one. Anyway, the original ship, the *Bounty*, tried to sail through those straits to get to Tahiti, but couldn't do it; the seas and winds were just too tough. Passages like those are a constant reminder that we are guests on this planet and have been given the technological knowledge to be able to travel around it in relative comfort for our body types. We use cruise ships and airplanes. Whales and other sea life, of course, are at one with the whys and wherefores of Mother Nature and the sea. They take the storms in their stride. Occasionally, we get to see a glimpse of their life as they surface to say hello before heading out to sea again. Seeing what Mother Nature can do at sea gives one a healthy respect for it. As a ship's doctor, I get to see more than the average traveler."

"Sounds like you've led quite the colorful life" Tina said.

"And are quite the eloquent speaker!" Jenny said with a smile. "Gives me a whole new… appreciation for you, Alan."

Tina gestured for him to follow.

"Come on, come sit with us, and tell us more of your stories."

Alan smiled and gave them a nod.

"Sure, why not? I've got some free time just now. So, where shall I begin?"

The girls, of course, were not concerned what they were told, so long as they were entertained, so Alan reached into his bag and retrieved his trusty notebook, one of a series of notebooks he'd kept for years and which went everywhere with him. He flipped through it, looking for inspiration for his story-telling. With a slight wince he flipped through ten or so of the latest pages in one turn, not wanting to share anything about Michael's murder or the investigation with this pair.

Then he gave a chuckle.

"Oh you'll love these, ladies… something to add a dose of reality to anyone tempted to put a doctor up on a pedestal. We do talk crazy, sometimes!… But… in our defense, paperwork can sometimes be filled out late at night, or in a rushed moment between patients."

Jen-Tina were very intrigued now, wondering what secrets Alan would divulge. He soon had then giggling like schoolgirls as he quoted from a catalog of forms completed by doctors filling out the paperwork which was then passed on to him.

"I'm sure my paperwork may not have been perfect at times," he admitted self-deprecatingly. "But I sure hope I never wrote anything as baffling as some of these guys…"

He grinned as he realized he had found the very quote to appeal to Tina.

"'She has had no seasickness, rigors or shaking chills, but her husband states she was very hot in bed last night.'"

Alan was gratified when of course the girls laughed immediately.

"Lucky man!" exclaimed Tina.

'So cute. So young!' thought Alan.

"OK. Here we go with another one… 'The patient refused an autopsy'….' the patient had no history of suicide'."

"But… don't you have to be…"

"Dead?… Yes, you have to be dead to have an autopsy… and if you have committed suicide," Alan confirmed for the refreshingly innocent Tina while Jenny rolled her eyes.

However, Jenny was also taken in by the next quote that Alan read out:

"'Patient has left his white blood cells at home along with all of his chemotherapy medications.'"

Despairing a little, Alan could nevertheless not help laughing as he read out one of his favorite quotes from his notebook:

"'Patient's past medical history has been remarkably insignificant with only a 40 pound weight gain in the past three days here on board.'"

In case this should be mistaken as quite normal, Alan puffed out his cheeks, bloating his stomach and jiggling his stomach with his hands. That of course had Jen-Tina giggling. He was very pleased with the reaction his stories were getting.

"Those are some of the better ones, but there were plenty such gaffes from supposedly intelligent doctors, let me tell you! Many patients were 'x-rated', although one hopes that does indeed mean 'x-rayed'. I certainly haven't met too many indecent passengers!"

The girls moved closer and Tina implored,

"Met *any*…? Got any really *juicy* stories?"

'Huh, if only they knew!' thought Alan, a little pained.

But instead of distressing the girls with tales of murder, Alan launched in tales from below deck, where many of the passengers would be surprised to know things did not always run along as harmoniously as the cruise lines would like passengers to believe.

# CHAPTER THIRTY

*July 22, 1984: Key West*

YOU HAVE A CREW on some ships that come from over sixty nations all housed and fed in the same place. There are battles that occur between traditional nationalities. This especially occurs if one group has gained the upper hand in management of a certain division or department. Traditionally on many cruise lines; there is an overabundance of Food and Beverage Department employees that come from either India or Central America. When there are Indians who are in charge of the kitchens, you can be sure that the few Pakistanis who slipped thru the hiring process do not feel terribly comfortable. The waiters often come from the Eastern European countries. There is often a mix due to the fact that many of these countries are changing borders rapidly.

When you have a loyal employee that has worked on the ship for ten plus years and he was originally from Yugoslavia that is now Macedonia that was part of Bosnia or Serbia a few years ago, one can understand how he or she might be a bit antagonistic toward a manager from another Eastern Bloc nation that took over his or her homeland politically.

The Nepalese are usually the security guards. In fact, the grunts in the security are retired Gurkas, the infamous well-seasoned fighters from the Himalayas. The chief of the security department is, ninety-nine percent of the time, from England. Guess things haven't changed much there, eh! Kitchen utility workers are often from Guatemala, Honduras, Nicaragua, and other Central American countries. They are often at war with each other.

All in all, there are not as many riots as one would expect. Occasionally a laceration needs to be sutured from a "friendly fork fight". Once we had an all out battle. The Russians won the battle, but most were thrown off the ship after spending time in the ship's brig until we got to the next port. Fortunately, we had just received our suture re-supply. They were using knives instead of forks.

Alan recalled one particular incident when trying to subdue a crewmember that was clearly psychotic with a shot of Haldol, and a different type of safety concern arose. The crazy crewmember was refusing to leave his bunk to go see the psychiatrist he had been scheduled to see on shore. The Nepalese and Philippino security guys were not able to subdue the man. His Romanian comrade did not make things easy, as he was aiding him. The nurse got the syringe of Haldol and brought it down to his cabin on the second deck. He turned around and stabbed her with the syringe. She was not a large girl, and the Haldol knocked her out for nearly three days. This is where Alan had to step in; after getting his nurse – a lovely young girl by the name of Mary – safely out of harm's way, and preparing a second injection. Alan had made use of some football skills, despite the fact that he had never played the game. When he was back in college, he had been just as tall as he was now, but much thinner. At his maximum, his college weight had only been about 175! So, football was out of the question – the opposing players would have just about snapped him in two on the first tackle. Yet, he had loved the game, and his analytical mind was forever studying the players and their movements.

So, when it came time to 'take down' this rampaging Romanian, he made use of some of those old plays he remembered. He went straight at the crewman, and then faked a move to the left – making it appear that he was going to go between him and his comrade – which made them smile. They shifted, clearly intending to 'sandwich' him between them. Meanwhile, two of the security guards moved around the three of them – just as Alan had directed – and began to line up to jump them from behind.

"Now we stops you!" the burly Romanian shouted.

Alan painted a surprised look on his face.

"Really?"

With that, he ducked down and rolled to the right! The two men slammed into each other; there was a loud 'clonk' as their heads banged together. A moment later, the guards jumped them, and Alan put the finishing touch to the 'dog pile' by adding himself to the mass of masculine flesh.

"Hold them, hold them down!" Alan shouted.

A quick alcohol swab to the arm, and he jabbed the needle into his arm.

"Arrgggg, vile monster!" the Romanian growled, trying to heave the others off of him.

For a few minutes, Alan and the two guards were bounced up and down as the crewman and his friend tried to throw them off. Finally, once the Haldol kicked in, the man calmed down, and his buddy – unable to move three grown men on his own – gave up.

Alan climbed off of the pile and stood up, wiping the perspiration from his brow.

"Phew, now that was an adventure in and of itself! OK, people, let's get this fellow out of here. And you," Alan added, pointing at the friend. "You are going on report! Interfering with a medical officer? Oh, this won't look good on your service record, my man."

The two guards hoisted the man up and carried him out, even as his friend rose and stood there, looking down at the floor with a rather sheepish expression and nodded his head.

"Yes, sir; sorry, sir."

Fortunately, not all crew interactions were so negative. There were also plenty of practical jokes; they were something Alan had been involved in since childhood. On the ships, some people didn't forget that childhood pastime. Sometimes it was the crew that short sheeted fellow crew members' beds, but more often it was passengers doing it to other passengers, wives and husbands included. Usually these jokes did not get so serious as to need the services of a doctor, but occasionally they did: cut fingers and the like.

Alan remembered two incidents that required his attention: one passenger having a severe fit of sneezing due to a sneaky application of pepper, and another getting a bad rash when someone slipped some sort of extract of peanuts (to which she was allergic) into her suntan lotion! Oh, did she need a lot of lotion, and her retribution against her 'attacker' (her sister) was swift and severe. The two provided the crew with hours of laughs throughout the entire voyage.

A number of times, Alan had heard – via the cabin stewards – of people blowing up condoms and then stuffing them in drawers, closets, and any place else they could think of. Ah, the silliness of some people. Of course, once word of that got – as they say – 'below decks' (to the crew), it was copycatted. There, as the crew has access to a more extensive array of supplies, the joke was taken to a whole new level – the condoms were filled with helium! For the rest of the voyage – and the next three after that – all manner of condoms went floating throughout the crew decks.

And then there was the couple from Atlanta, Georgia - Danica and Graham. He ran a steel pipe manufacturing plant that his former partners had bought him out of. Now, with the money from that little transaction, they traveled a lot! Danica had had some very good plastic surgery. At first glance, this 75 year old lady appeared to be in her 40's. Her hair was always done just perfectly, in typical Southern Belle style, and it covered any scars that might not be covered by the makeup.

Alan discovered the scars when she came to sickbay complaining of an earache. Of course, he had to examine her ears, and anterior to the outer ear, he could see the telltale signs of a face lift, as there was a technique that was used by many surgeons that left a scar along the hairline, down in front of the ear, then behind the ear, and then back to the hairline where most would hide the rest of the scar. Other surgeons used techniques that spared the anterior (front) of the outer ear. Alan had personally seen that that was a place that often got infected, or the scar would dehisce (spread out). He'd had a number of patients who had come onboard ships having recently had plastic/cosmetic surgery with this complication. In this case, it was of interest to know if this couple had had cosmetic surgery. It was Alan's job to be the informant to the nurse and a few members of the other crew as to his decision. So as not to breech patient confidentiality, he could not ask, so the diagnosis had to be one of an educated guess upon surreptitious clinical examination - that is, he had to make use of a good set of eyes. In this case, there was evidence of eye lid repair, nose, face lift and neck fat liposuction. The rest of the body was not examined for an ear infection.

Graham, also 75 years old, was in good physical shape. Alan recalled both he and his wife exercising in the gym on a regular basis. His plastic surgery appeared to be limited to a face lift, liposuction around the waist and a hair transplant. The excuse to examine his scars was a bad cough and upper respiratory infection. Once his shirt was off, it was not difficult to see the liposuction scars.

Alan's guestimate of Graham's age, with his silver hair, would have been early 50's without the knowledge of the scars. His facial scars were more obvious than those of his wife, as he did not appear to wear make up.

This active couple was a very nice pair. Their numerous travels gave them many interesting tales to reveal over the dinner table. The ship's doctor was almost always a well sought after host at a passenger's table; he gave the passengers status and usually some free medical advice. Alan had no qualms about including this charming couple at his table, as they were a guarantee of an interesting discussion.

One of those discussions was the revelation of a prank that they were involved in on board the Gold Line on a previous cruise. Apparently, they had a friend – Lady Penelope Something-or-Other - who traveled with them on many occasions. She was a very proper English lady who was already on board the ship on an extended cruise. She was unaware that Danica and Graham were going to be on the cruise. They had originally cancelled it due to some last minute concerns at his factory. In any event, their friend was not expecting them on board as the ship pulled into a port in Asia.

When they got on board, they were whisked to their suite and quickly donned some rather obnoxious disguises. Graham wore a moustache and a dark wig, bright plaid pants, a striped tie and mismatching blazer. He looked like the archetypical poorly dressed American tourist. Danica wore a black slinky dress, a pink boa, a large blonde wig and jewelry that was way too big for clothes and the person, as well as being totally inappropriate for the afternoon tea.

At the formal four o'clock tea, this couple sullied up to the bar, rather than taking a seat at a table, as most passengers did, save a few. They knew that their English friend would be at tea, as she was every day. From the bar in very loud voices, they ordered drinks.

"Because that tea ain't quite strong enough!"

When the drinks came, Danica complained loudly that there were no umbrellas in the drink. Of course, the bar staff and the officer involved were in on the prank. Danica went on with this prattle in a good American southern accent, at an obnoxious tonal level. Then the drinks were served.

Danica then remarked, again in loud tones,

"Where is my umbrella? I always gets an umbrella when I get a martini. Come on, boys, when I's paying $900 a night, I'd sure better get at least an umbrella."

With that, the bartender pulled out an umbrella – the kind like the crew set up on the beach – and hoisted it over the bar!

Lady Penelope's jaw dropped, and she nearly spilled her tea. That was it, Danica and Graham burst into fits of laughter, as did most of the crew and passengers assembled in the room.

Danica and Graham hopped off of their barstools and shed their disguises.

"Hello, Penelope!" they chirped, almost in unison.

It took a few minutes for Penelope to get sorted out, and then they all had a good laugh about it. All in all, it was one of the best pranks Alan had ever heard about. He was truly sorry that he didn't get to see it played out.

# CHAPTER THIRTY-ONE

*December 15, 2009: The Caribbean Sea*

ALAN REGALED 'JEN-TINA' WITH several more stories as the day wore on. As Tiffany had an important dinner meeting, they would not be dining together. Unfortunately, he happened to let that slip and the girls insisted he have dinner with them. As it was only a meal, he figured it was harmless enough.

"So, I understand we visit Grenada tomorrow," Tina said. "Isn't that a dangerous place?"

Jenny nodded.

"Yeah, didn't we learn in history class about that place? - Something about a war years ago!"

"I bet that's what Tiffany's meeting is about," Tina added.

Alan groaned. *History class?* Oh man, could they possibly say something else to make him feel even more downright ancient?

"Well, it *was* an island that had been left alone by the hoards of tourists for many years. Granted there are lots of tour boats that have invaded it lately, but for the most part only on the periphery."

"The what-ery?" Jenny said.

Alan laughed. These two really were something else – two of the American education system's finest they weren't!

"It means 'just around the edges'. The island has had its fair share of invasions for a good portion of its history; from the Carribs to the Dutch, the French and then the English."

"Who are the... Carribs?" Tina said.

"A fairly fierce indigenous people of the Caribbean."

The girls slowly nodded and let out a collective 'ahhh' as they gave Alan their full attention.

"Then of course, in recent history, it was ruled by a dictatorship for twenty-some years, and that was ended by the invasion of the US Army to free the island. That was under President Reagan: the stuff you learned in… history class. Of course, it was all to protect the medical students studying there."

Tina's brow wrinkled.

"The island has a medical school - why?"

"Well, it seemed that they had found a loophole way to get American students who could not get into US medical schools because of their grades, into the US medical system – for a while," Alan explained.

Jenny smirked.

"And how do you know about that, Doctor Alan? Was that your… alma mater?"

Tina smacked Jenny in the upper arm.

"Jenny, behave!"

Alan slowly shook his head in the negative.

"Oh, you are soooo bad, young lady! No, it was that it was common knowledge that the school had a less than stellar reputation, and they had ads in many of the medical journals requesting American doctors to come and teach."

Jenny giggled.

"Oh, I'm just kidding. So, is it a safe place to go now?"

Alan nodded.

"Yes; now, in the new millennium, many ships descend on the island's nice new harbor with its weekly invasions of tourists bringing greenbacks, McDonald's, and a way of life not unlike many of the other islands in the Caribbean."

"So, is that considered progress?" Tina said.

Alan shrugged.

"Oh… that's debatable."

"Have you been there before?" Jenny said.

"Yes, my first introduction to Grenada was when I had to get acute medical care for one of our passengers. I went with them to the hospital and then to the doctor's office aided by a local 'self appointed guide' who went by the name of Big Guy."

Jenny snorted.

"Oh really? And just how… big was he?"

"Big Guy was not big. He was rather diminutive, which is probably why he took the name."

Jenny laughed.

"Ha, I knew it! The small guys always have to compensate somehow."

"All right, all right, Jenny; enough, let Alan tell the story," Tina said.

"Thank you, Tina. Anyway, the ship's agent was busy delivering supplies to the food and beverage department, so Big Guy, who was a less than official guide, helped me and the patient on our way. I have to say, he drank a bit too much, and probably indulged in other intoxicants too, but he was very streetwise. As it turned out, the doctor I needed to get the patient to, was out at his weekend home. Well, that was no problem for Big Guy; he found out the unlisted number from a street network, we called, and went out there. The doctor was an American trained Gastroenterologist, originally-"

"A what?" Jenny and Tina said, almost together.

Alan laughed.

"Sorry - a doctor who specializes in diseases of the digestive system. Anyway, he was from the island, with a desire to help his people, and he was doing just that. Unfortunately he had a 'not too advanced' hospital in those days. Yet, our patient was able to get the treatment I felt was appropriate, and rejoin the ship without further problems."

"Well, that's good," Tina said.

"What about the island, and Big Guy; did you ever see either of them again?" Jenny said.

Alan nodded.

"Yeah, the ship I was serving on at the time went to Grenada every week for several months, and every time I would get a chance to go ashore, Big Guy was there waiting for the ship: ostensibly waiting to 'guide' someone, get some beer money etc. Over time, I learned more about the life of the average Grenadian through the eyes of Big Guy. I met his family, kids and friends. It was an education for me to learn how one survives on street smarts, some education and a good knowledge of the local plants and herbs that served as the family's medicine for the most part."

"Wow; do you think we'll see Big Guy there?" Jenny asked, wide-eyed.

Alan shrugged.

"Could be. Last time I was there, he was still plying his trade, and that wasn't too long ago."

"What about that doctor and his hospital; he ever get it improved?" Tina said.

"Actually - yes. Again, the last time I was on the island, I happened to swing by for a visit. It had been rebuilt and gussied up significantly."

The girls giggled.

"It was 'gussied up'? Sounds like a description for an old lady in a fancy dress!" Jenny said with a smirk.

Alan sighed.

"Oh, guess I'm showing my age, eh?"

The girls laughed harder, and gave him great big smiles.

"Oh, age is only a number," Tina said.

Jenny nodded.

"Yeah; what's that saying? Ah… you're only as old as you feel!"

"I seem to recall a joke that Rodney Dangerfield used to say," Alan said. "Let's see, it was – my doctor says I've got the body of a twenty-five year old; yeah - if he finds out what I've done to it, he'll kill me!"

That brought still more laughter from the girls, and that's all it took. Alan launched into a series of old jokes he'd heard from the likes of Dangerfield, Bill Cosby, Bill Maher, and others. As they were – ugh, young - they hadn't heard a lot of the jokes, so Alan was able to appear quite witty.

One of the advantages of serving on a cruise ship was the talent Alan had gotten to see over the years. Now, granted, some of the comedians were less than fantastic (to be polite), but there had also been plenty of great talent. He thought of it as much like how theatre companies would bring shows to Boston to try them out first, before taking them on to Broadway. It was a chance to see which ones had a chance and which ones were bombs!

Sometimes, the comedians were up-and-coming entertainers, trying their material out for the first time. Others were seasoned professionals who just wanted a change of scene; and then there were the talented comedians who had simply fallen on hard times.

Alan had talked to some of them – sometimes they'd had health concerns, or merely been seasick - and he learned just how serious comedy is! One lady comedian had told him that the entertainment business was a place where you get thousands (even millions) for your looks and talent, but only fifty-cents for your soul. It was also a business where you were only as good as your last show.

Frankly, it all made Alan glad that he was a doctor! At any rate, he and 'Jen-Tina' had a pleasant meal, and then went to the casino for some fun. Tina joined Alan at blackjack and Jenny went off to the craps tables. Considering her choice of wardrobe, he didn't think that wise, but who was he to say anything? She was in a strapless, backless, sleeveless top - aw heck, it was practically a belt! He was certain that the men at the table were totally delighted at having her as their shooter. Plus, she was wearing a little micro-mini-skirt and a thong. Every time she bent over to get the dice, Alan could easily see just how much she was peeling from her sunburn!

At one point, someone at the table shouted,

"They're coming out!"

Alan whipped his head around, quite sure they meant that Jenny's considerable... 'assets' had finally freed themselves of her virtually non-existent top! As it turned out, it was the casino employee and he was referring to the dice being thrown.

Alan looked at Tina, who rolled her eyes, and they both laughed.

"Ah, that's my sister for you."

"Yeah, but at least she's having fun."

Tina nodded.

"That she is; she's only spent *one* night in our cabin since the cruise started."

Alan tried to control his face; he didn't want his expression to betray the degree to which he was surprised, even jealous, and thinking of how he would not approve if that had been his daughter. After all, these days, young people were supposed to be free to... do as they chose, and passing any sort of moral judgment was considered inappropriate! How times had changed. That, too, made Alan feel old. Yet, in this case, he did *not* mind it one bit!

"Ah... well, she's... having a good time."

Tina smiled at him.

"That's the PC thing to say, Doctor Alan, but I can tell how you really feel; it's written-"

"All over my face; I know," he said quickly.

She laughed.

"True - very true! But no, it's *not* all right. I may sound like my father, but he was right about one thing – there's a big difference between just having sex and truly making love." She looked over at the craps table. "With Jenny, she hasn't learned that yet."

"Hey, she's still young; she's got time to learn," Alan replied.

"Oh, I hope so!"

Alan chewed on his lip.

'Yeah, there's always time to learn to love,' he said to himself. 'And, just because I love another, it doesn't mean I love Jo any less!'

'Love'? When had love come into what he felt for Tiffany? That thought shocked him and he pushed it away for now.

Some hours later, Alan and the ladies parted company; he returned to his cabin, Tina to theirs, and Jenny went off with one of the young studs from the craps table: a lanky fellow who'd had his hand on her behind during most of the evening. Switching on the light in his cabin, he saw the message light blinking on the phone. He crossed to it, picked up the receiver and punched the code. Standing there, waiting for the message, he looked through the sheer curtains over the windows. Ah, such a lovely evening with the twinkling stars and the soft moonlight reflecting off of the mirror-like surface of the sea. It was nice to see that the sea had calmed down: the waves were gone.

The message was from Tiffany; she would not be able to come by tonight. Alan understood; what with docking tomorrow in Grenada, she probably had a lot to do this evening and had to be up early in the morning. He smiled; she was being so thoughtful, concerned that he was upset about being parted for a single night. Since Jo had died, he'd spent plenty of nights alone: one more was no big deal for him.

## December 16, 2009: Grenada

THE NEXT MORNING, AS the sunlight filtered through those same curtains, Alan opened his eyes and looked out. Yes, they were at the island. As he really wasn't interested in partaking of any excursions, he rose and ate a leisurely breakfast at the late seating. The dining hall was practically deserted, and he was able to dine alone. He wanted that this morning; he needed time to think. Tiffany's message had said she might be busy most of the day, so it was up to him to continue the investigation himself.

The old lure of the land visits raised its head.

Often, when he was serving on the ships, he would be really pulled between staying on the ship and going ashore. Many times, there was no choice. A patient, an emergency drill, meetings with the captain and other officers, would develop, and the Doc would have to attend. That set up an entirely different set of feelings – frustration.

But the dragon this situation dragged up was the one where Alan had the choice of going or staying - plain and simple. Alan was always fascinated by all the ports; granted, some ports more than others - but ports in general and the surrounding countryside. Even if he had been to the same port twenty times, there was always something to do, see, and explore - meeting people, getting to know the local life, and just being more comfortable as a migrating visitor.

This 'dragon pull' is that ports all over the world have something special. They have seen visitors for centuries. This allowed mixtures of all kinds of cultures. Of course the fortresses and other historical remnants of the past remind one that ports are also battlegrounds.

Alan was sure that some of the nasty customs officials in some ports are direct descendants of one of the Mogul marauders. Thinking of that often allowed him to stay cool when dealing with a few of the officials in some of the ports. They could make it a less than an enjoyable experience. Those were the ports where he spent time doing the necessary paperwork on the ship, in much the same way as Tiffany had to do that afternoon.

Alan had seen Grenada many times; he just felt it would have been nice to go ashore and possibly run into some old friends. If he had had sufficient pre-planning time he would have tried to contact old acquaintances without cellphones and email addresses. But that wasn't to be.

Very well; he would be focused, and stay on board and review what was needed for the investigation. Step one: check out Mrs. Brightman and Mrs. Clapham, and see if there was a connection between them. So, once he was done eating, he again headed to the club with his laptop. He had to laugh to himself as he sat there waiting for it to boot up. He was becoming quite the regular here!

Once he was online, he sat back and tried to think. Okay, how could he check these ladies out? He had their addresses and phone numbers. Of course, these details were twenty-five years old; so they may not even be current. These women may not even still be alive! Still, he could at least do a search for the addresses and see what that yielded.

So, going to *Map Quest*, he typed in the first address: 1026 Cake Terrace, Sarasota, Florida. It took a moment, and then a graphic map of the area appeared. Using the zoom mode, Alan was able to get right down to the street level. Huh, just a regular old neighborhood: nothing special about the place – other than it was a corner lot.

He saved the image of the street to his computer, and then typed in the next address: 5325 Sally Lane. Pressing 'Enter', he waited for the results. He wasn't disappointed; the same sort of graphic was soon on his screen. Again he zoomed in, and his jaw dropped. This was not merely the same *sort* of graphic; it was the *exact* same map showing the *exact* same home!

Alan zoomed in to the street level, and studied the image intently; he didn't want there to be any mistake. No, it was true. Cake Terrace and Sally Lane intersected, and the two addresses were the same corner. Just to document the situation, he again saved the map as an image file to his computer.

"THEY LIVE AT THE same place?" Tiffany said, as they shared a pizza for lunch later that day.

Alan nodded.

"Yeah, I checked it several times; there's no mistake."

She snapped her fingers.

"They're partners! That's it, right? Think about it; one of them probably handles buying the antiques – from whatever sources she can find, and the other sells them in her shop."

Alan slapped himself in the forehead.

"Of course - a shop! Why didn't I think of that before? One of them must own an antique shop in the area."

"Or… they did own…," Tiffany said slowly.

"What do you mean? Oh, it's been twenty-five years; maybe they're not there any more; is that it?"

Tiffany nodded.

"Yeah. Oh, we should do a search on the property appraiser's website for Sarasota; see if either of the ladies still owns anything in the area."

Alan grinned.

"The old 'paper trail', eh?"

"Exactly! Come on; let's see what we can find."

After lunch, they went back to the club; Alan truly felt as if he should just have the crew rope off a section of the place for him permanently! They easily found the website, and did a search. Tiffany was right: Mrs. Abigail Brightman still owned an antique store in a small seaside community south of Sarasota called Venice.

Alan read over Tiffany's shoulder as she pulled up the information on the screen.

"Bev's Boutique, 1001 Inlet Circle, Venice. Venice? Does it have canals?"

"Who knows, but at least we have a lead. Huh, seems she owns several pieces of property all over the county! Wow, she's got to be quite the wealthy woman."

Alan looked over the list on the screen; Tiffany was right, the lady was quite the property owner.

"Check on Mrs. Clapham; see what she owns."

"You got it."

Her fingers just about flew across the keyboard for a moment, and then they waited for the results. When they came up, Alan was quite surprised – Mrs. Erica Clapham owned the house on Sally Lane, and nothing more.

He chewed his lip.

"Huh, seems the lady likes to keep a low profile. I wonder why?"

Tiffany grabbed a pad of paper and a pen.

"Well, let's write down some phone numbers, and we can call the town hall and other places to ask about the ladies. So far, they're the best lead we've found."

Alan nodded as he looked at his watch.

"I agree, and it's early enough in the day that we can make some phone calls. Hey, here's an idea: pull up the map of that Venice place, and get the area where their antique store is."

"Huh, what for?"

"Let's find out what other businesses are around Bev's Boutique, call them, and ask about the store. They might be able to tell us about the ladies."

"Ah... now I understand. Good idea, my man! Okay, let me see what I can find."

Typing in the address for the store, Tiffany pulled up the city map and then zoomed in on the neighborhood. The shop was located on a wide boulevard that ran from the beach area to the center of town. She clicked on the various parcels of land around the shop.

"Okay, we have a barber shop, a gift shop and the local drug store," Tiffany said.

"Ah, a barber shop – excellent!"

"What's so great about one of those?"

Alan grinned.

"Let me guess, you go to a stylist, a place like *The Hair Cuttery*, or something like that, right?"

Tiffany nodded.

"Yeah, why?"

"Oh, does this make me feel old! An old fashioned barber shop – especially in a small town – is perfect for learning about local gossip. So, I say we call there first."

"Ah... now I understand. Okay, I'll get the phone number and we can call."

Once they had the number, Alan got out his cellphone and dialed.

A moment later, he was rewarded with a voice saying,

"Yo, Carl's Clips; how ya doing?"

"Just fine, sir. I take it you're Carl?"

"You got it, fellow; and please, call me Carl – everyone does. What can I do you for?"

Alan tried to think – what was the right thing to say to get the man talking?

"Well, Carl, my name's Alan, and I just... retired. My dear... wife and I are on a cruise right now, and we were thinking or retiring to the Venice area."

"Ah, a wise decision; this is a great area – quiet, yet with enough fun so you don't sit around like a bump on a log!"

"That's what we noticed when we visited the area last winter; it just seemed delightful. Anyway, while we were there, we strolled down the main street and saw some of the shops – among them, yours."

"Did you come in for a shave and a haircut? I never forget a face, and your voice sounds *so* familiar!"

"Ah… yes, yes we did."

"I knew it! Alan… Alan Jenkins, clean shaven, long brown curly hair – just a little off the top. Am I right, am I right?"

"Uncanny," Alan said, rolling his eyes.

Carl laughed.

"And the boys here say I never remember: ha!"

"Oh, you certainly showed them up! Anyway, I seem to recall a little antique store in the area. Do you know it? Could you tell me anything about the place? I think it was owned by a Mrs.…."

"Brightman!" Carl said. "Abigail Brightman? Yeah, she's still around; the old… bitty… she won't ever die. You know, I don't like to gossip, but that gal gives me the creeps – the *drowned kittens* sort of creeps, if you know what I mean?"

"Oh yes, I certainly do. Why do you say that?"

"Well… I don't like to pass on rumors, but let me tell you about her…"

With that, Carl was off. Alan sat down, cradled the phone to his ear, and just listened. For the next hour, all he had to do was give a little 'ah-huh' or 'un-ah' every once in a while, and Carl was happy.

By the time he was finished and Alan hung up, he'd learned quite a lot about one of their prime suspects.

Tiffany snickered.

"What's the matter, 'old man', you a bit stiff in the neck there?"

Alan playfully battered her in the back of the head, even as he stretched his neck and turned his head. Using his left hand, he pulled his ear away from the side of his head and gave it a wipe.

"Brat! Oy, my neck is killing me, and my ear feels like it's been flattened to the side of my head. Man, that guy could talk a volcano into hibernating."

"But, I take it you still managed to learn something important?" Tiffany said.

Alan nodded.

"Oh yeah; he was quite the cornucopia of local lore. The lady in question – Mrs. Brightman - has been a fixture in the county for a good number of years, and she is one manipulative… lady! She's got her fingers in a lot of pies."

"What about her partner, Mrs. Clapham?"

"Now, there's the odd thing. As much as Mr. Busy-Body knew about Abigail Brightman, he didn't know diddly-squat about Erica Clapham! According to him, Mrs. Brightman has no partner in the shop."

Tiffany tugged on her hair and turned around in her chair to look up at Alan.

"I wonder - did Mrs. Brightman perhaps… eliminate her partner?"

"Tie up the loose ends, so to speak, and get rid of any witnesses…?"

"I know it sounds like something out a movie, but it's a possibility."

"Well, considering what Carl the Barber had to say about Mrs. Brightman, I can believe it," Alan said. "According to him, she'd eat her own young, if she'd ever had any!"

Tiffany stood up and paced a bit.

"Hmmm… maybe we should check and see if there's a *death* certificate for Mrs. Clapham."

Alan snapped his fingers.

"Good idea. Can you do that online?"

Tiffany sat back down at the computer.

"Let's just see what we can see, shall we? I'll try the records for Sarasota County first."

With that, she started typing. As it happened, there was only one family by that name in the county – a mother and father, and their daughter, Erica – and they had died some fifty years ago in a house fire!

Tiffany's jaw dropped, and she pointed at the screen, tapping her fingernail on the glass.

"What the…" Alan said slowly, his voice trailing off. "So… what does this mean?"

"Maybe we've got the wrong Clapham. After all, there could be someone else with that name. We've only looked in one place."

Alan slowly paced around the area, chewing his lip as he thought.

"Yeah… maybe… but, it could also answer some questions."

Tiffany turned around in her chair to watch him pace.

"Ah, I see what you mean; how the two ladies could share the same address, and why there are no records for her."

Alan nodded.

"Exactly, and why Mr. Barber Shop Man doesn't know one thing about her!"

Tiffany got up and moved to the window to look out over the water; then turned to face him.

"So… how is this a clue? What, Mrs. Brightman was – is – using Erica Clapham as an alias?"

"That would make sense. After all, we did find that they owned houses at the same address. Maybe Mrs. Clapham is a way for Mrs. Brightman to… I don't know; hide assets, to… serve as a cover for her smuggling operation."

Tiffany snapped her fingers.

"Yes, that's it exactly! It's just like that movie I saw, ah… 'The Shawshank Redemption'. Tim Robbins uses a dead man's ID to, ah… launder money and hide the illegal stuff the prison warden was mixed up in."

"Huh, okay; that makes sense. So, what's our next move? Can we prove it, and if we can, is it an important clue?"

Tiffany chewed on her fingertips for a moment, lost in thought.

"I don't know." She looked at her watch and let out a small gasp. "Oh man, I'm late; got another trivia contest to lead."

Alan gave her a friendly wave and a smile.

"Then go, go. I'll see what I can find out, and then we'll link up later; say… how about dinner?"

She bounded over to him, strained to reach his face, and gave him a friendly peck.

"It's a date; see you at first seating!"

With that, she took off, and Alan stood and watched her go. Yes - a fine figure of a woman. So, what was his next step in this investigation? Just as Tiffany had said: 'I don't know' - but at least he had all afternoon to think of something.

# CHAPTER THIRTY-TWO

*December 16, 2009: The Gulf of Mexico*

THE WHOLE MRS. BRIGHTMAN/MRS. Clapham thing was certainly a conundrum. When Tiffany had gone off to her duties, Alan lay back on his bed, this time remembering to kick off his shoes. He chuckled as he realized how quickly a woman's influence had once more domesticated him.

Hands linked between his head, twirling his feet at his crossed ankles, Alan cast his mind back. Mrs. Brightman really didn't sound familiar to him, except through Michael's stories. He couldn't visualize her. Yet, of course, he couldn't know every single passenger on board. It simply wasn't possible. Perhaps she had been one of the lucky ones who hadn't required the Doc's services aboard ship. She must have been on board several times as otherwise Michael would not have met her and begun his antiques dealing through this very useful channel. Well, it was too late now to ask Michael what the relationship was between Mrs. Brightman and Mrs. Clapham – if indeed there was any at all.

Alan did recall the incident with Mischa, and Mrs. Brightman's claim of someone being in her cabin, but he really couldn't picture what she looked like.

Alan snapped up into a sitting position so hard and so fast, it was like a rubber band being released; he'd remembered something else. That man – 'Dr.' Zetisman – he had said something similar one day up on deck. Alan's brow wrinkled as he tried to think.

What was it, what had been his complaint? Ah, his needles – the ones that clearly were not needed for insulin – he thought he'd lost one. Maybe someone had actually taken one.

Alan sat and chewed his lip. Was this connected to the murder; was it a clue? Had Mrs. Brightman/Clapham taken one of the syringes to kill Michael with? After all these years, it would be difficult to prove – one way or the other – and besides, 'Dr'. Zetisman was certainly long dead; so there was no asking him. Still, he would write up what he remembered and file it away.

Mrs. Clapham also was not too familiar to Alan, except through tales from the other staff and passengers about how 'difficult' she could be. She was an older lady with, so the staff said, more money than she knew what to do with. So one of the things she did with her money was to take regular cruises. From the tales of the staff unfortunate enough to be more acquainted with her, Alan easily recalled the vitriol which poured forth from this woman's lips at regular intervals. He thought now – not for the first time – what a pity it was that he couldn't prescribe anything to make her better disposed toward her fellow man (and woman).

Then Alan startled. *Some*one had liked Mrs. Clapham! There had been rumors on several of her cruises that she had her eye on a young member of the cabin staff, Toby.

"You just need to know how to handle her, and then she's a pussycat," Toby had said. "I think she's a total sweety, actually."

Alan chuckled, but the chuckle caught in his throat. Toby had been keen on Michael, hadn't he? He'd certainly appeared pretty cut up when Michael was discovered dead in his cabin. Thoughts whirled in Alan's head as he dismissed them, only to have them resurface again and again.

Alan clearly recalled the shock and distress Toby exhibited when he discovered Michael's body. But of course, that had been quite natural, hadn't it? It wasn't every day one stumbled upon a dead body. It was enough to disturb anyone, Alan conceded. It had never occurred to him up to that point that Toby might be gay, let alone keen on Michael! Yet there had also been the tone of voice that Toby had used in referring to Michael.

'I would never gossip about Michael', he had said.

That was fair enough, but Alan now recalled how there had been a hint of something more than affection and liking for a colleague in his voice.

Mrs. Clapham too had not initially seemed to be against Michael or his 'kind' as Alan later remembered her referring to them. This was starting to sound suspicious to Alan now. Had something happened to turn her against Michael? And if it had – on the very cruise on which Michael was murdered – was this significant?

Wracking his brains, Alan tried to recall more about Mrs. Clapham but, drawing something of a blank, he thought it was time to put in another call to his old friend, Bill. When he did, it was almost like Bill had been sitting on the phone waiting for his call.

"Hi, Doc... oh, Alan, I guess it is, now you're a man of leisure, huh?" Bill chuckled down the phone.

Alan returned the light laughter.

'Well, if you can call having a twenty five year old murder to solve being a man of leisure, I guess so,' he thought.

"What have you found out for me?"

At this, Bill sounded very pleased with himself.

"Well, it took a bit of digging, but I traced your deep cut for you – a hand!"

Alan sat up on the bed, suddenly hooked on Bill's every word. Just as Alan got excited, the voice on the other end of the phone seemed to trail off into uncertainty.

"Well – I *think* I've traced them... but, Doc – I mean, Alan – *you* didn't see this patient, according to the records. Your nurse did. It just needed a few sutures and a tetanus shot. It says here that Petra Gacek dealt with the only deep cut I can see for that period. So they can't sue you; it was nothing to do with you. As far as I can see, Petra did what was required, too."

Alan cut him short.

"And the cut – whose was it?"

The grin was evident in Bill's voice.

"Mrs. Clapham."

Alan's heart leaped.

"Well, well, well. Thanks, Bill. That was most... enlightening... Hey – while I'm on, picking your brains – do you recall much about Mrs. Clapham – or a Mrs. Brightman?"

"That's the strange thing..."

Bill's voice was exuding an unmistakable air of smugness.

"...It was Mrs. Clapham that was treated. That's in Petra's notes. But it was actually a Mrs. Brightman that paid for it."

Alan gave a long, low whistle, realizing a little late that this was down the phone, right into Bill's ear.

"Oh... uh... sorry. If you have any residual deafness of tinnitus, I know a good doctor that can treat you for it," quipped Alan.

Bill laughed.

"Well, I'm just glad to be of service, Doc – I can't believe the old bat is about to sue you twenty-five years on for a cut that was treated perfectly well."

Alan thought for a few seconds. Should he tell Bill what was really going on? Could he count on the man's discretion? Yet, why did it need 'discretion'?

Alan was simply doing some digging around. He didn't know for sure if he had anything, let alone a secure suspect, and so he wasn't about to go running around accusing anyone of murdering Michael all those years ago.

Alan made up his mind in a heartbeat. Of course Bill could be trusted.

"Well," Alan began. "Actually, I haven't been completely truthful with you," he admitted. "The inquiry... it was actually to see if there *had* been an injury like that... on the cruise... where ah... when Michael Hamilton... you remember him, I'm sure. Cruise director. Well, he died on board ship, and Bill... Now I'm pretty sure he was murdered!"

Now it was Bill's turn to give a startled whistle into the phone.

"Murdered, you say?... Th-that's major league, Alan... and twenty-five years on...?"

Alan nodded, although of course Bill couldn't see that.

"I know. I know. That's why I'm playing it careful. Don't want to stir up a hornets' nest until I've got my facts straight – but it's proved... interesting, shall we say, thinking back to it all. We all said, Bill – some things just didn't add up."

"Uh-huh," agreed Bill, readily enough. "But we all felt so safe on board. The idea of foul play... well, it was just unthinkable really, wasn't it?"

Alan agreed with a slight reservation.

"I know there was talk at the time about how the police investigation just... skimmed over some details, shall we say? – And I guess we were all eager to move on – both metaphorically *and* on to the next port. I admit, for a while, I dismissed the gossip of it being a suspicious death as the staff over-dramatizing, because they saw a murder as exciting, glamorous even."

Bill snorted a little derisorily.

"Yes, I remember thinking that it was all a bit distasteful – like they *wanted* him to have been murdered."

Alan agreed whole-heartedly with that.

"So, what had you changing your mind, Doc?"

Alan smiled as Bill slipped in his old familiar title.

"Well, I guess they had always been there at the back of my mind. The doubts. But then it all just came flooding back to me a few days ago. Maybe this is the first time my brain has had off, to ponder such things," he added, a little self-deprecatingly. "Suddenly it seemed to be obvious to me that Michael *was* murdered."

On the other end of the phone line, Bill gasped quietly at those words being spoken so openly – bluntly. Alan continued. Now he had begun to speak of this with someone who had been around at the time, he couldn't seem to stop. But Bill, puzzled, interrupted.

"And the deep cut you wanted me to research?... Surely you don't think Mrs. Clapham murdered Michael...?"

Alan frowned in consternation.

"I admit - I didn't really expect you to come back to me with *her* name. Someone like Dr. Zetisman was more prominent in my radar..."

"Ugh! Thoroughly unpleasant character that one," Bill made no attempt to disguise his dislike of a man who was an incredibly difficult passenger to deal with.

"Indeed," echoed Alan.

"So he had nothing to do with Michael's... uh... murder?... Next thing you'll be telling me is he was really diabetic with that giant needle of his!... So, say this Mrs. Clapham *did* murder Michael? – How did she do it?"

Alan sighed, somewhat deflated as now he had to get to the even less certain part of his story.

"That... I haven't worked out yet..."

"Ah, but you will!" Bill was brimming with confidence in Alan's abilities.

"Thanks for the vote of confidence, Bill – I'm working on it!... Well, catch you later. You sure have given me something to think about in old Mrs. Clapham."

The two said their goodbyes and Alan settled back on his bed, his mind whirling. So they *had* been close with the Mrs. Clapham/Mrs. Brightman thing – Tiffany *would* be pleased! For the moment, Alan cast aside thoughts of Mrs. Brightman as he already felt like he knew a little at least of her connection with Michael. But as he lay back on his bed, he wracked his brains, trying to summon up a picture of Mrs. Clapham – anything that would give him a clue about how *she* might be connected to Michael's murder – if indeed she was connected.

The main thing that sprang to mind was the afternoon, a couple of days before Michael died. Alan hadn't witnessed the exchange himself but he clearly recalled Mr. Sponecki, a regular traveler with the cruise line, recounting how surprised he was by the turn about in a fellow passenger, Mrs. Clapham's, attitude to Michael. It stuck in his mind due to the sheer humor of how people were often unguarded in their words around Mr. Sponecki as he had been deaf for years and many had been used to this fact, meeting him on many cruises. But, following treatment, his hearing was successfully returning, much to Alan's pleasure. On Michael's final fateful cruise, Alan recalled how Mr. Sponecki's hearing had been returned to near normal, yet he had not disclosed this fact to anyone, not even his family!

Alan chuckled now, thinking back.

"I'll tell them in my own good time, Doc. Anyways, things might change. I might lose it all..."

But both he and Alan knew that was, thankfully, unlikely. Mr. Sponecki was just taking his own sweet time to listen in on conversations and find out what people really thought of him.

"I might leave all my money to the cats' home!" he teased, causing Alan to roar with laughter.

"So, now your hearing is pretty hot, you must be realizing a whole new side to cruising, huh?" Alan chuckled, examining the man's ears.

"Ho-ho – you can say that again, Doc!... I've heard of 'spoiled little rich kids' but these ships – they seem full to bursting with spoiled rich Grandmas with manners no better than they ought to be."

Privately, Alan agreed to some extent, although he wouldn't admit it. His livelihood depended upon pandering to such people as well as taking care of genuine illnesses on board ship among the crew and passengers. Also, he couldn't resist a tease with Mr. Sponecki, whom, it was now revealed with his improved hearing, had a keen sense of humor.

"Oh, I dunno, Mr. Sponecki – how about I get you a dinner introduction at my table with Mrs. Clapham? I hear you two are firm friends after this afternoon! - Or Mrs. Brightman?... Michael Hamilton can introduce you two. He knows her very well and he tells us she is quite the sweetheart."

Mr. Sponecki all but spat on the floor.

"Mrs. Clapham is a despicable woman! You should have heard the things she was saying about Michael Hamilton. Now *that* would be one explosive dinner date."

Alan chuckled.

"Yes, I was teasing you. I heard some of what occurred this afternoon. Apparently Michael has upset Mrs. Clapham...?"

Mr. Sponecki nodded.

"Seems so, but the old... uh... well, she sure has changed her tune from yesterday. Why, it was only a day or so ago that she had both Michael and that handsome young cabin crew... can't remember his name – fauning over her.

"Toby?..." Alan suggested, thinking that was the most likely member of the cabin crew to be closely associated with Michael and to be referred to as 'handsome' by both men and women alike. He did seem to hold rather an appeal to both sexes.

"Oh yes, that's right. I'm still getting used to names now I can hear. Some of them are so difficult to lip-read, you know – especially the... *foreign* ones. Anyways, they couldn't do enough for her and she seemed pretty happy with their services that day. They even disappeared together – all three of them – for an hour or so. There were no excursions planned so I have no idea what they were up to."

Alan frowned. Michael always seemed to be pulling a disappearing act. It had not gone unnoticed by 'the powers that be', either. Michael would have to watch his step if he wanted to remain in employment, especially if he had now upset Mrs. Clapham. Alan knew what clout the wealthy passengers carried with the cruise ship authorities and a serious run-in with one of them could mean the end of one's career or at the very least a sideways shift to another ship where they would have to begin all over again getting to know the staff and building up relationships with them. Alan thought that would be truly horrible and he really didn't want to see that happening to Michael.

Just then, Alan shuddered and he came back to the present. Had it been the chilling thought that far worse than a sideways move had occurred to Michael or the fact that Tiffany had just entered his cabin and sat down on the bed beside him that had made him startle?

"Well hello there – I've had better welcomes than a shudder of revulsion," teased Tiffany, lightly rubbing Alan's arm.

Alan smiled and sat up, lightly kissing Tiffany's lips.

"Silly girl!" he playfully chided. "I was just resting my brain… it's been on overdrive today. You have to be proud of me, though…"

In the late afternoon sunlight pouring in through the cabin window, Alan excitedly filled Tiffany in on all that he had discovered that afternoon, both from Bill's phone conversation and his own deductions.

She was indeed suitably impressed.

"Wowee!... So – Mrs. Clapham, whom you don't really remember, was the one with the deep cut which might have been caused by the smashed glass in Michael's cabin? And she was heard arguing with Michael not long before he died - having been pretty friendly with him up to this point... and now you're saying that this cabin crew member, Toby, whom you had doubts about all along regarding his… *affections* – both he and Michael were known to spend a lot of time alone with Mrs. Clapham?... The same Mrs. Clapham we've discovered in Sarasota owning a house where a Mrs. Brightman also resides? And that same Mrs. Brightman owns property all over the city but Mrs. Clapham – a supposedly wealthy widow – owns diddly squat?"

Alan nodded, his mouth dry.

"That's about how it appears, yes."

He almost watched the light bulb appear over Tiffany's head.

"Oh, come on, Alan! There *is* no Mrs. Brightman and Mrs. Clapham – at least not both of them – Alan, they're not partners, or related – they're the *same person!*"

The revelation hung in the silent air as Alan digested this for a few seconds, the color draining from his face.

# CHAPTER THIRTY-THREE

*July 23, 1984: Galveston*

THERE WERE SO MANY cabin stewards on board ship, and many of them had specific duties that kept them well away from areas of the ship that the Doc frequented; as a result, he didn't ever get to know all of them. If they were responsible for cabins over on the other side of the ship, and they didn't have the misfortune to fall ill, Alan would have little cause or opportunity to meet them. The same could be said of many passengers too.

Now, Mrs. Clapham was quite notorious on board ship, because of her demands and complaints, which surpassed even most of the ridiculously minor things that would have rich passengers screaming about how they had paid a lot for their cruise and they were darn well going to get the best! Alan often thought to himself that these serial complainers knew the price of everything, but the value of nothing.

Mrs. Clapham was one such serial complainer. Alan recalled the cabin crew saying that there was even one occasion when she disliked how her bed sheets had been pressed. Oh if only she knew of the frequent 'apple pie bed' pranks that the staff pulled with each other in their quarters! He was surprised one of the cabin stewards that had felt the rough edge of Mrs. Clapham's tongue hadn't given her an apple pie bed of her very own; but then of course, Alan also knew how much power wealthy passengers wielded over the cruise line. It was not beyond the realms of possibility that Mrs. Clapham would see to it that any such prankster was fired, and unable to get another job on *any* other cruise line. *That* was the kind of value of money that she understood.

Casting his mind back, Alan recalled that Michael was said to have quite the knack of keeping Mrs. Clapham happy, which is why it seemed so odd to Alan to hear from Mr. Sponecki that she had been criticizing the tour director so openly and with such venom. Michael seemed to have quite a way with tough old women like Mrs. Clapham and his 'friend' Mrs. Brightman. He and the latter had met on a cruise many years before and Alan already knew that this had blossomed into a lucrative trade in valuable antiques for Michael. But now they were talking about Mrs. Clapham – and she certainly didn't seem to have been Michael's 'friend' towards the end of his life.

"It never seemed to bother her before now where Michael dipped his wick, so to speak," fumed the man whose hearing had recently returned to him, but who had been an excellent lip-reader, and apparently was well acquainted with Mrs. Clapham from previous cruises.

"Thick as thieves she was with Michael at one time – and that Toby guy... her cabin steward I think he is, but he doesn't seem to do much work as far as I can tell. He's certainly spent most of the last week with either Michael or Mrs. Clapham – or both. Giggling like kids."

Alan's interest was piqued just a little, but only because of the recent demise of the much maligned tour director.

"Then all off a sudden she was full of 'you queers are all the same', 'robbing rent boy' and a whole load of other insults I would never have thought she'd turn on Michael after how friendly they always seemed to be. She's certainly quieted down now that the poor S.O.B. is dead," Mr. Sponecki stated with some bitterness.

The Doc gasped a little, looking around to see if they had been overheard, and whispered, in the hopes that it would encourage Mr. Sponecki to do the same now that he could obviously hear so much better.

"I... I didn't realize... the crew thought they'd been subtle..."

Mr. Sponecki snorted a little in laughter but he did lower his voice.

"Doc – Michael was pretty easy to notice. And now he ain't here anymore... Meanwhile, Alfonse has been moping around like a whipped puppy with red, swollen eyes and you guys had a guard posted by the crew cabins. I'm guessing the leaders of the passenger grapevine missed the onshore officials coming aboard with the body bag, but Michael is no more, is he?"

Alan could only swallow a hard lump in his throat and give a little nod of his head in confirmation.

"Yeah," he managed, in a hoarse whisper, knowing that was probably not the official cruise line story, but Mr. Sponecki's candid speech had disarmed him.

Alan coughed a little, clearing his throat so he could speak clearly.

"Obviously, Mr. Sponecki – it wouldn't be good for that to become common knowledge on the ship…"

"Of course not," butted in Mr. Sponecki, before Alan could give an explanation.

Alan settled back a little more in his seat beside the elderly, but obviously very astute, regular passenger.

"I… didn't know much about how things were with Michael and Mrs. Clapham… and Toby, you say? – The cabin crew member?… I wasn't aware they spent too much time together – any of them."

Alan had temporarily forgotten the pained looks which had passed over Toby's face as Michael's body was discovered. A weepy Alfonse had again entered the lounge and plopped himself down on an armchair facing out to a flat, calm sea which somehow looked colder than Alan remembered it looking a day or so ago.

Alan feared that this may be the end of the informative conversation. But Mr. Sponecki slowly got to his feet, apparently having something else to share.

"Shall we take a walk onboard deck, Doc?"

Alan agreed immediately and the two men left the lounge, the Doc only pausing momentarily to give Alfonse a sympathetic shoulder pat and remind him,

"If you need anything – even just to talk – you know where I am."

Alfonse gave the Doc a grateful, watery smile and then Alan followed Mr. Sponecki for a walk on deck.

They carried on walking, both because they were too agitated to sit still for long and to avoid being overheard. The investigation into Michael's death had been completed – and quickly. Now they were on to another port, and as things became calmer on board once more and Alan had the space to think, after his welcome break with Christina, he had the strangest feeling that the investigation perhaps raised more questions than it answered. He had noted a few of these things down in the notebook now under his pillow in his cabin, but he didn't want to go and get it in case it broke Mr. Sponecki's train of thought and they didn't get a chance to chat on this matter again. After all, Alan's memory was pretty good, especially short-term. All that last minute studying for med school exams had honed that particular ability. He'd be able to make notes later.

As it happened, Mr. Sponecki was quite keen to share his observations about the Michael-Toby-Mrs. Clapham 'love triangle' as he laughingly called it before admitting,

"Actually, it seemed more like some kind of business deal to me. Antiques?"

The Doc gave a slight nod, although his brow was lined in consternation.

"Could be – although I didn't know Toby had anything to do with antiques."

Mr. Sponecki gave a low chuckle.

"Maybe he's a beginner and those two were – showing him the ropes? It seemed to me like he didn't know what they were talking about half the time. Something certainly seems to have gone wrong with a deal. Michael appeared quite shocked that Mrs. Clapham was annoyed with him. Kept telling her he got a good price or something – or she did. I – uh – I didn't quite catch that part of the conversation."

Alan was interested but not too concerned. Both Michael and from what he had heard Mrs. Clapham, could be volatile. A small thing could easily have been blown out of proportion, and if Michael thought he'd done what he was supposed to…

But still, he wanted to know more if he could, in view of what later happened to Michael.

"So – did you – get any details? Find out what they were arguing about?"

Mr. Sponecki shrugged.

"Not really - but the old girl seemed pretty upset about something to do with money, and she didn't seem to know who to blame but she was intent on laying it on either Michael or the other guy."

"Toby," Alan added, distracted.

"Yeah – well, he was the one that stormed off first. Said he wasn't being blamed for someone else's incompetence."

Alan relaxed a little.

"Ahh - so they could have been arguing about anything – maybe one of them gave her a bum recommendation for her last shore excursion."

Mr. Sponecki seemed unconvinced.

"Maybe – but she seemed pretty steamed up over a day trip."

# CHAPTER THIRTY-FOUR

*December 20, 2009: Miami*

THINKING OF THE PAST, some details coalesced in Alan's mind and he grabbed for his file folder. It hadn't meant much at the time, but now it was starting to make sense – or at least, sound possible. Michael had always said that his antiques contact was Mrs. Brightman. Could Mrs. Brightman and Mrs. Clapham really be one and the same? Could it really be that she murdered Michael? Why would she do that?

Opening his folder, Alan grew excited.

"Wait just a moment! I think I've got something here. Here, have a look at this ledger."

He held it up for Tiffany to see, and she sat next to him to look at it.

"OK, what am I looking at?"

"This is what was photographed on the film Michael had hidden in the model plane. According to this ledger, Mrs. Clapham was buying antiques all over the world, and then selling them – at a *loss* – in Mrs. Brightman's shop!"

"Ah… a loss; so, that means she… got a break on her… taxes, right?" Tiffany said. "I don't know too much about such things."

Alan laughed.

"Neither do I, but I do know that you're right! So, what if Michael found out about her little *accounting arrangement*? After all, she did say that someone was in her cabin, but that nothing was missing. So, maybe Michael slipped in, took pictures of her ledger, and then used that against her. Michael was a nice guy, but it was obvious he was no-one's fool when it came to business."

Tiffany slowly nodded. It did make sense.

"Ah… yes, that would explain why they – she – was paying him a monthly… retainer. He was blackmailing her, and these papers were the proof," Tiffany deduced from looking over the front page in Alan's file.

"I'd call that a pretty good motive for murder - wouldn't you?"

Tiffany nodded. She was sure that Alan was correct.

"Absolutely! So, what's our next move?"

Alan chewed his lip as he thought for a minute.

"Well… I guess we contact the authorities and… see about turning over our evidence to them. I've done the detective work; I don't relish the idea of a citizen's arrest or whatever it's called," he joked, trying to ease his rapidly beating heart.

After twenty-five years it seemed like he – they – had done what the 'authorities' had failed to do – find Michael's murderer. But any punishment would be up to these officials.

"Ah… I wonder who has jurisdiction," Tiffany said. "It's been twenty-five years; you sure the… what do they call it? Ah… the statue of limitation hasn't run out?"

Alan smirked.

"*Statute*, Tiffany, the statute of limitation, and no, it won't have run out. There's no statute of limitation on murder! I would say… we should call the FBI; they can advise us as to who has jurisdiction and how we should proceed."

Tiffany sat down at the desk and began typing on the computer. Her fingers tingled with the same excitement that Alan felt at being so close to apprehending Michael's murderer.

"OK, one phone number for the nearest FBI office, coming right up."

Alan moved to stand behind her and looked at the screen as she pulled up the website. He smirked.

"Yeah – hold the fries with that… Ah, there we go – the Miami field office – perfect! Get their number, and I'll call them right now."

Tiffany did so, and a moment later Alan was dialing. The operator came on the line after a few rings, and then Alan explained the situation. He was put on hold for a few minutes and then transferred to an agent who could discuss the situation in detail.

It took a while and Alan had to beat his way through a fair amount of skepticism to begin with!

Finally, again with a crick in his neck, a sweaty palm from holding the phone for so long and a flattened ear, Alan hung up and put his phone aside.

"Well, I bet you need a glass of water, after talking for that long," Tiffany said.

Alan nodded, even as he rubbed his neck.

"Yeah, I am just about hoarse from all that talking! But, it looks like Agent Collins is on top of this case for us."

"What did he say?"

"*She* said that she'd checked with the Maritime Authority as to jurisdiction, contact the Venice and Sarasota PD about checking on Mrs. Brightman... or Clapham, and look at all of our evidence."

Tiffany's brow wrinkled.

"Eh... how? Does she want us to email what we have to her, or turn it over once we land?"

"Both," Alan said, pouring himself a tall glass of water. "The electronic files are enough for them to start an investigation and then they'll need the originals once we land. Plus, she said I'd need to come into the office to give a deposition."

"Well, sounds like you've got quite the busy itinerary, once we land," Tiffany said. "Eh and here I was, thinking we'd get to spend some time together once you'd cracked the case. Looks like it's going to be the old 'wham-bam-thank-you-ma'am' routine, eh?"

Alan's brow wrinkled in confusion.

"Huh? Tiffany, I have to meet with the authorities! It's import-"

"Yeah-yeah, that old line; 'I have to help with a murder investigation'. Sheesh! Wish I had a dime for every guy who's said that to me!"

"I- oh, you little brat!" Alan said with a grin, as the 'light bulb' came on and he finally realized she was joking. "It's sass; you're sassing me, aren't you?"

Tiffany stood up, turned to face Alan, and gave him a very big grin!

"Gee, 'old man', do you have to be so slow on the pick up?"

Alan laughed, took her in his arms, and gave her a playful pat on the behind.

"Brat, a total brat; that's what you are!"

They embraced, kissed, and then sadly had to get back to 'work'. They emailed the documents to Agent Collins and then parted. Tiffany had to get back to her real work on board the cruise ship and Alan needed to unwind.

He felt completely drained! Yet, there was a final duty he felt compelled to complete: he called Michael's mother again to let her know what they'd discovered. The delight in her voice – however reserved she tried to remain – brought a tear of joy to Alan's eye. He promised to keep her updated on the situation, although he knew the police, once properly informed of the details he had, would contact Michael's parents, and then he went up on deck to relax.

Alan didn't know if it was the stress reduction from solving the case, or just being chilled out, but he fell asleep almost as his head went back on the lounge chair. He didn't even remember dreaming, and then he awoke hours later to the squeal of children playing.

Sitting up, he yawned, stretched, and looked around. It was late; the sun was just melting into the Gulf of Mexico. He didn't have to check his watch to know it was close to dinnertime – his stomach told him that. So, going back to his cabin, he did a quick check of his email – there was a message for him – then he got cleaned up, dressed, and headed down to the dining hall.

He smiled at seeing Tiffany waiting there at the doors for him; once again, she'd gone all out in getting dressed up. She was in a shimmering black and white gown. In a way, she sort of looked like a barber pole, but *what* a barber pole!

"How is my man this evening?" she said. "You look particularly happy with yourself."

Alan offered her his arm, and they headed into the dining hall.

"And why shouldn't I be? I'm on a great cruise, got dinner with a great… with a gorgeous girl-*lady* - and I heard from Agent Collins already!"

Tiffany's face went blank as he held her chair for her.

"What, so soon? What'd she say?"

"Not much; after all, it's only been a few hours. But, they did find Mrs. Brightman – still living in Venice – and brought her in for questioning. So, we'll see where that leads."

With that, they sat down to dinner, and had an exceptionally good meal. As it was the last night of the cruise, the entire wait staff came out and put on quite the show. They sang and danced around the dining hall – some had flaming baked Alaska on hats on their heads – and then the captain proposed a toast.

"Do you have anything special planned for tonight?" Alan said.

Tiffany slowly nodded.

"Yes, I have something very special."

Alan sighed and sat back.

"It's OK; I understand, you have duties to perform. Perhaps-"

She giggled and leaned forward, putting her elbows on the table – and her… 'assets' on display.

"Yes, I'm taking my *man* to see a show, and then… to his cabin – for the night!"

Alan shook his head.

"So-so-*so* bad! It's a date, my dear."

After dinner, they went to the main theatre and saw the final show; a revue of hits from Broadway – songs from *Rent, Little Shop of Horrors*, and many other shows. It was as good as any show Alan had seen on the cruises he'd worked. Then, it was up to his cabin, and Alan was very happy to see that beautiful figure of hers once again. A single zip, her gown fell away, and she was standing there in nothing but some black lace panties.

Oh, what a body!


THE NEXT MORNING, TIFFANY had to leave early; she had a lot to do before they pulled into port. Alan knew the drill. He packed his bags, left them outside his door and went to a quick breakfast. The whole passport and US Customs thing was going to take time – 'pencil-pushers' and paperwork always did – so he was in no hurry.

Sitting in the main entry hall, he had to wonder: had the police learned anything yet? He pretty much knew the answer to that question: no, they couldn't have! After all, it'd only been a single day; not even a full day. Still, he was anxious to know what they knew. As if in answer to that, his phone rang.

"Hello, this is Alan," he said.

"Ah, Dr. Mayhew, Agent Collins here. How are you this morning?"

"Fine-fine; just getting ready to leave the ship, as soon as I clear Customs."

"Excellent! I just heard from the Sarasota County Sheriff's Office. It seems they've found ID in the name of Mrs. Clapham in Mrs. Brightman's house; she was very vague about the whereabouts of Mrs. Clapham so it looks as if you may be right about her. She's an alias, I'm sure. Can you come directly to the office from the boat? We'd like to get your deposition and evidence on record."

Of course, Alan had expected that so he readily agreed.

"Yes, I'll catch a cab here at the dock and be there as soon as I can. Oh, and by the way, it's a ship, not a boat."

"Oh, there's a difference? Anyway - I'll see you later this morning."

With that, they said their goodbyes, and Alan saw that the passengers were beginning to disembark. Good timing all around. Getting to his feet, he looked around; would Tiffany be here to see him off? Would she... get off with him? No, that was too much to ask for. Yet, maybe all they'd shared meant he could ask... for something.

Moving down the gangway, he milled around with the crowd as they all tried to get out of the main building. Alan walked slowly; he... he really didn't want to leave; not... not like this.

"Alan!" came Tiffany's voice.

He smiled and spun around – even as she just about plowed into him! Throwing their arms around each other, they kissed and he slowly turned around, holding her in his arms. At last, after what seemed to be only a second, but his watch told him was nearly a minute, he set her down, and they parted.

"Trying to sneak away on me, eh?" she said.

He smiled.

"Again with the sass! I really must teach you a lesson in manners some day."

"Yeah-yeah, whatever, old man; you keep saying that, but you never do," Tiffany said, a sly grin on her face. "So, you're... off are you?"

"To see the FBI, yes; but... ah, I was wondering about something. Ah..."

"Yessss!" Tiffany said, almost jumping up and down on the spot in excitement.

"Well, your contract for this ship, when it's up, why not take a little vacation?"

Tiffany spotted a chance for one more tease – and a way to save face if Alan wasn't really asking what she really *hoped* he was asking.

"Not a bad idea. You... have any... suggestions on where I should go?"

Some of Alan's old reserve returned, hardly daring to hope she would want to see him again.

"New England is lovely this time of year, and... I'd love the chance for you to... meet my family."

Tiffany blinked her eyes – she seemed to be getting a bit misty-eyed.

"Alan, I'd... I'd love that. I'll give you a call when I get back after this next cruise, okay?"

"Sounds like a plan," he said, gazing down into those two sparkling pools of hers.

"In fact – I'll call you every day!"

A last kiss, a few whispered words, and then they slowly, reluctantly parted.

Alan moved out onto the sidewalk; the morning sun was hot in his face. It took a few minutes, but he finally flagged down a cab. After that, it was an easy ride downtown. So, what did the future hold for him? In the case of Michael's death – Michael's murder – he was fairly certain of where that was headed. It might have taken years to achieve, but Michael would get justice.

# EPILOGUE

*January 10ᵗʰ, 2010 Boston*

THREE WEEKS LATER, ALAN again found himself standing at the airport. This time he wasn't going anywhere, but he didn't feel so quite out of place and alone, either. He was there meeting Tiffany, excitedly thinking through all the things he would show her around his home town. He was thrilled that she had agreed to spend a few days with him on her shore leave, prior to picking up the ship for her next cruise.

Alan waited with a few others obviously there to greet friends and relations from the incoming flights. He had a clear view of the arrivals and he chuckled when he saw the unmistakable blonde head of Tiffany bobbing up and down, straining to catch a glimpse of him.

"Over here, Tiff'," he called, smiling as he recalled how that particular term of endearment had slowly crept into his emails and phone calls in the few weeks since he had last seen her on board ship.

With a happy squeal, Tiffany dumped her bag and ran, launching herself into Alan's arms, and he twirled her around, laughing.

"Oh my love, you keep me young!" he grinned, depositing her once more on his feet.

His grin only faded when Tiffany pressed,

"Yeah… eh… about that. You know it's not – the age difference – it doesn't matter to me… but, Alexa – has she calmed down yet?"

Alan inhaled deeply and tried to shrug off the question as Alexa's disparaging comments played in his head.

"Let's not think about that just now, huh? She'll love you when she meets you."

"She's agreed to meet me?" Tiffany asked, dubious.

Again, Alan was non-committal as he hailed down a cab and threw Tiffany's luggage into the trunk. He hurried to open her door for her as the cab driver made no move to get out of his vehicle. Finally, Alan got into the back seat beside Tiffany, having told the driver their destination. It was only then that he answered Tiffany – but not as she had hoped.

"Forget about my family for now. I thought you'd be itching to know what has happened on the murder investigation. It's been so difficult to get it all down in emails or to pass on the details in the few conversations we've managed to have – but it was quite a week in Miami, once I got ashore - meeting with the FBI and other authorities. Some of them were – to put it lightly – rather dubious about the whole matter."

Tiffany nodded.

"Well, you expected that. Getting them to believe that Michael's death was a murder at all, after all these years, was never going to be easy," she reasoned.

Alan smiled.

"We got a bit of a lucky break there, as it turns out. It seems that the little double identity trick was still going on. Probably after all these years, Mrs. Clapham had no fear that Michael's murder would be uncovered and maybe she got careless. Anyway, fortunately for us – and for the investigating police, not only was Mrs. Clapham's ID found in Mrs. Brightman's house, but there were a ton of documents that proved her antiques smuggling activity. It turned out - she had been stealing Russian national treasures since practically the Reagan era!"

Tiffany gave a long, low whistle. Alan, realizing that the noise had alerted the attention of the cab driver, instructed him to pull over.

"We can walk from here, thanks. I feel like a coffee, anyway."

The cab driver was mollified by Alan paying the full fare and he was soon on his way as Alan ushered Tiffany into his favorite local coffee shop. A few minutes later, over her macchiato and his double espresso, Alan resumed the report of the investigation so far.

"So, charging Mrs. Brightman with smuggling was pretty easy. But that's where the authorities happened upon a stroke of good luck. After all, what is a little charge of smuggling when someone is facing murder in the first degree?"

Tiffany had to agree with that.

"So, Mrs. Brightman would not seem to have much incentive to talk about Michael and his death. What happened to change that? I'm presuming she talked, since things seemed to have moved on even from our last conversation, Alan."

"They sure have!"

Alan was delighted to be able to fill Tiffany in on the latest details of the investigation.

"She had been smuggling antiques from Russia, right?"

Tiffany nodded, but didn't quite see the significance yet. Alan was happy to enlighten her.

"It seems that the government there wanted to extradite her back there to stand trial! So, when she was informed that she was facing *life* in a *Russian* prison, Mrs. Brightman suddenly became much more open to the idea of a deal. Given the passage of time, and the iffy case, the prosecution was equally open to negotiations."

Tiffany nodded, but with a small sigh.

"Well – twenty-five years on, I think we did a pretty good job of getting together the evidence."

Her ruffled feathers made Alan chuckle.

"Well – so do I… and so do the police. But honestly, even a second post mortem would have struggled to prove anything significant after all these years," he admitted, to which Tiffany had to concur.

"But Michael was cremated!"

Alan grinned.

"Yes, but she didn't know that! So, in exchange for letting her plead to manslaughter, she agreed to a complete allocution."

"So, did she… give any reasons…?"

The grin almost split Alan's face in two.

"She sure did! It seems we had it right; Michael had found out about her illegal dealings – using the Clapham alias to avoid taxes, import duties etc – and he had been blackmailing her for some time. So, she stole one of Dr. Zetisman's needles – you know - the enormous ones that I told you I was always suspicious of…?"

Tiffany laughed but part of her was disappointed that a man who had sounded a thoroughly unpleasant character was seemingly innocent. It was as if Alan could read her mind, as he at least in part shared those sentiments.

"Yes, while I'm not sure he can exactly be described as 'innocent', it seems that our Dr. Z. had nothing to do with killing Michael."

"Well, at least it wasn't Alfonse!" Tiffany chipped in cheerfully. "I told you!... So, it was Mrs. Brightman…?"

Alan patted Tiffany's hand across the small barista table.

"Apparently, she asked Michael if she could meet with him to discuss a re-negotiation of their 'payment plan'. While he was counting the money, she jabbed him with the needle, and pushed the plunger. All it took was air. No drugs. Michael lashed out at her, they fought, and then – in his death throes – he smashed the lamp and model plane. It was while gathering the money that she cut her hand, and then ran."

Relief at having solved the twenty-five year old murder case washed over Tiffany.

"Well, I hope she serves a long jail sentence," she asserted.

"Me too," agreed Alan. "But – given her age, I'd say she's looking at five to ten years max' – but even that may be enough to ensure she never sees life outside the walls of a jail again. I've called Mrs. Hamilton with the news, of course, but she didn't say much. You know how reserved the British can be! I *guess* she's pleased that Michael's murderer will receive punishment, but she didn't pass comment... Oh, she was polite, of course. Thanked us. But that was all."

"That doesn't matter. What matters is that the case was solved and that Mrs. Brightman will serve her sentence, regardless of whether she lives to taste freedom again. No-one knows what the future holds, Alan."

Tiffany, her small, soft hand cupping his larger, stronger hands in hers across the table, looked into Alan's eyes. Alan felt himself melting into those soft warm brown pools once more.

As for Tiffany and his... future with her - oh, that was a darkened highway stretching off into the night. He couldn't see the final destination, but he was willing to embark on the journey. Where it led, how long it would run – he didn't know – yet, he was anxious for it to continue. How did that song go: 'the rest is yet unwritten'? Well, how long he and Tiffany would share a life together was a story yet to be written, and it was time to pen the first page.

Manufactured By:    RR Donnelley
Momence, IL  USA
August, 2010